SPECIAL RELATIONS

'And then as if from a clear blue sky, she heard the question . . . "So how are you getting on with President Bradley . . . You both went to Oxford, roughly at the same time, I believe. So . . .?"

A thin, sharp blade seemed to enter her chest, below the heart.

"So, did you never meet, or have any contact?"

And there it was all plain and simple – the one question she should have expected, and hadn't. The interviewer was staring at her, his mouth slightly open in a half-smile. And you have only a split second, no time for thought on this one, Alison. This is live. And there are two or three million people watching you at this exact moment. *Answer the question.*

"I don't believe we ever did."

She knew it was the wrong answer, even as she said it. She knew – with utmost certainty – that she had made a crucial blunder. "You don't lie," the whips had told her, when she entered parliament. "You feign ignorance, stupidity, you avoid the question, if necessary you throw a fit and roll about on the floor screaming. But you don't tell a lie when there are people around who know the truth."

What have I done? she asked herself.

But she already knew the answer.'

Tim Sebastian was born in London in 1952 and is the author of five previous acclaimed novels. For ten years he reported for the BBC, mainly from Eastern Europe. He now lives in London, where he divides his time between writing and broadcasting.

BY THE SAME AUTHOR

The Spy in Question
Spy Shadow
Saviour's Gate
Exit Berlin
Last Rights

SPECIAL RELATIONS

Tim Sebastian

ORION

An Orion paperback
First published in Great Britain by Orion in 1994
This paperback edition published in 1994 by Orion Books Ltd,
Orion House, 5 Upper St Martin's Lane, London WC2H 9EA

Copyright © 1994 Tim Sebastian

A CIP catalogue record for this book is available from the
British Library.

ISBN: 1 85797 487 5

Printed in England by Clays Ltd, St Ives plc

For Peter

Prologue

June 1966

There's always a last day. But rarely, if ever, do you know when. Like the last day of your life. The last time you'll see a friend. The last day of summer.

Only in this moment does she know it, as the storm passes across the colleges and fields, along the Thames Valley.

She's running now, through the people on the street, no longer seeing or caring.

Each footstep takes her further from the year they spent together, the shared times and spaces, washing away in the rain.

'Stop her,' someone shouts. Because there's danger in her eyes and a wild momentum out of control.

You know it will go badly.

By the roadside little rivers collect, flowing down the main street towards the bridge. A soft night. Darkness at the edges.

Without warning she turns, thinking her name is being called, searching the crowd for his face.

Shaken, she steps off the kerb. Doesn't see the baker's van with the broken headlamps, that doesn't see her either, croaking its way half-blind up the High Street, spinning her body in the air, dumping it in the gutter.

Think on this moment – that a life might go so cheaply.

He can't help any more, for he's far away up the main street, out of sight. Off to a different world. He doesn't hear the sirens of the police cars or the ambulance, or the shouts of the crowd. And nor does she.

The news flashes city-wide that a student has been killed in a road crash. An eighteen-year-old girl. No name until the relatives are told. That's the rule.

He hears it on the taxi radio, riding out to the station, but it means nothing to him. There's no way it could be her.

Not a chance in the world.

* * *

So quietly, so carefully, the university professor of surgery walks down the lino corridor to the parents. Whispers. Says as nicely as he can, that the first reports were wrong, but it's only the prayers of the faithful that are keeping her. The damage, the shock. Would have killed many, if not most.

That's what he tells her mum and dad, in the darkened corridor of the Radcliffe, as they listen to the rain and the words, not understanding.

Dad has come straight from the office. He's so tired inside that shiny blue suit, hasn't shaved since dawn, keeps opening his mouth to say things only no words come out; and Mum is there from the kitchen. She was getting his supper, chops and bacon with mashed potato, way back in time, when things were all right. Before the telephone rang.

At dawn sister Jo arrives. Jo, in her last year at boarding school, still wearing the team tracksuit, a hairband. So much energy she can't stand in one place. Keeps going off to find someone, talk to someone, get something done. She'd been training for the match tomorrow.

The baker's van has hit them all.

Two police officers are there. A man and woman. They want to help, check details. Milky tea comes in plastic cups. The college principal. Also milky. 'Anything I can do?' The little rituals of sympathy. Thank you. Thank you so much. Dad, speaking for the first time.

Later they sleep on the chairs, the three of them, holding each other in a kind of semi-circle, as the light comes up over the city and the girl refuses to die. Refuses.

The professor wakes them at seven, managing to smile, telling them that a twenty-four-hour miracle has happened, the mind is somehow holding the body together. It's rare and extraordinary. But they shouldn't count on it to continue. There are no odds to weigh. No prognosis. They have no medical explanation for why she's here and not there.

He says that – and walks slowly back to his room, doing something he hasn't done since his student days, feeling the tears running down his cheeks, wanting the girl to live, wishing that after all he

2

had chosen another job. Miles away from a hospital. Miles away from the pain.

Mum and Dad begin to measure her life by the mealtimes she lives through. Lunchtime, teatime, suppertime. She survives them all, and at midnight the next night, the professor comes again. They've now identified extensive spinal damage. And he leaves them unintentionally with the question, they never thought to face ... would it be better if she died? Kinder. More humane.

Question for a couple in their late fifties, on a summer night in Oxford.

Jo goes in and talks to her. She talks through the tubes, past the bandages and the pulleys, to the closed eyes of her sister. She reminds her of the times they hurled pillows at each other, how they spied on the teenager next door who always left his curtains open, how well she had done at school, and how jealous Jo had been. In those days, long before.

She reminds her of all the dreadful boyfriends who courted her through the years. The spotty ones, the soupy ones, the ones who dressed up, and the others, whose hair Dad said he could stand on.

Time belongs to the heart machine and the jagged green line.

They are sleeping so soundly on the chairs, when the nurse wakes them. It's four or five, and suddenly she is paler and weaker, moving visibly away into the night. You can see there's no struggle. No pain. She isn't letting go. Someone is taking it from her.

Only they can't allow that. Dad sits them all by the bed. They hold her hand. They talk to her. Surround her. Rapid sentences. Anything they can think of. Like a crossword, fitting parts of her life, one against another. Up, down, across. So little in the way of clues.

They tell her how much they liked her friend – the tall American boy, six foot three from forehead to sneaker. The impulsive one from Kansas, the scholar who always said he could read her mind.

'We'll find him,' Dad strokes her arm. 'It'll be OK ... Can you hear us? Anything?'

Jo whispers ... 'They really loved each other. You know that don't you? Been together for a year now. Talked of marriage, I think. But he was going back to the States. Going into the Army. To Vietnam. Maybe they broke up. I'll try to phone.'

She returns later. 'They think he left already. No one seems to know. It's really awful.'

Two hours go by. The nurse looks in and then the professor but they don't interrupt.

There's a point where you reach the boundaries of medicine, the end of reason's road. And after that anything goes. You can pick any remedy, any hopes, or prayers. Any mystical utterances. Any appeal to the higher order of life.

That is your last right and they know it.

But what they don't know is that she is listening to them. The girl *listens*. She has no sight or power of movement. She has lost the means to communicate. And yet she hears the prayers and the exhortations. The memories of life. The family around her. The casualties she will take with her if she goes.

Outside, the professor removes his glasses and shuts his eyes.

Beside her bed, Mum and Dad are still talking.

If she can live through the night, she tells herself, she'll make it.

Chapter One

thirty years later:

'Let's go eat dinner.'

'Too much trouble.'

'I don't want to eat here.'

David Bradley looked across the table at his mother and recalled the conversation that had preceded their meal. It was odd how the roles had reversed over the years. Now she was the one to demand treats like a petulant child, she was happy to throw tantrums in the most public of places, she had to be bought off and distracted. And tonight of all nights, he would cheerfully have pushed her off a cliff, and laughed as she hit the bottom.

'Come here, Mother, I want to show you the view. There! Little further. That's it. Nothing to worry about.' And then a final heave as she leaned out over the gorge. 'Goodbye, Mother. Ha ha. Goodbye. Enjoy your dinner.'

Wonderful moment.

He looked round the restaurant. A meal for two in the Rio Grande Café in Bethesda, George Bush's old haunt – but that couldn't be helped. Meal for two with marinated steak and guacomole. Some beers, nachos, ice-cream for the old dear.

Total bill, somewhere around three thousand dollars.

That was when you added up the secret service costs, the Maryland police, the communications truck, the counter-assault team, and the medical wagon – all of which had turned out on a Sunday evening, because Mother wanted to eat out with the most expensively protected man in the world. Jesus!

You don't do this when you're president, he thought. Thank God the place had been half empty. Even so the secret service had needed two hours' notice, the kitchen staff and the patrons had all been suitably intimidated, and instead of being able to mix with some normal people instead of mother, he had been quarantined at a special table in the corner.

The only person who dared approach had been two years old

and nearly had her head blown off with a shotgun, because the parents forgot to ask.

One evening they wouldn't forget, thought Bradley.

When it came to the check, Mother's delicious sense of irony shone through. 'Let me pay, dear. It's been such fun. And I do like to buy my son a meal, once in a while, even though he's so big and famous.'

Bradley groaned. 'We have to leave, Mother.'

The old lady made a great play of handing over her credit card to the waitress. 'Such pretty girls,' she murmured. 'I do wish you'd find someone nice again.'

He nodded to the head of the secret service detail, and a handful of men in grey suits rose up from tables along the route to the door. Men of purpose. A customer began clapping and a few people cheered. Bradley grinned at the room in general. He was hard to take in at first sight. Just that bit too tall. Just the wrong side of six foot three. Just beyond what a normal clothes store can provide. Beyond normal range in size and bearing and now a president to prove it. The secret service had codenamed him 'Giraffe' and his mother 'Mouth'.

He knew but she didn't.

Thirteen minutes later the motorcade dropped Mrs Bradley at the Four Seasons Hotel. Thankfully, she refused to stay in the White House, or Blair House or any of the official residences. On her visits to Washington she liked to be 'her own mistress'. Bradley would sometimes wonder who else's she was. But he never made any attempt to find out.

What had happened to Mother, he would ask himself? What had happened to the quick-acting, quick-feeling woman he had grown up with? A mass of hair and ideas, a walking cocktail, fizzy and frothy, and wanted by everyone. Why had she reached an inter-section and rolled back down the hill?

'Mrs Bradley, ma'am.' A secret-serviceman helped her through the hotel door and into the lobby. Bradley felt a sudden stab of guilt as he recalled the way he used to run to her to say goodnight, every night, arms around her, holding so tightly, as if they were about to make separate journeys into the darkness and didn't know when they'd meet again.

Tonight she'd be alone in her suite – and he'd be alone in the

White House. And they'd journey a little further apart.

As for the country, he reflected – it was now nine thousand dollars poorer. The cost of a simple meal for two. No wine.

The first snow came in over the Chesapeake Bay sometime after midnight, carpeting wide tracts along the Eastern Seaboard. For just a few hours the city would be a thing of beauty, blind-white, untouched, the way its conscience never could be.

He had lain there for hours, knowing he wouldn't sleep. Pain, he had been told, creates its own calendar. Days and nights that he would grow to fear, because of the memories they induced. Fight it, they had said, on its own ground, in the quiet hours, in the shadows of dawn, whenever it strikes. Otherwise, you too will go under.

At five he got up and stood by the third floor window in his pyjamas. South over the lawn he could see the snow clearers at work along State Street, and in the distance the first of the morning headlights inching towards Capitol Hill.

And then, as he always did, he looked towards the park for the tiny pall of smoke from the ventilation duct. Often there were beggars, crouching beside it for warmth, coated in cardboard and newspaper, frozen against the ground.

Inside the White House, he thought, you could write and re-write history a dozen times a day. And yet a few yards from your window, a man with no home and no money would spend the night, trying not to die from the cold and the country's neglect. A man you felt powerless to help.

'I call it a magic carpet to nowhere,' his predecessor had said, as he packed himself and his tearful family into the limo, before heading out to Andrews Air Force Base and the last free flight home. 'That's what this job is. You turn dreams into speeches, and speeches into television. But don't think it's got anything to do with reality. Good luck! If you need anything, call someone else.'

He lay down on the bed, hearing the slow southern cadences as if it were yesterday. Only he wished it was.

For yesterday was Elizabeth. And today was the day she had gone. Two years past.

They had moved in, full of expectations about the changes they could make.

7

The removal vans, slick and practised, had departed by the time the inauguration was over. Elizabeth returned to find her own sheets on the bed, her own spaniel in her own basket, plenty of warm smiles and fine words. Washington's fickle, over-vaunted honeymoon in full flight, waiting as it always did, for someone to smash it apart.

And yet four months in, when the illness struck her, it seemed they had altered only the wallpaper and the height of the paintings.

He had hurried daily to the Naval Hospital in Bethesda, sat up nights with her in the suite, read out loud to her, because her eyes would no longer focus – and while the country had been with him, and the outpouring of sympathy overwhelming, the government had suffered. Behind his back the wrong decisions had been made, the wrong precedents established.

She had known it, and warned him, her political instincts somehow sharper and more finely tuned than his own. She had trusted none of them. And she had been right.

'When I'm gone,' she had said. 'You'll have to kick them into shape. You've been paying too much attention to me. They've been getting jealous – and going their own way.'

Right again – the way she always had been. 'I'm glad I never had to run against you,' he had told her.

'You did everything else,' she whispered.

It was the last joke they had shared together.

Five-fifteen. The green digits flashed on and off by the bedside light. Outside the apartment the building was still dark and empty. Only the secret service patrols and the duty officer in the Situation Room. Eight hours and he'd be in the air to Europe. Eight hours to the special summit in Berlin and some very urgent mediation. Russia and the Ukraine deadlocked over who controlled their nuclear missiles, who could fire them, who could bargain them away . . .

But he put it out of his mind. This morning was for Elizabeth. A few hours for her – and for him. He would shake himself free of the huge entourage, the secret service, the cabinet, the military aide, the whole circus – and head out to Arlington. It would be beautiful in the snow. Just the way Elizabeth had liked it. This was their morning.

He got up and went into the bathroom. It was the first room

Elizabeth had re-designed. And in that, of course, she was no different from any other First Lady. Nixon had ripped out Johnson's bathroom, Ford had ripped out Nixon's. At one time or another every first family had screwed around with the little room, inserting water jets into the floor, the ceiling, the walls. There'd been hard lighting and soft lighting. In the words of the chief usher ... 'there was more time spent on the shower than most of the legislation from Capitol Hill.' And still it wasn't right. The pipes gurgled and spat, the system was overhauled, replaced and overhauled again. But it continued to resist all treatment. Only Elizabeth had liked it. 'Leave it' – she told the usher. 'I like an eccentric bathroom. Tile it white and leave it.'

Now it was a standing joke between Bradley and the usher – Preston Harcourt – a stooping elderly figure from Louisiana, whom Bradley trusted more than the entire cabinet. Harcourt would let the president know when it was 'safe to take a bath', and lament the problems of living in public housing.

When he went away, Bradley would tell him ... 'You're in charge now, Preston. Don't let the animals in.' And Harcourt would grin with pride that the president of the United States would speak to him in such a way, with all the officials and senators around, and would shake his hand before heading out on to the south lawn, past the cameras and the invited flag-wavers, and on to the presidential helicopter.

Bradley fiddled with the shower controls, dried himself and picked up the internal phone. He knew Preston would be there. Preston would always be there. Especially this morning. He wouldn't forget.

'I'll be leaving in a few minutes.'

'Yes, Mr President.' The voice was still and cold.

Bradley was about to put down the phone when he had a thought. 'You're in charge,' he said and smiled into the receiver.

David Bradley had called the head of the secret service detail the night before, so they knew what he wanted. Distance, discretion. The minimum security package.

Just before six a.m. he rode down in the private elevator to the basement, skirting the situation room, through the ante-room where

9

his predecessors had once swam and played pool, and into the tunnel that led to the Treasury.

At the entrance two secret servicemen joined him, already in coats and scarves. A quick 'Good morning, Mr President.' For there was no time for pleasantries. They'd been told to take the commander-in-chief out into the big bad city, enjoying the highest murder rate in the United States. Light and shade on the three faces as they headed down the tunnel. Just the creak of leather on the carpet. Military rhythm – the way Bradley had learned it, then taught it.

This morning there was to be no backup SWAT team, no ambulance, no communications truck – just a White House sedan, warmed up on the east side of the Treasury. From there a fast run past the Lincoln memorial, Memorial Bridge, over the red-brick road to the cemetery at Arlington. Fast as the snow would let them.

As they came to the Treasury door one of the agents went on ahead, the other stood blocking his path. Only when the outside check was complete, did they hustle him to the car, not gently, not slowly either. Their business was his survival. No one said they couldn't bruise him along the way.

He got in behind the driver. But someone else was there as well. Bradley frowned. 'You didn't need to come, Bill.'

'With respect, sir.' The president's military aide, Lieutenant Bill Kemp looked down at the floor of the car. 'I had no choice.'

Bradley slumped into the corner. Kemp was the chain of office that couldn't be broken. Keeper of the keys, keeper of the codes, the man who carried a tiny suitcase around with him, known as the 'football', the president's Doomsday communications, the device by which he could launch America's nuclear weapons on any of their pre-arranged flight plans. It was, Bradley realised, part joke, part tragedy. With Kemp at his side he could sit on a highway and blow up the planet, on the move, they wouldn't even have to stop. You could hold a hotdog in one hand, and the button in the other. Ludicrous. But while America had the weapons, Kemp had the football and Bradley had them both.

The car turned right on to Independence Avenue and skidded slightly.

Unknown to Bradley the downtown area had been swept for the past hour by three separate teams, one posing as snow clearers, the others – local DC police. A special control point had been set up behind Arlington House, the Pentagon was monitoring air space, the vice-president had been alerted and a message sent to the chief of staff.

So while the passenger in the car had the honour to be the forty-third leader of the United States – a widower, a former governor of Kansas, a former US army colonel, a man with history and presence and bearing – he knew nothing of any of this.

He simply enjoyed the facilities of the most powerful country on earth. For the president to dispense with the secret service would be like announcing he was going to live in Takoma Park, or Dupont Circle, or Rockville. It couldn't happen. Wouldn't happen. Wasn't written in the book.

They had promised to give him discretion and distance. But they would give it their way.

Inside the cemetery grounds, he left the car on Sheridan Drive and told Kemp to stay in it. There were crows calling out from the trees as if in warning. But when they stopped the silence was complete. He could hear only the muffled sound of his boots on the snow – the two agents fifty yards behind.

At the top of the hill Bradley moved on to the stone parapet and looked out over the city, still half-dark. The monuments were visible only in miniature, Capitol Hill, the flat sprawl of the Pentagon to the right. And in front of him a great sweep of white, that undulated through the trees, as far as he could see, broken only by the thousands of grey-stone graves in perfect lines. Twenty funerals a day, they had told him. The cemetery would be full in thirty years.

It took him a moment to find Elizabeth's headstone. The wind must have blown the snow against it, for the lettering of her name had been obscured. And he took off his glove, sweeping the surface clean with his bare hand, crouching beside it, making sure it had not been disturbed.

For the first time he looked round to see who was buried beside her. An army lieutenant, a midshipman killed in the second world war, someone else in Korea, someone in the Gulf. It was like crossing through time.

Elizabeth would be at home here, he thought. The army nurse who he had met on her second tour of duty in Vietnam, who had been wounded by shrapnel in the thigh, who had attended the most violent of deaths – and laughed at her own, when it stood before her.

She hadn't wanted to be buried in Arlington, but with her war record she had the right. Bradley had insisted on it. He'd never told her, but he needed her close – still, after all this time. He needed her physical presence.

He got to his feet and thought back to the funeral. Not since Woodrow Wilson had a First Lady died in the White House. And never had it been so public, with hourly bulletins on the networks, with the switchboard inoperable from the weight of calls, with no place to take your tears. Caller after caller, message after message. Politicians from every country, in every language. It seemed as if the whole world had come to lay its sorrow at his door.

He recalled how Elizabeth had foreseen this as well – and reminded him of his duty. 'Tens of thousands of people are dying daily across the country,' she had told him. 'They'll be looking to you to show strength and dignity and encourage them to do the same. You owe them that. It's your role. That's what the country requires from you. Don't go to pieces on me.'

The cold pressed down on him as he stood there. He realised suddenly he had brought no flowers, and then smiled at himself for forgetting that as well.

'Whatever else you do – don't bring me flowers,' she had said, the day before she died. 'You have other more important things to do. And besides,' she had added, 'I'll be watching.'

'You talk as if you're just catching a train,' Bradley had said to her.

'That's all it is, my dear,' she had replied. 'That's all it is.'

Bradley walked on after a few minutes. He always went to the Tomb of the Unknowns. Even in winter they changed the guard every hour. As he arrived to the east of the amphitheatre, he could see the ritual was about to begin.

A soldier of the US Third Infantry was taking his twenty-one paces in front of the tomb, pausing twenty-one seconds, then marching back. The snowflakes had stuck to the back of his greatcoat. Bradley could see the young face, reddened from the wind.

If the guard even noticed him, he didn't show it.

The president watched as the replacement was led out and his rifle inspected.

In the distance he could hear two voices in conversation and assumed they had left open the door to the guard house. And yet he gradually realised that through some freak acoustic inside the amphitheatre, he was listening to a secret service conversation.

'Bradley's lost it. Look at him, he's a broken man.'

'So would you be,' came the response. 'He'll come through.'

'Maybe.'

'He's gonna get the sympathy vote next election. No doubt about it.'

'If he runs. Personally, I don't think he will. The guy's finished.'

For a moment Bradley felt the anger exploding inside him ... those two little bastards ... But then he turned back to the ceremony at the tomb. The inspecting officer had finished the ritual. The rifle was jerked slickly back into the soldier's hands.

He wanted to go now, impatient suddenly, the mood lost. If the secret service thought he'd rolled over – they wouldn't be the only ones. He knew he'd let things slip, failed to concentrate, failed to watch his back.

In Washington a slip could rapidly become a slide. Lies became facts, simply by being repeated. A weak president could be shelved or bypassed, or as some of his predecessors had found out, violently removed. And yet he wasn't weak. Look at the years in the Army, the service in Vietnam. The man who they'd had to promote, because he was better at giving orders than taking them. 'Colonel Impulse', they'd called him, because he could think on his feet, change orders, change tack, throw a whole campaign in the air and conjure a new one.

And now he was commander in chief and the secret service had him finished. If he couldn't impose his own agenda, someone else would impose theirs. It was the wolfpack in suits and ties – same ethics.

Bradley knew he should fear the system, as well as seeking to control it.

He looked back over the cemetery, the gravestones protruding over the snow. Below them were men and women who had fought. Now he'd have to do the same.

Chapter Two

At a quarter to five the White House chief of staff, Harry Deval, looked over to his wife Jane and touched her gently to make sure she was asleep. He always woke at the same time, savouring the pre-dawn light, the stillness. It was the only time he got to think about what he was doing, to ask himself basic questions. The only time he couldn't run away from the answers.

Nearly, so nearly, he had thrown everything away. The family, the house, all those lives and faces that connected with him. You, Harry. You nearly let it go.

He got up and stood looking at Jane. Someone else had pushed her out of his life. For that whole year. A woman who had felt so different in mind and body, who touched him on so many levels, who gave him what seemed to be a second chance, and didn't ask him to choose.

But six months of joy had been followed by six months of guilt and shame, and Harry hadn't been able to live with himself, let alone anyone else. So he'd broken it. He'd walked away. On a night when he'd cried and she'd cried and he thought life would never again be worth living.

Only now, in the first light of morning he thanked God he had.

On the landing he passed his son's room and stopped. Even at that distance he could hear the boy's gentle breathing. Another hour and he'd be up too, charging round the house getting ready, or most likely refusing to get ready, for school.

Sometimes Harry thought he was past coping with an eight-year-old. He remembered the first time he'd been to Jason's class. It was father's day and they had all perched uncomfortably on their sons' school chairs, at their sons' desks, while the teacher had talked about loving and nurturing, the way American schools always did. Harry had looked round to find he was about fifteen years older than the other dads – except the ones on second or third marriages. They all had thick heads of hair, slim waists, bagless eyes. Christ – it had

14

been a shock. Harry was already spending ten minutes each morning deciding where to place which hair. And then in the car he had tried to console himself. He could still stand on the touchlines and yell for the football team. He could still run around at Halloween with flour on his face.

He went into the room and touched the boy's face.

This too, I would have thrown away.

It took him just a few minutes to get ready. Then, without a sound, he tiptoed down the stairs, opened the front door and eased it shut behind him.

The Washington snow was thicker than he'd expected. It would be a day at least before they made any serious impression on it. Snow clearing wasn't DC's strong point, he reflected. Nor were roads, nor was crime, nor drugs – or anything else for that matter.

He had met her in the same kind of snow, just a year ago. She, an administrative assistant in the Old Executive Office building that housed the overspill from the White House.

She too, would walk to work, and had laughed when he'd asked if she needed help with her handbag.

One year ago.

Now Harry wanted her transferred. Didn't want to meet her in the canteen or the corridor. Best if she moved on of her own accord.

At the bottom of Massachusetts Avenue he caught a cab, told the driver to stop on C Street, and walked the rest of the way to the south-west entrance.

Even the chief of staff shows his laminated identity card, and has his name checked against a computer listing. Just in case he isn't chief of staff this morning, in case he's been the victim of a swift and silent coup, in case the president has suddenly taken against him, while having his supper or picking over his breakfast. They were all things that had happened and would happen again. Harry Deval knew that because he'd helped organise them himself.

Holding office in this building was about as safe as cleaning windows on a fifty-floor skyscraper. You were never more than a step away from disaster.

He entered by the west wing and made his way to the office in the south-west corner. Only a small staff room separated him from the president. Inside were a handful of paintings, western scenes loaned out by the National Gallery of Art. But otherwise the room had little colour. It was here that Deval had been sworn in by the deputy executive clerk two years earlier and nothing much had changed. The windows still carried thick, dark blue drapes, edged with ribbon, a large built-in desk spread itself along one wall, and some wing-back chairs, sat upholstered in loud stripes. The effect was cramped and dark – but the position was what mattered – proximity to the president, proximity to power. As they'd said in Carter's era – 'nothing propinks like propinquity.'

At the sideboard he opened a packet of Lavazza coffee and spooned it into the espresso machine.

There were plenty of notes on the desk – the list of people and policies that would have to be traded during the course of the day.

For a moment though, while he waited for the coffee, he took out a small photo of Jane and Jason and stood it on the window sill.

The affair was over. They were all that mattered now. He'd got away with it.

Chapter Three

Bradley was back in the White House long before Washington's alarm clock went off – the seven o'clock shuttle out of National Airport en route for La Guardia.

Due to noise restrictions the plane is prevented from taking off earlier – so, when finally released it climbs hell-bent on vengeance over the pleasant and expensive north-western suburbs, shaking breakfast coffee cups right along the Potomac.

And while it shattered the sleep of tens of thousands of people each morning, it failed once again to wake the president's mother.

Ruth Bradley also missed the eight o'clock shuttle and a few others besides, until sitting bolt upright in her suite at the Four Seasons Hotel, and staring at the telephone beside her bed.

Had it rung or not? Too much dreaming. She looked over towards the dressing table. The bottle of Jack Daniels was no dream. And then as if to answer her question the phone rang again.

'It's Emily, Mrs Bradley.'

'Is it morning again?'

'Afternoon. You said to wake you at twelve.'

'Lord save us, I'm late.'

'The party doesn't begin till seven. We might just make it.'

Mrs Bradley sank back on to her pillow. 'Where would I be without you, Emily, dear?'

'Asleep. I'll be round at six. Bye.'

Emily Laurence put the phone down and shook her head at it. The president's mother was about to live up to her reputation – scatterbrained and extremely difficult. Unfortunately, when she visited Washington it fell to Emily and the rest of the administrative section to see she was managed, muzzled, and the unavoidable damage contained.

'Mother Wolf' as she was known, was quite capable of doing to the administration, what another wolf had tried to do to little Red Riding Hood.

17

The result was that Bradley rarely found time to see her – crises would be automatically triggered by her footstep, cracking on to the Tennessee marble floor of the cross halls. She once confided to Emily that the whole place seemed on the verge of total panic. 'Don't they ever plan anything?' she asked. 'Dear God, my poor son seems in a permanent state of nervous exhaustion!'

But Bradley often succeeded in getting her out of Washington. He had sent her to Paris to check on the number of US women employed in international organisations. He sent her to a funeral in Africa, to a party in Egypt. And she had gone to them all with an agenda entirely her own. 'Dig and delve,' she would say. 'That's my role. Find out what's really going on.'

Emily well remembered what she had found out in Egypt – that the US ambassador had been having an affair with a local telephonist. At three o'clock in the morning Mrs Bradley had just happened to be looking out of her window and seen the two of them 'all over each other' in the courtyard below. It had taken two days of blunt talking to stop her blurting it out to the president when she got home. Little wonder that most White House staffers treated her like an elderly Titan missile, that should have been bargained away in the arms talks years ago.

By two o'clock she had bathed and made ready her shortlist for the evening. Three pairs of shoes, three outfits, a few earrings and diamonds, all carefully laid out on chairs, a selection from which the final ensemble would be chosen an hour before departure. That would of course depend on mood. And mood, she reflected uneasily, might well depend on Mr Jack Daniels.

She looked at the bottle, but left it where it was. In the old days before her husband had shut her out, she hadn't needed the alcohol. But that was another life. He hadn't wanted much to do with her after the children, simply hadn't wanted 'to live that way'. No family life, no involvement in the daily household. Gradually there had formed around him something she called 'the exclusion zone' that left the two of them no place to meet. In the end they shared nothing except a roof; and in summer when the sun burned deep into the Kansas plains he would stay out on the farm, and they wouldn't even share that.

Two years earlier he had come to Washington for the inauguration of his only son. He'd come for the funeral of his daughter-in-law, and he had turned away and cried into his handkerchief by the edge of the cemetery. In that moment she had wanted so much to reach him, and yet it was far too late for that. He had long since removed her from his heart and she knew the process was irreversible.

She glanced at her watch. Perhaps a short stroll would be the thing. From her window she could see the Biograph cinema across the street, and Mrs Bradley cringed deep inside. On her last visit she had fancied a lunchtime movie, didn't matter what it was, just somewhere to go for an hour or two, to dilute the loneliness. She had waved away her state trooper and stepped inside the 'dear little place opposite', only to discover she was in the middle of the purest imaginable pornography. What was a normal cinema in the evening, filled its seats by day with titles such as 'Bat Bitch' and 'On Golden Blonde', unadvertised except to the cognoscenti. She had hurried out, her hand over her face, praying most fervently that no one would recognise her.

The memory put her off a walk. Besides, the snow would make the streets so hazardous. She turned and looked again at the bottle of Jack Daniels.

Channel Seven News led that evening with the story of fresh snow-falls and Mrs Bradley had begun to wonder whether the party was a good idea.

'Emily, I've been thinking . . .' she said, as the young White House staffer barged through the door to the suite, nose red, eyes watering.

'We're going,' said Emily, reading the signs correctly. 'Everyone would be mortified if you cancelled now. Besides it'll be fun.'

'I'm not so sure . . .'

'Fun, Mrs Bradley, and of great value to the president. You know what an asset he feels you are on the social circuit.'

Ruth Bradley brightened. 'I suppose we must all do our bit,' she sighed. 'Help me choose what to wear.'

'Which is the warmest?'

'You're so practical Emily. I want to look . . . fun.' She smiled indecently. 'Isn't that what I'm supposed to look?'

Emily ignored her. She wasn't going to walk down manipulation alley – not this early in the evening.

As they rode down in the elevator, Mrs Bradley dabbed at her forehead in the mirror. 'Remind me who's going to be there, my dear?'

'It's a twelfth night party, Mrs Bradley. Each course at a different house. So the guest list is a little unpredictable. I think it's a great idea. All the places are in Georgetown ...'

'Oh God ...'

'What's the matter?'

'If it's Georgetown half the women will tell you they have to leave early because they're ovulating, and the men will be claiming they have to be in the Situation Room at five a.m. They've just managed to squeeze a few hours into their busy schedule. How nice. We'll all be awfully charming. It'll be like swimming in jello. So tasteless somehow ....'

'It's Washington, Mrs Bradley. Everyone talks about everything.'

'Well I don't.'

The hell you don't, thought Emily. That's why I'm here. To keep your trap shut.

The car moved off on to M Street and turned right on Wisconsin Avenue. Emily hoped the food would be worth it. She felt like a guard-dog, looking after an elderly poodle. Still, even guard-dogs got fed.

Washington's north-west ghetto has much to recommend it. It's the one remaining point on the capital's compass where the police do not yet record a daily homicide, stabbing, knifing or other such tiresome distraction. The north-west is for the white minority, with chocolate box mansions and cobbled alleys. To look at some of the houses, Emily reflected, you might wonder if the art galleries of Europe had been plundered by their occupants. Everyone, it seemed, had bought their little piece of genius, a Picasso, a Cezanne, one even sported a Turner, part of the Rouen collection, a pale beacon of distant, unaffordable magic.

Below it sat a Washington lawyer, shrimp in one hand, glass in the other, next to him a middle-aged brunette, puffed up in a dress that reminded Emily of one of those driver-side airbags, another lawyer beyond her, and finally Ruth Bradley. She had chosen the red outfit, she said, because it went with her hair. For the hundredth time Emily listened and said nothing. Mrs Bradley's hair was bottled blonde.

Despite the feigned reticence the president's mother greatly enjoyed her entrances. The moment she appeared in the doorway the other guests would immediately stop talking, stand up and clap – giving her an opportunity to tell them 'not to make such a silly fuss', but to wait around looking touched and tearful while they did.

They all had the same background, fed on cotillions, holidays in Baden-Baden, friends in Hyannisport who knew others in Bar Harbor, who were wintering in Florida, before travelling on.

To Emily their lives were like the lyrics of a song she had once heard – and in her mind she was almost setting them to music. Only then she looked across the table and spotted trouble.

It had arrived in the form of a memorable face. You know the way some faces are like landscapes or moons, wide and open – others sharp and chiselled, pointing forward. Faces that are going some-where. Well this face was definitely going somewhere. It belonged to a man who blew in late through the door, a mass of nervous apology, a wet stripe on the side of his suit, a trickle of perspiration sliding past the ear. He had fallen down in the snow, he said. Couldn't find a taxi, couldn't find a car, revolting day all round.

Emily saw the hostess wrapping him in the gentle embrace of ownership, her hand lingering an inch above his damp buttocks – and she knew then he was trouble. You learned to look out for such people, you learned to fence them in, rope them off, divert and distract them wherever possible. To her, he had 'Press' written in every ingratiating, sweating pore.

She would have warned Mrs Bradley. On later reflection she should have tugged her screaming into the nearest bathroom and rammed the warning down her pearl-encrusted throat . . . only there wasn't time.

'So how's the president?'

Someone always starts it. Emily had been looking round the faces, knowing full well who would do it first. At every social event from brunch to bar-mitzvah – you gave the president's mum a little space, a little time to strut and preen – and then you stuck it to her. Let's get political. Let's have a bit of dirt on Mr President. She had seen it so many times around the country. Only in Washington it was more finely honed. The knife was sharper, slid in more easily. Sometimes you didn't even notice the primary incision.

The wet stripe on his suit had all but dried. The shrimps were little mounds of crackly carcass on the table. He wouldn't have long before they moved off to another interior-designed banquet – and the process began again.

The president's mother turned her gaze to see who had launched the enquiry.

'Pete Levinson, Mrs Bradley. Good to see you.'

'And what do you do, Mr Levinson?'

'I'm a writer.'

'Anything I might have read?'

'Only some menus.'

Everyone laughed. Relief not humour.

'I worked one summer as a waiter,' he went on. 'Now I'm an assassin – a film critic. I attack all the people who're more talented than I am.'

Mrs Bradley smiled politely and was about to turn her head ...

'You were going to tell us how the president was?' he raised his eyebrows expectantly.

'Was I? How silly of me. Well ...' Emily tried to flash a look of warning, but Mrs Bradley wasn't in the receiving mode. 'I sometimes feel so sorry for him,' she said and gave a deep sigh. 'Every time I go round – there seems to be some kind of panic on.'

She looked round the expectant, silent faces, knowing she should shut up. God knows, Emily had monogrammed the rules into her backside. But then you couldn't just be the president's mother and say ... 'he's fine. Everything's fine.' It wasn't normal and to Mrs Bradley it wasn't very nice. She did so enjoy being liked. She liked the invitations, the company – even the superficiality of being someone. She wasn't going to live any more through her husband – she might as well live through her son.

Emily looked across at her, feeling the danger. 'Goodness,' she said, 'we should really be moving on. Can't miss the main course, can we, Mrs Bradley?'

But Mrs Bradley was sailing under her own steam, careless of the rocks that threatened her passage.

Chapter Four

Preston Harcourt had spent most of the day packing Bradley's suitcases. For the travelling wardrobe is substantial.

As well as everything else, the president has to be a male model. Obviously, the little TV make-up kit is always at hand to enhance nature, but the clothes are highly symbolic. Most people, say the statistics, look for two things – the body language and the coat on your back. You could in theory be a monkey, released from the Washington zoo – but if you spoke clearly enough in eight-second soundbites, and wore a stiff white shirt – hell, the world could be yours.

Preston, of course, didn't think that way. Preston packed for emergency summits or natural disasters – for the tropics or the arctic. Only he had the right to close the lids and send the luggage on its way.

Molly Parks had helped him – the White House seamstress, who spent her days, mending sheets and towels and keeping the inventories up to date.

Just before lunch she had taken away one of Bradley's pullovers to repair the sleeves.

'Can't you get him to throw this thing out?' she asked Preston.

Preston shook his head. 'Only Mrs Bradley could have done that. We used to have a deal. She'd steal the clothes that needed mending from his wardrobe and pass them to me. That's how I used to get them to you. Now I'm the thief.' He put on his glasses and examined the pullover. 'He won't let me get rid of anything any more. Not now she's gone.'

'What time's he leaving?' Molly asked.

'He'll leave when he's ready.' Preston consulted the daily White House schedule, issued to all members of the permanent staff. 'Eight o'clock tonight,' he said. 'That's if he ever gets through with his meetings.'

The door to the Oval Office had been shut for hours. A secret service officer stood guard in the outer vestibule, waiting to be relieved. It looked as though no one was going anywhere.

Sometime mid-afternoon the White House maitre d' had arrived to find out the president's requirements for dinner. But he had been waved away and had returned to the kitchen.

Inside the office Bradley turned back from the window and regarded his cabinet colleagues with some disdain. The meeting had been a mess. Little jabs of interdepartmental blame had been traded back and forth by one secretary after another. Each argument had been countered, each fact disputed. The results – highly inconclusive. Bradley decided to get rid of them. He nodded to Harry Deval.

'Thank you, gentlemen. I'll be in touch later. Clark, would you wait a moment please.' Clark Norton, the secretary of state, basked briefly on the sofa, while the rest of the team filed out. Harry Deval examined the faces. There wasn't a man among them who didn't want to be included in the inner circle. The jealousy was intense. At the White House the only weapon is information – the more you have, the more powerful you become. You can sell it, barter it or use it as a lever. The trick is pretending you have more than you do.

Bradley sat at the desk.

'Why shouldn't I go to Europe, Clark?'

'You don't need to. I can go. Defence can back me up. It hasn't reached the stage where presidential intervention is necessary. It's that simple.'

Bradley smiled inside. The secretary of defence would have blown up like a Cruise missile, at the suggestion he 'back up' Norton.

'The British don't share your view . . .'

'The British don't have . . .'

'Let me finish, Clark . . .' The president stared angrily across the desk. 'We have an escalating conflict between Russia and the Ukraine, over who owns the former Soviet missiles. This dispute has been going on unresolved for well over two years. Now there's a new Ukrainian president who's threatening to back out of negotiations and seize what he can for himself. The Russians want us in, the British want us in. My cabinet is as usual divided. Some say it's day, others think it's night – but you want me to stay here. Why? You signed off on this weeks ago.'

'Situation's changing. Much more fluid. We don't want to expose you to something that could blow up in your face.'

'Go on.'

'We need you in the wings, Mr President . . .'

'If I stay in the wings it may be too late to get in on the game. I have to influence things before it gets that far.'

The president picked up a paperweight and toyed with it. 'I don't need to remind you Clark that there are few things more dangerous at the moment, than the old Soviet missiles. You yourself are aware that many more of them are unaccounted for, than we have ever made public. Something approaching a hundred, I believe, spirited away from the former Soviet Republics and now in China, North Korea, Iraq – and those are only the ones we know about.' He put down the paperweight. 'If we don't act quickly in any and every nuclear dispute, the consequences could be horrendous.'

'I agree.' Norton spread open his palms. 'And that is exactly why we should keep your intervention until it's most needed.'

'Thank you, Clark.'

There was a moment of silence before Norton realised that the conversation had ended.

He stood up, almost painfully thin, a wide academic forehead, thick glasses. 'I take it then that you'll still be going?'

'D'you find it difficult to accept that decision?'

Norton opened his mouth to speak, but thought better of it. Bradley was suddenly very dangerous. The question was like thin ice and he was being invited to skate on it – did he feel strongly enough to resign over this issue? He could hear his own heart beating. Maybe he'd underestimated Bradley. Maybe there was steel left in him after all.

'Of course I accept your position, Mr President.' He attempted a smile. 'I simply felt it my duty to provide you with all sides of the argument.'

'I know you did.'

The meeting was over. Deval opened the door and nodded at Norton as he went through. He turned back to the president.

'You've got an enemy there.'

Sitting by the fire, Harry chose his moment. 'Why are you going to Europe?'

Bradley smiled back. Harry was probably the best friend he could have. It went back nearly ten years to the time he had first run for governor in Kansas. Deval had been one of the powerful State 'interests' he'd needed to win over. By this time he had left State and gone back to the family law firm, trawling in big money. It was money Bradley needed for his election campaign; money and the right introductions. Deval's clients had ranged from the rich to the disgustingly rich. Useful investors, anxious to help build a Republican party that could throw off its cold-war image, and move the economy out of the mud.

Looking back, Bradley realised it had been more than a political partnership. The two men had come to like each other very much. Their wives had become the closest of friends. Since Elizabeth's death Jane Deval would often come over to the White House in the evenings with Harry and Jason and go round the private apartment, turning on lights and televisions and calling out to each other, as if it were a home again. She had even put up new pictures in the central hall on the second floor. Jason had brought a painting from school. They played board games on the living-room rug.

Bradley enjoyed those times. He enjoyed having someone to confide in.

'I need to reassert myself. I need to get out of the past and find a way into the future. Maybe this trip'll do it.'

'Why this trip?'

'I don't know.'

Deval stood up. 'So catch the plane, Mr President.'

'Stay in touch, Harry.'

'Don't I always?'

Chapter Five

'That wasn't a good idea.' Emily sat back in the limousine, scowling. It was lucky the woman couldn't see her face.

Mrs Bradley reddened. 'I only told him David was hurting a little . . .'

'You did what?'

'I told him he was lonely.'

'Jesus, you said that about the president?'

'I'm his mother for God's sake!'

'What else?'

'England. I said I'd been to England.'

Two alarm bells began jangling in Emily's head.

'Any details?'

Mrs Bradley went silent.

'Let me tie this one down. When I went out to the bathroom this guy Levinson started pumping you . . .'

'No! Well, yes . . .'

'All information has to be cleared with the press secretary. We don't just go round blurting everything out. I thought I'd made that clear. Did you say anything else about the president?'

'Of course not.'

There was silence in the car. Emily didn't believe Mrs Bradley. She had a mouth big enough to walk in and sit down. But the instructions were to use mink gloves. God Almighty, you couldn't leave her alone for a second.

'I'm sorry if I spoke harshly, Mrs Bradley.'

There was a few moments' silence while the older woman savoured Emily's apology.

'That's quite all right, dear,' she said. 'But you must remember that if it wasn't for me – there wouldn't be a president Bradley – now would there? Mmm?' She smiled victoriously. 'Well then, where are you taking me for my main course?'

* * *

'Boeuf en croute,' announced the new hostess. There was a ripple of amusement. The lady was from Alabama and despite being the wife of a former assistant secretary of state, she pronounced it 'Bof an Kraut.'

Mrs Bradley stifled her own snigger with a napkin and surveyed the woman's discomfort.

'What a treat, my dear,' she said. 'One of my favourite dishes.'

Emily looked down at the table. Beside her she could see a man tying his shoe lace, contorted with laughter.

This time the guests were more varied. A film actor had flown in from Los Angeles, a fashion model sat mummy-like at the end of the table, picking at a carrot, while her escort finished his plate and began eating from hers.

The talk, though, was standard Washington – high people caught in low places. Emily noticed they didn't tone it down for Mrs Bradley. And she was loving it. As the beef slipped down effortlessly, the knives and forks dissected the well-known names of the capital. There was scandal at Landon School, a male teacher arrested in a drug bust, wearing women's clothes, a senator who'd felt obliged to swear on a pearly-white Bible that he wasn't homosexual – 'As if anyone cared,' said the model, the daughter of a noted anti-abortionist who'd gone to Europe 'to do just that' – a former member of the House armed services committee who confessed he'd once sold secrets to France, 'probably for the food,' said the actor. Each had a tale to tell, except Mrs Bradley, who could really have told a tale, thought Emily. And maybe already had.

They left first, because Emily thought the conversation was taking some wrong turns. The room seemed to be a little full of democrats, fast losing their inhibitions and their tact. She had already picked up some loud whispers about how 'Bradley should sort himself out. Time for weeping was over.' Definitely the moment to go.

'We won't stay too long,' she said as they drove to the last house.

'I always enjoy dessert,' replied Mrs Bradley. 'Sweet tooth, you know.'

If the president's mother had a sweet tooth, it was the only sweet thing she had, Emily reflected. By that time she was tired and the rich food sat uncomfortably in her stomach. She wouldn't be sorry to get back to the town house in Alexandria, where she could shut out the whole evening, put on an old Tom Lehrer record, and think about returning one day to New York.

She was, she told herself, an American. Washington wasn't America. Washington was sleaze and counter-sleaze, big bluff, big pain in the arse. She felt sorry for Bradley, though. That was something else. But Washington sucked.

It was the grandest of the three mansions and absurdly extravagant. The gravel drive was already over-parked with limousines and foreign sports cars. In the powerful arc lights Emily could see that a once beautiful house had been painted primrose yellow. Who the hell would paint a house in Georgetown yellow?

Mrs Bradley was about to ask the same thing, only she remembered exactly who it was.

Larry D'Anna was one of the most flamboyant characters in Washington. During most of Reagan's second term he had been in charge of the Department of Commerce. Or more accurately his wife had been. She would tell him what to do, and then go do it, without him – she it was who decided who to stroke or mug, whose hands were to be held or slammed in the door. Under her care Party funds had never been in better shape – and membership, as the card adverts used to say, had its privileges. For a time Larry was one of the kingmakers in the cabinet. High-profile, loyal but incontrovertibly stupid – in other words a perfect sacrifice for the time, when the administration needed one and the public demanded one.

Of course, in Reagan's final term many lambs were ritually slaughtered on the altar of the latest embarrassment. When Larry's turn came, he was said by the leak machine to have miscalculated badly over the Savings and Loan scandal. He had to go. Most people were aware that Larry possessed no more than the barest understanding of the scandal – and that too was perfect. He couldn't even deny his way out of trouble. In the best White House tradition he duly learned of his dismissal on NBC Nightly News – and was asked to surrender his White House pass as he left that evening.

After that, Larry and Judy covered their pain behind their yellow brick walls and went on much as before – only with one exception. They made a private vow to get even. None of their guests ever knew about it. The parties went on as before and they still turned up, marvelling that the D'Annas had remained so loyal. 'Way to go,' said the faithful. 'Helluva guy.'

In fact Judy and Larry were doing nothing more than waiting for their moment.

But Mrs Bradley had no inkling of this as she swept into the hall. 'Lord,' she whispered to Emily, 'it's like a florist shop.' And so it was. Bouquets and vases, spread around, with everything but taste in mind. Thoughtful little combinations of red and white roses – the kind most people order for funerals. Or were the D'Annas trying to tell them something? Mrs Bradley didn't know and didn't much care.

She was far more interested in piling chocolate profiteroles into her bowl, and moving on down the table to the tiramasu.

Here, of course, the conversation was politically more correct, but that much duller than in the other houses. Entertaining catch-phrases like 'budget deficit' could be heard through smacking lips. As she looked round for diversion, she was surprised to find Pete Levinson standing by the fruit salad, spooning cream over fresh pineapple.

'We're not supposed to meet twice in one night,' she said, conscious that Emily was close by.

'Fate is sometimes generous,' he remarked, smiling.

Mrs Bradley saw a set of good white teeth and approved. In the old days when she'd bought horses for the farm, she had looked at the teeth before anything else.

'I guess it's very presumptuous of me,' he said, 'but I help out at a homeless centre in College Park. Everyone would appreciate it a great deal if you could come by, sometime. Kind of shows the guys that the government hasn't forgotten them.'

'I'm afraid that won't be possible.'

They both turned round. Emily had returned with a red face and a glare that embraced them both.

But Mrs Bradley looked at Mr Levinson and liked what she saw. His suit had dried. His hair had been re-combed, and those teeth really were quite marvellous.

She missed entertaining male company. In fact she'd almost forgotten what it was like.

So she ignored Emily and looked straight at Pete Levinson with the beginnings of a smile in her eyes.

'That would be very nice,' she said firmly. 'I'd like that.'

Across the room Larry D'Anna turned his back and smiled down at the cheesecake.

Chapter Six

David Bradley remembered all the advice about departures. 'Take the steps at a restrained run. Even if you have to sit panting in your seat for the next half hour. The country wants a guy who can get up steps in a hurry, who's fit, goes jogging. No human weakness, OK? Look what happened when Carter flunked the marathon.'

The south lawn was floodlit by the television lights as he made his way swiftly to the microphones.

'Take one question. Give 'em a soundbite and then head for the chopper.' Clifton Till, the large, rotund Press spokesman was beside him all the way.

Bradley smiled into the lights, seeing no faces, hearing the shouted questions, coming at him like missiles.

'How serious is the situation between Russia and the Ukraine?'

He recognised the voice of a network anchor. That was an easy one. But then these guys were hired for looks, not brains.

'As we understand it, Bill,' he frowned as if to signpost the message. 'As we understand it – there's considerable tension between the two States. They've asked us to try to mediate the dispute, and we'll do our best. We don't like quarrels over nuclear weapons. That's why we're going to talk. It's also,' he tried smiling a little reassurance – 'It's also a long overdue opportunity to meet the Ukrainian leader and I'm looking forward to our discussions.'

Anodyne crap, he thought and walked away, saluting the guard at the foot of the helicopter. Everytime you opened your mouth, you risked hanging yourself a thousand times over. If it wasn't serious, why were you going? If it was serious, then Americans would be phoning the White House to ask if it was safe to go to bed. You couldn't win. You just had to hold back the flood, for as long as you could take it.

It's like Beirut, his predecessor had told him. Once you take that oath, there's no safe place to stand. You can go hide in the dog kennel, but the switchboard will find you, because some astronaut decides to call from outer space, or the vice-president wants to know if he's allowed to unzip his pants and take a pee ...

The helicopter pulled slowly away, turning left of the Washington monument, heading south-west towards Andrews Air Force Base. It was a clear, cold night. No further snowfalls were expected till the weekend. Bradley watched the lights along the Potomac and put his hands into his coat pocket. He knew it was there, even before he touched it – a small thin chocolate bar, which Preston always bought him before a journey. To Bradley it was a little piece of the outside world. True, he could order himself a thousand chocolate bars from all over the world – but this one always came from a tiny vendor on K street that Preston would pass each day on his way to work. And it made Bradley think back to the time when he could walk a public street without bodyguards and without a bullet-proof vest. The restrictions weren't easy.

The day before, he had asked Harry to get him a hotdog.

Deval had smiled. 'You can pick up the phone and order one ...'

'I want it off the street. Plenty of mustard and onion, wrapped in tin foil. Tastes different.'

And Harry had brought back several and they'd eaten them in the Oval office.

'I told the guy, this one's for the president, so make it good,' Harry laughed. 'He said I should jerk off somewhere else. If the president wanted a hotdog, he'd come and get it himself.'

'Might just do that ...'

The helicopter was coming into Andrews and he could see everyone in their places. The White House protocol, the military aides, the Press yet again ...

'They have to film every departure and landing,' Till had explained, 'in case the plane crashes.'

'We wouldn't want them to miss a scoop like that, now would we? I'm lucky they haven't yet found a way to film in my bathroom.'

'They're working on it,' Till replied. 'Believe me, they're working on it.' He had a sense of humour that Bradley enjoyed and counted on.

'OK – let's do it.' The president stepped out on to the runway.

He was about to climb the steps to Air Force One when he glimpsed Preston, standing a little way back among the service personnel who always see off a presidential plane.

He stopped and went over to him. 'Preston,' the voice carried loudly enough for everyone to hear. 'You're in charge till I get back. You hear that?'

Even in the icy wind, the old man's smile shone back at him across the tarmac.

They were well over the Atlantic by the time Bradley found himself alone.

Norton had gone back to his seat. Till was briefing the Press corps, about how the meeting was 'key', but not 'make-or-break.'

'Walk the tightrope again, Cliff,' had been the instruction. 'Lean a little this way and that. Let them have some positive expectations, but don't say we're looking for a breakthrough.'

'That's not a lead. They can put that kind of thing half way down the page. These guys need a lead.'

'Float the idea that we'll use the economic aid as a lever. "Administration weighs tough measures." That should hold them.'

Bradley closed the blind in the little conference room and turned down the light.

With his eyes shut, he could see once again the cemetery at Arlington, the stark simplicity of the gravestones, standing in thick snow.

Why am I going on this trip? The Cabinet's right – I should be dealing with all the domestic problems, getting my act together, getting control.

You have to move on.

Bradley opened his eyes. Air Force One was turning gradually in the Atlantic Jetstream.

He wasn't sure if he'd heard a voice – or said it himself.

Chapter Seven

The duty officer in the Situation Room called well after midnight.

'What is it?'

'Sorry to wake you, sir. The Brits are going to announce a new prime minister – 0600 Eastern Standard.'

Harry looked at his watch. 'What the hell's going on there?'

'Embassy in London says John Gordon'll be resigning on the grounds of ill health. Heart trouble.'

'He only just won an election.'

'Sudden heart trouble.'

Harry raised his eyebrows. The duty officer sounded like a machine.

'Are they saying who'll take over?'

'It's a lady called Alison Lane.'

'A lady!' Harry almost choked. 'You'd think they'd learned their lesson last time round.'

'She was health minister. No one we've dealt with.'

'Has the president seen this?'

'It's been received on Air Force One.'

Harry was well aware that once the White House accessed the communications satellite, transmission would begin in less than two thousandths of a second.

'I asked if the president had seen it.'

'Hold the line, sir, I'll check.

The voice came back in an instant. 'The president's sleeping, sir.'

'OK, then patch me through. He'd better hear this.'

'Go ahead, Harry.'

'How's the flight?'

'It *was* fine. I particularly enjoy sleeping nights.'

'New prime minister in Britain. Thought I'd let you know since you were going to see Gordon in Berlin, and I know how well you got on with him.'

'I love all Labour prime ministers.'

'Anyway this might delay the start of the summit.'

'What happened to Gordon?'

'Probably the stress of the election. But you'll like this one. The replacement is the health minister – lady called Alison Lane.'

'Say again Harry. I think there was some interference.'

'Lane. First name Alison.'

'Jesus Christ!'

'David? Wait a minute! David?'

But the line had gone. The connection with Air Force One had been severed.

In the darkness of the bedroom, Harry replaced the receiver. He could feel Jane moving beside him.

'Did you hear all that?'

'I'm asleep. I never hear anything.'

'He hung up on me.'

'Maybe he was asleep too. You should try it sometime.'

Chapter Eight

The winter day threw itself at the British mainland like a hostile invasion. Gale-force winds, driving rain, bitter temperatures.

Alison Lane switched on the radio at dawn and groaned at the weather forecast. The moment she stepped out her hair would be blown upside down, her dress would fly over her head, and she'd look like a scarecrow, with her knickers on show for all the world to see.

This day of days.

She turned over and faced the bare wall. Some people had wailing walls, great walls, border walls – this was a thinking wall. Plain white and kept that way, a wall on which she projected her friends and enemies.

And now she knew who they were.

There hadn't been much in the way of sleep. Too many powerful images, too many shocks to the nervous system.

At eleven o'clock last night she had learned of her victory. Not a noisy triumph, but a quiet one, bitter and sad. Labour's all-day emergency conference at the Queen Elizabeth Hall had broken up with speeches about unity, and carrying forward the Party's programme, and what a tragedy it was that the new leader, elected a fortnight ago, had been struck by a second heart attack. Much anguish, much wringing of egos, and then a vote. Labour had a new leader. And Her Majesty's government had a new prime minister.

The car had taken her from home, through the darkness to Whitehall, the wheels swishing on the empty wet streets. Inside she was led rapidly through the dimly-lit hall, past the portraits of former prime ministers up the stairs to the private apartments.

His wife had opened the door, dabbing at her eyes, daughter in the background, the moonlight shining in through the little skylight in the hallway. 'He's expecting you, go straight in,' and then the bedroom, the familiar balding head and glasses, the face so white and tired on the pillow.

John Gordon, the first Labour Prime Minister in seventeen years, beaten only by his heart.

'You weren't my choice, I have to tell you.' He pursed his lips. 'But no one listens to you when you're on your way out. Besides, ...' the eyes targeted her forehead, 'you seem to have prepared the path pretty successfully.' Statement of fact. The cool, clipped Edinburgh dialect. No emotion. He'd leave that to his family, thought Alison. It wouldn't come from him.

'You might have waited though. Some of the doctors think I'll make a full recovery, given time.'

'John, we have to push the programme forward. You've been in bed two weeks. Ever since election night. People are getting restless.'

'So much for hero of the hour.'

'There had to be contingency plans ...'

'Contingency be damned. When was I to have been booted out?'

'Not booted out.' She held his gaze. 'Only if you didn't make a quick recovery. And so far you haven't. But you must have known, yourself ...'

'There's a difference between suspecting and knowing. I'd like to have played my hand for myself.'

Mrs Gordon put her head round the door. 'Two more minutes.' She looked hard at Alison. 'That's all you can have.'

Her husband coughed and shifted on the pillow. 'I'm away to a nursing home in the morning. The announcement will be made at eleven, if that's acceptable ...' A single eyebrow rose. 'It's a pity you'll have to jump in at the deep end, but then there is only a deep end in this job. The summit in Berlin, Foreign Secretary's away in India, all the economic measures ... it's always the same – just when you think you've hit the bottom, you hear someone knocking from below.' He sighed, but the expression was blank. 'I shan't miss it,' he said very quietly. 'I wanted you to know that before you celebrate.'

As she got out of bed a sharp pain stabbed at her back. And yet Alison barely registered its presence. The pain was old and familiar – a little like the physiotherapist who came twice a week to treat her. Old Lillian, who looked so gentle and benign, until her fingers stiffened like claws and dug out the pressure points. Old Lillian who would cover up the pain and send it away for the day.

Alison crawled out of bed and went to the wardrobe. Like many women in public life, her clothes were numbered and rotated regularly. The problem was she kept buying the same things – same black and white ensembles, same dark coats and jackets, to the point where one set looked very much like the other.

She surveyed the row of outfits and fished out a hanger. There was little point in trying to please other people. One man's classically-dressed woman was another man's frump. Besides, Labour still contained plenty of the old bags, who hadn't brushed their hair, or put on make-up in fifty years and bitterly distrusted anyone who had.

But today she would see the Queen. The words sounded like a nursery rhyme. They couldn't possibly be true.

In the little kitchen she made toast and coffee and ran through the morning in her mind.

She had already called Mum and Dad, woken them at midnight, listened to the thrill and anxiety coming down the line in equal quantities.

'Be careful,' Dad had said. 'Watch your back.'

'Listen to your father ...' from Mum. And she had laughed because you could never be prime minister in your home. You'd always be the girl who grew up, the girl from Christmases past.

But then the excitement began to wake inside her. God, there was such a hell of a lot to get through ... the packing for Downing Street, the summit in Berlin. She didn't expect the doorbell.

'I'm not dressed, Keith.'

'Best news of the day.'

She opened the door. He was hiding behind a bouquet of roses.

'Been a long time, Alison. Congratulations.'

She laughed. 'Three days, Keith. That's all.'

'Well, it's felt like a long time. To me, anyway ...' He came into the living room, took off his coat and sat down. Alison wasn't sure she liked that. Wasn't sure that, since she was now prime minister, he shouldn't have asked. Or was that being stuck-up? And yet there *was* a difference. Had to be.

'Thanks for the flowers.'

'Are you pleased to see me?'

Alison stood where she was and asked herself the same question.

Keith Harper, Labour's chief whip, was about ten years older, a man coloured wicked grey, MP for Wigan. She had known him since her earliest days in the Party, but it wasn't until three months ago that they'd gone out for dinner.

It was clear even then that Labour was heading for victory, but clear too that Gordon wasn't going to make it. Not for long. The doctors had already made loud noises of protest about his blood pressure. If he went on like that, they said, he'd enter parliament in a hearse.

'We have to think ahead,' Keith had told her, 'and fast. We're looking at options. People options. Are you interested?'

'Christ!'

'I take it that means yes.'

'Christ, yes!'

'Party's in a mess. There's a few too many of my front bench colleagues from North of the Border. Looks like the bloody Scottish National Party. We need someone who's English, not one of the leftists, but plain English, with a lot of charm, and some winning ways ...'

She just kept smiling at him. *This* was what she'd wanted. This and only this.

They had gone to a small Chinese restaurant in Whitechapel, to be certain no other politicians would see them. Just the few remaining yups from the East End, who'd moved out there when it was fashionable, and got stuck when it wasn't.

Keith had been amusing company, talked about all the women MPs as 'perfumed farts', told her there'd been quite a lot of talk in the Members Tea Room about her legs, and a 'good solid bust' and how that wouldn't be at all a disadvantage when the shoving began.

She had looked at him across the table and laughed. God, she'd been excited. He was a good-looking man. Large grey eyes. Bit of a paunch. But she didn't mind that. Strong, dry hands that held hers tight as they walked back to the car. He was a powerful figure in the North, good Union credentials, worked his way through the Party machine. And now he sat on all the committees that mattered. He was mediator, negotiator. He could deliver influential factions, when it counted. A deal-maker. A queen-maker, the way it turned out.

Which was why she took him back to her flat for coffee. Only coffee hadn't been enough for him. He'd wanted to get his hands all over her 'good solid bust', and she hadn't been at all prepared for that. She should have been. God knows there'd been enough amateur gropers in her time to start an Olympic sport. But she hadn't expected it from Keith.

It was bloody awkward. She needed him, needed his friends and his contacts. And yet, even in her excitement, something had told her not to give in. Keep him at bay, don't let him have it, let him work for it. If he gets it now – *you* might not get it at all.

'Listen Keith,' she'd whispered. 'Not while all this is going on. Let's see where we stand. If it goes through then you won't be able to stand the sight of me . . . take it slow, love . . .'

He had taken it. She wasn't sure how. Dented male egos could sometimes lie down and play dead, only to return with renewed vigour. At any rate, he had made some more coffee, and they'd talked for another half hour, and she had tried to give him a big kiss on the cheek and a friendly squeeze.

Only now he was back. And that ego was alive and well in his eyes.

She answered his gaze. 'Am I pleased to see you, Keith? Was that the question? I'm sorry – bit preoccupied this morning . . .'

'I want us to go and celebrate, love. We did it.'

'It's too soon.'

'I meant, you know, when things have quietened down a bit.' The smile contracted.

She shook her head, trying to clear the thoughts. She didn't want to lead him on any more. He might just as well know where he stood. This was the morning for a new start, new decisions.' Listen love, I don't think there *can* be anything between us. You know what I mean?'

'No, I bloody don't know what you mean. You said . . .'

'I didn't say anything Keith, and maybe I should have done.'

'Listen you . . .' and his index finger was suddenly out there pointing a foot away from her . . . 'so what were all the friendly glances about, the holding hands . . .'

'Oh, grow up! You think just because you hold a woman's hand you can get her into bed?'

'We had an understanding. I thought ...'

'You thought too much!' There was silence for a moment. She would make one more attempt to do it nicely. 'You know, we're going to be far too busy for anything like that. Don't you see?'

'What I see is you trying to patronise me. Three weeks ago, you held out the possibility that you and I could have some kind of relationship.'

'Did I?'

'You know bloody well you did.'

She looked at him coldly. You didn't speak that way to a prime minister. He would have to learn that.

'Now get this straight, Keith. You are bloody married. OK? Keith Harper. Married, right? So let's just start living in the real world and get on with it.'

'I'll tell you something about the real world, Miss Prime Minister,' and his voice had gone very quiet. 'I'll tell you about all the strings I pulled, going back thirty years, the favours I called in ...'

She looked at her watch. 'This is getting monotonous. I have to go to the Palace, I have a news conference, a meeting of the cabinet. And tomorrow I leave for Berlin. We'll talk when I get back.'

'Couldn't stop you talking three weeks ago – the way you were, dribbling with excitement ...'

She smiled. 'Three weeks is a long time in politics. You know that.'

Chapter Nine

He wasn't going to watch the announcement; wasn't going to watch her swan into the Palace ...

As he walked he could feel the bile rising in his throat, a searing cancer of disappointment, spreading out across his body.

The smell of that woman, the touch of her, the way her index finger would idly caress his palm ... Jesus, fucking ... !'

Two schoolchildren looked round. The street was filling up. Control yourself man. You're chief whip. You're a school prefect. Head of punishments ...

But I wanted that woman ... more than anything, I ...

He couldn't go back to Downing Street. Not with all the cameras and crowds, the whole pissing circus, dancing attendance on her.

There was a meeting all morning of the Policy Committee where he was supposed to sit in. Business as usual. But he couldn't face it. He'd been amazed at the number of committees that had to be attended, with all the bloody civil servants, telling them what they were supposed to do and how to do it.

Keith turned left past the Ministry of Defence, and then up Whitehall towards Trafalgar Square. On the corner was a café. He went inside and sat by the window.

Alison could be a real bitch when she wanted, a real 'Lah-dee' with her university accent, and all that legal training. And yet he couldn't remember a pull like that. Deep down in the gut where it ached. Not since university when girls seemed to grow on trees and you just reached up and plucked them down ....

He'd always watched her, but it was the last three months that hooked him. The phone calls, the private chats.

She wasn't beautiful, but she reeked of it. Sensuality. He played the word a couple of times in his mind, rolling it around.

You would go to bed thinking of her, wake up with her still there, fixed in the mind, mouth slightly ajar, lips wet, the way she did when she was thinking.

'Coffee, love ... ?' the puzzled face of a young waitress in view, looking down at him.

His marriage had faded so fast. Denise. Blimey, I even have to think to remember her name. She'd been fine as the wife of an MP, but when he'd started work in Downing Street, it had become too much for her. She'd begun buying new dresses, talking too much to her friends, wondering why she hadn't been invited to this dinner or that cocktail party. She could be so ... he didn't want to say 'common', not even to himself. Because common had always been good. Common was real and British. *He* was common. But things were different now, and she had stayed the same.

'Got a phone here?'

The waitress pointed to the corner and Keith went over and dialled a local number.

'I haven't got time for this,' the man answered.

'Course you have. It's breakfast, that's all.'

'Only on the worst bloody day of the year! Look Keith, I'm in the bloody radio car in five minutes for the *Today* programme, then I've got to be at Number Ten. So have you.'

'I'm asking as a favour.'

'You've asked a lot of those recently.'

'You took your time.'

'I'm a cabinet minister.'

'Only just!'

'That's neither here nor there.'

Tom Marks, the Trade and Industry Secretary beckoned the waitress over and ordered brown toast, coffee and orange juice.

'Bloody hell. You've changed.' Harper sniggered. 'I remember when it was all bangers and lashings of bacon and fried bread. What happened. You meet a nun?'

'I didn't come here to discuss my diet. What's this all about?'

'Difficult time, this. Party's only been in three weeks and we get a change of leader. People can get over-excited, you know what I mean. Sometimes they think they can jump the queue, get up a rung, curry favour with the new lot. Others, well, others might feel they can throw some weight around.' He shrugged. 'Keep an eye open for me, would you ... ?'

'What?'

'You heard.'

Marks spread a thin layer of butter on the toast. 'You call me out this morning of all mornings, to ask me to keep my eyes open, watch over my colleagues ...'

'One in particular.'

Marks pushed away the plate. 'I don't think I'm hungry any more. I don't think I'm having this conversation.'

'Listen, Mr Industry Secretary, sir, we had to push her in fast. OK? The old boy's heart wasn't dancing the right rhythm, was it? So we pulled a lot of strings and got it through. Compromise candidate. That's how she was sold. And a lot of people's noses are out of joint.'

'What are you saying?'

'I'm saying. Keep an eye on her. If she's not right for the job, then we have to move fast. We've been out of power for seventeen bloody years. If she can't hack it, let's get rid of her at the first opportunity.'

Marks drew in his breath.

'What are people saying about her?'

'They say she's got nice tits. What d'you think? It's too early ...'

'Don't tell me you weren't on the phone half the night, canvassing opinions.'

'All right I'll tell you this. My friends, the people I normally have breakfast with ... we all think the party had to go forward. Instead of people with egg on their ties and slogans, we needed brains, university education, funny accents. Doesn't matter. What matters is we stay in power and try to do something.' Marks summoned the waitress and asked for more coffee. 'What's up then?'

Keith looked away. He hadn't realised how angry he was with Alison. After all the backing he'd given, the days and nights, canvassing up and down the country, the arm-bending and back-scratching. All the broken nights and broken weekends, he wasn't going to take rejection from her. Not now.

Marks sipped his coffee. 'What's the matter, Keith? Don't like her so much now she's got what she wanted? Having second thoughts are we?'

'Hard to tell. Maybe I'm not so sure.'

45

'We can't start changing bloody leaders like dirty shirts, you know. I called in a lot of favours to get her approved.'

'I know that. I'm just saying keep an eye on her.'

'Christ, you people are odd . . .' Marks shook his head. 'Give the woman a chance. She's bright, she's done her time. And the punters like her. When did we last have a Labour leader, anything like as popular out there?' He waved at the rain-spattered window. 'And the other thing. She meets everyone on their own ground. She doesn't have to talk down, and doesn't have to talk up. She's as close as we'll get to classless Britain. Which is more than can be said about the two of us.' He sighed. 'I have work to do – unlike some people.' He went over to the door and was about to step outside when he changed his mind and came back to the table.

'I know what this is about . . . You've been trying to pork her. That's it, isn't it? You were coming on to her for months only now she's told you where to stuff it . . .'

'Don't be stupid.'

Marks stood looking down at him. 'That's what this is about. This "I'm not so sure" nonsense. Well, let me tell you something, my friend. We've just switched Party leaders, because of a little revolt in which you and I played not inconsiderable parts, mm? Labour has a new prime minister and she's going to be bloody good. And even if she isn't, the public aren't going to know, 'cos we aren't going to tell them. Am I getting through to you?' He leaned down and put his elbows on the table. 'We've got four whole years before a General Election and Alison Lane is going to fight it for us . . .'

'Unless . . .'

'Unless what?'

'Unless there's a major scandal.'

Marks sat down the same side of the table as Keith. As he did so he moved closer to him, speaking almost directly into his ear.

'There isn't going to be any scandal,' he said quietly. 'Is that clear? Not for your sake. Not for anyone's.'

Chapter Ten

'I hope you enjoy the job.'

It seemed such an odd thing for the Queen to say. Almost as if Alison were taking up the post of cook. She had half expected her to add ... 'We eat at seven. Please be punctual.'

The audience had lasted only twenty minutes. 'I shall look forward to our meetings ...'

And that had been the signal for departure. When Alison thought back, she hadn't really said anything at all. 'What a shame it had been about Mr Gordon ... we do wish him well.' Nothing of substance, not even a comment that the world was in a dreadful state ...

Ah well.

And then it was the cameras and the interviewers. The set pieces for the main news, the impromptu mix and mingle at Number 10. The standard assurances about continuity for the sake of the markets – and meanwhile you set about trying to undo everything the last incumbent had done. 'Mr Gordon was a wonderful leader. It's a very sad day for the Labour Party.' But by late afternoon you forgot he ever existed.

Politics was the sea lapping on the beach. It didn't care whose feet got wet.

A funny little note was delivered. Message about salary, cheques to be signed by the Paymaster General. £4780 per month – the salary of a prime minister, debated and decided each year by the House of Commons.

That would please the bank manager, the grizzled old sod.

She recalled opening the account at a branch in Tufnell Park, soon after moving to London and her first job.

'I get a lot of young people in here,' the manager had said. 'They all want to borrow money, and all of them tell me they're going to be rich and famous. What are you going to do?'

'Probably go on the game,' she told him with a straight face.

'In that case . . .' and there'd been the semblance of a distant smile, 'you'll undoubtedly be a better proposition than most of our other clients.'

Bloody hell, Alison, she thought. Bloody prime minister. You!

But the euphoria didn't last long. From early morning, sackfuls of ministerial baggage (and she included in that, some of the ministers themselves) were dumped at her door for intervention or approval. And three times a day, at one, five and eight, the little green vans would go out again from the Cabinet office, carrying back the prime ministerial responses, the communications of government to its arms and legs and other sensitive parts.

It was, she reflected, a tiny staff, with which to handle the onslaught. About 100 people, from the private secretaries, through to the telephonists and messengers. Just 100 people to keep Britain at bay, and the government from tripping itself up.

As she walked through the door, it had been like a first day at school. All the 'little friends' to be introduced, someone to tell her where the lavatory was, a row of assorted instructors, who'd coached all the others through the course, and finally the head teacher, in the shape of her predecessor's principal private secretary, Dick Foster. He had taken her over to a corner and given her the tightest handshake of the morning.

'Hallo, Prime Minister. There's me and two others you have to see. And then the day's yours. Word of advice. Government is government whether you're Labour, Tory, or the progressive Martian party. Government takes place not on a tennis court or in the tube – but in this building. There are committees, there are permanent secretaries, under-secretaries, sheep and horses – all of whom are there to serve you, according to long-established procedures.' He had coughed, as if to punctuate the little speech. 'Shall we do the tour?'

They had begun at ground level. 'You'll want to meet the garden room girls first . . .'

'The who . . . ?' She had winced visibly.

'I'm sorry. It was Lady Falkender who gave them the name. The secretaries. Their room looks out on to the garden.'

They had stood up when she'd gone in. Three rooms with low ceilings, and the lawn backing on to Horseguard's Parade. Quiet and orderly, with a plaque on the wall, showing that the King had sheltered there during the war.

'Gina, Alice, Susan . . .' the private secretary reeled off the names like a waiter reciting dishes of the day. 'Some of them will be travelling with you. So you'll get to know them all in time.'

And then on through the labyrinth. It was a maze of staircases and corridors. 'Plenty of exits if you want to make a dash for it,' the private secretary had smiled. 'Tunnel to the Foreign Office, exit through the Cabinet office into Whitehall. Straight into Number 11, and Number 12 too, if you want.'

She had taken a quick look at the chief whip's meeting room, with the long green drapes, and the green-backed chairs. She noted the credit card sized security permits, and the keypads on the walls.

'By the way, do call me Dick, Prime Minister.'

She had tried hard not to laugh, but then given up the battle. 'I'm sure I won't need to,' she told him.

When they'd recovered they made their way to the prime minister's study on the first floor. A long narrowish room, with three windows looking out over the garden to Mountbatten Green and St James's Park.

She'd been there only once when Gordon had offered her a Cabinet job. She recalled the beige carpet, with the small green flowers, the gold-framed mirror and the fireplace with the pillars. But the cricketing print behind the chair had gone, a left-over from the last Tory incumbent.

She sat on one of the red velvet window seats and stared out.

'I suppose I ought to go over a few mundane details,' Foster said. 'One of the WRAF's normally comes down from Chequers to look after your cleaning and stuff. She'll do the shopping as well if you give her a list. Of course you can go out if you want.' He chuckled. 'I didn't mean it to sound like Pentonville, but you'll probably get mugged by the first crowd that spots you – figuratively, that is.'

'Quite.'

'If you're not having lunch in the House, the steward'll make something in the flat. That's what Gordon did. Alternatively there's a canteen in the Cabinet Office, which isn't bad. But I don't think PM's normally go there.'

'When do I get the boxes?'

Foster sat up straight. 'Immediately, Prime Minister.' He pointed to one of the battered red objects sitting on the desk, with the words 'Prime Minister' embossed on it. 'We fill those up day and night. Please call for them when you want. And of course the duty clerk will bring them up overnight and leave them just inside the hallway of the flat.'

'It's not locked?'

'Never has been in the past.'

'So I shouldn't wander round in the nude.'

'Well, er ...' Foster turned red. 'I really couldn't advise you on that one, Prime Minister ...'

'Depends who has access, I suppose. By the way who does have access?'

'Well, whoever you want, really. Apart from me there's the other private secretary, political secretary, parliamentary secretary, chancellor ...'

There was a knock at the door. Foster moved across to open it.

'Oh yes,' he smiled, 'and of course the Director General of MI5. I'd better leave you.'

'Morning, PM.' The new arrival shut the door behind him. 'I've brought you some reading matter. One or two bits and pieces about the people you might be choosing as ministers.'

'How thoughtful, Sir Henry.'

He allowed himself a broad smile.

She'd seen it first, some twenty-five years earlier. He was just Henry in those days. The 'Sir' had come later.

Alison recalled an invitation to London, a couple of weeks before she'd left university. She was walking slowly and with considerable pain, but she wouldn't use a stick, not that day. Not in front of those people.

It was a long summer afternoon, and she was shown into an office off Birdcage Walk, where the London sun streamed in and turned all their faces into silhouettes and shadows. Typical lunchtime faces, mottled red, drinking steadily into their forties. There was tea and polite, inconsequential chatter about old college days. But it seemed clear that her interlocutors knew plenty about her, knew she was going on to study law, knew she'd become a barrister – but just wanted to put to her 'a little proposition' if she could spare the time.

'I'm here, aren't I?' she told them.

Indeed, they replied. Indeed she was. Cheeky as well.

Odd how the light had stayed in her eyes during the conversation. No one had asked if it was uncomfortable for her, or suggested pulling down the blinds, or moving her chair. She realised later she would be hard put to identify any of them, if ever she had to.

And in the end what had stuck in her mind were the individual words and phrases like 'trust' and 'loyalty' and 'defending democracy'. Not said in a hectoring or unpleasant tone, but almost as an idle conversation, a discourse on the modern world and the duty of the individual.

And when she'd drunk a cup of tea and the shadows had lengthened, they all stood up and thanked her for coming.

Of course the meeting would not be discussed outside that room. Not by her, not by them either. If people say things and other people understand them, they need never be repeated. That was the doctrine. That was the litany. 'We're all grown up. Aren't we?'

'You didn't ask about my accident,' she said as she left the room.

Sir Henry held the door. 'You appear to have made wonderful progress, Miss Lane. I'm sure we all look forward to your complete recovery.'

When he spoke then and in years to come, there always seemed to be a sentence missing. Something he was going to say and then changed his mind. A phrase or a word that would indicate what he really meant. A little key to his mind and his intentions.

As time passed she looked forward to their meetings. Always at his suggestion. Lunch mostly, or a drink in the early evening. A quiet exchange of information. Who was up? Who was getting there? Who were the oddballs, the question marks? They trusted her to see the dangers. Admired her insights. Flattered her when the physical pain became almost unbearable, and she would hold out her hand for reassurance.

Sir Henry could be a comforting figure – when it pleased him.

And when you've established such a relationship, it's hard to break it. For he treated her so gently. A fine lunch in genial surroundings, drink first, three long courses, sometimes a little bunch of yellow roses. Brandy, if she wanted to go all the way.

It was the subtlest of pressures. A secret life within a normal life. A private undertaking. A caring hand to help her up the steps, on which she had experienced the misfortune to fall.

She knew what he was doing – and decided early on to let him do it. She knew he liked her, more than that, would like her a lot if she let him. But that wasn't part of the game.

The game allowed them some fantasy – some flirting, a little challenge, in which both got what they wanted, without ever getting it all.

Soon after entering the Labour Party she had run for the leadership of the Labour council in Islington. Trendy borough – made up of Tories who couldn't be bothered to get into their sports cars and vote – or the good old hard left, who were fighting for London, inch by inch as if it were Stalingrad.

She didn't really stand a chance against their candidate. Not as a Labour moderate. Not until a letter came through her door on a Sunday morning, two weeks before the vote.

It was nothing less than a thorough-going investigation of corruption in the borough, and the officials who had been involved in it. No signatures. No sources. But staggering in its detail and range. Inside the envelope were copies of fake contracts for work never done, fake payments into non-existent accounts, there was money laundering on a scale Alison had never imagined. Many of the names were low-level council officials – some she would have expected. The one at the bottom of the list took her breath away. It was the candidate she was up against. And now she had the knife to gut him.

She remembered sitting on the floor of her bedroom, hearing her heart thumping out a march of triumph. She had no doubt who had done the research. Sir Henry had indicated more than once, that he was watching the local councils, the hard-left cells, the people who might cause trouble if the day ever came, when there was real trouble, and the trouble came to London.

Even then Alison took nothing for granted. She checked several of the cases herself, ran the information through the computers, saw how the links emerged. And on election eve she called a Press conference, climbed out of her trench and slaughtered the enemy. The result was the largest majority in the history of London council elections.

'Lane Walks It,' said the local paper – and so she had.

Three weeks later, after a decent interval, Sir Henry bought her a champagne lunch at the Reform Club. And even though they had never kissed and never would – she was his, and he was hers.

He sat opposite the desk as she leafed through the files. Occasionally she raised an eyebrow. There wasn't much to surprise. Some excesses here, some deficiencies there. If you wanted a Cabinet you had to have a group that reflected society as a whole. Not many angels to be found.

'What do you think?' he asked, after ten minutes of silence.

She smiled. 'Well it varies – either a girl too many, or in one case,' she grimaced, 'a girl too few.'

'Quite.'

She handed him the files.

'I should put them out of your mind for now. It's Berlin tomorrow, isn't it, and President David Bradley,' the name came out very slowly. 'First time in thirty years, I fancy.'

'You don't forget these things do you?'

'How do you feel about it?'

She got up from the desk. 'I've tried not to think about him. Tried to pretend that it never happened, that he and I never happened.'

'And now?'

She surveyed the white telephone on her desk, with the finger pads reading 'White House' and 'NSC ADV'. It had been installed by a US communications team and was a direct line to the National Security adviser and the President. She hadn't dared touch it.

'Now?' she looked up. 'I'm terrified.'

Chapter Eleven

Keith Harper had held the job of chief whip for just under three weeks. But even in that time it had opened a door into the world of rumour, deceit and treachery that he had always suspected lay hidden beneath the solemnity of Westminster.

Not only was there no disappointment. He had found the job a positive delight.

For the whip's office is the prime minister's intelligence corps, the ears and eyes of Downing Street, acquiring knowledge of the most intimate nature, for use when needed. In parliamentary language that is 'persuasion'. Cross the river and most people would call it intimidation.

One of the tasks of the chief whip is to maintain a book of secrets, into which he and his staff enter the personal circumstances of the Party's members of parliament. The pages often detail the records of chance indiscretions, of mistresses, of weekends, clean and dirty, – no everyday story of gentle-folk, but as one member put it ... 'the meat in the scandal sandwich.'

This book of books is kept in the chief whip's office at No.12 Downing Street, but Keith had taken the precaution of copying a few names and addresses into his pocket diary.

Now as he looked through it, the name of Cindy Tremayne bounced off the page at him – as he recalled the vivacious, black-haired Londoner and the circumstances that had earned her a place in his book.

Cindy was a very bad girl indeed, who had begun keeping some very good company. Long ago she had been the girlfriend of a prominent member of the Shadow Cabinet, a highly qualified nurse, and then later a physiotherapist working at several private hospitals. But the money had not been enough – and when she lost most of her limited investments in the late eighties, it was time to make use of some old political contacts. She was discreet, she was fun. She was caring and soothing.

'You should be in politics,' an MP once told her after she had soothed him on all fours.

'I am,' she replied, untying his wrists. 'Just as much as you are.'

Keith thought back to the time he had met her. Cindy was tall like a tree, shaped like a sculptor's dream. Plenty on which to hang both your hat and your heart. Just the kind of person a tired, front-bench politician far from home, could fall for.

The trouble was that one of them in particular had rapidly become a pest, writing her letters, ringing all hours, threatening to throw himself off balconies and under buses.

And Cindy, being sensible, not wanting scandal or complications, had called the whip's office and told them they had a problem.

Keith was grateful. The Party was grateful. The MP was quietly de-selected some months later by his local constituency. It was all clean and well-handled. Cindy was class. Cindy could be trusted. And among her unusually large and attractive assets they noted her common sense.

Now, as his bitterness towards Alison Lane intensified, Keith realised Cindy might have some additional uses.

He went back to the phone and dialled a number in central London.

'Cindy, you may remember we met a few months ago. Party work. You were most understanding.'

'I do seem to recall something ...' The voice was even, non-committal. Cindy knew all about telephones.

'So we have some work we might be able to offer you on a confidential basis.'

'Perhaps you'd like to come round.' Keith thought she was laughing.

'I'll do that.'

Cindy's apartment was on the eighth floor of a block off Gloucester Place. Not poor, not rich. Too close to the railway line if you were fussy about locations. But then if you were visiting Cindy, location didn't really matter. She opened the door in a plain dark blue suit – to all the world, the head of a major corporation, a lady of means and breeding.

She led him inside. No swing of the hips. No sexual aura. On the contrary, no hint of anything. The sitting room was furnished by

55

Scandinavians, plenty of pine, the rugs carried geomteric patterns. The atmosphere was clean and cool. This was a place where you brought your own fantasies. A clean slate. No pressure, or influence. The client was king. And Cindy was the queen.

'Won't you sit down?'

'I wanted to thank you for handling that matter a little while back.'

'Thank you for thanking me.' She smiled for a moment and the dark red lips closed soundlessly together. Keith had the distinct impression the clock was now running.

'I came to ask if you were interested in a project I had in mind. It's going to take quite a bit of preparation. But you have the tact and the qualifications.'

'In principle I'm interested in many things. Who is the gentleman concerned?'

'It's a lady.'

The smile returned and after they had talked a while longer, Cindy Tremayne was still smiling – to herself. It wouldn't work, she decided. But she wouldn't tell him that. The whole project would die a death by itself. All the same, it was intriguing the lengths to which politicians would go.

It was close to eight when he got home. Three bars behind him and a day he wanted to forget. She was there in the hall as he fumbled with his keys.

'You've been drinking.'

He looked at his wife and began to laugh. She had such good instincts, such a cutting intellect. Good old Denise. The first person to get an 'O' level in her road. Postman's daughter from Liverpool. Never missed a communication.

'Well done, love.' He started to clap, but she walked away, back into the kitchen and he followed her, more in search of food than anything else.

'You'll have to get it yourself.' She pointed to the fridge. 'I bought some fish today. Fish is good for you.' She was painting her fingers.

'Where you going?'

'Pictures. I'm meeting Iris.'

She went upstairs to change and he stayed at the kitchen table. Bugger Denise. Bugger Alison. It was going to be such a boring, bloody evening. No one to shout at. No row. But then, he reflected, in the last few weeks they'd even stopped arguing with each other. Denise was usually in bed when he left in the morning, she was usually back there, by the time he got home. She had even installed a television on the chest of drawers . . . 'liked watching things lying down.'

He took off his jacket and climbed the stairs in search of even a minor argument.

As he entered the bedroom he could see her by the basin, naked from the waist up. Probably going to wear her boob tube. Big girl, our Denise, he thought. Not like Cindy, but two good handfuls there, all right.

She swung round, her mouth turned down at the edges, as if she didn't like what she saw.

'What are you staring at?'

'Nothing.'

'Good. Cos nothing's just what you're going to get. You haven't bloody been near me for months. So don't think you can just stumble up here with your mouth hanging open.'

'At least it's not a permanent state with me.'

She walked purposefully towards him. He couldn't take his eyes off her swinging breasts – so he missed the hand that came out and slapped his face. Hard. Right on the mouth.

He stepped back, intending to swipe her in return. And then all he could feel was the anger. Anger at Denise. Spite for Alison.

Slowly, almost carefully, he took her arm and pulled her on to the bed.

'For God's sake, Keith . . .'

But he couldn't hear her, pushing his weight on top of her, grabbing at her underwear, pinning her shoulders on the pillow. All he could think of was that this was for that bitch Alison, who wouldn't let him near her. The only thing he wanted was for her to see him now, in this little bedroom, riding away for all he was worth, with stupid Denise moaning like an old steam train. God, he wished Alison were there.

Eventually he got off and lay on his back, his trousers still round his ankles, underpants half down.

Denise sat up and rolled her tongue around inside her flushed cheeks. After a while she said quietly ... 'I don't have to go to the pictures. We could stay here.'

No we couldn't, he thought. It was bloody awful, the way it always had been.

Chapter Twelve

Sir Henry hadn't dreamt for years. Old men, he told himself, aren't supposed to have dreams, not in their striped pyjamas, with the pills and potions at the bedside, and a body the other side of the mattress, called a wife, snoring into the early hours.

What possible use were dreams?

And yet he had one. The quite discernible merging of fact with fiction. A face and a conversation, and a warm female body that wasn't a wife and didn't snore, and possessed a name he'd known for so many years.

He hadn't wanted it that way. That's what he told himself, as he made his own piece of toast, retrieved the *Daily Telegraph*, and waited for the official car.

But he'd had 'a thing' about her for as long as he could remember.

In the dream, Alison had wanted to show him her new flat, somewhere near Regent's Park – with trees and a lake clearly visible from the front window. As they'd got out of the car she had taken his hand and smiled so warmly that he'd felt himself go weak with pleasure.

'My dear, you look absolutely splendid!'

Her eyes had laughed back at him, the blonde hair falling forward, across them, the mouth glossy with pink lipstick.

As she'd walked up the steps, he couldn't help admiring the shape of her, the 'bloody fine hips', the extra inches here and there that only seemed to offer extra pleasures. This was a woman of plenty. The mouth too generous for politics, the voice too soft, but that word 'plenty' kept revolving in his mind.

The dream must have been late afternoon, for the flat was dark enough for him to hide his excitement. His face had gone red, must have gone red, for all the thoughts it contained.

'Have a look round,' she called out. 'Won't be a minute.'

Hang on, Henry, he told himself. Steady, old boy. Don't do anything stupid.

'Aren't you going to come into the bedroom?'

Oh God. 'Yes, coming.'

She's in the bathroom. Get on the bed, man. Get ready.

And now she's coming out and she's *fully dressed*, all business-like and official.

'What are you doing, Sir Henry?'

'I thought we were going to ...'

'Of course not. How could you ... ? No!'

'I don't quite understand.'

'Which part of 'no' don't you understand?'

'Well, all of it really.'

'You *are* a dirty fellow, aren't you ... ?'

And he had woken there in a hurry, hoping to God it wasn't true, hadn't happened.

He had tried to forget it, wash and dress, think out the day ahead. But it hadn't been the first dream like that. Several times, in fact, over the years they'd known one another. And each time it took a day or so to get over ...

Of course nothing had ever happened, or would happen. He knew that. Something had always stopped him this side of good taste, of propriety.

But because he could never have Alison Lane, he wanted to be a part of her life, to control it. He wanted very much to use her.

When the car arrived, he sat in the back staring at the newspapers, not reading them.

They bore little relation to the facts that he knew. On every page – 'the prime minister thought this ... or the prime minister thought that ...' People wrote about Alison Lane as if they understood her priorities, her motives. But they never even touched the surface.

He could recall their first meeting so well. His colleagues had been horrified by the extent of her injuries. Why was he summoning such a woman for interview? It would be years before she'd be well again ... one operation after another.

'We need fighters,' he'd told them. 'Think what she'll be like if she recovers.'

And then in the years that followed he had helped to re-build Alison Lane. Not just her politics – the unseen hand in the back-ground – but her confidence, her strength.

The injuries, of course, had done her no harm in parliament. On the contrary they were the political capital that got her noticed in the first place. She was the instant role model, self-made woman, the fighter come back from the dead. She couldn't help but make it.

He recalled the decision to steer her towards the Labour Party. They needed some footholds in there. Real ones. People with prospects. And she hadn't taken much persuasion. Not after the Vietnam war; not when the health service started running down. A home had been suggested to her in Labour – and she had willingly gone to live in it.

To every wing of the Labour party she had appeal – to the sufferers, because she had – to the carers, because she did, to the bright intellectuals because she could argue round corners and out of blind alleys. She was New Labour Party, and in the mid-eighties fitted neatly into the Kinnock re-organisation. She didn't talk in slogans. She either made them up or carried them herself.

It was a march that clinched it. Two thousand people crossing central London to campaign against Health Service cuts – and Alison at the head of them. She shouldn't have gone. She really wasn't up to it – in the cold of a January afternoon. The doctors had all said it was too much for her. Go along at the beginning, was their advice, or make a speech at the end. But don't walk it. Too soon after the latest of so many operations. Too dangerous.

He recalled the photo of her next day across the front pages of the tabloids – a young woman in excruciating pain. A young woman, after major surgery on her spine, and the painfully slow healing of her legs. A woman sitting on a park bench, with tears running down her face, eyes tight shut, a walking stick clasped in her hand like a cross.

Alison Lane, it said. Fighter.

The car took him down a ramp to the underground entrance of MI5. He exchanged it for the lift – and that, in turn, deposited him on the seventh floor. He liked the view – a wide sweep of the Thames at Vauxhall, the trees along the Embankment.

A better view than Downing Street and more power at this desk than at any in Number Ten. More real power.

And yet, as he looked out, he had the uncomfortable feeling that relations with Alison were about to change. In Berlin she'd be meeting the only man in whom she'd ever invested her heart. Inevitably it would upset the quiet, unstated arrangement he'd enjoyed. Had to.

For more than twenty years Sir Henry had played the role of elder companion. A position of trust from where he had watched her mental journey – the way she had put aside David Bradley and the emotions he had woken in her.

But the recovery had been patchy. She hadn't faced it, he decided, hadn't understood it as the natural selection of the sexes. She had simply buried it roughly, haphazardly in a shallow grave.

For a long time he stared out as the boats puttered below and the traffic stood clogged along the bridges. If you could turn back rivers, he thought, maybe you could turn back time.

In the years to come he would always think back to this moment, when the idea first hit him.

Chapter Thirteen

It was seven in the evening before the pile of papers cleared in front of her and Alison knew she had to talk to someone.

If there was to be a meeting with David Bradley she'd have to ensure the past was straight in her mind. Only one person could help her.

She phoned through to the private office. Dick Foster, picked up the receiver.

'What time is the plane tomorrow to Berlin?'

'When you climb on to it,' he said amiably. 'For the rest of us ten o'clock.'

'Is it full?'

'If you mean Press, TV, a couple of ministers in dirty raincoats. Yes, full as can be.'

'Dick, I need to go and see my dad in Brighton – just for half an hour. Can you get me there and back in time?'

Foster was an experienced civil servant and unlike most of his colleagues, he enjoyed exceptions to the rule. After one day he decided he was enjoying Alison Lane.

'Can you leave in fifteen minutes?'

'Dick?'

'Yes, Prime Minister?'

'Don't take this the wrong way. But I think I love you.'

London's like a car park, she thought, as the police cut her a path through the traffic. She stared out at the faces of the ordinary drivers, some curious, others angry. Bloody politicians, servants of the bloody public, forcing us to wait while they swan their way through. She could almost hear the words, watching through the bullet-proof glass as their lips moved and their eyes followed.

Through the East End, through Whitechapel and Bow – and she could pick out the Chinese restaurant beside the cinema, where Keith Harper had taken her, a few weeks back, when they planned and plotted, and never really believed she'd drive past in a Jag, leader of the pack.

You never let yourself believe until it happens. Not any more.

City Airport now and as the car turned on to the tarmac an RAF helicopter landed to the west of the main terminal. The pilot kept the rotor at full speed.

Alison tied a scarf round her head, got out, reached for the arm of her bodyguard.

'Thanks, Jim.'

Just a twinge of pain when you're in and out of cars all day. Good to have a strong arm to hold on to. Now and again. It's not a sign of weakness, they'd said. You can do it, you have nothing to prove. That's what they'd told her at Stoke Mandeville hospital, where she'd forced them to make her walk.

It doesn't hurt to take someone's arm.

'Ready, Prime Minister?'

She loved helicopters, really loved them. Better than all the ferris wheels at all the fairgrounds. The power to land or stand or hover. Power and speed. She gave the pilot a thumb's up, and the Sea-King lifted into the early evening, the sky clear and the freedom to go where she wanted . . .

These were the treats of office, she thought. Maybe she'd get used to them. Maybe she never would.

Thirty minutes later they clattered in high winds along the south coast, swooping down on to a playing field beside a black windmill. The sea was just across the road, the sun already below the horizon. Time, told in a picture.

It was only a ten minute journey, but it was the ten minutes at the edge of daylight when the darkness seeps in from the east. Beyond the cliffs the sea and the sky had somehow merged solid like a curtain, preparing to shut off the day.

They turned off the main coast road, climbed a hill and halted beside a bungalow.

'I'll wait for you here, Prime Minister.' The bodyguard opened the door and helped her out. Instantly she could smell the salty air and hear the waves and the seagulls, out over the channel. The path was slippery and she took it slow, trying to remember the last time, hearing the little sounds domestic – television, kettle, the clatter of dishes. Her mother must have glanced through the window for there was a sudden shriek, the door was flung open and the old lady was in her arms, laughing and crying ...

'Dad, Dad, look who's here.'

She could see him struggling out of the armchair.

'Wait, don't get up ...' hurrying towards him, helping him to his feet. Dad in his old green cardigan, smoothing down his hair, shaking his head in disbelief.

'What do you mean ... don't get up? Wouldn't I get up for my own daughter?'

For a moment the three of them hugged each other in the middle of the sitting room.

'Sit down, girl. Take the weight off your feet. Heavens, you'll stay and have some tea, won't you?'

'It's what I came for.'

'Such a treat,' her mother said. 'We haven't been able to think straight all day. Sitting beside the radio and television. Heavens above!'

'Was I all right?'

'All right? I should say so. Your Dad's like a dog with two tails when he talks to his friends ...'

She laughed. 'But they're all Tories ...'

'Not any more,' said her father. 'Not after I've finished with them.'

She watched him across the tea table. The shaky hands, the face thinner, greyer. And yet the eyes had lost none of their intensity. He would always know her. He would know why she'd come.

As her mum cleared the table, he said quietly ... 'this trip to Berlin ... you'll see David, won't you?'

'I have to talk about it, Dad.'

'Not if it hurts. I don't want you to go through it again.'

'That's just it. I've left it too long. But in the last two years, ever since I've started seeing him in the papers and on television, I knew I'd have to bring it into the open.'

'Why? ... Why do this to yourself?'

'To understand. To understand the reasons he went away ...'

The old man turned and looked out over the garden. 'You know why he went. There was a war. It's not that at all. It's the accident, isn't it?'

She didn't answer.

'You can't blame him for what happened . . .'

'I know that . . .'

'But you do. Still. You blame him for all the suffering you went through, the operations . . .'

'It's easy for you . . .' She stopped suddenly. It was as if she'd struck the old man across the face. 'Dad, I'm sorry. I'm so sorry – I didn't mean that. I know how much you suffered, you and Mum. I'm sorry I said that.'

'Doesn't matter,' he patted her arm, the way he had done when she was a child, 'doesn't matter.'

Mum brought the tea. Niceties on a tray. Everything in a bowl or container. Sugar and jam, hot buttered toast, chocolate biscuits. Tea for children.

Alison poured. For a moment, none of them knew what to say.

She looked across to her Dad. It had always been easier to talk to him.

'You know . . . I've thought about this for so many years . . . the two of us saying goodbye like that. He never knew what happened to me, did he Dad? You never heard from him – letter or anything?'

'No love. I don't think he ever knew.' He shook his head slowly. 'You must have hurt him very badly all those years ago . . .'

'But he never wrote.'

'He respected your feelings. The man had his pride.'

'Dad – what could I have done? Turn up at the barracks with a zimmer frame and a stupid smile, saying 'hi, remember me?' I was a wreck. I loved him too much to impose that kind of thing on him.'

'We were all injured. It happened to all of us. Besides, he was a good boy. He'd have wanted to know.' Her father turned away and looked out over the garden. She could see his mouth tighten, the lips like thin lines, the way they always were when he became upset. 'David always made his own decisions,' he said. 'I saw the way he used to look at you . . .'

'Your father's right.' Mum was sitting on the edge of the armchair. 'I remember saying so many times . . . you ought to call him. But you wouldn't have it. And yet he had a right to know.' She bit into her bottom lip and Alison could see the moisture in her eyes. 'You

66

can't go on blaming him, my love. Not after all these years . . .'

The old lady wiped her eyes with a ragged, check handkerchief made from one of Dad's ancient shirts. She could never bear to throw anything away.

The prime minister's VC-10 pointed down the runway towards the rainclouds, north of London. It was loaded and full – the defence secretary, the foreign secretary, the Press spokesman, the Press themselves, all strapped in by RAF stewardesses and given triple measures of alcohol – a ritual designed to keep them enthusiastic and compliant.

They reached cruising altitude over the Thames estuary, heading east towards the Kent coastline.

Alison sat alone in the forward compartment, wondering what she would say to David Bradley, trying to push back a whole crowd of memories that seemed to be clamouring for attention.

An RAF steward appeared round the curtain. 'There's a call for you, Prime Minister. It's from the chief whip's office – Mr Harper, I believe.'

Alison looked up sharply .She didn't want to be interrupted. Least of all by Keith Harper. 'Tell him I've gone out for a walk.' She could see the puzzled face turn red. 'Tell him I won't be back for quite a while.'

Chapter Fourteen

David Bradley hadn't slept since Harry's call to Air Force One.

On arrival in Berlin he cancelled the meeting with the Chancellor, cancelled the city tour, cancelled the Reception for the Russians.

Alison Lane had jumped out of his past, where she'd been shut up, bolted and kept out of sight. She didn't belong in the present.

And yet, how could he have missed her rise to power? The answer was immediate. Easily. He didn't know the names of three quarters of the British Cabinet, let alone any others. Wasn't any need to know, unless they came to visit or shot someone. Alison had done neither.

'I'm sick,' he told Till. 'Got the flu. Tell 'em I'll be OK tomorrow.' But he had his doubts about that.

Alison Lane.

It was like opening a grave.

Remember that last afternoon? He did remember.

He was leaving Oxford to go into the US Army. He'd told her he didn't have a choice. *He* didn't. He wanted to stay with her because she was his home, she was the place he laid his head, where he stored his hopes and dreamed his dreams. But it was 1966. It was Vietnam. And he had to go. America's war. He couldn't sit in a library while his countrymen were going off to get killed. Couldn't drink himself silly at pubs and parties and read out essays in cozy tutorials. He'd drive himself completely insane. Just couldn't do it.

Vietnam. 'Nam.

He shook his head, tried to slow his breathing. Seemed like ten centuries had passed since then.

He could recall the anti-war movement, just getting up to speed, marching through the colleges of Oxford. Meetings, demonstrations, the sit-ins. And there he'd been, out on his own. The only one who couldn't see the big, bad Truth.

'But I have to do this,' he told her, the day before the summer term ended. 'And you have to think it through and find a way to accept it ...'

'I can't accept it. How many times do I have to tell you? It's morally indefensible. It's stupid. It's a waste of lives. And it's a waste of you. I thought you were cleverer than that. I thought you wanted to study and learn and be someone ... that's the person I've ... that's what you said you wanted ...'

And she'd been right, hadn't she? They'd all been right. Only he couldn't have done it any different.

Even if it happened again, he'd go. Stupid war, stupid motives, ideal for a stupid bastard like me.

'You'll see it my way in the end ...' he'd said as they walked across Magdalen Bridge that last afternoon.

'If I was someone else I would – but I'm not.'

'Try to understand!'

'I can't.'

Final footsteps to the coffee house, out again into the rain.

'Won't you say goodbye to me, Alison?'

'I ...'

'Alison?'

And suddenly he couldn't tell where the rain ended and the tears began, running together down her face as she held him for a few seconds and then broke away.

'Alison!'

Seeing the long dark raincoat, disappearing down the street, the crowd opening like a mouth, taking her in ...

You have to let her go. You have to ...

Thirty years on he felt the sweat break out on his forehead as the moment came back.

I made a choice, didn't I? Terrible as it was, I made a choice and I had to live with it.

Three decades with no letter, no phone call, because that was how she'd wanted it.

He could still remember the way the hurt had stabbed at him. Even in battle he hadn't been able to shake the thoughts of her. The softness of her. Not for so many years.

But when the hurt had blurred and blunted, there had still been the favourite memories.

Like the winter weekend they'd spent at her aunt's house in the middle of what would have been a field in any other country – but in England was a swamp.

'I've put you, David, in the attic,' Auntie had raised one meaningful eyebrow. 'And you, Alison are next to me.' The eyebrow had become a no-nonsense challenge.

And there it was. The England of old ladies with big mouths, of relentless wind and rain, of darkness by teatime, of jelly called jam. How, he had wondered, could it also have been the England of Alison Lane?

Bedtime was decreed by Auntie after the radio news at ten o'clock. 'Quite enough misery for one day,' she had observed. 'Alison?'

And that had been the signal for the long march upstairs.

He hadn't been able to hide his disappointment, sitting downstairs, reading over *The Times*, the dogs, snoring and farting beside the fire.

Alison hadn't given him a sign of anything. Three weeks since he'd met her at a college dance, written her notes that hadn't received an answer, met her in the street and been brushed off. And then a letter in the college mailbox ... 'I'm going to spend the weekend at my Aunt's. If you'd like to see some English countryside, meet me at the station, Saturday 12 o'clock.'

Jesus, what an adventure.

And now zero. Zilch.

Eventually he had creaked his way to the attic. The light was broken, and the room was freezing, so he felt his way to the bed and decided to sleep fully dressed.

But when he climbed in, someone else had got there first.

'Ouch. Who is it?'

'It's my aunt. Be quiet.'

'What are you doing here?'

'Writing an essay. What d'you think?'

'I think you get a kick out of danger.'

'Don't you?'

'But I can't even see you.'

'Then imagine.'

'I'm American. We don't do imagining.'

She had laughed.

'You seem to know a lot about this kind of thing.'

'I'm *good* at imagining. What are you good at?'

'Can't you tell?'

'Not so far.'

He had never thought it would be something to laugh about. He thought it would be something you took with great intensity, with a kind of hallowed reverence, with lots of heavy breathing and deep stares.

But laughter?

She had gone on giggling, silently for about ten minutes. And in the end he had joined in.

Only one Alison in his life.

And then one Elizabeth.

Admit it now, that it was never the same. Of course – not the same. But nowhere close. A different level, different planet.

Elizabeth had been so organised and ordered. Submerged in blood at the Field hospital. So full of goodness.

Stand them side by side in your mind.

And Alison was breathless and unpredictable. Elizabeth was steady and calm, with all the values and morals that would, assuredly, have taken her to a better place.

When they married, there had been no place for friendship with Alison. They could never have met as friends, sitting across a coffee table, politely holding forth about their families, or politics – done lunch, exchanged season's greetings, phone call for the birthday.

Better the break, sudden and complete. That's the way she wanted it. Better they try to pretend it had never happened, the way he did try, over the years.

So many times, though, watching an English film, reading an English book – he would see her face and try to blot it out.

There never was an Alison Lane. Never knew her, never wanted her. Never heard the name. Repeat after me. Learn by heart.

Like an atheist, going every Sunday to church – he had recited the words – and believed not a single one.

Chapter Fifteen

The Russian leader was in a hurry and a bad temper. The two were closely connected. He hated to be late, liked to spend time combing his thick, grey hair, liked to check his suits were pressed, shoes gleaming.

'When you've grown up in a pisshole in the Urals,' he would tell Katya, 'such things are important.'

And yet that morning he had been unable to get up. She had tried at eight and at ten, and then again in desperation at 11.30.

'Why didn't you wake me before?' he had bellowed.

And she had smiled at him and replied quietly that she had.

He remembered now – sitting through the night, as if in a long tunnel of vodka, swimming down it with his two old friends from the Party school. No Party any more. No school. Just two friends – and these days you were lucky to have any at all.

Shilov swore at himself in the mirror. He'd tied the tie wrong. Look at it – bright blue Italian silk – hanging like a rope round a cow's neck. I can't escape my past, he thought suddenly. I come from a country where, according to the old saying, people always clambered up your arse to remove a tooth. Everything done in the most difficult fashion.

Only now you had to maintain appearances. Take Russia's new armies of smooth, silky tongued capitalists – all suited by French tailors, all with tassles on their shoes, and judging by the country's performance, without a fucking idea between them.

'I'm damned if I know where they're getting their money,' he had told Katya. 'I haven't got any. The country's pissed it all away years ago, and yet these little bastards drive BMWs and gamble all night at the Hippodrome.'

'Strana Chudyes,' she had said to him quietly. 'Land of miracles.'

'We could do with some,' he had replied. 'Especially now.'

When he was dressed, she looked at him, brushing his collar, straightening the tie. He was still a good-looking man, overweight, suffering a little from what Russians call 'mirror-disease' – when you have to look in one to see your feet. But then, who wanted bones?

'So we leave in thirty minutes,' she said to him.

'I know. I know. Always you are the planner – the details.'

'Just as well, don't you think?'

'You are an extraordinary woman. I become president and yet it is you who has the brains. Brains and beauty. I just have a loud voice, so all I do is shout out the things you tell me to say. If anything ever happens to me, you should take over. The Parliament respects you. The intellectuals respects you . . .'

'And the "narod" – the people? Did you forget them?'

'Ah, the people.' He grinned at her. 'The people will love you the way I do . . .'

'You are a sentimental fool . . .' She led him into the small kitchen of the private apartment. It was modern and comfortable, with pine units fitted the year before by a Finnish contractor.

'You're worried about this meeting, aren't you?' she asked, making coffee.

'The meeting – no. The meeting will be all friendship and smiles. I'm more worried by what happens after it – when none of the promises are fulfilled and it turns out we have brought home a piece of paper as worthless as the ruble. This is what worries me.'

'So why do it?'

'I had to suggest international mediation. Nuclear weapons are everyone's issue. The Ukrainians have surrounded most of the silos that we still have on their territory. They're refusing to let supplies in or personnel out. This is very dangerous.'

'So talk to Klimak.'

'I can't talk to Klimak. He makes no sense. Now he is president of Ukraine he has become even more insufferable. Sits in Kiev stirring his nationalists. The only hope is that the Americans and British will put some pressure on him – we all need dollars these days. Maybe Klimak will listen to that kind of reason.'

'And if he doesn't?'

'We are both threatening to leave our great commonwealth of independent states.' He snorted. 'A meaningless gesture, since without Russia and Ukraine – there can be no commonwealth.' He shut his eyes and fell silent for a moment. Then he reached for her

73

hand. 'It's good that you are coming with me, Katya.'

'Why?'

'Because I love you.'

She smiled. 'You won't have time to love me on this trip.' And then she looked into his eyes and the smile left her. 'These worries inside you, I can feel them, my dear. There is something you don't wish to tell me.'

He got up and held her head against his shoulder. It was the way he had said goodbye to her the first time they had met, more than thirty years before.

'I'll tell you,' he said softly. 'But there is no reason for this, no evidence, no facts. And yet I have the strongest of all convictions that this is a one-way journey ... that I will not be coming back.'

The captain pushed away his food half-eaten, and decided to pick a fight with Chukovsky.

'So, Colonel, when is this pointless exercise going to come to an end?'

Chukovsky looked up expressionless from his book. The captain was an arrogant little pisser from Moscow, serving the last two months of his military service. Then he'd probably go home, borrow Daddy's Mercedes and drink himself into the ground. Our great élite, he thought. Same people, only now they had a lot more money to chuck around. Didn't just *dream* about it, sitting a couple of thousand miles away in bank accounts in France or Cyprus or Liechtenstein – now they could spend it out in the open. Like this little shit's family. Gold rings, gold watches, probably had a gold condom in his wallet. He went back to his book, only the captain wouldn't leave it there.

'I mean – here we are, Colonel, seventy metres below the Republic of the Ukraine, next to a missile that's spitting smoke and is fuelled up ready to go. Only problem – there's no one to fire it at any more. So why not just turn off the lights and go home?'

Chukovsky put down his book. 'Where were you before this, Captain? Lunatic asylum? Lavatory? Maybe you were in the zoo. You see, I'm trying to work out why you're such a fucking idiot. Finally, after all these years we're coming down the mountain. Can't you see that? Only it's hard, because we've never done it before –

and none of the ignorant bastards in power ever thought we would. So they quarrel like kids. Who's going to get the toys? Have you got more toys than me? The great cities of Moscow and Kiev, scrapping in the street, over a bunch of rusty missiles. No wonder there needs to be a summit in Berlin ...'

'And after that we'll get out of here ... ?'

Chukovsky went back to his book. 'Tell you what, Captain – give the chief of staff a call. No really! Ask him. He's probably got fuck all to do – same as you.'

The captain stood up. 'Think I'll open the tin can and have a walk up top. Volodya will be awake in half an hour. Then he can take over. Not that there's anything *to* take over.'

Chukovsky heard him get in the tiny lift, heard it rattle up the shaft, heard it clank to a halt on the surface.

On a television monitor above the console he could see the captain standing on the green metal platform, in the clearing. There was nothing to show it was a silo – or anything at all for that matter. He was always amazed the army could find it. And yet every day the unmarked buses brought the three-man teams for their twenty-four-hour shift, then picked them up when it was over.

Otherwise they were nowhere. A hundred and eighty miles south of Chernobyl, in a wood.

And now the captain was 'having a walk.' Chukovsky nearly laughed out loud. You couldn't have had a walk in the old days. You couldn't even have pissed against a tree, for fear of being spotted from a US surveillance satellite. Especially this silo. This was one of the ones they hadn't declared in the arms talks, slipped it in under the net, built it in a hurry when the US satellites were playing up, back in '86 after the space shuttle disintegrated. The Americans hadn't been looking at anything for a while.

He put his feet on the console. This was really the silo that got away. Just a hole in the ground with a great fountain pen sticking up inside. The captain had said it was ready to go. Chukovsky wasn't so sure. So many components, always something going wrong. Never the proper personnel to service it. Who was to say, it wouldn't behave like any other piece of machinery Russia produced? When you wanted it, it lay down and died.

Nearly three p.m. – half-way through the twenty-four-hour shift.

75

The air was stale and damp. He cleared up the plastic plates from the meal and threw them away.

Maybe the captain was right – turn the lights off and leave.

And then he glanced again at the monitor.

In the days that followed he realised he could easily have missed it. Why look again? Nothing to see. No one around. Nowhere to go.

For a moment he froze. And it's probably conditioning, he realised. You see all manner of strange things on television screens. You're used to it, you grow up with it . . .

But the sight of the captain, writhing in apparent agony, scrabbling at the lift button, a low line of armoured cars and troops in the distance – this was something you didn't see. Only in nightmares. Only for the mentally deranged.

Chukovsky snatched at the console, pressing the lift override, bringing it down fast, and then pulled the red lever to the side – the hydraulic mechanism that would swing a three-metre thick steel lid across the silo, blocking out the world, making the installation impregnable.

'Volodya – get in here,' he shouted to the sergeant in the sleeping quarters.

At the bottom of the narrow shaft, the open lift came to a halt. And as he leaned forward in the semi-darkness Chukovsky could see the captain had passed out. There was blood spreading across his open shirt . . .

Christ and the resurrection.

'Volodya!'

The docile sergeant appeared, dazed, still sleepy, staring at the captain as if not understanding what he saw.

'Help me lift him, man. Quick.'

They dragged the captain through to the control room and laid him on the floor. Chukovsky could feel a heartbeat – but it didn't seem strong, didn't seem regular.

Volodya brought the first-aid battle kit. 'What the fuck's going on here?'

'Shut up, and help me dress this wound. No, fix this. It's morphine. He'll need it if he comes round.'

He looked at the captain's inert face. The colour had gone. Sweat had formed on the forehead and upper lip. As they cut away the

76

shirt he could see thick, dark blood coming from a hole, below the ribcage. How the hell do you stop it?

Chukovsky hurried to the central console and lifted the emergency telephone. His eye caught the television monitor.

'Yop tvayu mat!'

It was the Russian expletive that exhorts you to commit an unnatural act with a close relative.

But then that was understandable. To Chukovsky the sight on the screen was as unnatural as they came. A row of armoured cars, lined up around the silo shield, some fifty infantrymen bearing the blue and yellow colours of the Ukraine, and an officer who strode towards the camera with evident pleasure, removed his revolver and shot out the glass.

Seventy metres below, the screen flashed and went black.

Chapter Sixteen

The room was full of traps. Building blocks, a train, crayons and balls. Little landmines in the darkness. Harry Deval picked his way round them, pulled the cover over the boy's legs and watched him kick it off again in his sleep. A good reflex, he thought. Don't accept things from people who stand by your bed late at night. Now there was a lesson in life.

When he came out, Jane was waiting for him on the landing.

'You only see him comatose, these days,' she shrugged. 'When was the last time you guys had a conversation?'

Harry took a deep breath. 'Is this something new?'

'What do you mean?'

'Is this a new complaint, or are we going back to the old one?'

'I'm just saying . . . I think you should see more of each other. Go to a ball game, roll around on the floor, go eat pizza . . .'

'You're right.'

'So?'

'So nothing. You tell me how to put in less hours. What kind of job do you think this is?'

'You always say that . . .'

'The job doesn't change . . .'

'Well maybe I do.'

They didn't talk for a while. It was Jane who broke the silence.

'Did you reach David in Berlin?'

'Nope. I was tied up. He was sleeping. Besides he was pretty strange last night, hanging up on me like that. I mention this prime minister's name – and that's it, he's gone. I tried thinking what it was that freaked him out – but who the hell knows? He's an odd kind of guy these days.'

'So are you.'

'Yeah, but at least I'm getting better.'

She grinned at him. 'That's what you think.'

'Maybe there's something in her past.' Harry stared at the ceiling.

'Maybe he knows something about her. I should run her through the computers . . .'

'You mean you don't have better things to do. Is that what I pay my taxes for, so you can check up on friendly leaders?'

He looked up sharply, but she was still grinning.

'You know there are times when you really piss me off.'

She got up and went over to him, running her hands over his balding head.

'Hey you know I don't like that.'

She took his hand and led him towards the stairs. 'Come on, Mr Sensitive. I'll make it up to you. Haven't seen that pathetically grateful expression on your face for a long time.'

They both lay awake for a while, not talking.

'Who are your friends, Harry?' she put her head on his chest. 'There must be people you do talk to.'

'Get serious. You don't have friends in this town.'

'I mean the people you eat with, drink with . . .'

'They're not friends. Mostly I'd prefer to eat without them. They're the people who smile at me, want my job, want information, want access to the president . . .'

'No friends among them?'

'Maybe one or two. But how do you tell?'

'And David?'

'David's a friend.'

'Why? Because he doesn't want your job?'

'Maybe.'

'Do you want his?'

Harry didn't answer. He glanced over to her, wondering what lay behind her question. He really hadn't looked at it that way.

The snow froze again during the night and at five he woke, realising the room was unusually cold. The ice had scratched patterns across the window panes – from inside! The power was out. Washington's fragile electric system had bowed once again to winter. That's what you got for having overhead power cables. Jesus, it was cold!

He dressed in a hurry and made his way downstairs. Every room was freezing. Coat, hat, scarf – and all the papers he had brought home and hadn't read.

On the street, he could see the Dodge, icicles hanging from the headlamps. Still dark, fresh snow on ice, no lights in the houses. Like the end of the world.

Third try and the car started, and he kept his foot on the pedal, till the heater clicked in and the temperature arrow began to rise. As he lifted the handbrake, there was a creak of protest from the frozen suspension, and a spin from the rear wheels.

Some fucking superpower, he thought, if I can't even get up the hill.

Swearing and stamping his feet, Harry coaxed the car to the top.

Five minutes later he was at the bottom of Massachusetts Avenue, and it was then that he saw her. Not her face. Just the hair that bounced thick and free down her back, the handbag over her left shoulder, the sheepskin boots that they had chosen together in a shop, well out of town.

He didn't look at her until he was past, until he could see her in the rear mirror. Had she recognised the car? She'd sat in it often enough. Jesus! She was too far away for him to see her expression.

It took Harry at least a half hour to calm himself. By then he had forgotten all about the check he'd intended to run on Alison Lane.

Chapter Seventeen

Ruth Bradley couldn't remember the last time she had woken up with a man on her mind. Over the years she had woken up with one or two in her bed – discreetly, of course – and for no other reason than a very passing infatuation.

But this was different. Pete Levinson had been so charming at the party, and seemed so interested in *her*, and hadn't gone droning on about the presidency, and the greater glory of the nation . . .

The point was she had been able to turn off the damned performance for a while, and when that little minx Emily had not been watching, she had actually managed to relax and talk normally.

. After all, you can't spend your life, guarding against a chance word. You had to be able to trust someone. And anyway, the presidency *should* be more open. There were far too many secrets in this world. She would talk to David when he returned from Europe.

For once Ruth Bradley didn't feel like breakfast in her room. She went downstairs to the coffee shop and sat for an hour, glowing brightly, with a copy of the *Washington Post*, crumpled beside her plate of croissants, and a vague, watery smile, just in case anyone recognised her.

It reminded her of sitting in bars all over the world – mostly on her own. Jack would never leave the farm, and when David was a child she had decided that if they were to see anything of the world, they would have to see it together. That was when the loneliness had set in.

Wherever they went, David would be in bed by nine or ten and Ruth Bradley would be sitting at midnight in the hotel bar, the perfect image of the American tourist, her maps, guidebooks and camera laid out on the table, and her heart crying in the wilderness.

On his thirteenth birthday she had taken the boy to Paris. It was late summer and she diligently led him to the art galleries, to the Tuileries Gardens, to the Bastille. But after the first few days she could see that his heart was elsewhere. The tall, awkward teenager had become captivated by the daughter of an American couple, staying in the same hotel.

The girl must have been at least three years older than David – even wore a little make-up. Not a beauty, but a wild, smiley, do-anything kind of creature, hair in thick brown bunches, constantly on the move, curious about everything she saw.

Paris to David Bradley was suddenly the girl from Fort Worth, Texas, who told him that when he grew up, she'd buy him a fifty-ounce steak and take him to Billy-Bob's saloon, where he could try his hand on the rodeo.

And then one night, she pushed him up against the wall outside the hotel and ran her tongue over his teeth, telling him she was just checking his dentistry. And he informed his mother the next day that he wouldn't be going with her to the galleries, or the race track at St Cloud, but he and his girlfriend were going to take a riverboat from the Pont St Michel and wouldn't be back till dinner.

From that moment on, Mrs Bradley had looked on her son as a man, or rather a man-to-be. Little David, who was now big David, had acquired new confidence. When he walked he left footprints. When he touched lives, they stayed touched.

She looked round the coffee shop, remembering a newspaper article about the types of men who became first or second husbands.

David was always a first and only husband. A once-only husband. He wasn't nice and accommodating. He wasn't soupy and soft, didn't wear tassles on his shoes, didn't work out or eat bean sprouts. Didn't need to. He came ready-made, tough, decisive and frighteningly bright.

For years after that Paris trip, the letters had kept coming from Fort Worth in Texas.

On his eighteenth birthday, David had flown down there, eaten his fifty-ounce steak at Billy-Bob's, and a week later flown back to Kansas.

His mother had stood at the airport barrier with her head on one side, and her eyebrows like question marks. 'Well?' she had asked, 'Aren't you going to tell me.'

'Can I put down my suitcase?'

They had got in the car and he had turned to her and said

simply ... 'didn't work out, Mom. She still wanted someone three years younger.'

So the letters had stopped coming. But Mother Ruth was proud of him.

Later, of course, David went away on his own or with his friends. And so did she. There were causes and charities, excursions with the Audubon Society, treks in search of moose or eagles – and when the self-pity inside her reached intolerable heights, then there was the occasional night of hurried and largely incompetent passion.

She never really knew what to do, she told herself. The basic outlines, yes. But the details. The fine tuning. There would be plenty of shifting and groaning, and the men would grab her hands and try to show her what to do with them. But it was like gardening. You could either get the thing to grow – or you couldn't. And mostly, Ruth Bradley couldn't. Not for them. And not for herself either. Where, she often wondered, were the dark, delicious secrets that people were supposed to take with them to the grave? All she had was the memory of a few embarrassed conversations like ... 'I didn't mean to hold it so tight.' 'Never mind. It was my fault.' 'No, no. I was on edge.' 'Just tired. Maybe it'll be all right in the morning.' Oh God, Oh God, Oh God!

Gradually, the glow left Ruth Bradley, as the sludge of memories drifted past her.

Idly she picked up the *Washington Post* and glanced at the front page. 'Party Coup Brings New British Prime Minister.' Another woman, it seemed – but then who cared about Britain these days?

The photo looked nice enough, blonde hair, kind of fixed smile, pretty enough ...

She turned the page, but then something made her turn back.

The picture was interesting. Must have been taken on a day out, for the wind had caught the woman's hair, thin, fine hair ...'

And then something caught Mrs Bradley's memory deep inside. Wait a minute. Wait, wait wait.

I know this face. Somewhere I have met this woman.

She ordered fresh coffee and sat thinking harder than she had thought for a long time.

It was the set of the face – that was it. Determined. Forceful and yet there was a smile never far away, if you knew how to get it from her.

David's words. God Almighty – David's friend. The friend from Oxford they had met so many years ago when he was over there. The ghastly meeting with her parents ... Mrs Bradley's mind had started to race.

She checked the name in the paper. Alison Lane. That was it. Alison.

My God, My God – this is incredible. I have to tell someone.

She looked around the coffee shop but there was no one in sight.

She read the story through twice. This was so ex-tra-ord-in-ary.

The bill came and as she got up to leave, her eyes became fixed by the passage of a rose, seemingly in free flight above her head, a pink rose, on a long stem, its leaves still wet, falling so slowly towards her, on to the table cloth. She looked at it for a few seconds, before seeing the hand that was attached, the blue shirtsleeve and the silver cufflinks.

To be fair to him – and most people weren't – Pete Levinson had entertained strong reservations about going to the hotel. He hadn't much enjoyed the twelfth-night party either. Old ladies, he told Larry D'Anna, weren't his style.

'But this old bird is something else.'

'You mean this old bird's son is something else.'

D'Anna smiled agreeably. 'That's what I said.'

Of course there was something in it for Levinson. And Levinson was in a needy state.

At the age of fifty-three he had discovered that the world of the freelance reporter can suddenly turn cold and inhospitable. Charm and the suntan from the ultra-violet lamp in his bedroom, were no longer enough to run the Porsche 944, the apartment on Capitol Hill, and the precious club afternoons out in suburban Maryland and Virginia.

It hadn't helped much that Levinson, who wrote for the *Washingtonian* under the pseudonym 'Count D', had torpedoed his own career by writing a story so disastrously inaccurate, that a number of influential people had seriously considered cutting him into little chunks and serving them up at the Baltimore aquarium.

The story had begun with an impeccable rumour that a man of

high standing called Richard C Whittle was visiting massage parlours from Washington all the way to the Great Lakes, treating himself to the extras – even dreaming up a few of his own.

Levinson had names and addresses. With a little work on the story, he even got some credit card receipts, autographed by Whittle with unashamed, ballpoint clarity. All of which should have told him something. For if Mr Whittle was indiscreet enough to go round using his credit card at such establishments, then there was the slimmest of chances that he wasn't the same Mr Whittle, Levinson thought he was: that is Richard C Whittle, secretary of the Navy, and a close friend of the president.

Now the real Whittle lived on the East-West Highway in Chevy Chase, never married, indulged in pyramid selling for Amway, and thought the whole incident was hilarious. When all the reporters and cameras turned up at his door, he 'just couldn't see what all the fuss was about.'

But his namesake at the Pentagon took an entirely different tack. The magazine story landed on Washington like a giant cowpat, spattering the filth as it went; and lawyers for the Navy department went in search of colossal damages. By lunchtime on publication day they had secured well over a million dollars and a retraction statement, broadcast by WTOP throughout the day.

As for Levinson, the city's insiders said his arse had been kicked so hard 'he'd had to go look for it in Wisconsin.'

Only the intervention of Larry D'Anna prevented him from being cast into outer darkness. But then D'Anna never knew when he might need a journalist, particularly a poor one, the kind who would eat out of your trouser pocket, and insert his tongue into whatever crack or orifice you suggested. Larry's words. Larry's style.

What he needed, he told Levinson, was some intrusive surgery on Bradley's private life. The time as a student, the early childhood. 'I want smoking bimbos ... I want to know if this guy farted out loud at a cocktail party. I want all the cracks in the mirror – and if there aren't any, I want to put some there.'

'This was all done when he got the job,' Levinson had protested.

'Bullshit! The guy's wife was badly ill, so the press laid off. That was the unwritten rule. We know bupkus. Bradley had the softest ride of any president in history. They virtually left the past alone, out of respect for his lady, and the illness and all that.'

'What makes you think there's anything there?'

D'Anna had grinned. 'There's always something there. Look at your own life, huh? Just find it, Pete. I don't care how.'

Levinson could recall the conversation word for word. He'd told D'Anna he drew the line at old ladies. But who cared what he thought? There was a job to be done.

'Mrs Bradley – a wonderful surprise.' He bared as many teeth as he could.

'Are you in the habit of throwing roses around hotel coffee shops?'

'I was carried away ...'

'Oh please!'

Levinson realised he was in danger of overdoing the treacle.

'Let me be honest with you, Mrs Bradley ...'

'That would be nice.'

'May I sit down?'

She nodded towards the chair opposite. She was so excited by the news of Alison, that she'd have offered the doorman a seat.

'I was looking for you because I thought we might have dinner together?'

'Why would we do that?'

'Perhaps because we had such an enjoyable conversation the other night. I wanted to tell you more about the boy's club I'm involved with. It seemed to me that you might just welcome a simple dinner and some conversation – instead of all the gala performances you're required to give around town.'

Levinson had the gift of being able to blush at will, and so the colour was coursing like a torrent into his cheeks.

Ruth Bradley surveyed him thoughtfully. He really did talk bullshit ... flinging roses around, having a simple dinner, some conversation. If that wasn't a come-on, she didn't know what was. And yet, she was in such an excited mood. Could she tell him? No, no, of course not. Out of the question. But why not have some fun, for God's sake? What was she waiting for? A man who would build her a doll's house full of light and pretty dresses, fields of happiness stretching away to the horizon? Who was she kidding? Life was three-quarters over and if she didn't go out and grab some good times, she'd lie in her box and regret it forever. She knew she would.

Besides, he had such good teeth.

She leaned across the table and lowered her voice. 'What are you doing now?'

They went on to have a wonderful lunch. Galileo's restaurant, off M Street, with all the Northern Italian dishes Ruth Bradley could have imagined, and there was Campari to start, champagne to follow, red wine to savour, and brandy for nothing more than the joy of the moment. Whichever it was.

They had laughed and talked. God how they'd talked! It was so easy to talk to a man like that. Such a wonderful listener, with no axe to grind and you didn't have to watch . . .

Oh God!

At six o'clock that evening, she sat upright on her bed in the Four Seasons. What the hell had she said?

Maybe she had just thought it. The name Alison Lane. Not said it out loud. But hadn't there been a moment . . . ?

She recalled David's lecture to her when he took office. Nothing about his former life. No loves, no friends, no cute little memories. Presidents don't have pasts, except the ones the White House press office authorises. Break that rule and no one is safe – no contact, no girlfriend, no distant relative. 'The public domain is infinite.' Those had been his words.

Ruth Bradley felt very sick. If she'd had a gun, she reflected, she would have blown her brains out in that very moment, all over Georgetown.

Chapter Eighteen

'How long have we known each other, Peter?'

The British ambassador in Berlin toyed with his brandy glass and wondered what was coming. He had known Clark Norton for more than fifteen years on the diplomatic circuit. Quite long enough to form a deep and enduring dislike of the man. But since when did that get in the way of a good contact? And good contacts didn't come much better than the US secretary of state.

He smiled across the study at Norton. 'Been a few years, hasn't it? Paris first I think. You were the rising star in the political section, while I was sent out to buy the bloody croissants.'

'But you did it so well.'

'You're very kind, Mr Secretary.' It was only half a joke. Norton really liked his title. Flattered him. Made him feel someone.

'Wonderful dinner, Peter. And wonderful to see you again.' His mouth expanded to approximate a smile. 'Perhaps we should join the ladies in a minute. But I thought it would be good to talk.'

'Of course, anything worrying you?'

Norton crossed his legs. 'There's no chance of us being heard is there, Peter?'

'What d'you mean?'

'I mean you haven't got any kind of devices?' His hand described a circle around the room and gestured to the old black labrador crumpled by the floor. Brits always had to have something to dominate.

Peter shook his head.

'It's just that I wanted to get your reaction to an idea. Kind of an international position, if you know what I mean.'

'Whatever I can do to help. You know that. We've done one or two trades in the past, I seem to recall.'

'I want to make a bid for the presidency.'

The ambassador tried not to move a muscle, but he could feel his hand tighten on the brandy goblet.

'That's ...'

'I wanna make a bid, because Bradley's weak and damaged, and I have to distance myself from him, before he goes down the can.' A thin line of moisture appeared on Norton's upper lip. 'For Chrissake Peter, we need some leadership round here. Bradley's never recovered from his wife's death. I'm sorry about that. But this country needs a firm grip, and if I'm to get in the right position, I have to start now.'

'What can I say, Clark? That sounds a ... er exciting prospect.'

'What about, internationally?'

'You know us. Special relationship and all that. Every support.'

'Every support?'

'Of course.' Peter frowned. 'When the time comes.'

'I may need your help before then.'

The dog stirred in the corner, and yawned.

'In what way?'

'Bradley was in England as a student.'

'So?'

'There must be records about his time there?'

'Hang on a moment, we went down that road once before, if you remember. Clinton never forgave us.'

'This is different, Peter. This time, the right guy's gonna win.' He rose abruptly and smoothed down his trousers. 'I'm glad we had a chance to see each other again. It's always good to know one has friends abroad. So much more trustworthy than those at home.'

'Politics, Clark.'

'Where would we be without them?'

Chapter Nineteen

He thought Cindy Tremayne was really something, sitting there in the restaurant, with tits that could re-float a battleship – bobbing and buoyant, two separate invitations to make a bloody fool of yourself. He grinned across the table – but she wasn't reciprocating.

To her Keith Harper was cheap and a bit brash. Got himself a new job in the Party, come up from nowhere very nice, didn't mind bragging to anyone who'd listen.

And she'd done plenty of that.

He'd taken her to the Carvery at the Tower Thistle Hotel, where the greedy bugger had stuffed himself with roast turkey and potatoes, biggest plateful she'd seen in her life. Looked as though he hadn't eaten for a year.

She hoped fervently he'd be too bloated to take her to a room after lunch, like several other MPs she could name. But, on reflection, it wasn't his style. He was too mean to pay for sex. His kind would would rather look for strays and pick them up when they were down.

Coffee came and Keith turned to business. He had called in some favours, he said, got her an interview at the physiotherapy clinic – the one that pampered the very influential, 'including,' he added, 'the lady I work for. It's a poncey sort of place, but they're professional. I take it you still know the moves?'

'They're not moves. It's technique, skill . . .'

He had a sudden image of Cindy, naked on all fours, tying the hands of an MP with a leather thong. 'Of course.'

She took a gulp from the wine glass. 'How close do you want me to get?'

'Where no human eye has been before.'

'You have to be joking.'

'Don't even think it. The aim is to cause considerable embarrassment . . . that's why we're having this conversation . . .'

'And you'll take the pictures to make sure of it.'

'We'll need evidence, that's perfectly true . . .'

She looked out over St Katharine's Dock – the play-boats, the toys for the rich. One or two of the MPs kept discreet little cabin cruisers moored along the jetty. That's when they weren't over at her place, being little boys again – or girls, dressing up and preening. So many times she'd wanted to burst out laughing, at the sight of their bare bottoms in the air . . .

Cindy turned back to Harper. 'It isn't going to work.'

'Why?'

'Because she's going to tell me to piss off – that's why. The moment I start pawing her, where I'm not supposed to, that'll be it.'

'I'm not so sure.'

'Well I am. And then what's going to happen to me – get locked up in the bloody Tower, I expect?'

'I said we'd take care of it. We did last time, didn't we?'

'Last time was different. I came to you. Besides, I've never done anything like this.'

Harper inclined his head slightly. 'That's not quite true, is it Cindy?'

'Of course it's . . .' and Cindy really had to think hard to remember this one. How many years ago? Christ, he had done his homework!

She had been eighteen when a female teacher had tried it on. 'A' level college in boring old Bournemouth, where everyone and everything seemed to have retired. Only not Miss Simpson, deputy principal, in her late twenties, with her wide-blue eyes and short tennis skirts. Cindy had been invited to play singles on a Sunday afternoon and when the game was over, she thought nothing of entering the shower with Miss Simpson, watching her long black hair matting under the warm water, feeling the hands soaping her back and then her buttocks and thighs – hands that were so assured, so knowing.

The older woman had moved round, just as competent with the front of her body – the nerve-endings, the paths to pleasure . . .

Cindy could still hear the urgent flooding of the water, still feel the fingers drawing patterns on her body – the sense of being engulfed by new and illicit ecstasy. Miss Simpson had used the erotic weapons for which Cindy had no defence.

91

'I've always found difficulty saying no,' she confided later to a friend, 'it was easier just to go along with things.'

And things had gone along pretty pleasurably until, three weeks later, the affair had become public. A male staff member had forgotten to knock at Miss Simpson's door one evening, and had entered to find the hand of the deputy principal embedded down the front of Cindy's jeans. Worse, Miss Simpson had been unable to extricate her hand, without first loosening Cindy's waistband – a fact that had only served to prolong the embarrassment.

Of course, Miss Simpson was asked to resign and did so, and Cindy, after a talk with the college doctor, and some pastoral care from the parish priest, was allowed to stay on. Scandal committed, scandal buried. The rite of passage through the British provinces.

And now, some twelve years later, the government chief whip was recalling the incident at lunch by St Katharine's Dock, which meant he knew how to dig dirt and wasn't fussy where he looked for it. And in that case, thought Cindy, maybe, just maybe he was ruthless enough to make the scheme work.

Looking up from the table, she smiled at Harper, as if to show him, she wasn't even vaguely surprised.

'I think all that history is my business,' her eyes locked on to him across the table. 'We can all handle confidential material. I expect my own records are just as interesting as yours. That isn't the point. What is – is that I've thought about it and I'll give it a try. But if it does go wrong, I want out, and I want money to start a life somewhere else. Long way, away.'

'Agreed.' Harper gestured at the waitress to bring the bill. 'Only it isn't going to go wrong.'

He paid in cash, and steered her through the tables, watching the heads turn, the jealous glances, tourist and businessman transported into instant fantasy. That's what Cindy did for people. Brought those fantasies to life. Perhaps, she'd do it for Alison Lane. Who could tell? Maybe *that* was her thing, after all.

As they got out through the swing doors, he held on to her arm.

'Excuse me . . .' she turned round sharply.

'I just wanted to say one thing, Cindy, before we go our separate ways. I wanted to emphasise the importance of not mentioning this to anyone – and I mean anyone. You do see that, don't you?'

Cindy freed her arm. 'I hardly think you have to remind me of that.'

'Because if you do,' Keith ignored her, 'I'll close you down for good. No work, no favours. And a lot of aggravation that a single girl in London would be wise to avoid.' He handed her an envelope. 'All the details you need are in here. Your appointment's tomorrow. Please be there on time. They appreciate that kind of thing.'

He watched her drive away in the taxi. Of course, if it did go wrong, he reflected, they'd both be on their bike.

Probably to a place where you couldn't even buy one.

'Cindy Tremayne? What a pleasant name!'

'Thank you.'

'I've had a look at your qualifications and the ah ... letter you brought with you. That all looks perfectly in order ...' The director of the Harvey Clinic gave a little cough. 'Of course we don't normally discuss these things, but I can't tell you how fortuitous your application is. Most fortuitous, in fact. One of our longest serving physiotherapists called in a few hours ago from hospital, I regret to say, to inform us she'd been in an accident. Apparently she was pushed to the ground by a mugger. Fellow tried to steal her handbag, and when she resisted, struck her on the knee with a cosh. I gather she's in great pain – may even have fractured the bone ...'

'How awful!'

'Looks as though she'll be out of commission for weeks.'

'I see.'

'Thing is, if you'd come yesterday, I'd have told you we had no vacancies, and to come back another time. So you see ... one man's ... or rather one woman's misfortune ...' He laid his hands on the desk, white hands, perfectly manicured, the tip of a handkerchief protruding from his sleeve, 'One woman's misfortune is another's er ... good luck.'

'I suppose it is ...'

'Yes, well.' He stood up straight against the side of the desk. 'We shall of course want to see you at work for one or two sessions. Shall we say ten o'clock tomorrow morning. A little trial period, if that's acceptable to you ... just a week or so. And then we'll review things at the end of the month ... Miss Primp will discuss the ... ah terms of the engagement ...'

Cindy stood up and held out her hand. The director smiled smugly. 'We don't shake hands in this establishment, Miss Tremayne. We work with clients who don't normally like that kind of familiarity, unless of course they happen to be from the ah ... continent.'

'I quite understand.'

'Good day, Miss Tremayne.'

It took an hour to fill in the forms, under the painstaking direction of Miss Primp. Miss Fatarse, more like, thought Cindy. And it was only as she walked away down the drive that she reflected in any detail on the circumstances of her engagement. What a wonderful coincidence that a long-serving physiotherapist had been injured in an accident. What perfect timing. What organisation.

Of course it was further evidence that Keith Harper was a man who got what he wanted. And if you stood in his way, he would sweep you aside.

It wasn't that she minded any of that. Cindy enjoyed high stakes, always had done. She enjoyed the feeling of standing on a tightrope, beating the odds. That was her life. The risk. The subterfuge.

All the same, she told herself, it would be prudent to make some travel arrangements, should the need arise.

Chapter Twenty

Alison Lane barely noticed the landing in Berlin, or the bulky German chancellor with his hand outstretched in welcome, blue raincoat almost touching the ground, full of sincere greetings and profound hopes. And wasn't he always?

Dick Foster sat beside her on the short journey to the city – and she took refuge in his low mumble, going over the programme, the people she'd see, the agenda.

He was like a priest intoning a private prayer, as she stared out at the neon lights and the crowded cafes along the Ku-damm.

'Give me half an hour,' she said as they reached the hotel. And Foster had rightly interpreted the look ... Don't interrupt me. I've got things on my mind. You know what to get on with.

She had shut the bedroom door of the suite and sat by the window, feeling the flush spread out over her cheeks.

Don't know if I can do this, she thought suddenly. Don't know if I want to. The mind isn't supposed to remember pain. That's the safety mechanism. But why can I feel it now, advancing like an army?

She opened the window and the cold air leapt in at her, bringing the noise of traffic and sirens as another delegation arrived. Little Berlin on the street far below. Out of reach.

We're none of us supposed to have lives, she reflected. Not the leaders. Not the heads of government. We're offices, we're chairs. We can't feel and we can't react. People write to us in their thousands about poverty, injustice, unhappiness. And we get up in parliament and tell them how well we're doing. We pick up babies in a crowd and kiss them, because we haven't time for our own.

That's why I grasped this job. I didn't want to feel any more. I didn't mind missing out on happiness. I just wanted to avoid the pain. I can't go through it again. I have to be the armour-plated bitch, they all think I am. And maybe it's true.

She picked up the phone and called Foster.

'Where's Bradley staying?'

'Hilton, I think. Want me to fix up a call?'

'No. Just wondered.'

'Right.'

'That's all, Dick.'

'Yes, Prime Minister.'

'Call you when I'm ready.'

'Of course, Prime Minister.'

Lying on the bed she remembered the first time she had seen his picture after Oxford. A magazine article ten years earlier about the soldier governor, the Vietnam hero from Kansas – and where better they had asked, to find a real cowboy?

She had felt a physical jolt, felt his hands, felt the rain as it washed away her dreams on that early winter evening in Oxford. The city where you came to learn of what had been and what might be.

And she could hear that voice as if it were yesterday. The voice that always said to her ... 'I can reach you, Alison. Wherever you disappear in your mind, wherever you hide your thoughts, whenever some hurt or some disappointment sends you running deep into your imagined cave. I can always reach you. I always will.'

She remembered the two of them, promising things they didn't know about, giving gifts that weren't theirs to own. How could we have said those things, said them with all the certainty of true ignorance? We found answers where there are only questions. We made plans and dreamed dreams as if they were the currency that could buy us a future. If you voiced the words – they'd come true.

I always said that to him, she recalled. 'Tell me it'll happen, David, and it will.' Only he wouldn't. He'd play lots of games but he wouldn't play that one.

For him the plans were intentions – that life would honour or dishonour according to rules of its own.

He knew it – and I didn't. He said it would happen if it was meant to. Does he think the same now?

I really believed that when my studies were over, I'd go to America, I'd go to the war, I'd find my soldier, with a book in his hand instead of a machine gun – and I'd take him home. And we would live that ever-after kind of life, whatever it was, under the tall skies, in certain hope of happiness and light.

And then the feeling of pride when he'd been elected president. What a night it had been. Quiet, silent pride, for her alone. David, David, you did it!' ... said only to herself, as she stared at his face on the screen. Hadn't a little voice said to her even then ... 'If he can do it, so can you?'

She got up, went into the bathroom and stared at herself. I know who *you* are, she thought. I recognise you from the papers. You're Prime Minister Alison Lane, nobody's lover, not for a long time ... A life on the outside.

But I no longer recognise the person you were in Oxford and maybe that's why I'm here. I want to find that woman. I want to know if she's still around. Because she was happier than me – and she knew how to love. And I think I can learn from her.

When I move, he thought, a thousand people have to move with me. Half of them arrive before I do ... they build little communication cities all over the world, so I can talk to anyone I want. And if that's not enough, they spend days discussing where the nearest hospitals are, in case someone decides to shoot me.

If I want to step over to a crowd, then the people will suddenly find themselves abused and threatened by men with plastic earpieces, ordering them to take their hands out of their pockets.

That would be all right for four years. But it isn't going to stop there. When I finally kick the bucket, they'll want to know from the Almighty well in advance whether I'm going up or down. If they haven't sanitised the area first, they'll tell him to back off. The secret service can do that.

Bradley looked around the crowded, makeshift Cabinet room. They had taken over the entire ninth and tenth floors of the Hilton. He had filled the place intentionally. Didn't want to do any thinking. Didn't want to reflect on the reason he'd come to Berlin.

Everyone seemed to be talking. You couldn't think a single coherent thought with this crowd around; secretary of state, press secretary, deputy chief of staff, jackets off, ties loose, gin and tonics and beers in front of them. All boys together. Night away from home. In charge of a country, sure. But what the hell, they were going to have a good time.

He had asked if Alison Lane had arrived. Just an innocent inquiry. But why should it be anything else? There wasn't any guilt, was there?

Christ, thirty years earlier, it was she who had broken it off. She and the circumstances. He had finished his studies at Oxford and was heading for the Army. She was going to call. That was the deal. She would make contact. But she never did. Deal was off.

Funny people, us Americans, he thought. Life defined in deals. Deals made, deals broken. Round the corner, though, there'll always be another . . .

'Wanna drink, David?' Clark Norton from State had a voice that could cut diamonds.

'I think we'll settle down, gentlemen,' Bradley addressed the whole room. 'As you know I have a morning meeting with the Russians. It's a friendly. That's fine, but let's agree a position.'

They straightened up, put down the drinks, pulled out folders and yellow pads. The class was back in session.

Bradley knew all about the danger of friendly meetings. It was like exhibition boxing. You still fought and you still wanted to win. And at this level a wrong word, a wrong impression, an emphasis or a nuance misunderstood – and the whole conference could jump off the cliff.

It would be the same with Alison. So careful, David. So careful. For when you've loved a person, they leave something inside you – a presence, powerful yet dormant. Only if it should ever wake, he thought, it has the potential to shatter your beliefs and certainties and drag you from your orbit, right out into the unknown.

Twenty minutes later, a political aide brought a note to the president.

'Gentlemen,' he interrupted Norton in full flight. 'I'm gonna stop you here. The British prime minister is on the telephone. We'll resume in ten minutes . . .'

The words weren't an invitation to be silent – they were an invitation to leave. A clear order to get out.

Rapidly, the five Cabinet members shouldered their jackets, collected their papers and headed for the door, exchanging puzzled looks. Something was wrong because prime ministers didn't call without warning, and presidents didn't get rid of their staff when they did.

In the secretary of state's suite the Cabinet put down their papers and breathed a collective sigh.

'What the hell's he up to?'

'Did you see his face?' Norton stood by the window and gazed out. 'He looked nervous ... who knows ... ?'

'Who cares?' said Till. 'Let's deal with the Press. We need some stories and we need some photo-ops. This isn't a summit unless it's on television.'

Norton threw a folder at him. 'Make it up, fellah. You usually do!'

Till stared down at his yellow pad. Like all Press secretaries he considered it was better not to lie unless he had to.

But, hell – it made the job more fun.

Chapter Twenty-one

Only Foster stayed behind in the room. He had scheduled the phone call, completed the formalities. Yes, the president would be happy to speak with Prime Minister Lane. One moment please.

She took the receiver. 'Thank you, Peter.'

'Goodnight, Prime Minister. If you need anything . . .'

What I need, she thought, is to put down the phone and stop shaking inside. I need to black out the past, and look only to the days ahead. I need to speak to the president of the United States about an international crisis – not because I loved him thirty years ago on another planet.

As she gripped the receiver, she saw herself standing, decades ago, in an old red phonebox off the Oxford High Street . . . picture so clear.

David had returned to the States because his grandfather had died. And he had written to her saying . . . on May 21st, I'll call you at the payphone beside the King's Arms, exactly midnight your time, seven p.m., Eastern Standard. Don't get drunk. Don't pick up anyone. Be there, OK?

She had been there. An hour early, in fact. Whether by Greenwich Mean Time or Eastern Standard, walking up and down in the sub-zero temperatures of an English spring.

Bloody country, bloody phoneboxes. What am I doing?

And she could hear everyone else's conversations through a broken window pane . . .

God the things people *said* to each other!

Of course midnight found some little wimp, standing, pouring out his miserable, wimpish heart to a girl called Tiggy, who clearly didn't want to know. There were plenty of 'please, Tiggy's, and 'be reasonable, Tiggy's, and 'let's give it another go, Tigs.'

All so clear, even with such a distance in time . . .

And then the wimp had given up and she took possession of the box, ready to defend it whoever came.

He would ring late on principle. She had been so sure of it. But he was right on time.

'Al!'

'Don't call me Al, David.'

'How about "Ally"?'

'What's wrong with Alison? Been all right up till now.'

'Too long. I think you're an Ally.'

'Sounds like a narrow passage.'

He laughed.

'I didn't mean it like that. Can't you raise your mind above waist level?'

'It's kind of stuck down there.'

'Oh, very nice. I'm not standing in this phonebox to practise pornography . . .'

'You got something better to do?'

'As a matter of fact, there's a guy waiting outside who looks really gorgeous . . .'

'Remember I come from a violent country . . .'

Her turn to laugh.

'I'm not good with rivals . . .'

'Then don't think about it . . .'

'Why did I call you?'

'No idea. Tell me.'

'Uh-uh. I've told you too much already. I want you to put down the phone, walk straight past this Adonis creature, or whatever his name is, go back to the room, lock the door, and read a book by the gas fire . . .'

'What are you going to do?'

'Oh take a walk past the red lights and the ladies with white boots . . .'

'Goodnight, David. Don't bother coming back.'

''Night. I'll see you next week.'

As she left the box, the wind had raced up Broad Street, grabbing at her hair and her coat. Only she didn't feel cold. She could move with the wind, sway with the wind, ride it all the way to the little room across town . . .

And now?

Calm in the room, suddenly. Little pieces of history moving out of the shadows. Berlin – where she had brought her memories.

'Alison?'
    'Yes?'
    'My God, I can hardly believe this . . .'
    'I know.'
    'You sound exactly the same . . .'
    'I haven't said anything . . .'
    'But you do . . . . .'
    'What . . . . sound like a silly student, you mean?'
    'Never that . . . I don't know what to say . . . am I going to have to
beg to see you?'
    She laughed. 'I might like that. Do you want to see me?'
    'D'you need to ask?'
    'We could go on throwing questions at each other all night.'
    'Is that a formal proposal?'
    'David, I'll see you in the morning, OK?'
    'Breakfast here is at seven . . .'
    'I'm not sure . . .'
    'I could have you forcibly detained.'
    She smiled at the phone. 'All right.'
    'You can bring your chaperone. But I don't bite in the mornings.'
    She knew all about his mornings. 'Goodnight, David.'
    'I'm glad you called.'

Only why had she called? He sat still for a long time, repeating each
word.
    She still fenced. Still had her edge. To Alison conversation had
always been a martial art. And she, such an elegant practitioner. It
made her attractive, sexy. She would lock on to you with her mind,
applying a little pressure here, little pressure there. It was intensely
physical.
    Now, after thirty years, she was rolling back history – a whole
lifetime – calling to see who he was. Old friend or adversary?
Business or personal? It was that simple – and that complex.

At two in the morning he telephoned Deval at home in Washington.
    'How's Jane?'

'Pissed at me because I work too hard.'

'How's Jason?'

'Asleep, thank Christ. Otherwise he'd be pissed at me as well.'

'Then work less.'

'There's a job to do, David ... and you're so fucking needy. By the way, you OK? You didn't sound so good on the plane.'

'I realise I've been a pain in the arse these last two years. Elizabeth's death hit me harder than I thought, harder than I could even admit to myself. But I feel stronger now. When I went out to Arlington, it seemed for the first time as if I could let her go. Almost as if she were telling me to let her go, and get on with being president.'

'David ... Jane wants to talk to you.'

'Put her on. I like talking to a pretty woman at night ...'

She giggled. 'And I like talking to a real man. Not the kind of animal I'm married to. What are you wearing?'

'Nothing. Can't you tell?'

'You want me to fix you up with someone?'

'Sure. You busy tonight?'

'You mean to tell me that the cast of thousands you employ can't even get hold of a couple of Frauleins. They're not trying. You should sack the whole crowd of them.'

'I intend to. Time I waved around my little wand, don't you think?'

'Depends which little wand you had in mind ...'

'Jane!'

'David!' She laughed. 'I'm a doctor, remember? I'm used to discussing these things ...'

'Are you going to bill me for this consultation?'

'Isn't that the American way?'

He paused for a moment. 'Jane what would you say if I told you I was interested in someone ... ?'

'If it isn't me, I'll tear her eyes out.'

They both laughed across the Atlantic.

'David, if you're interested in someone who you think could make you happy, I have only one thing to say to you ... go for it. You've been sad long enough. You deserve it – and you also need it. Too many nights on your own aren't healthy. And yes, this is a consultation, and yes I'll be billing you ...'

'And what if she turns me down?'

'Am I talking to my eight-year-old son or the president of this God-fearing nation?'

'I've been out of the game a long time ...'

'Then get back in. Who's going to turn you down?'

'The lady who just called.'

'Tomorrow's another day, honey.'

'Goodnight, Jane. Tell Harry not to work so hard.'

'Goodnight, Mr President.' She laughed softly and with evident pleasure.

Chapter Twenty-two

He didn't look much like the president of Russia, sitting on the bed in his shirt-tails and stripy underpants, scowling at the floor. All day long his energy had been flagging, through the plane journey, the buffeting by the winds, the meetings with all those extra bright diplomats Russia never knew it had ... and finally his strength had collapsed.

Katya put on her nightgown and went over to him. She laid a hand on his forehead and felt the fever.

'You're not well. "*Ty ustal kak syem chertyay.*" You're as tired as seven devils. Sleep! Tomorrow's very important.'

'Of course, yes, how good that you reminded me. I was planning to play tennis in the morning and then take a swim in the afternoon ... so thank God you told me.' The anger was barely controlled. It was not a tone Shilov often used with her. And then, quite suddenly, it had disappeared. He turned and gripped her hand ... 'Katya, I'm very sorry. I don't know why I spoke like that. The journey ... I ... please forgive me ...'

'Forgive you?' She smiled. 'Why should I forgive you? You're just as bad-tempered as when I first met you. Always getting drunk and apologising for it. Ahhh ...' She put her arms round him. 'Go and bark at someone else. But if you don't go to bed, you won't be able to.'

She patted the presidential behind, and he walked stiffly into the bathroom. It was the size of a small swimming pool in Moscow. Suite of Honour or some such nonsense in the Grand Hotel. East Berlin, of course. Not that there was supposed to be a difference any more – but there always would be.

He looked round at the gold-plated taps, the Italian tiles, the crystal glasses. Ample proof that the East German authorities had been corrupt and insensitive on a massive scale – building vast, opulent hotels to impress Westerners, and making their own people stand in line for a lousy sausage. The Party had had it coming.

Only, what a legacy! Half-empty, overpriced guest houses – and a few thousand nuclear missiles, being squabbled over for ownership. And now they came to Berlin, not as proud possessors of the largest country in the world, but a selection of bankrupt bureaucracies, begging bowls outstretched to the British and Americans.

Christ, it was humiliating!

He splashed cold water on his face, and stared at the mirror.

Time was when he too had been a good and faithful Party member. Hardly something to be proud of. Hardly something to shout about, either.

All those years reciting nonsensical claptrap about the proletariat, and the victory of socialism. He was as much to blame as anyone else, wasn't he?

And yet, you couldn't fight the Party from the outside. Gorbachev had known that. You had to take it over and destroy its entrails from within.

Only now there were other dangers . . .

'Come to bed for God's sake . . .' he could hear Katya calling from the bedroom. 'Stop daydreaming.'

He shuffled back to the room and got into bed beside her.

'Did you read the report I gave you?'

In the darkness she turned towards him. 'You mean the shooting at the missile silo? Yes, of course . . .'

'I'm amazed Klimak had the nerve to come here. He blatantly attacks one of our nuclear installations, claims it's his, and refuses to allow medical care for the wounded . . .'

'That's merely his negotiating position. He would obviously try to seize some advantage before the talks. I had expected something like that.'

'But I have to respond. Don't you see? I have to send reinforcements. If I'm seen to be weak, then my position at home becomes even more dangerous. I have very little room for manoeuvre.'

'Wait a day. This will all come out in the conference.'

An hour must have passed, maybe more, when something woke Katya and she sat up in bed, wondering where he was, seeing his silhouette by the window.

The pale streetlamps led all the way down to Unter Den Linden.

Cars were swishing past in the light rain. Berlin, still alive in the darkness.

'What is it, my dear?'

He smiled and pulled her close. 'You know what I'd like? Now – this minute. Just to go for a walk – the two of us. Take a look at the Brandenburg Gate without the people there. I know we've seen it in the ceremonies, we passed it in the motorcade. But just to stand and stare at it for a few minutes. You and me. Is that so much to ask?'

'Yes.' She ran a hand over his face. 'Much too much. You wanted to walk on different streets, the secret ones, the dark ones, the ceremonial ones. You wanted big fanfares and television cameras. You wanted people to listen when you speak. There's a price for all that.'

'No more midnight walks?' He shook his head. 'When we were students we used to walk half way across Moscow in the rain, or the snow. We used to pass the Lubyanka in terrible fear, thinking what would happen if someone stopped us. D'you remember the day, a man came out and told us – we should get away from the building and quickly, and it would be the worse for us if we didn't . . . D'you remember that? You didn't stop shaking for three hours.'

'It was like living in a minefield. We never knew when we might make a mistake – an unguarded word, a joke. How many times did we lose our friends because an unknown informer had reported something. My God . . . when you think back, Dmitry. Whatever problems we face now . . . it has to be better than the way it was. And to have a revolution without blood? This is something so extraordinary, for us, for Russians . . .'

'You're right, of course you're right . . . but I wish sometimes we were different people. I wish that we didn't have to create with one hand and destroy with the other. Always this has been our pattern. All through history.' He put both arms around her and gripped her tightly. 'You know something . . . I don't believe in revolutions without blood. Oh yes, the communist party is dead, Gorbachev resigned, the Soviet Union is like a black hole in the history of the world – but the blood will flow again. You saw what happened with our parliament. Maybe in drips, like the rain, or the patter of a tiny stream, but in the end there will be a river, and rivers flow into seas

107

with their waves sweeping over our country ...'

'Stop ... stop ...' She could feel him shaking. 'It won't be like that. Not this time. This is different. Civilization has moved on. The other countries will help us. Never again, Dmitry. Never again.'

Katya got him back to bed and held him tightly beneath the blankets, and then she moved her hand up under his pillow and touched cold steel. Without hesitating she clicked on the light and stared at the small, black automatic pistol.

'What the ... ?' he turned round, blinded for a moment by the bedside lamp. Then he saw what was in her hand.

'Put it away, Katya, and go to sleep.'

'Why did you bring this?'

'Why did I bring this ... you know why I brought it. Look at the people around us. What have we been talking about? Our history, the violence ...'

'There is a whole army out there to protect you ... bodyguards, KGB, police ...'

'And one night a man may come through them all, past the guards, through the security, and he may open this door and stand looking down at us. What then? Do I throw a pillow at him and say my prayers ... ?'

'It can't happen.'

'That's what Julius Caesar thought.'

'It won't happen. Please get rid of it, Dmitry. I'm serious. Give it to security. Trust me.'

'I need ...' But he caught the expression in her eyes and knew he couldn't refuse her. In all the forty years they had known each other he hadn't been able to say no. Not when she really wanted something. Not when she knew she was right ..'

'All right, all right. I'll do as you say. Now go to sleep and let me do the same.'

He turned off the light and listened to the rhythm of her breathing. After a while it became slower and deeper and he knew she was sleeping. Katya had always possessed such wisdom. She had saved him so many times when his temper got the better of him, when he would have alienated his friends, when he was unable to see the way forward. She had been the powerful one. Her intelligence and her intuition, married to each other, had made for an unbeatable combination.

Only this time he knew she was wrong.

Chukovsky had watched three people die. Friends, hit in a convoy that had come under attack in Afghanistan. And it hadn't really struck him until much later. So much had been going on – the scramble to the field hospital, the shouts and instructions, the hard committed faces of the surgeons fighting death on its own ground, body by body. That is hot death, he thought – where you die in a hurry, in uniform, for a cause. And everything that can be done *is* done.

Not like now. Not like the captain – stretched out, quiet, motionless on the floor of a missile silo, seventy metres below ground. No assistance. No flurry. Cut off from the world and now, clearly, about to depart it. That would be a cold death. The worst kind.

Chukovsky could still feel a pulse, weak and hesitant. He and Volodya had managed to stop the bleeding. But there was no more they could do. Their communications with the other silos were down. Even the ground-wave emergency network was inoperative, or perhaps, he thought wryly, had never worked at all.

Now the three of them were at the bottom of the silo, out of contact, probably surrounded by half the fucking Ukrainian army. And who was coming to their rescue? Who even knew about them? What the the hell did it matter to anyone if the Captain lived or died?

Only it mattered to him.

'Colonel, you should eat something.' Volodya appeared with a bowl of stew.

'What time is it?'

'Seven.'

'Is that morning or evening?'

Volodya laughed without humour. 'Morning, I think. Here,' he handed Chukovsky a spoon, 'it's not bad. A lot better than my mother used to make.'

'Doesn't say much in this country.' He went over to the captain and checked his temperature, and listened to his heart. They had given him shots of antibiotics, and tried to get him to swallow some water. Thank God, he was unconscious. At least he was out of pain. And if he had been awake, what could they have said to him? 'We're doing all we can. Don't worry, comrade. Help is at hand.'

He sat at the main console and ate the stew. You lost all sense of time below ground. But there were some things, he thought, that you could see with greater clarity. Like the sense of futility, the waste of the captain's life.

Not that he had known him well. They'd only met each other a couple of months ago. And yet there was something about him that he'd admired. Sure, he was brash and loud, and couldn't wait to finish his two years in the army, to get out and make some money.

But he was different from many of the Russians. He didn't just sit moaning about the prices in the shops, he had schemes and dreams. Each day seemed to bring a new one. Big talk. Wild talk. Fifty projects a second. And although most of them would be forgotten the day after, it was exhilarating to listen. The future meant a goal, an event, achievements – not a tragedy waiting to happen.

Russia needed people like that, if it was ever to climb out of the hole it had dug itself.

Chukovsky felt the anger rising inside him. Why should a man like that have to die, in some stupid, pointless confrontation? And if he died, how many others would die, and how would the youth of Russia ever realise its dreams? It seemed to him that the Captain was a symbol of the future they *could* have. And he went over and knelt beside him ... 'Don't die, young friend,' he whispered, 'don't die. We'll find a way. You have to go on living. You must.'

At the console he could see Volodya fiddling with wires and switches, a metal plate had been removed from the installation.

'What's going on?'

'Checking the communications.' Volodya put down his screw-driver. Instead of the usual blank indifference, his face showed genuine puzzlement. 'I can't quite work out why no one is replying to our signal.'

'Because we aren't sending one. That's why. Our own transmitter is fucked. You said so yourself, an hour ago. '

'That's the point.' Volodya shook his head. 'It isn't fucked. We're sending fine. We're even receiving.' He turned a dial. 'Listen to this.' And suddenly the tinny voice of Moscow radio filled the room. A woman's voice, clear and well-modulated, discussing the opening of a new play.

'I don't get it.' Chukovsky slumped in the chair. 'Why don't they check in with us. Brigade headquarters are supposed to signal every three hours to make sure we're on line.'

Volodya picked up the metal plate and screwed it back into the console. 'They don't want to know,' he said casually. 'For some reason,' he raised his eyebrows and sighed, 'they just don't want to know. Isn't that a scary thought, Colonel?'

Chukovsky shook his head. 'It wasn't till you mentioned it.'

Chapter Twenty-three

She awoke in a hurry. Hungry, but not wanting food. Her throat dry, but not thirsty. She could feel the sensation of a storm building from a long way, away.

Alison, you wanted this day for so long. What will you do with it?

She chose a dark skirt and crimson jacket. Red for action. Red because it was urgent and immediate. Red – to camouflage the blushes. She took a gold link necklace that Dad had given her when she'd come out of hospital, and a signet ring from Mum. And now you're on your own . . .

In the office suite, Foster was skimming through the traffic from London, the Press summaries, the transcripts of the late night news programmes. A garden room girl was taking notes.

'You'll have to give some interviews this afternoon, Prime Minister.' He was jotting notes on a pad, trying to get what he called 'an armlock' on the day ahead. 'Got to hit the evening bulletins. As you see, we're mostly on the inside pages and quite a long way down the TV running order. But we'll build on that. Since this is your first Foreign, we're going to make you 'super stateswoman' today. Start pushing a few themes. Perhaps it's something you and Bradley can agree on. Remember he'll be getting quite a bit of coverage from our lot, as well. Can't be seen to lag behind. No sudden initiatives that we haven't been told about. No rug being pulled from under our feet. Americans are good at that . . .'

He rambled on, crumbs from his toast cascading over the blue worsted trousers, mouth awash with ideas and coffee.

She heard most of it, forcing herself to concentrate, forcing the past out of her mind, willing the present to take its place. Power and responsibility. That's all there was to think about. The reason she'd been chosen. The reason for doing the job. The same discipline that had made her get out of a wheelchair thirty years ago and walk – that's what would see her through. What was she expecting from this meeting, from David Bradley? Nothing, she told herself. Nothing at all. She shut her eyes for a moment. I wish that were true.

Quickly out of the car, into the hotel lobby. One deep breath and just do it. Foster struggling to keep up. A wave from a familiar figure. Ignore it. Christ, it was the Italian prime minister! Too late, you're in the lift now, secret service escort . . .

And then she reminded herself . . . It's only David. A boy you once knew. Just a boy . . .

On the presidential floor the morning rush hour was breaking around them, the quick and the late, the paper carriers, the shouters, the orderers, the deciders. Everywhere she looked the place was running on coffee in plastic cups.

A plain white door opened into a crowded room and she stood there, not hearing the noise, searching the faces. It wasn't the man in the White House photos, or the magazines, that caught her attention, but the voice that had never changed or varied. A quiet voice for a president, quiet for a military commander. But a voice that could carry endlessly across time. If you shut your eyes for just a moment, she thought, then the years in between might never have happened.

'David . . .' In the few steps it took him to reach her, she saw only the smile of honour . . .

'Prime Minister,' he took her hand. The room stopped talking.

She could feel the instant warmth, the strength behind it, always so open, so approachable, always touching and holding . . . And the sheer size of this gentle giant. 'You're like a house.' She could hear her own voice, laughing the words on a summer afternoon decades ago. Sounds from another time, the stirring of a wind.

He was saying something else, but she couldn't hear him.

I know why it happened, she thought suddenly. I wondered if I'd stare at him and ask myself . . . .was this the man I knew? But I don't. I know him. An old face is like an old map, drawn long ago. The landmarks don't change . . . it's all still there . . .

She hardly saw the other people, other hands shook hers, and David was leading her down the row of food, the silver trays, the fruits and rolls and scrambled egg . . .

Clear your thoughts, she told herself suddenly. Otherwise you'll be the breakfast . . .

For a moment, she seemed to lose her balance, but his hand was there, solid beneath her arm, and the smile never wavered, or the words of welcome, the constant stream of introductions.

They sat on sofas – all so deceptive, she thought. So low-key, almost casual. And yet each of us is like a guard dog. At any moment we can bare our teeth and fight to protect what's ours. Till then we're happy enough to jump up and lick each other's faces.

She looked down the row at the American Cabinet. Americans are very focused and very organised. When they sit at a table, it's expected there'll be a winner and a loser. And they don't play for the fun of it ... all this he had told her so many years ago.

Think hard, Alison. Take it point by point. She could feel her concentration returning.

Norton was speaking, laying out the American position, sur-rounded by coffee cups and yellow pads and hangers on ...

And David was watching from the sidelines.

It was a standard American approach. They set out their points as if everyone else had already agreed them, and twice she was forced to interject, to clarify, to diverge ...

His eyes never seemed to leave her ...

The talk was sharp and detailed. Thank God she had read all the briefs, thank God for Foster, thank God for ... the man sitting at the end of the table ...

And then Norton came down to the bottom line.

'OK, this is our position. We're not about to get involved in this dispute. No peacekeeping between Russia and Ukraine. No green line. No troops. Period. We tried that in Yugoslavia, we've tried it in lots of places since the cold war. Doesn't work, and no one thanks you for it. We're here to offer assistance if they can sort out their problems – or take it away if they can't. That simple.'

'We look at it differently,' Alison shifted on the sofa.

'And what way is that?' Norton threw a look at the president, but the president ignored him. He drained a glass of orange juice. 'Prime Minister, would you care to share your thoughts with us.'

'We have a lot of thoughts. And a lot of facts,' she looked straight at Bradley. 'Money, straight money, aid, handouts, whatever you want to call it – none of it buys stability or democracy. Never has done. Not in any of the regions it's been tried. And especially not here. We can threaten them with cutting off aid from now until Christmas – and it won't make the slightest difference. These people have their own agenda, which has nothing to do with putting food in the shops or balance of payments – or any of the things that get us voted into office ...' she smiled, ... 'or out.'

'What then?' Norton grimaced across the coffee table.

'Pride. Honour. Power. It's trying to persuade these people that their ultimate interest lies in peaceful relations with each other ...'

'And the best incentive for that is the dollar. We *buy* their co-operation. That's the language they understand.'

'Wrong ...' she could see Bradley begin to smile. He was enjoying the argument. 'Oh, they understand what dollars are. They'll take all you've got. And it may change what they eat, or what they drive around in, but not the way they think ...'

'So what will?'

'Diplomacy, cunning, understanding.'

Norton pushed away his cup. 'Sounds pretty damn wet to me.'

He looked towards Bradley for support. But the president seemed deep in thought, a thin smile was threatening to appear at the edge of his mouth.

'I think we have to listen very carefully. We're not dealing with rational people. We're not dealing with people who grew up with good educations and plenty of liberal thinking. We're dealing with very biased, ultra conservative old foxes, who still think they can play small town politics, and use their missiles when things get tough. It's very tense ...'

'I'm sure we're grateful for you bringing that to our attention,' Norton let out a sigh. 'You Brits ... you always look at it from too many sides. We need some clear thinking here, not a dopey kind of wishy-washy approach ...'

'Mine isn't.'

'The hell it isn't.' Norton laughed hollowly. 'We got enough talk-shops around the world. We don't need the British Labour Party opening up another. I seem to remember you guys would have given the missiles away to the Soviets years ago. So don't lecture me ...'

'Clark ...' The president's fist descended in a straight, conclusive line, and came to rest on the coffee table. 'That's enough, Clark. I think you should apologise to the prime minister ...'

'What the ... ?'

'You seem to have gotten carried away. Your language was undiplomatic.' The room had grown very quiet. It was unheard of for a president to rebuke a senior adviser in front of the Cabinet, let alone a foreign leader.

Alison sat up ... 'I'm sure no offence was intended. I certainly took none. Please continue, Mr Secretary ....'

Norton opened his mouth and hesitated ... 'I ... I regret if I upset anyone. I merely wished to make a point.' He looked Bradley straight in the eye and stood up. 'Excuse me. I have some important arrangements to make before the conference gets underway.'

Bradley poured himself another orange juice and waited till Norton had left. 'That's it, ladies and gentlemen, thank you. We'll stop here for now.'

The Cabinet and their advisers shuffled out. Foster threw Alison a raised eyebrow, as if to ask ... 'D'you want me to hang around?' She shook her head. And then quite suddenly a palpable feeling of rage burst inside her ...

Not only had David embarrassed his own staff, he'd stepped into a battle she could easily have fought for herself. Fought *and* won. Damn, damn him! She didn't need his intervention. His patronage. Or his help.

He closed the door and turned to face her, seeing the anger alive in her eyes.

'Alison ...' Take it slow, for something is terribly wrong.

'I appreciate your help out there. But I can look after myself ...' Slowly, she says it, each word stressed.

'Alison.'

'What?'

'We haven't seen each other for thirty years. Do we have to start like this? I'd have said the same thing if it had been the chambermaid in there. Norton was rude and boorish. I won't tolerate that kind of behaviour ...'

'You were patronising me. This is business. What you did was personal ...'

'Alison, please sit down ...' He tries to smile, but he can see the fury, taste it ...

'This can't happen again. It was totally unacceptable. The past is past. We have jobs to do. There's no sign we're going to agree on anything at all ...'

'Wait a minute!'

'What for?' And the anger is there, coloured on her face, white hot, stored for years.

'I don't understand why you're upset.'

'Then you don't understand anything.'

'Tell me!'

'I ... I couldn't even begin.'

'Listen to me. For thirty years I've been asking myself ...'

'Leave it,' the voice is cracking at the edges. And now for the first time there is almost unbelievable pain in the face. 'I don't want to open this box and nor do you. You should apologise to me and to Norton.'

'What I say to my Cabinet is my affair ...'

Her mouth closes very tight. Bradley can feel her slipping away.

He tries a final plea. 'You're acting as if we're strangers, for Chrissake.'

'That's exactly what we are. So leave it at that.'

'I have to talk to you.'

She turns and moves away. 'Goodbye, David.' And the anger has gone, replaced by something much worse, indifference, ice-cold.

Her back is already turned, her body through into the doorway, legs in black stockings leading her to the lift.'

Christ, Jesus. I don't believe this.

As he stands there alone, shock and disappointment crowd into the room beside him.

'I haven't felt so insulted in my entire career.'

Cliff Till considered the secretary of state's words with some scepticism. Norton was a tough, old-style campaigner. He belonged to the backbone of the GOP. Floated around for years with the highest of the high. Dinners at the White House, trips and Martinis on Air Force One, all the badges, T-shirts and pens he could want. A lifetime of politics that would have taught him how to kick and be kicked. And yet the public dressing down of a Cabinet member in front of a foreign leader – that had to be close to a first.

'Well, there are two ways you can handle this.' Till blew out his cheeks.

'Continue.'

'Stay or go.'

Norton moved his lips in the kind of mechanical gesture, often associated with a smile. And yet there was nothing even remotely friendly, happy, or contented about it.

'I'll take the third option.' He stood up. The decision was made. As far as he was concerned, Bradley was for the cooking pot.

Chapter Twenty-four

The hurt came back to him.

Like the time she had once scorned him in Oxford. The day he thought he'd lost her.

They had gone to see *Clockwork Orange*, which he hadn't enjoyed. She, by contrast, had loved it.

In the pub opposite the cinema she raved on about the symbolism, the double meanings, art.

'I thought it was pretentious crap,' he said and instantly regretted it. He could still see her face tighten, see her flounce up from the table, pushing her way out of the crowded bar, him following, people looking round . . .

'What's going on?' He had caught up with her on the street corner.

'I want a walk. I don't want to discuss it any more, OK?'

'You can't walk on your own. It's late.'

'I'll do what I bloody well want.'

She caught a bus into the town centre and he stood watching the vehicle lights rock away down Hedington Hill into the darkness.

At midnight, he was looking out of the bedsit window, in the terrace off the Cowley Road. No one knew they stayed together. She always said her parents would disapprove if they found out. So she kept on her room in College. Kept up appearances.

At 1.30 she turned the corner at the bottom of the road, and he hid behind the curtains hoping she hadn't seen his face and the concern that was stamped all over it.

'What happened?'

'Let's just go to sleep.'

She had turned her back to him, but he moved close in, his arms tight around her.

'Take no notice of me.'

'Difficult when you share my bed.'

'I expect too much. I've no right . . .'

'Did it matter . . . what I said about the movie?'

'Yes. No – it just shakes me when we don't think the same about things. I'm used to us sharing things. And then something like this happens and I start to have doubts.' She put a hand on his arm. 'Just forget it.'

Only you never do, Bradley recalled. Even with all they'd had, Alison was like walking on a glacier. There was always a chance the ice would crack.

He looked out of the window over Berlin, recalling the student in the bedsit off the Cowley Road. There was no way of knowing if, this time, she'd come back.

At his disposal was all the power the world had on offer. He could destroy markets, start wars, summon anyone he wanted. He had only to command and the genie would deliver. Anyone, that is, except Alison Lane.

'Prime Minister, the BBC are here for the interview.'

'I'm not doing the interview.'

'I'm sorry, Prime Minister, I don't quite understand. We *agreed* to it this morning. It's very important we put across our position.'

'You do it then. Something just came up. Do I have to tell you how to do the bloody job?'

'We need to make an impact on the main news tonight.'

'Then dream up another way. I'm not doing the fucking interview. Is that clear enough?'

Foster retreated in a hurry.

It didn't take much, she thought. Just a trigger. A hair's pressure and the control had gone. All the mental reconstruction of thirty years. Collapsed.

She breathed deeply, trying to make her thoughts stand still. How is it that he can do this to me? Why can David Bradley reduce me to behaving like a wounded animal?

She went over to her dresser and looked for a handkerchief. Her face was wet. Wet! She went into the bathroom and stared into the mirror. Tears had mixed in with the makeup.

'I don't know what's happening to me . . .'

She rubbed her face with a towel and repaired the damage. There hadn't been any tears for a quarter of a century. This wasn't the day to start again.

Chapter Twenty-five

'Sir Henry.'

'My dear.'

The head of British counter-intelligence hadn't announced his arrival in advance, never did, never would. Simply turned up in Downing Street or Berlin or countless other places, when he wanted. And you don't say no to this man – not unless you feel yourself in a stronger position that most of the British prime ministers this century.

He perched his black-striped bottom on the coffee table.

'I thought I'd better bring this in person. It's a report from our ambassador here.' He got up and handed her a few sheets of paper from his pocket. 'There's no file – no numbers. You'll see why.'

She read the document through and handed it back.

'I have to let him read it, Sir Henry'.

'That wouldn't be clever.'

'He's . . .'

'President of a foreign power.'

'An ally. The most important one we have.'

'Of course he's an ally. Insofar as there are allies these days. But he's also the leader of a country, that we know to be conducting industrial espionage on our soil, that we know to be attempting to put some of our companies out of business in the Far East, so that their own can take over, that deliberately withholds . . .'

'And we're not?' Alison felt involuntary anger.

'You read the reports . . .'

'Those you show me. What about those you don't?'

He looked away. 'We've known each other a long time, Alison.'

'That's not always a good thing.'

'This is background, my dear. An example of gross disloyalty from one of the president's closest colleagues. All right, his secretary of state. It's appalling, it's unpleasant, but it's standard politics. Nothing more. The reason I thought you should see it, is in case there's some impact on the summit. If you want my opinion – it could be useful in the future.'

'I see. You want to keep your options open.'

'I don't want to blow our sources, either our man here in Berlin – or Norton himself. There's our own interest to consider, beyond any notions of . . . how shall I put it, friendship between nations.'

'You wouldn't mind an operation against the Russians, would you?'

'I didn't say that.'

'You never *say* anything, Sir Henry. But you might want to leave open the possibility that it could be useful to your interests.'

'To our interests, Alison. To the National Interest . .'

'As you see it.'

'That is the duty I'm empowered to perform.'

She paused for a moment. 'I take your point . . .'

'Let me make a point about allies, my dear. They're always more trouble than enemies. Our problem is remembering which lie we've told to whom. And as far as the Americans are concerned, we really don't count for much these days. We need them a lot more than they need us. Their weapons, their intelligence, the satellites . . .'

'All the more reason to buy some credit.'

He smiled. 'All the more reason to exploit whatever leverage we have. Let's make sure we get the best price for our goods . . . your decision of course . . .'

'I said – I take your point. It's bad enough to be a Labour prime minister, dealing with a Republican president. We're not exactly natural allies . . .'

'I wouldn't say that . . .'

'Then you exceed yourself . . .'

He got to his feet. 'In that case, I apologise, Prime Minister . . .'

Alison turned away towards the window. 'Have no doubt that if it comes to a choice between my past friendship with David Bradley and my duty to this country – my duty will be paramount. I hope that's understood.'

'Perfectly.'

Sir Henry slept badly on the flight from Berlin, his mind turning new circles. He didn't need to be told that Alison had already seen

David Bradley – nor that the meeting had gone badly.

Even so, she had surprised him. The new edge in her authority. She was sharper, more combative. For years he had thought he controlled her, politically, even emotionally. Now he couldn't be sure. Her rebuke had caught him off guard.

And yet it emphasised something he had known all along – that power was nothing more than a matter of perception. You didn't need to prove it. Rarely if ever did you need to use it. The trick was in persuading people you had more than them.

Alison was trying that trick for herself, and when it came down to the wire, who controlled whom?

By the time he reached it, the house in Holland Park was in darkness and his wife had gone to bed, leaving a plate of cold meat on the kitchen table.

Sir Henry ate thoughtfully, scooped himself two wedges of Stilton from the sideboard, and sent it down with a brandy and ginger ale.

It had been his nightcap for years – his routine. Often the one constant in a life of shifting lines and allegiances.

And yet there was a strange contrast between his professional and personal lives. At home there had always been Wendy and *her* routine, her sessions as a magistrate, her concerts and the dinner parties she gave for her friends.

Although they still slept in the same bed, they had shared no intimacy for years. Neither of them missed it. They had simply moved on. Life was cushioned and comfortable. They were companions, talking to each other, sharing four walls, friendly but conspicuously unaffectionate. They had tiptoed away from their sexuality. She wouldn't come in when he was in the bath, he would stay outside while she dressed. After a while, if you didn't look, it wasn't there.

Which was perhaps why he had failed to anticipate the changes in Alison Lane.

Sir Henry had never possessed knowledge of a searing and urgent relationship. He knew all about manipulation. He knew about Swallows and sexual tempting. But the process by which two human beings can eat out their hearts in the search for one another – this was closed territory. Unfamiliar, and in his case, largely unexplored. He had no idea how an old and powerful liaison could drastically alter a person's outlook.

Alison had said that if it came to a choice between duty and David Bradley – the duty would hold sway.

How could he be sure?

He recalled her face in Berlin, flushed, motivated . . . moved. Yes, that was it – moved, the way he hadn't seen it for years.

How could she be sure, either?

In the darkness of the bedroom Alison stretched out her feet, as if to make certain there was no one beside her.

Tonight, she thought, as every night, the British prime minister tucks herself up, kisses and hugs herself, tells herself how well she's done and goes to bloody sleep.

'That's it. What did you expect?'

'I didn't expect anything.'

The conversation began way down inside her.

'If you didn't – why the big fuss? The great buildup? Mm?'

'I thought if I saw him again, I could let it lie, finally, bury it, once and for all.'

'And can you?'

'I want to. I tried earlier . . .'

'Can you?'

'I have to . . .'

'*Can . . . you?*'

'I don't know.'

Only then did the voices quieten and let her sleep.

Chapter Twenty-six

'So you want me to return to Washington, Mr President?'

'It would be best, Clark. Under the circumstances. You can announce a new initiative on the Far East talks if you wish. But I want you out of here.'

'May I ask why?'

'That should be obvious. Your comments to the prime minister were really quite offensive. They displayed the kind of inflexibility we've been trying to move away from.'

'I'm sorry you felt that way. If you wish me to offer my . . .'

'We'll talk when I come back, Clark.'

'Of course, Mr President.'

Norton chuckled to himself and relaxed as the Atlantic flowed beneath him. The more distance between him and the President the better he felt. He knew he'd sailed pretty near to the storm, but he didn't think Bradley would fire him. That would upset the right wing of the Party, and Bradley wasn't strong enough for that. No – it had gone just right. He'd keep away from the White House, but stay close enough to gather some dirt. That was the object now.

He shut his eyes and replayed the conversation. It was typical of the slide at the top. Bradley was a sap. If you couldn't speak your mind to the fucking allies – who could you speak it to? It wasn't even as if Britain counted for anything these days.

Weakness. Indecision. Those were the hallmarks. Maybe it was time for a gentle word with the approachable Harry Deval. Maybe he too was fed up with Bradley. Maybe he had his own ambitions. It would be worth finding out.

The stewardess arrived with lunch and Norton smiled down at the plastic tray and the fruits of a first class meal. He stuck a fork into the smoked salmon and rolled it around his mouth.

How nice that Harry had fixed things up, after that little affair he'd been so careful to hide. Of course it was stupid to get involved in the first place.

Norton shuddered for a moment at the thought of what would happen to him in similar circumstances. Darlene had told him she'd cut it off with a rusty knife if she ever caught him at it. And he believed her. Darlene was like that. Led with her mouth, and the rest of her tended to follow. She didn't threaten for fun.

But Harry, well Harry had been really dumb. Dumb to do it and dumb to shit on his own doorstep. Of course the lady had needed some comfort when it all ended. Ladies were like that. She had really needed to talk to someone. And so the little word had spread, as words so often do around buildings, and closed communities.

And in the way of these things the little word had eventually come to him. Not to be used, of course, but to be filed away as part of that Washington compendium of useful facts that you keep close by you for quick and easy reference.

His father had taught him that. Keep good records. Always keep records.

Norton smiled at the memory. His father had died six years earlier, but not before he had destroyed the records that could have gotten him indicted by a grand jury. Records about his dealings as a long-time Washington lobbyist. Records of the receipts and the payouts. Records of the famous people he had made rich. And the riches he himself had acquired.

Records were all very well, until the day someone else saw them. Harry Deval would find that out.

Chapter Twenty-seven

A long line of BMWs and Jaguars stretched up Whitehaven Parkway towards St Patrick's – the Episcopal day school and parking lot for the children of north-west Washington.

Harry could see a senator from South Dakota gesticulating into his carphone. Young blonde mothers stood outside chatting in designer sweats, hairbands. What did they find to talk about? It wasn't as if they ever did anything. Washington's houses and gardens were tended by armies of central Americans and Filipinos – most illegal. The actual owners barely took off their gloves, except to sign cheques.

These days, of course, it was PC for mothers to stay home with their kids. Ten years ago they'd have been social outcasts without a salary. No salary. No status. No one to talk to at cocktail parties. Now all it took were a few medical studies, and the stay-home mums got rehabilitated ...

Washington and its fashions.

Jason was at the back of the homecomers, tall for his age, his jeans half way down his bottom, shirt out. Harry thought he looked like a businessman after too much dictation with his secretary, but he wasn't going to tell him that.

He opened the car door and handed him a tuna sandwich. There'd be no point in conversation until the boy had eaten. God knows what they did to them at the school. Their blood sugar levels were zero by the end of the day.

They turned off MacArthur Boulevard, through Foxhall, towards the American University.

'Where's Mum?'

'Working.'

'What?'

'She's a doctor, remember? You guys should talk more ...'

'I know that ...' Jason dropped a blob of tuna on the seat, hoping Harry hadn't seen it.

'Remind me to bring a towel next time.' He grinned at the boy.

'Look, Dad ... it's just that Mum usually comes on a Friday. You never come ...'

'I come sometimes.'

'Bull ...' Jason stopped himself just in time.

Harry was about to rebuke the boy but he changed his mind. They saw each other so little, the last thing he wanted was a fight. He'd start shouting, Jason would clam right up, and they'd sit in Pizza Hut like an old married couple, not saying a word.

'How was the sandwich?'

'Fine.'

'You still hungry?'

'Sure.'

At least there were some certainties left in life.

They drove to the Cheesecake Factory in Chevy Chase. Harry ordered a hamburger and fries, Jason chose salad.

'What's with this salad?'

'Cholesterol, Dad.'

'I don't believe what I'm hearing. Sounds like a bad TV ad.'

'No really. You have to watch that. Mum said so ...'

Harry folded his arms. And people thought the White House was tough. 'I'll think about it.'

Jason smiled. Like his mother he had the knack of knowing when he'd won.

The bill came and the boy leaned his head on Harry's arm.

I'd pay for moments like this, he thought ... I swear there are times when I could tell David I'm finished. I'm done with the intrigue, gonna stay home.

And then he saw her, saw the hair, saw the profile, the same profile that he'd held and hugged and watched in the semi-darkness. She was sitting in an alcove table and an electric jolt seemed to be stabbing at Harry's chest, his hands and jaw frozen, his life in his throat.

'Dad ...'

She was talking to a man, in blazer and green pullover and the worst thing of all was that he knew him too.

A journalist from the White House Press corps. Investigative type. Little digger, little ferret, little rat. The worst.

'Dad, are we going?'

They were sitting so comfortably. Warm and happy. Coffees and Danishes on the table in front of them.

And she was talking away, nineteen to the fucking dozen. And he was listening.

They had cleared away dinner and the television was fighting for dominance. Jane punched the remote and switched it off.

'What's up, Harry?'

'I worry about everything.'

'Why?'

''Cos everything's fucked up. All kinds of strange things going on.'

'Like what?'

'You don't want to know.'

'I'm your wife . . .'

'That's why you don't want to know. If I had the choice I wouldn't want to know either.'

She stretched a hand out to his arm. 'I could help.'

'I wish that was true.'

It must have been three when the phone rang. He had it instantly in his hand. Christ Jesus, who the hell . . . ? If it was her calling . . . But the voice wanted Jane. It was the intern at Sibley Hospital. Jane gave some instructions, asked some questions. Harry could hear the names of drugs, doses, checks every fifteen minutes. Someone was having a far worse night than him. She hung up and lay down again, facing the wall.

'Is the patient gonna live?'

'For a while.'

'Doesn't sound very optimistic.'

She turned towards him. 'Never is, Harry. Not in this job.'

Chapter Twenty-eight

Way back in the seventies Ruth Bradley was said to have 'electrocuted' Kansas City.

That was the view of the exclusive Women's club she set up, and the deputy chairwoman – a lady with no less a name than Champagne Tripp – who had meant to say 'electrified', but was too far gone to notice.

The occasion had been the club's gala dinner, one summer evening in the Hilton Hotel and a Tribute to Mrs Bradley's skill and leadership.

'You have done for women,' Champagne had smiled down from the podium, 'what Werner Von Braun did for rockets. Put us in orbit – where we can't get kicked around any longer.'

Mrs Bradley cringed deep down in her soul. God, the woman was an embarrassment. Drunk out of her mind and ludicrous with it.

All these years later she could remember the stupid sequins groping across her yellow frock, her bosom pouring out like some creamy trifle and the piggy eyes, questing for a suitable male to take her home.

'Anything with three good legs,' Champagne would declare to anyone who was listening, and collapse in squeals of laughter.

The rule was that members could invite husbands or boyfriends – or neither. And a smattering of docile, compliant tuxedos would sit through the evening, grinning and hating it. But, mostly, the women came by themselves. After all the club was about female bonding, 'fellowshipping' – women with an identity of their own and nothing to lose but their men.

At least, Mrs Bradley reflected, it had filled up the years – or part of them. Filled the place that an interested and involved husband might otherwise have occupied.

When she thought back, the club had lasted no more than five or six years. People had married and moved away, married again and moved somewhere else. It had been an effort just to update the mailing list.

Take Champagne Tripp herself. She had used husbands the way most people used airline upgrades. Everytime she got a new one – the seat improved. 'Never marry for money, honey,' she would always say. 'Marry where money *is*.'

Somehow though, they never completely lost touch. Champagne was incapable of forgetting a birthday, an anniversary, even a mother's day. Gaudy cards would arrive with absurd, outlandish inscriptions – from Santa Fe or Sausalito, or Vegas. Evidence of the winding path on to which lust, or money, had led her.

In the end, though, Mrs Bradley stopped opening the envelopes, re-directing them instead to the garbage compactor, wishing the tiresome woman would leave her in peace. Until, that is, one arrived with a Washington postmark.

What the hell was Champagne doing in DC?

She prised open the scented red envelope and looked inside. No card this time, but a lengthy, rambling scrawl over three pages, also scented, in which Champagne had detailed her latest catch.

'My dear, he's like a tiger, leaping on me all times of the day and night. I'm thinking it's safer not to bother with clothes and simply walk round the house stark naked. What a delicious idea! Would you come for the weekend???! Oh, stop it, Champagne . . .'

Mrs Bradley skipped a page of antics . . . who in God's name was this tiger?

Her eyes halted at the top of the last page . . . 'Of course, he's very well connected. Well, he would be, wouldn't he? I mean – not like David, of course, speaking of *connections* (!!!), Mrs First Mom . . .'

And there it was – three lines down. Mr Tiger ran a large and very powerful firm of Private Investigators. He was the mole inside, but more often in the street outside, Washington's number one bedrooms. He *knew* the city, biblically, biologically, scandal by scandal. Knew its fancies and foibles. He had studied that quintessential link between power and indiscretion. The high risk business – and the people who loved to play it.

That, thought Ruth Bradley, was the reason she had been thinking of Champagne Tripp. And that was why she needed her.

* * *

It took five minutes of gooey platitudes, before they could get down to business.

'I've been a little indiscreet.' Mrs Bradley coughed delicately.

'A man?'

'Well, it wouldn't be a dog, would it?'

'You mean you fucked him, honey.'

'I did not.'

'Then what does this "indiscreet" mean?' Champagne gave a little giggle.

'It means . . .' she tried again. 'It means I said some things I wasn't supposed to say.'

'Oh. That kind of indiscreet. I thought this was gonna be the fun kind.'

'Is there a fun kind?'

'You better believe it. Keeps me and my honey in . . .' she nearly said champagne, but giggled again instead, '. . . in the pink, mmm?'

'I see.'

'Now you just tell me what I can do for my old chairwoman. You know Ruth, there's nothing I wouldn't do for you. That was the club motto. And that's how I feel still. Us club girls have to stick together.'

'You're so right,' said Ruth Bradley. 'You are *so* right.'

They met the next day in the bar of the Willard Hotel. Champagne was in a pink trouser suit with a zip down to the crotch, half-opened either by strain or omission.

Mrs Bradley thought strain. No one could be that obvious.

She ordered two Bloody Marys and bounced on to the seat. By the second bounce she was already talking.

'You're in trouble, honey. This check you wanted on Pete Levinson – looks like shit on a windy day.' She removed the giant celery stick from her glass and chewed at the end. 'I got them to do this one fast. He's not a nice guy, Ruth. I think you should know that.'

'How not nice is "not nice"?'

'Big time.'

'I tried calling the number he gave me. But there isn't even an answering machine . . .'

'There isn't even a Pete Levinson . . . I'm sorry, honey.'

'What do you mean?'

'I mean that Pete Levinson is a stooge. A reporter, by trade. He screwed up badly a few months ago, with that Pentagon story. Case of getting the wrong man. You must have heard about it?'

'I try not to read newspapers – far too depressing.'

'The reason he's a stooge is that he's friends with one or two of the old Republican crowd. People who got thrown out in the final years of Bush – people with grudges. Plenty of grudges.'

'Go on.'

'It seems there was this plan to get even with the Party. Get at David – and more importantly, use you to do it. Levinson was told to make goo-goo eyes at you and find out any dirt he could on the president. It seems you've been pretty forthcoming. He left for London yesterday.'

Ruth Bradley shut her eyes. 'Is there anything I can do?'

'How much did you tell him?'

'I said David had once been in love with the woman who's now prime minister of Britain. I said he probably still is.'

Champagne toyed with the remains of her celery stick. 'That could be very embarrassing,' she bit off the end, 'for both of them.'

Mrs Bradley stayed at the bar longer than she'd intended. Long enough to realise that she had now divulged her secret to two people. In Washington, just one would have been lunacy. Two was suicide.

Chapter Twenty-nine

From his first-class compartment Pete Levinson stared out at the frontal depression of south London.

He hadn't been to England before, hadn't expected the desolation of terraced houses and terraced faces, as the train tore past them.

And yet it fitted in with all he'd heard. Brits didn't matter any more, didn't work, ate lousy food. They were living proof that you couldn't cash in your history. The more you had, the more it cost you.

He took out a notebook and wrote the thought down. Catchy little phrase. If he found the time maybe he'd do a colour piece on the side. 'Ignorance,' he recalled his first editor saying to him, 'ignorance is liberating. You're not restricted by facts or knowledge. You're a free man. And frankly Levinson,' he'd added, 'you're just about the freest man I ever met.'

As the train rattled on, he shook his head at the window, checked his reflection, smoothed the hair. The good thing was being free of Ruth Bradley.

She had really tied on a few at the restaurant in Washington. But she hadn't enjoyed it. There was an air of desperation about her, loneliness. Dying to talk to someone – perhaps for years. It only took a man with a suntan, and a few doses from the coloured bottles. She'd have woken up later and realised what she'd said, poor old fart. But he didn't have much choice.

That same evening he'd gone to D'Anna and told him about Alison Lane, and watched as the most ridiculous of smiles had spread itself across the man's flabby face.

'Bradley knew Lane at Oxford? You have to be kidding.'

'That's what she said.'

'What d'you mean "knew"?'

'She loved him.'

'Jesus!'

'Really loved him – that's what she said.'

134

Larry had begun walking up and down the room. 'This is one hell of a fucking story. What happened to them. How d'it break up?' His eyes seemed to enlarge. 'Get yourself over to England and do some checking. And Pete . . .'

'Yes, Larry.'

'I said checking. No fuck-ups on this one, 'cos your arse ain't exactly bullet-proof these days. You with me? By the way what did you have to do to get her talking, uh? A little magic-in-the-sack, uh?'

Larry was a creep. And yet Levinson was well aware he hadn't landed this assignment because of his reporting talents. In that, he'd already proved himself pitifully incompetent. D'Anna had chosen him for one reason only – he knew how to ingratiate himself with women. He was a cheap charmer – and when it came down to it, he admitted to himself, a dick for hire.

'When you come back,' D'Anna had said, 'you can pump Mrs B some more. And I mean pump.'

'Anything but that, Larry.'

'Anything, including that.'

He dozed for a while, waking as the train pulled into Brighton station. The air smelt fresh and the wind gusted him down to the seafront, blowing away the tiredness from the journey.

It was going to rain. Maybe it was always going to rain. A few tiny women were out with dogs, too cold to lift their legs . . .

As he walked along there was something one-handed about the place. What sort of major resort had two piers – one working, with lights and music, the other broken up by the sea and the storms, a mass of rusting girders, sitting just along the beach.

Why didn't they do something about it? In the States they'd have built a leisure complex, bars, a casino. Americans would never tolerate crap like this on their doorstep.

He rented a car and took the coastal road to Newhaven. The wind never stopped and the rain came and went and came again, unable to make up its mind.

When he reached the port, he made his way to the headland and walked along the harbour wall. In the distance the white cliffs rose sharply like the roof of a warehouse, and the sea went from light to dark green, as it stretched towards the horizon.

At the edge of the beach was a sprawling amusement arcade, again half-working. The tea was only half tea, the hotdog was cold and he took a diet coke because they 'wouldn't have been able to fuck that up.'

Britain, he decided, wasn't for him. No sunshine. No suntan. No buzz in the air.

Back in the car he ran a comb through the ruffled brown locks, and studied the map. It was easy. Take the coast road again, west to Saltdean. Up a hill. First house on the left. Soon be dark.

'Who is it?' The old woman's voice was barely audible behind the front door.

'I'm an American. Pete Levinson. My car broke down. I'm sorry, can I use your phone?'

He could hear her whispering.

'What's that you say?' A man's voice now, hesitant, wary.

'My car broke down. May I ... ?'

The door slid open on a chain. Levinson could see an eye looking him over. Finally it opened all the way and the two old folks were standing there, sharing a nervous smile. Didn't want to seem inhospitable. Wanted to help. But wished he hadn't come. He could see it in their gestures.

'I'm sorry to disturb you.'

'That's all right.' The lady beckoned him in. 'Cold night. Here, I've got the number of a garage.'

'Thanks so much.' Into the sitting room and he was taking it all in, the awful flowery chairs, a couple of vases, dining table ...

'The telephone's here.' The old man in the green cardigan pointed to a little table. He'd seen him looking round.

Levinson dialled. 'I think it's the fan belt. Ford Escort ... where am I?' He turned to the couple. 'I'm sorry what's the address here? Right ... uh-huh ... twenty minutes. OK.'

He hung up and turned towards them. 'They say it'll be twenty minutes.'

There was a moment of silence. They really didn't want him to hang around.

'I guess I'd better ...'

'Would you like a cup of tea, Mr ... ?' The lady smiled thinly. She couldn't bring herself to be rude. The husband glared at her.

'Pete Levinson, Mrs ... ?'

'Lane,' the smile held. 'Margaret Lane.'

He combed his hair in the bathroom and by the time he came out there was tea on the narrow kitchen table. Careful Pete.

'Milk, Mr Levinson?'

'Pete, please.' And as he looked up to answer, he could see the pictures on the cork noticeboard beside the dresser. A girl in her early twenties, standard beach picture, awkward pose, sixties hair – the crooked smile. Yes, yes! Jesus, yes ... !

'Are you on holiday, Pete?' She poured milk from a small jug.

'Just a few days. Came down this evening. You know, just on a whim.' Cool Pete. Your hands are shaking. Slow it down.

'Where are you staying?'

'Haven't thought.'

'There's the Grand in Brighton or if you're touring inland, the countryside, the White Hart in Lewes is very good. I mean the food. Rooms as well, but ...'

'I'm sorry, Mrs Lane' and the little boy blush began to seep in over his cheeks, right on command, 'but I couldn't help noticing your picture up there. It looks like a lady who's pretty much in the news right now ...'

The couple exchanged a glance.

'I mean, you said your name was Lane, after all.' You could have bottled the silence in that kitchen, he thought. Bottled and frozen it.

'Mister Levinson.' The father didn't look pleased. 'I'd thank you not to mention this to anyone. Parents are supposed to be a little bit in the background in cases like this.'

'No, no. I understand. Of course I do. I guess I just wanted to say congratulations. And, and ... you must be very proud.'

The old lady flushed. 'We are jolly proud. Aren't we Jack? It's wonderful news. I don't mind telling you that at all. And simply marvellous for the country.'

She was a stalwart – this one. No Ruth Bradley beating in her breast. Wave your whistler at this one – and she'd chop it off.

The father shifted his chair back. 'Look I don't mean to be unfriendly, but we've an early start tomorrow . . .'

'Please. I understand perfectly. It was great meeting you all.'

Mrs Lane showed him to the door, and walked a few steps down the path.

'I hope you didn't think we were unfriendly. We've always been fond of Americans. It's just this sort of thing is so new to us . . .'

'You've been very kind . . .'

'Goodbye, Pete.'

He turned to go. And this, he knew, was his last chance.

'As a matter of interest, Mrs Lane, why did you say you were fond of Americans?'

'Well, a long time ago Alison . . .'

'Margaret!' The father was standing in the doorway.

She stopped in mid-sentence, awkward suddenly, embarrassed. 'Well, goodbye then.'

Levinson raised his hand to wave and let himself out through the little garden gate.

He didn't look back, until he got to the end of the road.

And then it was that wonderful feeling, where you know you've something so special in your pocket that it's beginning to burn your nuts off. A story that would motor its way into the headlines. Christ, a real-live, prize-pinching mother of a scoop. A gift seized from heaven itself. I love you, he told himself, checking his reflection in the car mirror. I really, really love you.

Levinson just had time to open up the bonnet up and check that he'd mutilated the fan belt sufficiently, for the mechanic not to become suspicious.

'I didn't like him.'

'He was nice. Friendly. Americans are like that. You've just for-gotten.'

Alison's father hadn't forgotten at all. 'Different breed this one, if you ask me. Too slimy for his own good. Surprised he didn't slip on the path.'

'Jack, that's awful.'

'I think he was snooping.'

'What on earth for?'

'Because Alison's in the public eye. That's what happens. Reporters and people like that start digging . . . she warned us.'

'But how would he get the address?'

The old man sat in his favourite armchair, thinking it through. 'You hire an enquiry agent for a day. Anyone can do it. We should tell someone, just in case.'

'But Alison's in Berlin. We can't ring her there.'

'I know that.' He slumped deeper into the chair. 'Who was that friend of hers? Fellow who's now chief whip. She always spoke well of him. Harper, wasn't it?'

'You worry me with this kind of talk.'

'I'm only going to tell him what happened.'

'I don't think you should. Not without talking to Alison.'

But the old man was already looking through the diary beside the telephone, hunting for the special code that would put them through to Keith Harper, or anyone else they wanted in Downing Street.

Chapter Thirty

'You did exactly the right thing. Thanks very much.'

Keith Harper put down the phone and returned to the kitchen. Denise had cleared away his plate.

'It was all cold.' She scraped the leftovers into the bin. 'Who was that?'

'Work.'

'And how is Miss Work?'

'Don't be stupid.'

'Well, someone keeps calling all hours of the bloody day and night.' She cut the raspberry ripple into slices and gave him one. 'Not that I care.'

'It may have escaped your notice, but I am chief whip.'

'Ooh, sorry, sir, sorry, Mr Whip, I'm sure. If you ever took me to any of the parties or all these other things you go to, then maybe it *wouldn't* escape my notice.'

He couldn't answer that. Couldn't tell her he was ashamed – ashamed of the seventies dresses for sixteen-year-olds, the talk of make-up and television. The baby-doll face that now only pouted or cried.

Of course he'd loved her in the old days. She'd been pretty and lively and funny. She used to go canvassing in outfits that would have got her arrested in the fifties. She had once stretched up to kiss a baby, enabling the party manager to remark that he now knew for certain she wasn't a real blonde.

But it had all been fun and light-hearted. Denise was a cuddly, affectionate little creature, knew bugger all about politics. But backed her man, got him dressed up, got him envied, flirted and joked and played around till they elected him for her sake. The local party in Wigan loved her. She was a shocker when shockers were in. In the old days.

Wasn't her fault Alison had come along.

Wasn't his fault either.

He put the remains of the raspberry ripple in his mouth. 'I have to go out for a while.'

'Go, then. I'm not stopping you.'

Cindy Tremayne had made progress.

Not only had she passed her initial tests at the clinic, but she had passed into the affections of the Director's secretary – Miss Primp.

She it was who insisted on scheduling the most important clients. She it was, who had to be impressed.

The breakthrough had came early that evening, when Cindy had finished an appointment with the bottom-heavy Mrs Riverton-Fforde.

Rivers, as she was known in the clinic, was loaded with most things, including cellulite – but a sense of humour was not among them. So it was with considerable relief that Cindy pummelled the woman into silence, rubbed her down like an old carthorse, and pushed her out into the evening, to spend money and complain somewhere else.

Exhausted, Cindy retired to the staffroom, lay on the sofa and shut her eyes – a state of grace that remained uninterrupted for at least ten minutes, before Miss Primp's otter-like moustache appeared round the door.

'I say, Cindy?'

'Yes, Miss Primp.'

'D'you have a moment?'

As she led Cindy to the consulting rooms, she explained the reason for the summons.

'My back,' she passed a hand round and tried to rub her cocxyx. 'Where exactly does it hurt?' Cindy felt for the base of the spine.

'Bit lower.'

'There?'

'Bit more . . .'

Cindy removed her hand. Any lower she thought and she'd be half way into the colon.

'You'd better take your clothes off and let me have a look.' A smile crawled across Miss Primp's face.

Cindy turned down the light to shield her eyes from the sight of the middle-aged carcass. Lord save us, she thought, the old bird was wearing cami-knickers.

'It's nice when you dim the lights like that,' Primp stretched out on her front, peach-coloured bra, ankle-stockings.

'Now what kind of pain is it?'

'Dull ache, mostly. Probably the way I sit. So uncomfortable these new chairs. I tried putting a cushion ... outch!'

Cindy's fingers dug towards the thoracic nerves. 'I think we're getting somewhere ...'

'I think it's ...'

'Lower. I know, you said so. Let me explain something about the spine Miss Primp. The nerves all connect up to various organs of the body. The cervical nerves do the head and neck, biceps, wrist extensors. Down here we have the lumbar nerves – they look after the leg muscles. Little further on – the sacral nerves.'

'What do they do?'

'Bowel, bladder, feet – and, of course ... the sexual function.' Cindy let the words drip off the end of her tongue. 'One doesn't go messing around down there.'

Primp had started to breathe heavily. 'Quite.'

'But to an expert, it's possible to diagnose the source of the strain and carry out a course of regenerative work ...'

'Yes ... ?'

'Yes. It takes time, and obviously each treatment has to be carefully planned.' Cindy left her hand on Miss Primp's buttocks and knelt down till her face was next to the older woman's. 'It's important not to rush these things, Miss Primp.'

'I ...' the breathing was coming now in jerks.

'I think we should plan your treatment together, and have a full session next week. You know my timetable. I shall be happy ... her hand carressed the buttock, 'to help in whatever way I can.'

'That's most awfully kind.' Primp sat up. Cindy could see the perspiration on her upper lip, the flush of excitement.

She recalled what a colleague of hers had told her a long time ago. 'People are like cars, Cin. Put the right key in and you can turn them on. No different at all. Just find the key.'

And now she'd found the key to Old Primp. When the time was right, she wouldn't hesitate to use it.

It was nine o'clock that night, after a long day on her feet, if you please, when Keith Harper called.

'You free tonight?'

'Why, are you lonely?'

'Not me. There's a man I want you to go and see. I'm not even sure you'll find him. But it's important.'

'Where'm I supposed to look?'

'He's either in Brighton or a town called Lewes. Sussex.'

'Sussex! You must be mad. D'you know what time it is?'

'It's worth . . .'

'I'm not even dressed and you want me to drive down to Sussex. I couldn't even be there before midnight.'

'Just wash your hands and get going. I was about to say it's worth a grand.'

They settled for fifteen hundred.

Two cups of coffee and twenty minutes later, Cindy was sitting in her white Toyota coupé, heading south over Westminster Bridge. She glanced in her mirror. Big Ben was like a great lighthouse, warning of the dangers of London.

When she'd first come to the city, she had taken to walking round the square at night, wondering what sort of people worked there.

Only now she knew. That was the trouble. Knew more than she'd ever wanted.

Cindy plugged in the CD player and switched on Dire Straits. Fast now, through Kennington, Lewisham, Croydon – the car, cutting through the cloudy night. It wasn't going to work, she told herself. She wouldn't find the American, wouldn't deliver him to Keith Harper and worst of all – wouldn't pass go and collect the fifteen hundred.

What kind of world did these people live in?

And yet it wasn't any stranger than her own. Over-fed women who came to lie on a massage table, because they wanted company, and were scared of being fat. Politicians, who paid out crazy money to unbutton their pants in front of someone who wouldn't laugh. Now this fellow – who by the sound of it, had been snooping in the right place and needed to be 'talked to'.

'Gently, carefully, Cindy, the way you do so well.'

She had put on the soft, black leather trouser suit for this job –

white turtle neck, her long, black hair let down over her shoulders. A touch of foundation. No powder, for her skin was without blemish.

But where the hell was he? Would he think small or big?

She headed the White Toyota towards Brighton.

An hour and a half earlier, Pete Levinson had driven along the coast road, looking for somewhere to celebrate.

The Grand sounded just right, fitted his mood. It was a grand kind of day. After all, he'd found the parents, found the photo, got a hint of the American connection. By the time he'd written it up – his way – the story would sit up and bark from here to Cincinatti. He'd be back in the groove, ready to forget about creeps like Larry D'Anna.

The Grand was just the place – the white facade, the doorman, the please sir, yes sir, of course sir. This was more like it. Some respect. About time, Pete my love. You've earned it and you're back where you belong.

Then there was room service, a bottle of champagne and an ice bucket to cuddle.

Only one thing he still wanted – but then he always wanted that.

It must have been 11.30 when someone knocked at his door. By that time he was only half-drunk, toying with a lobster claw, wondering how he'd spend the riches that would surely come his way. The girl asked if she could trouble him for a couple of minutes – she was doing a survey of hotel guests – what they liked, what they didn't. How their visit could be improved. She was sorry it was so late.

In her hand was a clipboard and pencil, but the smile told Levinson all he needed to know. He didn't mind what bullshit excuse she gave. If she wanted to come in, he wasn't going to stop her. If she charged, what the hell? This was his day.

As she stood in the doorway, he could have sworn the black leather moved and stretched, as if it had a mind of its own.

Chapter Thirty-one

It was only the clock on the wall that told him it was dark. But for just a moment Chukovsky fancied he could hear the wind in the forest clearing high above them, the calling of the birds, the rustling of the night creatures in the undergrowth.

Sometimes on the dawn shifts, he had left the dank confines of the silo and gone up top to watch the stars. And it seemed the supreme irony of all ironies – that here, laid out for him, was the beauty of the universe – and he held in his hands the power to destroy it.

On a night three years ago, he had stood in that clearing and made himself a promise. If the order ever came, he would disobey it. If they threatened to shoot him, he would die where he sat. But there was nothing that could make him contribute to the ending of the world, and the extinction of mankind. Not he. Chukovsky. Not this man, out of all of them.

And yet now, that thought seemed so remote. Tonight there was violence all around them. And in a little while, laid out at his feet, in a rough, army blanket, the young captain with his big mouth and his big ideas would die. He had crossed the river many hours ago, and you couldn't get him back now. He was already on the other bank and he'd go without ever once looking back.

Poor captain. Or was it those he'd left behind who would find themselves the poorer?

'Volodya, buy me a coffee. Leave the fucking radio. Do something useful.'

The big sergeant sighed and stood up from the main console. 'I can't get away from the idea that they're ignoring us.'

'Why should they?'

'Easy. Here's the picture at Brigade Headquarters, OK? I've got it all worked out. They look at the map – and they see us fine. Silo 312. Bad scene. Sending out emergency signal on the hour, every hour. Ukrainians have marched on it – shot up the captain and now they're sitting on top of the place – like a hen laying an egg. What do they do? They hear you bleating away. Captain's about to shove it, you're hysterical. And they can't do a thing. They're not exactly going to ask you to open up the bloody lid and let in a doctor – are they? Uh? Be realistic, Major. They just don't know what to say. So they shut up.'

'Get me some coffee!'

'It's true. I'm certain of it.'

They couldn't have said when he died – which, to Chukovsky, made it all the more poignant. Somewhere between four and seven in the morning, when the first fingers of light would have been pointing through the trees from the east.

Volodya had checked him. 'He's gone.' The two-word epitaph. Soldier's tribute. 'Been there, done that, gone away.'

This one, though, the most meaningless of all the journeys.

For some reason he could remember the instructions they'd been given about death. 'Meet it head on. Climax of a glorious, courageous duty. Celebrate the departure of another exemplary patriot, whose name will be forever, and ever and ever . . .'

That was the great thing about the Soviet Army. There'd been instructions for everything. What to feel, what to say, how to direct your energies. Or not.

He remembered the way they'd leafed through the rule book, presented to each recruit with all the solemnity of a public lavatory. 'Don't masturbate in battle,' read clause 74A. They'd fallen about laughing at that one. Bound to be plenty of time for the old, right-handed two-step when the great push came and the shells started falling. First thing you'd think of, if things got tricky. Put down the Kalashnikov, whip out the dong. Doesn't every soldier do that? Battlefields of rhythmic wristing. What a hoot!

Only the laughter hadn't lasted. This wasn't a fun army. You'd only had to go to Afghanistan to realise that. Think of the sickos you met there.

Plenty of them had been on drugs – cure for fear, cure for boredom, cure for sex, cure for loneliness. The longer you could be parted from your mind – the better the system had worked. Even the officers had been at it.

By the time they'd come home, the only thing there wasn't a shortage of was narcotics. How else d'you get an army of brainwashed illiterates to go up into the hills to be shot at?

And now? Now at last there was something to fight for and the captain had been the first casualty.

Chukovsky sat in the chair by the main console and shut his eyes. Of course the fighting would have to go on. But finally there would be some accountability. Some justice. Instead of being screwed around by nameless bureaucrats, there was the chance to do something right.

For the moment they would wait for rescue. But when it came, there wouldn't be any official commissions, or diplomatic exchanges, there would have to be an immediate investigation into the captain's murder. Culprits handed over. Here on Ukrainian territory. Otherwise . . .

'Volodya!'

The sergeant looked up, disinterestedly.

'What kind of arms do we have here?'

'A little of everything. Pistols, sub-machine guns. For some reason there are even a couple of hand-held anti-tank missiles. Think someone was doing a private deal . . . .'

'Make sure it all works.'

'Why?'

'Because I tell you to.'

They took out the weapons and put the captain's body in the cabinet where they'd been stored.

They covered him with a sack – and as a last gesture, Chukovsky folded one of the army greatcoats and laid it beneath his head.

If they didn't do something now, he decided, that's what all of Russia would be like.

Not caring for the living. But disposing of the dead.

Chapter Thirty-two

He wasn't used to having doors slammed in his face. Didn't happen much to presidents. Not in the open, at least.

Hadn't happened much to plain old David Bradley, either. Came out of the army after Vietnam, married the nurse who'd stitched his arm. Service wedding, statutory kiss, walked beneath the sabres. Happy ever after.

No place for rejection.

Not until Alison Lane.

The elaborate convoy was heading out of Berlin for the first session of talks. Behind him all the secret service trucks, the 'wacko' car with the nuclear buttons, A Lincoln limousine, shipped out specially from Washington, just in case he wanted to stop by the roadside and launch a missile before lunch. What a fucking waste of taxpayer's money!

Lousy mood you have there, Mr Bradley. Can't forget her standing there, telling you to shove it; the past is past, and you should think of your duty.

This from the new Labour prime minister of Great Britain and Northern Ireland – the lady you used to buy sweet and sour pork from the Chinese take-out – the lady you took to bed on a Saturday night, or Sunday night, or Monday ...

But what did you expect?

No, really – what? To bridge half a lifetime in a single day? And think of this ... maybe she's right. Maybe you simply forget the past, get on with your lives and responsibilities ...

Isn't that the rule?

There's no place for the leader of one country going soft on the leader of another. No precedent. Too many conflicts of interest. Too many judgements clouded.

The rules, Mr President. Remember the rules.

He looked out at the thick woodland, the narrow roads that had once belonged to the miserable, little state of East Germany.

Look at the way *they'd* obeyed the rules.

Wasn't the duty of a leader to re-fashion rules? To *set* precedents, not follow them?

If I want Alison Lane ...

But it doesn't work that way. Not with her. For there's a whole wagon-load of pain that's travelled with her for years.

What happened to you, Alison? Who happened to you?

The setting was not what he'd wanted. The bleak, 19th-century castle of Babelsberg, stuck on a hillside overlooking a lake. Like the backdrop to a Wagner opera.

For weeks now the advance security team had been crawling through grass and climbing trees. Not even a hostile crow had come their way. It was declared safe. The 'protectee' could come.

And yet the difficulty of bringing four world leaders to a single place was scarcely believable.

The US delegation was frankly a disgrace. He'd asked to see the list, despite Harry's reservations. Four hundred people, for Chrissakes, right down to the lady who did his makeup, and made sure his three clean shirts were out there and ready in the holding rooms.

No wonder Reagan had loved the job. It was all acting and image. It was the feel-good factor, the comfort zone – or any of the other wacky concepts the media men liked to fling at him when he rehearsed a public appearance.

'Mr President, you still look like a soldier going into battle.'

'That's what I trained to do.'

'We have to sell you as the man who went to battle and won. You have to look like a winner – at all times – the guy on top. Not the guy under fire.'

They talked crap. But then the business was crap. So they talked the truth. He'd learned all that during the campaign, watching the public chew up the ones who didn't have the body-language right.

'Not too hard, not too soft,' came the instruction. 'You don't want to be like Bush and remind American women of their first husbands.'

'I'm here now,' he would say. 'So let's get on with the job.'

'Say that in your second term,' they'd reply. 'This is just a practice run '

* * *

And when she came he couldn't help the smile, realising the contrast with his own arrival. No security blankets, no young, grey-suited agents, ready to throw themselves in front of a bullet. But just a woman, with an elegance and calm that set her apart – almost alone. She left the car by herself, with a dark blue coat buttoned to the neck, black leather boots – and the fine blonde hair, blowing all ways in the wind.

Elegance and calm. She'd always had them.

'Shall we do the cameras?' He waved a hand at the wall of lenses.

'Is there a choice?'

'Always.'

He watched her gradually release a smile and turn to the photographers.

'Should we shake hands?'

The smile fled.

'There doesn't seem much point.'

They entered the hall and at once whole clusters of aides and ministers and interpreters were crowding in on them. He wanted to pull her to one side, find a quiet room, ask what the hell was going on in her mind. But the Russian was arriving and the Ukrainian would be there any moment. And there was a block in her eyes that he couldn't surmount.

I need to reach you.

But in that moment, he was powerless to do it.

A large, square table occupied the raised centre of the room. Eight seats – two each side. It was like a chess game in a vast auditorium – only if anyone lost, the entire game would end in failure. Four winners or four losers. No draws. No extra chances.

He'd shaken Klimak's hand outside. Ukraine's president, with his brushed crewcut. A rough hand. Once belonged to a miner. Once to a communist. Now he was anything they wanted if it kept him in power. The man was small and wide, but it wasn't fat. There was bone and muscle – and a brain, said the briefing, that would understand power and pressure and politics, and wouldn't lie down.

'You talk, we'll listen. I understand that's the way our people have set it out?' Bradley looked round the table.

Shilov nodded.

Klimak grinned. 'Are we to understand ...' his hand took in the British and American delegations, 'that you are together or apart? We,' he glanced at Shilov, 'are apart.'

'We represent independent voices in an alliance ... .' Bradley leaned forward, but Alison took the ball.

'Our politics are very different – our rules are different ...'

'So are our capabilities.'

She stared at him sharply.

Klimak laughed. 'Perhaps we should mediate between the two of you ... uh? We have experience of alliances, my friends. Very bad experience. That is why we left. You would do well ...' he stopped himself.

Old habits, thought Bradley. Start of the old lecture. Hasn't yet learned the new script. 'We're here because you requested a meeting – shall we leave it at that.'

The Klimak grin.

Shilov shifted his papers. 'Mr President, Miss Lane, President Klimak,' he sighed. 'Let's not waste time on the jokes and pleasantries. Klimak may enjoy this, but the situation is serious. The argument centres on the twelve missile silos, currently located in the Ukraine ...'

'You told us there were ten,' Bradley's fist hit the table. 'What is it with you people ... ?'

'That was my predecessor. You didn't expect that the communists would tell you the truth ... '

'Should I expect it from you?'

'I am telling you now, Mr President.'

'How many more surprises are there?'

'Ask Klimak.'

There was silence for at least twenty seconds. Across the table Bradley caught the interpreters exchanging glances. He hoped Alison wouldn't break the silence. You had to create some tension. Let Shilov and Klimak find something useful to say by themselves ....

He watched her sit back in the chair. She understood implicitly.

The Russian opened his briefing book. 'Our position is very simple ...'

Bradley chuckled inside.

'We are willing to decommission the silos, remove the weapons and have them destroyed, according to our international obligations ...'

'They're not yours to decommission.' Klimak was still smiling. 'The missiles are on Ukrainian territory. Therefore they belong to the Ukraine ...'

'They belonged to the Soviet Union and Russia is now the legal successor ...'

'My friend,' Klimak looked pityingly at Shilov, 'we all belonged to the Soviet Union. Times have changed. Now we belong to ourselves. We're human beings again. What's left on our territory is ours.'

'That is presumably why you have surrounded our silos, and in one instance – shot and wounded our military personnel.'

'A local misunderstanding. The officer has been disciplined. You are free to send in a medical team at any time ...'

'And open up the silo, so that you can overrun it.'

'Our silo, my friend.'

Alison sat forward. 'What if the area were to be cleared and an international team came in – and decommissioned the silos?'

Klimak looked at Bradley. They both realised she had made a mistake.

Shilov shook his head. 'You will understand, Miss Lane ...' it was clear from his voice that he doubted she would ... 'the missiles contain certain examples of technology that are the property of the Russian people. We cannot therefore simply allow international personnel – however, well-intentioned,' he bowed his head in her direction, 'to examine the missiles at will and acquire this technology. We're not yet so far down the road. I hope I make myself clear.'

'But you're content to leave your soldiers wounded, and possibly dying ...'

'That's a matter for Klimak's conscience. If he withdraws from the area, we'll tend the injured ...'

'How can you sit here ... ?'

'Prime Minister Lane! I would remind you this is not a road accident in Chelsea!' He paused to let her see the anger in his eyes. 'You may be glad that we left the men where they are, since the choice is between that – and handing the missiles over to Klimak. We, at least have proved a certain responsibility ...'

'Responsibility ... At this moment you possess 176 nuclear-armed ICBMs, carrying roughly 1,240 warheads and anywhere up to 600 additional warheads ...'

'Impressive, isn't it?' Klimak smiled amiably.

It's like bloodletting, thought Bradley. You bring out all the poison, release it from the system – jab by jab. And either you find a cure, or the patient dies. Even with all the preparations, the briefings, the assessments and strategies – you often don't know what's down there until you start to probe.

'I've heard enough for now.' Klimak pushed his chair away from the table. It was like a boat casting off from the jetty.

'Before you go ...' Bradley raised an eyebrow. 'Before you go, President Klimak may I suggest we at least keep our ministers and experts busy. I believe there's a useful area for the working parties to explore.'

'What?' Klimak stayed where he was. But they were all watching him.

'The setting up of a joint Russian-Ukrainian scientific team, to handle transition arrangements ...'

Klimak turned away in disgust.

'Just one word of warning ...' Bradley stood up. There were times when they had to know where you were coming from. You had to remind them who was what in the big, outside world. 'The United States, at least ...' he glanced at Alison, 'is not prepared to see a nuclear confrontation that would endanger our interests and those of other countries. Not when the Cold War has ended and our people are looking forward to a new stability. That is not acceptable to us. Period. There must be a solution ... We are required,' he let the word hang for a moment, 'we are required to find it.'

'I made a fool of myself, didn't I?'

She sat in the ante-room. Bradley gestured Norton and Till to leave them.

'It's your first summit. And no, you didn't.'

'Thanks for not helping me.'

'I learn by my mistakes.' He gestured to the sofa. 'Sit down for a moment.'

'Will they come to the evening session?'

'Hell, yes. This was just theatrics. Plenty of politicians don't think it's a proper meeting unless someone walks out. It just opens the bidding. To them it's part of the ritual – like shaking hands.'

She coloured. 'I'm sorry I refused outside. That was churlish. I was still angry with you.'

He joined her on the sofa, but said nothing. You couldn't pressure Alison Lane. Neither the teenager – nor the adult. Questions only brought more questions. If you wanted an answer, you waited for her to give it.

She got up and went to the diamond-shape window. Outside, past the security cordon, she could see through the trees, down to the lake, an old iron bridge, its superstructure shaped in a semi-circle.

'The Glienicke Bridge,' Bradley had come up behind her.

'Where they used to hand over spies?'

'All the fun has gone.'

She turned to face him. They were closer, he realised, than they'd been in thirty years . . .

'I can't go back, David.'

The voice and the unexpected kindness in it, took him off guard. 'I never said . . .'

'Listen,' she said quietly. 'Don't say anything. Just listen to me. I know what I see in your eyes, and it wouldn't be fair if I didn't tell you this. Our meeting is chance. One in a thousand. But it's still chance. I won't read more into it than that. Last time I saw you, I was angry and I'm sorry for that. Maybe I was still working things out in my mind. Maybe I wasn't clear. Perhaps not even until the summit – when I saw what we had to do. How important it is . . .'

She looked hard into his eyes. But she couldn't read them. He was motionless, silent, as if a shield had come down in front of him.

'There's also a degree of pain in this, which you can't guess at – and for the moment I can't tell you. One day. But now isn't the time, David. There's too much to do.'

'I think you should give us a chance . . .'

'It couldn't be, my dear. Just couldn't.'

'I'll fight for my chance, Alison.'

She went over to the door and opened it. 'Then you'll be fighting yourself.'

* * *

Till knew what he'd seen.

He sat in the fifth car of the US convoy, waiting for the president – and the return to Berlin.

The private meetings, the phone calls. He checked his notes. But Bradley wouldn't be that stupid, would he?

And yet look at Kennedy.

That was the strange thing about politics. Despite all the checks and balances, the men and women involved in it, acted as though they were totally unaccountable. Professionally and personally. Do what the hell they liked.

Oh yes, they would say, we're accountable to the people. The great American public.

Sure.

Since when did the people get to hear what was going on?

So maybe it wasn't so far-fetched. Bradley and the prime minister. Double the risk, double the fun. Perhaps people got off on things like that.

Chapter Thirty-three

'I'll do the interview now, Dick.'

'I don't understand, Prime Minister. I told them it was off.'

'Then tell them it's on again.'

Alison disappeared into her room, sat at the dressing table, and retouched her makeup. Decision time. That was it. You make your decisions and you go forward. And she had told David Bradley, where she stood. No return to the past.

'I'll fight for my chance, Alison ...'

She wished he hadn't said that. A long time ago, so many, many years back she could recall telling him ... 'when you fight for something, David Bradley, you always seem to get it. Don't know what it is about you – but you always get your way. Always win in the end.' It had been a source of pride to her when she'd said it. Now it seemed like a curse.

The BBC had asked for the 'friendly' interview. Here she was, they said, just three days in the job, attending summits, caught up in the tussle of international politics. Long way from Education Secretary. How did it *feel*? This was the Sunday morning chat programme. Bit of news, bit of colour and informality. Plenty of *feeling*.

She didn't mind that. All they wanted was for you to resemble vaguely a human being, smile, laugh, and appear to know what you were doing.

Only, don't ease up. Every interviewer believes there's an extra nugget to be extracted – just by them. They want to make news. They want their name in the headlines – and you're the vehicle to get them there.

She knew all that. Five minutes in they had covered the 'meteoric' rise, looked at the dangers of Russia and the Ukraine – now they'd be heading for the final straight.

'Thank you, Prime Minister, etc etc ...'

But the interview was running longer than scheduled. Perhaps another item had fallen through. And then as if from a clear blue sky, she heard the question ... 'So how are you getting on with President Bradley? Things haven't always been smooth between a Labour prime minister and a Republican president, now have they, Prime Minister?'

'The world's moved on,' she stiffened slightly. 'Of course there are differences of opinion. That's healthy in an alliance. But we have many points of common ground. We share the same concern that the nuclear dispute between Russia and Ukraine, should be settled as a matter of urgency. That's why we're here.'

'I meant more on a personal level.' The interviewer crossed his legs. 'You both went to Oxford, roughly at the same time, I believe. So ...'

A thin, sharp blade seemed to enter her chest, below the heart.

'So, did you never meet, or have any contact?'

And there it was all plain and simple – the one question she should have expected, and hadn't. The interviewer was staring at her, his mouth slightly open in a half-smile. And you have only a split second, no time for thought on this one, Alison. This is live. And there are two or three million people watching you at this exact moment. *Answer the question.*

'I don't believe we ever did.'

She knew it was the wrong answer, even as she said it. She knew – with the utmost certainty – that she had made a crucial blunder. 'You don't lie,' the whips had told her, when she'd entered parliament. 'You feign ignorance, stupidity, you avoid the question, if necessary you throw a fit and roll about on the floor screaming. But you don't tell a lie when there are people around who know the truth.'

What have I done? she asked herself.

But she already knew the answer.

Sir Henry knew it too. After years of watching Alison, and watching all the other politicians, you know when there's a turning point. You see so many scandals break and wash away the people caught up in them. You almost get used to it.

And yet this one seemed so unncecessary.

He leaned across the breakfast table and reached for another piece of toast.

Wendy put down her coffee cup. 'I thought she was rather good. A lot more capable than some.'

He nodded and spread the marmalade in thick dollops. Wendy had never understood anything.

Pete Levinson saw it – out of the corner of his eye. He hadn't known whether to watch the show – or watch Cindy. So he'd looked at both.

Cindy had been going through her second, morning exercise routine, dressed only in an ankle chain and a headband, and a lesser man, he told himself, would have missed the brain-shocking importance of what Alison Lane was saying.

He sat up straight in the bed and hit the television remote control, trying to read her face, seeing the lie, as if imprinted in the middle of her forehead.

Cindy was now doing handstands against the wall.

Jesus Christ! It was enough to make anyone go crazy. He'd come back to Alison later.

In the bungalow, a few miles along the coast, Margaret Lane, got up and turned off the set.

'Why did she *say* that? She didn't have to. It was an old relationship, finished thirty years ago. Normal, natural. She could have told the truth, brought it into the open. No one would have cared.'

Alison's father got up and went to the window. 'It's not over. That's why she said it. It's never been over. She's my daughter. I know her.'

They didn't speak again. Margaret Lane disappeared into the kitchen and began peeling potatoes. He found her there a half hour later, her face streaked with red and distorted by the tears.

Chapter Thirty-four

At dawn, on his fifty-first birthday, Harry defined the rest of his life.

You will never again have so much power, so much anguish, so much guilt.

Two days since he'd seen her in the restaurant in Chevy Chase. Two days of waiting and asking himself. Why would she be talking to the little Ferret from the Press corps?

He fancied he had heard his name, whispered and sniggered across the table.

Christ it was humiliating.

He went into the bathroom and splashed cold water on his face. A worried, hunted creature stared at him from the mirror. So who do you blame Harry?

Fucking idiot that you are.

He could hear the dull thud as the two thick wadges of Sunday paper landed in their polythene covers on the front porch. And maybe there will come a day when I don't have to run down and tear open the pages, scanning each column like a thing demented, to see whether they've found me out.

But not today.

Only when he'd covered all the sections did Harry relax. A day of rest had been ordered by the doctor who lay beside him. Jane Deval, prescribing a family outing, morning till night. So he could throw away the papers, and forget about heading into the White House.

That's what she'd said.

By the time she came down it was eight-thirty and he was making french toast and frying bacon.

'Boy, even the smell of this is life threatening.' Jane opened a window and let some of the smoke escape. 'Did you have to start a fire on your birthday?'

Harry wasn't to be distracted. 'Your order, madam?'

'Go easy on the heart attack. I want juice, bran, and a cup of black coffee.'

'I'm sorry, madam, we don't serve crap like that. This is a restaurant for people who eat. Grass and other fringe dishes are sold down the street.'

'You're crazy. I have to do something about you. People keep telling me you're a lousy ad for my medical practice. They look at you and think, that's a hell of a doctor he's married to. She can't even put him on a diet.' She was grinning now. 'Why shorten your life? I could give you ten extra years ...'

'Yeah – it'd feel like twenty. I wanna go out in a blaze of calories. Like a kind of dietary supernova.'

'What's a supernova?' Jason had shuffled in, wearing pyjamas. 'And where's the french toast?'

They took the toboggan to Battery Kemble Park and watched the boy, falling all over the hill, chased by dogs, shouting to his friends.

They said hallo to a White House staffer and his family.

They nodded to a teacher from St Patrick's, his wife, ridiculously overdressed in a yellow ski suit.

'Fifty-one.' Harry shook his head. 'Where'd it go?'

'Your waist.' Jane laughed. 'C'mon it's at least twenty minutes since your last meal. Let's go eat lunch.'

Harry couldn't remember a happier day. They had brunch at Houlihans, with tables of food and pitchers of beer that seemed to stretch well over the State line. We'll do more days like this, he thought. When this is all over ... when I can start again.

Get yourself a life, Harry. Get it now, while you still can.

He had almost fallen asleep back home when the phone rang.

'For you.' Jason couldn't have cared less.

Harry put his hand over the mouthpiece. 'Didn't you ask who it was?'

'Some guy.'

'Hallo?'

'Harry, it's Clark Norton.'

Harry closed his eyes. 'I thought you were in Berlin.'

'I was. President asked me to return home. New Far East initiative ...'

160

'Right, right, right. I believe I heard something about that.'

'Can we have a talk?'

'Monday, ten o'clock suit you?'

'Now, Harry.'

'Clark, this is my birthday.'

'Congratulations. Give me half an hour Harry. I'll come round.'

He climbed into his oldest coat, two sizes larger than he was now and walked Clark Norton down the street.

'What's on your mind?'

'I got sent home, Harry, like a schoolkid who'd fucked up on his homework.' Norton's foot kicked at a ridge of snow. 'That's what's on my mind.'

'President's call, Clark. Nothing to do with me.'

Walking past sleepy, snowy houses, some kids throwing snow-balls, only the temperature was rising.

'Harry, Harry.' Clark smiled and patted Harry's shoulder. 'We're in this together. All of us. It's the way things are.'

Harry stopped and turned face on to Norton. 'What the hell are you talking about? You get sent home . . . and we're suddenly all in this together? What's that supposed to mean?'

'Part of the general malaise, my friend. A symptom of the way this administration is going. You know what I did? I talked tough to the new Labour prime minister . . . Alison Lane. Labour for Chrissake. Half-pink, half-any colour they can find. And we're supposed to pussyfoot around these people? Jesus! Memories are short in this town. So what happens . . . the President tells me my behaviour's offensive and I'm to go home in disgrace. For what? For Chrissake.' Norton pointed his gloved finger through the air at Harry's nose. 'That's why I say we're all in this together, because something is plainly very wrong with the guy. And you should know about it.'

Harry turned away and began to walk down the street away from Norton.

The older man slithered after him. 'Well, Harry?'

'Well what, Clark?'

'I think we should at least discuss some strategy here.'

'I have nothing to discuss with you. The president makes his decisions and as far as I'm concerned that's it. You want to make a case out of that, you go to him, tell him to his face.' He shook his head. 'Because I will, Clark. I'll go to him and tell him about our little conversation.'

And suddenly the mood had changed and Norton was smiling the little smile he saved for those occasional little Washington triumphs. They could have been two men enjoying each other's company, out for a stroll – suburban DC, little friendly argument, some banter. Only it was way past that.

'I don't think you will, Harry.'

'No?'

'I don't think so. Because I don't think you would want a certain story coming to light and upsetting that nice family you have back in there ...' he jerked his finger in the direction of Harry's house, 'and that attractive and very competent wife of yours ...'

Someone seemed to be squeezing Harry's stomach and he was fighting for breath.

'I'm sorry, Harry, did you say something?'

'Spell it out, Clark. Let's hear what you have to say.'

'Only to point out that we have certain things in common and that we might be able to serve each other's interests over the next two years. So it wouldn't be a good idea to go talking to teacher out of school. Do I make myself clear? The lady we haven't yet spoken of, is, as you can understand, in some distress and feels it might be cathartic to let her feelings out. I have, of course, counselled against this. I ...'

'Get out of here, Norton.' Harry's stomach seemed to be expanding, tearing, some kind of hook deep inside ...

'Think about it, Harry.'

'You're scum, Norton.' Harry turned and walked away. 'That's what I'm thinking about.'

'Be careful, my friend.'

He could hear the words, following him up the hill, settling on his back.

'Do you often keep secrets from me?'

He smiled. 'Course I do. It's my job.'

She turned away in bed and faced the wall.

'What happened today, Harry? With Norton.'

'We talked. He's a pain in the arse. Should be put down.'

'I said . . . "What happened, Harry?"'

She didn't use that tone very often.

He stayed silent for a moment, turning his body, pressing against her back.

What was he to say? Listen, it's all one big mistake. I'm not really the person you thought I was. But please keep your mouth shut and don't talk to any of our very influential friends. Dry your eyes and let's go back to being the statistical exception you always thought we were – a happily married couple.

Instead he ran a hand through the hair on the back of her head. 'I turned fifty-one. I had a wonderful birthday.'

But even as he spoke, the nausea was rising in his throat.

Chapter Thirty-five

In the late afternoon they switched on the special lights in the Babelsberg castle, as the temperature plummeted across central Germany. The clouds hung thick with snow and the wind beat around the chimneys, shaking the trees. From outside only the cars and the lighted windows could be seen. A tiny village, iced in, cut off from the outside world. Four leaders at a table – winter at the door.

He could see the deep trenches below Alison's eyes – the skin pale under the spotlights, hands too busy with papers and pens. Nervous, damp hands that left a ring of moisture on the leather folder beside her. Only the face betrayed no emotion. And this, he thought, is a trained, political animal. Knows how to behave, controls the mouth, the body language – only the fine blonde hair seemed to go its own way, curling in irregular tufts at the side, untamable, as it always had been.

And yet he knew what she'd said on television. They'd flashed it from the embassy in London. Full text, without comment. Had it in his pocket. The phrase that denied him once and for all. 'I don't believe we ever did.' Why in God's name had she said it? Sooner or later, someone would talk. A friend from the old days, a tutor. Sooner or later the Press would get on to it. And how do you answer then? What was he to say if asked the same question? Go along with the lie? Challenge her in public? This was a nightmare, scheduled and waiting to happen. Worst of all ... it needn't have happened. She could have said '... I knew him, we talked, had a few drinks.' Now it was the worst of all worlds.

In the middle of a summit.

The president turned his eyes towards the Ukrainian leader. The Russian sighed. Alison spoke first.

'I understand some useful ground was covered by the working parties, this afternoon ...'

'They speak in the dark.' Klimak tossed his head back. 'They talk about technical details, removal of warheads ... .but the essential questions have not been resolved ...'

'Ownership of the missiles and the technology.' Bradley put down the papers. It was time to open the bidding. The Russian and the Ukrainian were there as dealers. One had a product, the other didn't. They would now have to bargain to divide it or dispose of it. These two men hadn't come to Germany to start a war. They'd come to set a price. You have to keep that in mind. The only thing at issue was the price.

He rubbed his eyes. 'What do you want, President Klimak, President Shilov – what do you want?'

The two leaders looked at each other for a moment, expressionless. Shilov raised an eyebrow.

'I want our share of the missiles,' Klimak folded his arms.

'What for?'

'Because they belong to us.'

'What do you want the missiles for?' Alison leaned forward.

'To protect our security.'

'Guarantees would protect your security.'

Klimak laughed. 'Look at the Soviet Union. Full of guarantees. To you, to us, to everyone. What are they worth now? There is no Soviet Union. Tomorrow,' he looked hard across the table towards the Russian president. 'Tomorrow there may be no Shilov.'

We'll get a price, thought Bradley. But not this session. Maybe not tomorrow either. They'll play it as far as they can, posture, threaten, go through the ritual ... Not surprising since this is the only chip they can cash in. Seventy years of communist rule and all they can sell are the weapons. This is the last, best deal they can hope to make.

'I'm hungry,' he said simply and gathered his papers. 'What d'you think – our people will let us take a break for lunch?'

'Take the rest of the day.' Klimak wasn't smiling. 'Frankly I have become bored with this discussion.'

'We shall try to be more entertaining.' Shilov got up. 'I'll have some clowns sent over to your hotel. Or do you have sufficient in your delegation?'

'Be careful, my friend. This is more serious than you ...'

'Gentlemen ...' Alison was standing, looking round at the faces.

165

'Forget I said that. We have to do better than this. I think our people deserve better.' She left the hall before anyone else could move. Never mind entrances, she thought. Making a bloody exit is just as important.

'I needed to talk to you.'

He had knocked at the door of her delegation, and she had duly excused her staff.

'Good. This summit isn't going anywhere.'

'Forget the summit. I want to talk about you.'

'No deal. For God's sake, David. We have something fast approaching an emergency and you want to talk about me. No. I'm not available. I'm not even here. D'you understand? If you want to talk summit – fine. If not – I have work to do.'

He stood outside in the corridor.

You should give her up now. This is all the excuse you need. Agree with her, tell her she was right, tell her goodbye. We all make choices ...

And yet after two years in the presidency, you get used to having your way, all ways. He knew that. Knew the strength of his authority. You're not encouraged to accept restrictions.

'Presidents are powerful men. They end up getting what they want.'

He'd heard that during the campaign. Advice from an old CIA agent, who'd spent years in the basements of Washington, working on projects, far away from all the oversight committees and special prosecutors – projects, that somehow, somewhere, a president had whispered he wanted.

This time Harry would tell him ... 'Don't even think about it. She's outside limits. You can't do that.'

Only no one says 'can't' to the president. People have tried persuading, arguing, but in the end no one says 'can't'. The president is elected by the people. He's the symbol of the people's will and the people's authority. You don't say 'can't' to the people of America.

Alison was everything he wanted.

Including unattainable.

Chapter Thirty-six

'Been a lousy day, Dad.'

'I know.'

'You saw the TV interview . . .'

'What made you tell them that – about never having met him?'

'I've been asking myself all day. I panicked. It's too close, too intense. I suddenly felt that if I said anything, even the slightest thing, it'd all come tumbling out . . . and then they'd never leave us alone. Can't you see it? Unmarried prime minister, widowed president. They'd have us in bed together before tomorrow's headlines.'

She could hear the old man sighing. 'Would they?'

'I had to make a decision, then and there. Whatever I did would have been wrong.'

'I suppose we should have expected it. I mean they know you were at Oxford, same time and all that . . .'

There was silence for a moment. 'I think I'm losing it, Dad. The summit, David. It's like an overload, seeing him again. He's amazingly impressive in the negotiations. In everything really. Just the same. Only more. That's what's so difficult. I don't know how to . . . half of me seems to have gone back in time, keeps telling me . . . go get him, he's yours, nothing's changed . . .'

'Easy, love. Take it slow.'

'And then there's the bloody summit, going nowhere . . .'

'You'll do it.'

'I wish I believed that. I keep telling myself what I should be doing. And yet I don't quite get there.'

'Tell me, then.'

'I can't help being struck by him. God knows, the men since haven't exactly beaten a path to my door.'

'I seem to remember you slamming that door . . .'

'Did I? I sit here, thinking – look at what you've got. The job they'd all kill for. Leader of the gang, and then I go to bed at night.

And who do I talk to about it? I ring you. Maybe I talk to Dick
Foster. But he doesn't talk back . . .'

'It's the life you chose.'

'What? David in his castle, me in mine . . . to be alone?'

'It's too late for David. You're on opposite sides of the world.
You've got to accept that.'

'I have, Dad. I was only talking.'

'Are you all right, Prime Minister?'

'What if I said "no", Dick?'

He blushed. 'I, er . . . I'd see if I could help in some way?'

'What if I said I wanted you to take me out on the town, candle-
lit restaurant, jazz club, dancing till dawn? What then, Dick?'

'I would make all the necessary arrangements, talk to the protocol
office. We could . . .'

'I didn't mean that. Can I be very personal for a moment? I
meant, would you like to take me out? On a date. You know . . .
you're a single man and I'm a single woman. There's nothing in the
rules . . .'

'But I work for you!'

'I know,' she smiled. 'But if you didn't?'

'I really . . . erm, I never thought, Prime Minister.'

'Thank you, Dick, that's all I wanted to know. Thank you for
being so honest.'

'Is there anything else I can do?'

'Goodnight, Dick. Get some rest.'

Chapter Thirty-seven

Dear Harry . . .

'Who's your letter from, honey?'

The moment he saw the handwriting, he had gone down to the den, well away from Jane, heart clumping down the stairs after him. He knew who it was, although she'd never written before, swore she never would . . . 'I couldn't do anything to hurt you, Harry. Not in a million years . . .'

Bitch.

Dear Harry,

'I didn't want to write, but Clark said you wanted to know how I was. I never realised you told him about us. I didn't think you told anyone. But in a way I'm glad you did. Well, I'm lonely Harry and I miss you, the times we had together, the dinners, the walks. I've never felt so intimate with anyone in my entire life and I don't just mean the *physical* . . .'

He shut his eyes.

'Couldn't we just meet for a half hour? I want to talk to you, not to get in the way. But we have so much, you and I. I can't believe you have that kind of relationship with your wife, and I know you need it. The magic that we made together. I can't stop thinking about it.

'Anyway find me just a tiny corner of your day. Meanwhile, with love . . .'

Christ, there was more the other side.

'PS . . . Clark Norton is such a nice man. I thought he was just passing on a message from you, but he's taken quite an interest in my career and says I'm under-employed for my talents in the EOB. Would I like a spell at State. Jealous?

'PPS . . . I love you.'

I hate you, thought Harry. Almost as much as I hate myself.

Chapter Thirty-eight

Keith looked out of the window. Far below, the Gloucester Road was blocked solid with traffic. Rain was spitting and jumping off the sidewalk.

'Who are you?' Pete Levinson threw the question at his back.

He turned and examined him across the clinical neutrality of Cindy's living room. She had done a good job, tracking him down, getting him to London – peeled and packaged.

'A friend.'

'I've never ...'

'A new friend. Isn't that nice?'

'Depends.'

'On both of us, Mr Levinson. Let's just say I have some influence in this town.'

Levinson swallowed. 'Are you police?'

'More influence than that.'

'I'm leaving. You can't keep me here.' He stood up.

'I wasn't aware we'd kept you anywhere.' Keith smiled and nodded over to Cindy. 'I'd have thought our hospitality has been pretty generous.' He raised an eyebrow. 'So far.'

'So what do you want?'

'We have a proposal.'

'I'm listening.'

'First we want to listen to you. What you're doing here, who you're seeing, what plans you may have?'

'That's my business.'

Keith turned to Cindy. 'Can we have some coffee, love?' She detached herself from the sideboard and disappeared into the kitchen. He took out a notebook. The pages were empty, but Levinson couldn't see that from where he was sitting.

'Last night you visited a Mr and Mrs Lane, claimed your car had broken down. Snooped around, asked a lot of questions ...'

'I'm a reporter.'

'Who for?'

'Magazine.'

'Good circulation?'

'Very.'

'I'm so pleased.' Keith's smile hadn't wavered. 'There's a procedure here, Pete – you don't mind if I call you Pete, do you? Have you ever worked abroad?'

Levinson shook his head. Keith had guessed well.

'So you don't know about our regulations. Reporters,' he closed his notebook. 'Reporters need accreditation.'

'I'll send an apology.'

'That may not be enough . . .' Cindy returned with a pot of coffee. 'But don't let's talk of things like that, Pete. Let's talk of how we might help each other.'

He poured the coffee into tiny blue cups and handed one to Levinson. There was something he recognised in the man – a chancer, a trader, a man of the streets. Some people look at you head on, others don't look at you at all. Levinson looked through you – to the angle beyond. We're not so different, thought Keith.

He took a sip of coffee and put the cup down. 'You went to Brighton to get information about the prime minister's parents, or about the prime minister herself. Right Pete?'

'I . . .'

'Let me finish, Pete, and then we'll throw this open to the floor, OK? You're doing a story about Alison Lane. Where she came from, what her home was like, background. Quite understandable. She's only just got the job. It's very simple. And what I'm proposing to you is also very simple. You want a story and I want to give you one. What could be a better arrangement than that?'

Levinson showed his much-vaunted teeth and grinned at both of them.

Cindy couldn't help a little fondness for him. Pete was very good at what he did, and very appreciative of what she did back to him. A real meeting of bodies, she reflected. It was something that Keith Harper, with all his party funds, couldn't buy, couldn't create and probably wouldn't even recognise if it crawled up into his pants. Pleasure.

* * *

They ate lunch in, Cindy showing skills she didn't often use, pouring claret and brandy, while Levinson drank himself into a happier and more talkative frame of mind.

He was a gift. Keith had known that instantly. Much better to leak a story through the American press than going to the British tabloids. Fleet Street was too tricky, too close. A tiny elite knew everything. Downing Street's Press office called them 'the sharpshitters' and hid behind trees when they walked past. There was only one imponderable about them. Would they knee you in the groin – or stab you in the back? And could they do both at the same time? You didn't leak through them. Not the big stuff.

But if a damaging report on Alison were filtered through the Americans, no one would suspect the Labour Party. And even if they did, the route would be too circumspect, too difficult to trace. When you had a story that flew – then so did the dirt, the recriminations, the bloody witch hunts. Much safer to come from the States.

As Cindy cleared away the food, Levinson began laughing quietly, as if enjoying a private joke.

'Yes, Pete?'

'Eating here, like this, the three of us ...'

'Why is that so funny?'

'You don't want to be seen out with me, do you? Uh?' Levinson's voice had risen slightly, but it wasn't the wine talking. 'It just kinda hit me. That must mean your face is pretty well-known outside this apartment.'

Keith didn't move.

'That's OK. I'd do the same if this was Washington.' He shook his head. 'But you're good. No, really. I mean it. You find me, you organise this stunt – both of you. OK, I don't know what your game is. You don't tell me. But I figure one thing, and maybe this'll surprise you. You guys don't know what I know – about your own prime minister.'

'Really?' Cindy leaned forward and filled the American's goblet. She'd seen it so many times before. Another half bottle of fine champagne cognac in the wrong throat. One of the oldest of the truth drugs, prising inhibitions away from worried minds.

Keith tried to steady himself in the lift on the way down. But the drink and the excitement seemed to boil over inside him. Pete Levinson hadn't just sung his heart out – he'd performed a fucking aria. Sweet, sweet music, and more lyrics than he could ever have dared to hope for.

'I've got you,' he whispered, opening the main door to the apartment block, stumbling out on to the wet streets.

'Who's been telling lies then Alison, my love? Who's been fibbing on television? "I don't think I ever met David Bradley." ' His voice reached an imitation falsetto. 'And now we have you, my little vixen. Fellow students at bloody Oxford, living and screwing together. Christ – what a story. It'll be the bloody crucifixion all over again, from hell till Tuesday.'

He hailed a taxi and took it all the way home.

'Denise! Denise!'

'Stop shouting.' She appeared in her dressing gown at the top of the stairs. 'You're pissed.'

'Let's go out to eat.'

'You're too pissed.'

'Make me a coffee. Then we'll go.'

It was all right until half way through the meal, when the thrill of vengeance seemed to wear off.

Denise had ordered the best bottle of white wine in the Italian restaurant, wouldn't go home, chattered incessantly about her sister's hairdressing salon. A wedge of veal had stuck between her front teeth and he couldn't take his eyes off it. Suddenly it all seemed so clear. Things weren't ever going to change. He didn't want Denise, he wanted Alison. The closeness that had developed between them during the election campaign. If she were here now, they'd be sitting, almost nuzzling, talking about the rat-pack, who was up or down, who was up whom – all that kind of thing, the lifeblood of British politics, the things that counted – not this nonsense about the price of a perm.

Even now, when he thought he could wreck Alison – something told him to wait. Maybe if he went to her, said he understood how she felt, but just to give him some time, and see how things panned out ... then maybe after a few weeks they could ...

Denise was smoking – she had that annoying habit of talking while the cigarette was between her lips. 'So why the dinner out then? What's the big celebration? Something gone right for once?'

'I don't know. I really don't. Just needed to get out.'

'Thought it might be that you wanted us to try again.' She hung her head. Question disguised as statement.

'I . . .'

'Don't say it if you can't.' She shrugged. 'But you're still the only person I care about. I wish I didn't.' She fumbled her wine glass but eventually got it to her mouth. 'You know the place where you could try, if you wanted to, don't you?'

He knew that all right. He could see the wide, bouncy bed, with the television opposite, the dressing table, crowded with her bottles and potions. That's where you tried and failed. And that's where you knew about it first.

And what if Alison turned him down again? Would he simply dump Denise and live on his own?

Could he leave the silly creature to fend for herself. What kind of bastard could do that? One like me. The answer was immediate. No hesitation.

'Let's go.' He helped Denise to her feet, put the coat around her shoulders, steered her through the door.

By this time she was quite drunk, so when they got home he carried her upstairs and laid her fully clothed on the bed. The face was a mess. Smudged lipstick, runny mascara – a mess outside and a bigger mess within. The mouth seemed to be moving silently, but there were no words coming out. He took off her shoes, switched out the light and went downstairs to the kitchen.

Night of decisions then, Keith Harper. What do you really want?

I want Alison Lane to call me and say she wants me to come round, that she needs me, that we could be happy together, after all.

That's what I want.

He sat there, maybe for an hour, listening to the kitchen clock. In the end he poured himself a whisky and by the time he had drunk it, he'd decided what to do.

He'd talk one last time to Alison. Just for himself. Just so he'd really know.

After that, for all the hurt and disappointment, and for the life that could have been and wasn't going to be – then and only then – he'd break her.

Chapter Thirty-nine

Shilov sat on his bed and worried about himself. Was it a new worry? An old one? Was the Slavic melancholy descending on him with the winter? Try as he might, he couldn't shake it.

'There have been three attempts on my life since I became President . . .' He turned to Katya.

'Two of them were entirely frivolous . . .'

'How can you call them frivolous?'

'My dear, a man who charges at your bodyguards wielding an ancient Cossack spear is hardly serious. Nor is a madwoman trying to throw a brick at your car as it passes beneath her flat.' She smiled.

'And the third?'

'The third was not frivolous, I grant you. A bomb discovered in anyone's car is not frivolous.' She chuckled. 'Even if it was incorrectly wired. My dear, with such skills available in our country I am convinced you have nothing to worry about.'

'I believe you.' He inclined his head towards her, eyebrows raised. 'I always believe you, my dear. I gave up the pistol, remember?'

She rose and walked around the bed. Little did anyone know that the wife of the Russian president had spent the morning, sewing a new zip on his trousers, because the Russian tailors that her husband had brought with him from Yekaterinburg insisted on using buttons. Buttons for the president! At a summit! And they had fallen off. Christ arise!

'Somehow I have not seen you worry like this before.' She frowned. 'Is there anyone in our group you don't trust?'

'Ha! I am at a loss to find someone I do trust. This is the great irony of all ironies. Everyone thought the plotters and conspirators in Russia were all communists. So what happens when the communists disappear? Just as much plotting as ever. More, in fact. Open season. Trust is a luxury we don't yet enjoy in our country.'

'It's not that bad.'

He smiled and stroked her hand. 'Let's hope so.' Leaning across, he kissed her cheek an inch below the right eye. His favourite place for more than forty years. 'Let's hope so.'

Harry Deval was known as a slab of genuine Washington. A tough, experienced lawyer, willing to offend all kinds of people if the cause was right. Over time he had represented the presumed crooked and the barely innocent, the sinned against, and the sinners, the people who inhabit the city's greylands – the legal-lands, where day is night if a lawyer says so and a jury believes it.

Law was life in Washington, Harry reflected. Lawyers did your business, they often did your family. They most certainly did your death, and frequently your taxes. 'Enter a law office,' he used to say, 'and it's one-stop shopping – all the pains of life under the same roof.'

The pain that day came in the shape of Clark Norton, ushered into Harry's west wing office, with minimal formalities.

'I don't have time for you.' Harry stood up.

Norton grinned. 'Then I'll come back later.'

'I won't have time later, or tomorrow, or at any time in the future, Clark. Do I make myself clear.'

'Perfectly.' Norton let his thin, blue-suited frame fall into a high-backed armchair. 'I want to know about Alison Lane ...'

'British Embassy is on Connecticut Avenue. Four dollar taxi ride. I'm sure they can help.'

'No, Harry!' He sounded like a whining schoolboy. 'I want to know about Alison Lane and our president. Rumour has it, there was once some kind of relationship between them.'

'Ask her.'

'Someone did. On television in fact. She denied it. My information is that she lied.'

'Too many rumours in your life, Clark. Why not get yourself some facts? Can't help. Sorry.'

'Help is required on this one, my friend. Think about it, Harry. I'd like some answers please, by tomorrow.

Harry moved to the door. 'Get out of here, Clark.'

'I'm sorry you feel that way.'

Harry's secretary appeared in the doorway from the outer office. 'Sorry to bother you, Mr Deval.'

'What is it, Jean?'

Her eyes took in the presence of Clark Norton and flashed Harry a warning.

'Would you show Mr Norton out?'

She returned ten seconds later, without him. Her voice descended into whisper. 'There's a lady in tears in the outer office. She's from the administrative section, says she's a friend of yours. A Miss ...'

'Show her in, Jean.'

Harry faced the window and clutched his stomach. He could feel his temperature rocketing, could feel all the walls of all the castles falling in on him, all defences breached. I can't do this, I can't go on like this ...

'Hallo Harry.'

As he turned again, she was sitting in the chair Norton had vacated, hair long and lush over the plain white blouse, red eyes, red nose, handkerchief in hand.

A full-scale assault on his conscience.

'I didn't mean to cry. It was just the thought of seeing you again.'

'Why did you come here?'

She opened her mouth wide. 'Why did I come here? Harry, you asked me to. Clark Norton fixed the time and made the appointment on your instructions ...'

Worse than he'd thought. The sound of more walls tumbling.

'Listen to me. I'm sorry for what happened. More sorry than I can tell you, but there's something strange going on with Norton. I made no appointment. I never mentioned you to him. I gave him no messages for you.' He drew in his breath. 'Which means he's playing some game of his own to get at me ...'

'I don't understand.'

'Don't you? Don't you ever read the papers or the scandal sheets? That's what this town is about. Who's ...' he nearly said 'fucking' but stopped himself. 'Who's dating whom, who was seen where, who's split up. Careers are broken that way. Lives irreparably altered. That's called sport in this city. That's how you play power. That's what's being done to you and me.'

'But why would Norton do that?'

'He's in trouble with the president, wants my help. I'm not playing along.'

178

'But he seems such a kind man.' She dried her eyes with the handkerchief. 'You seemed such a kind man.'

Don't get into that Harry. Lovely as she looks. Vulnerable. All the reasons you went for her. Don't touch that one.

'Listen, I have to ask you something. Did Norton introduce you to any reporters?'

'Only one. Guy from the *Post*. Peters, I think his name was. Only because he's doing a feature about White House staffers ... you know, like about the footsoldiers, the people who work away in the basement but never get any recognition ...'

'Did he ask about me?'

'Well, only in passing. You are the chief of staff after all ...'

'But no other references ... nothing about you and me?'

'No, Harry.' Hurt across the eyes. 'And I wouldn't have told him anything either. But that was only a pre-interview. We're going to meet next week and do a full interview then.'

'Cancel it.'

'Why?'

'I'm sorry to say this, but you have to leave town for a while.'

'But ...'

'I know I have no right. Now especially. If I could do anything to change what happened... But there are some strange political games going on at the moment. This could get really messy.'

'You mean, for you.'

'For both of us. For the president.'

She stood up. 'I want to tell you something, Harry ... aside from all this Clark Norton business ... you really hurt me, the way I would never have hurt you. You said the kinds of things that married people shouldn't say to anyone. Not if they intend to stay married. Of course I was wrong to get involved with you, so I have to blame myself. But I couldn't help it. I loved you. And you took my love and made me feel it was going somewhere.' She swallowed hard. 'And then you dumped me.'

She looked round for her handbag and picked it up off the carpet beside the chair.

'I'll think about what you've said. But there's no point making any promises. You and I made plenty of those in the past. And look what happened to them.'

He watched her walk through the door, couldn't help following the sleek shape, the sculpted legs ...

You're sick, Harry. You wrecked a beautiful woman and you still can't take your eyes off her.

Chapter Forty

By 6.30 most of the lights in the clinic had been doused. Cindy looked out of the staffroom window and caught sight of the director hurrying across the car park towards a white Jaguar.

Inside the car, she saw him lean over and kiss a bearded face, and for a moment she wondered if the shy woman, introduced to her as his wife, knew about the liaison. But what did it matter? Open anyone's life, really open it – and there'd be plenty to shock. People were always more than they seemed – more dangerous, more irritating, hungrier ...

She sighed and buttoned her white coat, ready for the last session of the evening – Miss Celia Primp, the clinic's appointments secretary, fawner and gusher to the rich and famous.

This was the promised hour when she would explore Miss Primp's spinal nerves – and beyond; when Miss Primp, would be at her most sickeningly persuadable.

From early morning Cindy had watched the woman blushing and simpering in expectation. The red cheeks, the moist lips, the pouting at her tiny mirror. Even the director hadn't known what to make of it.

'You all right, Primp? Seem a little hyped-up, today.'

'Nothing, Mr Thomas. *Really.*'

Cindy headed down the corridor towards the most private of the consulting rooms, a white, windowless square, often used for the trainees. The table was in the centre, under a narrow-beam spotlight that could be brightened or dimmed by a foot control. Like all the rooms there were pictures of Arcadian landscapes, mountains, lakes – and a CD system, complete with the sounds of whales calling to each other. Maybe the patients identified with them, thought Cindy. After all, one or two were about the same size.

In the old days, when she'd trained, Cindy had taken the job seriously. She had her regulars and favourites. It was a very private, even caring kind of work, based on trust. Many people felt vulnerable when laid out on the table. They wanted to confide, they wanted to release pain both from the body and the mind. Some would weep silently as she rocked them from side to side.

Even the men behaved in those days – once you laid down the rules.

'You have to get across the idea,' the instructor had declared, 'that this is massage. Just massage. Right? Not massage and a blow-job.'

And by and large things were all right after that. You had to remember, though, that the masseuse, by the nature of the job, held a powerful position. In many cases she was more intimate with a patient than their spouse. But as always, you trod a narrow line. Touch them in one place and it was therapeutic, move your hand two inches to the left, and you could end up in the Magistrates Court.

As she opened the door Cindy could see that Primp had let down her hair from the grenade in which it was normally housed. She was lying face down on the table wearing what looked like a silver 'body'.

To Cindy she seemed like the kind of furry toy, children refuse to throw away – some of the stuffing had shifted, some had come out, nothing was quite where it should have been, and where it had been twenty years before.

'You'd better get undressed,' Cindy turned up the lights. 'We don't do treatments with a 'body' on. Just step into the changing room here, take your clothes off and put on the sheet that's hanging up. I'll be with you in a moment.'

'Yes, of course.'

A cloud seemed to pass over Primp's sun. She hadn't been expecting the business-like tone. Nothing for nothing, thought Cindy, we have to play hard and soft. That's the only way it'll work.

Primp emerged from the changing room, looking like the ghost in a school play.

'Lie on your front, please,' Cindy suddenly wanted to laugh. 'That's right. I'll just work in some lotion and we'll take it from there. By the way, is there anything I ought to know about you health-wise? Injuries? Bruises, any areas I ought not to touch.'

'Oh, no.' Primp sounded breathless. 'Nothing like that. I mean I'm really fine ...'

182

'You were complaining of terrible pain in the lower back . . .'

'I meant apart from that.'

I'll bet you did, thought Cindy and bent to the task. With her foot she turned on the CD, and the mournful notes of Albinoni seemed to drip from the walls. Lights down a little. Dig deep around the spine. Come on, old bird. Let's get you in the mood.

'All right, Miss Primp? Don't worry if you fall asleep. Plenty of patients do, you know. And tell me if you feel cold.'

'Oh, I won't do that . . .'

Cindy began a gentle rocking movement. This was going to take time.

'I like to have a friendly relationship with my clients.' She poured more oil on to Primp's mole-infested back.

'I do so agree.'

'Trouble is some of my clients are so . . . well, withdrawn.'

'Then we must see you get some others . . . Ooh yes, Cindy,' Primp had suddenly felt the impact in the sacral nerves.

'I'd like that. I mean you have some pretty important clients here . . .'

'The most important in the country.' Primp's voice lapsed briefly into its tart professional mode. 'Only the cream, in fact. Mr Thomas is most insistent . . .'

'And then there's the prime minister, isn't there?'

'Yes, but she's . . .'

'Anyway, I'm sure there wouldn't be any chance of working with her.' Cindy let the music have its say for a few bars. She lifted the sheet from Primp's back. 'Would you like to turn over – towards me, please?' The furry animal, with the misplaced stuffing, rolled on to its back. 'That's better.' She replaced the sheet. 'Would there?'

Primp looked puzzled. 'Would there what?'

'Be any chance of working with the prime minister.'

'I'm not . . .'

Cindy lowered the sheet and let her hand mark out a line between Primp's newly-exposed breasts.

'I'm sorry, what did you say?' The hand seemed to be losing its way somewhere around Primp's navel.

The woman's breathing had grown almost louder than Albinoni, much louder than the little voice. 'I said I'm not sure that wouldn't be an excellent idea.'

Cindy's hand continued its downward path.

Of course, they had an agreement of the best kind. The unspoken kind. The kind of professional confidence and trust, between a medical practitioner and a patient, sealed in a top London clinic.

The details remained to be worked out, but it was all going better than she could have hoped.

Only that, to Cindy, was an uncertain sign. In her life something good was inevitably followed by something bad. And for that reason, and for that alone, she made her way the next morning to a travel agent in London's St John's Wood, paid in excess of 1,200 pounds, and purchased a round the world ticket through Air New Zealand, valid for a year.

It was good to have that in your pocket. Risk was all very well. In fact she knew she thrived on it.

But risk-takers had to be careful. Particularly those who would seek to lay a hand on parts of the British prime minister. And not just any hand. And not just any parts.

Chapter Forty-one

The dinner party had felt long and rugged like a walk in the hills. Sir Henry took off his jacket and sat in the kitchen looking at the floor.

It wasn't that Wendy's friends were dreadful – they were just so *good*. Came from good families, did good works, said good things about other people.

Of course they knew what he did. That was all in the public domain these days. And they assumed it was also 'jolly good' for the country, for the state, for the world in general. He had ended up longing to tell them that they used to cosh the bloody confessions out of Soviet illegals, and went around the world gayly blackmailing and suborning with the best of them. All *good* fellows, every one of them.

One day. He smiled inwardly. One day.

Wendy came in, after seeing out the last couple. 'Don't bother with the clearing,' she grinned, enjoying the joke. They both knew that he never helped with the chores. There were some things a man of the house simply wouldn't do. Not if he had to work like a dog. Not if he had a certain status. She'd understood that when they got married – and she hadn't sought to change him.

'Brandy?'

He nodded and opened his briefcase. The Director General is still the only member of the service allowed to remove files from the building, and he spread the grey covers on the kitchen table, because he was too tired to make it to the study. Wendy would no more look at them, than attempt a climb on the north face of the Eiger. After forty years it was just one of the many unspoken agreements between them. In fact they were all unspoken agreements. Some days, he reflected, they barely conversed about anything.

The files dealt with surveillance on Keith Harper and the girl – Cindy Tremayne. They were detailed, terse and included the transcripts of telephone calls, and intercepted mail. There was also a page devoted to the American, Pete Levinson, with some supplementary background supplied by the FBI, through the National Security Agency. Sir Henry made a note in the margin, to do the Americans a similar service over the next few days. Gone was the time when you chalked up favours – now you paid for them pretty much on the nose, otherwise they didn't come again.

He could see where it was going, see the plan. Harper was a ruthless bugger, ruthless and hurt – and that combination was ... difficult. Yes, difficult was the word. Unpredictable. Because the hurt drove the aggression. And hurt came in odd waves, subject to odd moods.

And yet it wasn't a bad setup. Without knowing it, Harper was running the kind of 'sting' operation in which MI5 had long special-ised. He was good too. Could almost have been recruited a few years back ...

'You looking after your young lady then?' Wendy turned round from the draining board, stacking plates.

'What d'you mean?'

'Don't shout, Henry.' She smiled pleasantly. 'I only meant the prime minister. Isn't that the young lady you're supposed to be looking after?' She turned back. 'Must be odd for you, working for a woman, mm?'

'She's quite well-behaved ...'

'I assumed she would be.' Wendy finished the dishes and put away the tea towel. 'All your women are – aren't they Henry?' She kissed him lightly on the cheek. 'I'm going to bed. Goodnight, my dear.'

He stayed where he was for a moment, then reluctantly closed the files and replaced them in his briefcase.

He couldn't help it – the files gave him a buzz, Alison Lane gave him a buzz – but Wendy didn't. Not any longer.

When in God's name had it happened? At what point had the work and the fantasies taken over and the beautiful woman upstairs gone and sat in the shade? At what point had they stopped investing in each other and sought solace elsewhere?

You're a fool, he thought. You didn't even realise, until it was too late.

Such a waste.

Chapter Forty-two

'I don't understand.'

Dick Foster's face took on the colour and texture of well-cooked gammon.

'It's quite simple. I don't wish to take the call.'

'But it's the president of the United States.'

'I don't wish to take the call. Do I make myself clear?'

'Perfectly ... but I ... I don't know what to *say* to them. I've got the deputy chief of staff, telling me to expect the call. *Expect.* This is really quite irregular.'

'Point out I'm engaged in very difficult domestic negotiations. There's a crisis in London. I'll see him later at the talks. Does that sound better?'

Foster's mouth described a few strange, but voiceless movements.

'Thank you, Dick.'

She closed the door on his departing back.

I can't speak to Bradley. Not now. He doesn't want to talk about the summit. He wants to talks about us. What us? Everytime I think about him it's like standing in quicksand. Sometimes I'm proud, sometimes I'm angry, sometimes I just wonder how he could have got where he has without me. Why didn't his life fall apart when we split up? Why was I the one, slammed into the gutter along the High Street in Oxford?

There's no forgetting him. Not after all this. But I have to find somewhere in my life to put him, somewhere safe and out of the way – like an old field at the bottom of the garden, with trees around it, so I can't see him from the house – and he can't see me.

She brushed her hair and tried to punch the summit into her mind.

Keep in mind the central idea. They've come for a price. They've come to deal.

And then she remembered. Even that thought belonged to David Bradley.

* * *

The telephone buzzed to tell her the car had arrived. In ten minutes they'd be moving out again to the Babelsberg Castle.

'Security's been tightened.' Foster sounded tired. 'They've already cleared the hotel foyer, guests are being kept behind barriers and those here already, have to stay in their rooms. Germans have laid on extra police outside and the crowds are under video surveillance.'

'What's going on?'

'No idea. Maybe some hoax calls. You always get them at summits.'

She hung up and checked her briefcase.

Downstairs Foster did the same.

If you'd taken the bloody call from the president, he told her in his mind, we might have found out what it was about. Bloody woman. Bloody prima donna.

He couldn't help the old prejudices rising to the surface. True, she was clever. True, she was attractive. But she wasn't consistent. Women never were.

He remembered his mother warning him about minxes in skirts. And she should have known.

Shilov glanced out of the ninth-floor window of the Grand Hotel.

'It's so odd to hear them talk about German security.' He turned to Katya. 'The last time we talked about German anything – it was the Nazis. That's what I grew up with. Hitler's Germany.'

'You of all people have to move with the times.'

He laughed. 'What is it with you? Always, you have to keep my nose on the path. Plenty of wives would say simply . . . yes, darling, or whatever you say, darling. You've never said that.'

'If I did you would go even softer and sillier than you are.'

'That's not how the country sees me.'

'They don't know you like I do.'

He pulled her towards him. 'Katya, Katya . . .'

Her eyes softened. 'There's no time for that Katya nonsense. You have a summit to think about. How long is this bastard Klimak going to hold out?'

'The working parties have made some progress . . .'

'Then maybe he will deal.'

'We will both deal. That was never in doubt. Neither of us can go back with nothing. It's just a question of how much we pay ...' He broke off as his personal bodyguard appeared in the doorway. 'The foreign minister wishes to see you urgently.'

'Then show him in. Must I sign a form?'

The minister hovered in the doorway in double-breasted suit.

'Katya Borisovna,' he bowed briefly towards the president's wife. 'Speak, man.'

'Most interesting news. The defence ministry reports Klimak has begun pulling Ukrainian forces away from the missile silos ...'

'Ha!' Shilov turned and beamed at Katya. 'You see, you see what I was saying. The bargaining's begun.'

Bradley's call reached her in the limousine as it pulled away from the hotel. There was no preamble. No preparation. Out of the corner of her eye she could see Dick Foster trying to disappear at the edge of the seat.

'I hope this isn't a bad time.'

'It feels like it.' She shifted uncomfortably.

'I'm sorry. You're the only identifiable human being on this planet, who's so far refused to take my call.'

'What's it like being God?'

'I didn't mean it that way. I wanted to tell you I'm sorry. I was behaving like a kid. It wasn't the time to be talking about relationships.'

'Nor is this. You have to see that. It shows we have duties which go beyond ...' she looked at Foster's profile, 'it shows there's no place for other things ...'

'I can't accept that ...'

'I suppose gods find it difficult to accept what mortals tell them ...'

'That's not what you feel ... you forget, I've done a little exploring inside your head.'

'Old paths, David, they're out of date. And now I have a summit to go to ... so do you.'

'I'll get back to you one of these days. If it kills me.'

Official tone now. 'Thank you, Mr President. I'll let you know when there's some progress.'

She replaced the handset, and looked over at Foster. He had shut his eyes in the hope he could feign sleep. But his breathing gave him away. Short, nervous gasps, like a spaniel having a bad dream.

'Dick . . . ?'

The eyes opened a fraction.

'Must have dozed off, Prime Minister. Sorry.' He sat up.

Alison raised an eyebrow. 'You're going to have to lie a little better, Dick, now that you've heard the conversation.'

Chapter Forty-three

They liberated the silo on a cold afternoon, with the sun standing sullen in the corner of the clearing and the cool dampness of death on the trees around them.

There's no triumph here, thought Chukovsky as he blinked into the grey daylight, and grasped the hand of the air corps major. But there is shame and anger. And there's payment for both of them.

The body-bag came out, Volodya, directing the soldiers ...

'This is a great day,' the major wore his smile tight like a belt. 'They've pulled back to within two or three kilometres of the silos, leaving us a corridor, and permission to fly three helicopters in.' He chuckled. 'We brought six – the Hinds, gunships.'

Chukovsy hadn't known what to think when the radio message came through. Was it genuine? Who was giving the orders? Finally there had been confirmation from the other silos in the region. And he had taken the lift to the surface and gone back to the world with a vengeance.

The commandos had set up a tent. Inside it – a map table, communications post, canteen – all rudimentary.

'Right.' Chukovsky sat down in the only available chair. 'As the senior officer here, I'm taking command. Notify Moscow that my captain was killed in an act of cold-blooded murder. Representations must be made to the Ukrainian foreign ministry and the culprit handed over for court martial within forty-eight hours.'

The major didn't move.

'Why d'you wait?'

'You exceed your authority, Colonel. This is my command, my post, my men .... '

A flush had started to spread across Chukovsky's face. He could feel the beginnings of a fever. 'Damn you – we have to secure the area. We need more troops. More helicopters ...'

'I can't do that without direct authorisation from Moscow.'

'Then get it.'

'They won't agree. It's too sensitive. For God's sake, there's a fucking summit going on in Berlin . . .'

Chukovsky slammed his hand on the table. 'If we don't act now, then by the morning the supply route could be closed again, and we'll be trapped inside. You can't go on hiding in silos. My God – we're the forces of the Russian Federation. Doesn't that count for something?'

'You play with dangerous toys, my friend. You should show more responsibility.'

'An officer of mine has been killed in an act of war. What more d'you need to . . . ?'

'Soldiers die – even in peacetime, Colonel, or have you forgotten some of the little adventures we used to carry out in the name of the great Socialist motherland? Uh?'

'Then now is the time to force a stop.'

The major shook his head. It struck him that the two of them were like pots, boiling side by side on the same stove.

Risky.

He hadn't been so happy since God alone knew when. The news from Ukraine was the breakthrough he'd almost stopped believing would happen. Now the summit could move.

Me and my premonitions, he thought. I'm too Russian. Too dark. I've forgotten how to be content. We'll get the session over, then Katya and I will slip away, lose the bastards, take a little journey with a bottle of wine and some chicken. An adventure. A night-time feast – like the old days.

He stood in front of the mirror and rubbed his hands in delight.

This time she tied the tie for him. 'You never get it right.'

'Still not bad for a fellow who used to drive a tractor . . .'

'And might do again soon.'

He grinned. 'If I do, you can sit on my knee.'

'Your stomach has beaten me to it.'

They opened the suite door and moved out among the body-guards.

No more doom. Thank God.

Into the lift. One of the bulky men seemed to have bathed in eau de cologne. Shilov caught his wife's eye and winked. Just because they were in the West they had to smell like French whores.

Outside, can you believe it? Sunshine even. Not a trace of cloud. The kind of day you killed for in Moscow.

Through the empty foyer – out under the canopy. Wait a minute. The way I feel. Look at the crowds. Listen to the cheering. I'm a popular guy. Man of the people. He looked at Katya, this would be fun.

Shilov bypassed the car. The tallest of the security men blocked his path. 'Not a good idea, sir. Extra security. You know the American warning . . .'

'I'll judge the warnings. If you can't talk to people – you shouldn't be in power . . .'

Out there on his own suddenly, the security men hurrying to keep up. And they tell you the biggest nightmare of all is a man in the crowd, with bad intentions . . . .

Katya's face borrows a frown. The security chief turns to her . . . 'Please get him back.'

And he's over by the barrier, heart expanding with all the goodwill of the moment, Russian hospitality and peace to all mankind.

Down the line he goes, like a small tank, elbowing his own security, thinking he'll kick them later for getting in the way. Child's hand, woman's hand, a camera, two cameras . . .'

He hears Katya's voice in the background. Wonderful! After all the dark days, the crises, this is why I went for the job. A little adoration isn't a bad thing.

More hands and cameras.

And then he stops for a second because the sound drowns out and it isn't a camera in front of him, four feet back, not in that shape, with the eyes beside it, looking beyond this world, and way too far into the next.

And Shilov – trained as he is by years of Soviet treachery and danger – reaches into his jacket to the gun he always carries, and knows in that second that it isn't there.

Katya, he wants to say. Katya, I gave it up because you asked me to. Katya I need . . .

But there's no time for him to turn, as the eyes in the crowd find their focus and the bullet travels . . .

That this should happen to the President of Russia, he thinks, just a few yards from his wife, on the best day, for so many, many months.

Please, just an hour, a field, bottle of wine, Katya ... please!

But the thoughts were silent, and lost in the screams and the terrible shouting, as they closed around him, the sudden violence and the shock reverberating along the street.

No one heard them except Katya, running, running towards him.

It came at them on the emergency defence channel.

Unreal. So unreal when you sit in a wood and learn that the world has thrown itself out of the window.

'Can't believe this ...' The major kept repeating it, the words slurring round and round.

'They're saying injured. Badly injured. Christ! Taken to the Charite hospital in Berlin ... Fuck!'

'Quiet, I can't hear ...'

They had all gathered, drawn by the alarm in the voices, soldiers, officers, the commandos on guard, standing in the half-dark clearing, knowing they'd remember the moment.

Same bulletin, repeated, minute by minute. And they waited for the orders. Countdown, thought Chukovsky. He could just picture the chaos in Moscow, the scramble to take power, the shouting, the garbled orders given and withdrawn, no one knowing what to believe. Panic across the jagged, snowy rooftops. Good city not to be in that night.

And then it came, authorised by a whole clutch of them, because no single man had the power any longer to take a decision. Not these days, when power was shared, when power was a broken instrument that might or might not work on the day you wanted it.

There it was – general state of alert ... 'To all the Forces of the Russian Federation, to the border units, the internal troops, to the airforce and navy, both in and outside Russian territorial limits ...' The voice droned on, reciting the endless units.

Chukovsky stood up. 'That's it, Major. I think we know who's responsible for this. And now I'm *taking* command and securing our position. Time we got some responses from the Ukrainian authorities, may be with a gun or two up their backside.'

The major said nothing. Out over the clearing the darkness had come in and lain across them. There were many hours to go till morning.

Chapter Forty-four

Katya stood up, straight and proud, as Alison entered the hospital waiting room.

'I'm Alison Lane.'

'Thank you for coming, Alison Lane.' The English was effortless. Katya gestured to the row of chairs.

To Alison it was a macabre little room – the place where you sit waiting for news of lives and deaths. Like the departure lounge in an airport – who's leaving, who's delayed. Only here, no one's hurrying to catch their flight, and any delay is welcome. 'Travelling today?' people ask. 'Hope not,' is the best response.

Contrast the stillness here, she thought, with the clamour now being raised across the planet, people in all countries, shot out of their daily routine by the news of a single bullet in Berlin.

Beyond the partition wall lay the man it had struck, and beside her the woman.

'Today he was very happy. That's why he went out to the crowds. He loves to do that; says it's the best part of the job. He thought there'd be a breakthrough at the summit.'

Katya had stopped crying. Or maybe, it occurred to Alison, she hadn't yet begun.

'I'm being asked to make a statement.'

'What are the doctors saying?'

'The doctors say nothing.' Katya sat up. 'That's because they know nothing. They're still assessing the extent of the wound. It may be some time.'

'Then there's little you can say.'

'I have to say something. He's the president of the largest country on earth. Anyway ...' she shrugged, 'the days of silence are over. The people elected him. He belongs to them. They've a right to know.'

'D'you know what's happening in Moscow?'

'Some of it. The rest, I can guess. Of course they're already blaming Ukraine and Klimak ...'

'He's left for Kiev.'

'Good. For now I'm more worried about our own people. We've got to prevent any reprisals. I don't trust the vice-president. He blows in so many winds he can no longer stand straight.' She shook her head. 'He even asked me what I thought he should do ...'

'So you told him?'

'Of course. Dissolve the parliament, I said. Call in the military and intelligence chiefs, make sure the country stays calm and disciplined, that nothing is done in haste ....He said yes, yes, yes. Which means no, no, no. I may have to return to Moscow myself and carry a message from the president.'

'But he's unconscious ...'

'Exactly.' She gave a thin smile. 'Isn't it fortunate that I can read his mind?'

They called her away to visit the visitors – the German chancellor, the mayor, the chief of protocol, like schoolboys, she thought, come to confess they've broken your window. No, they hadn't detained the person responsible. But they would. They really would. Rest assured. And then the head-hanging ritual ... 'So very sorry,' 'thank-you,' 'if there's anything ...,' 'Thank you again,' 'anything at all ...'

Just turn the clock back an hour or two, she told them silently. Not much to ask. Give him back to me, without the stains on his shirt, and the sightless eyes. Give him back.

But they simply bowed in their collective helplessness and looked at the floor.

'May I suggest something?' Alison leaned forward.

'Please.'

'That you go in and talk to him.'

'Why?'

'I said I knew something of what you're going through. And I do. Many years ago, when I was a student, I was hit by a truck and not expected to live. My parents gathered at my bedside and talked to me, and refused to let me die. I heard what they were saying. I couldn't move, but I heard almost every word. I believe it was that which gave me the strength to pull through.'

'You recovered well.'

'Not entirely.'

'Why?'

'It's another story.'

'Ah.' It was Katya's turn to stretch out her hand.

'He *will* make it.' Alison got up to leave.

'You're right. He's certainly obstinate enough.' A smile appeared in Katya's eyes. 'Besides, he always said he wouldn't trust me if I were left too long on my own.'

Outside the hospital Alison tripped and fell getting into the car, twisting her back, wincing at the pain.

'I'm fine, I'm fine ...' But Foster was already racing round to help her up, two German security men bearing down, out of nowhere. You could see it in their faces – please God, not another accident.

'Really. It's perfectly all right.'

But the pain travelled with her to the airport.

It sat there, bringing back that sense of utter despair which had hit her thirty years before.

She recalled the first time she'd tried to sit up in bed after the accident. 'Why can't I? What the bloody hell's going on? Je—sus!!' The shrieks had summoned the ward sister, two nurses, a houseman on duty on the floor below. 'I can't do it. I can't do it.'

Trouble was, the mind doesn't leave it at that. Body's failed, it says, tut tutting, standing all smug beside you. Only maybe it's your failure, in some small way. After all, you didn't look where you were going. So you brought it on yourself. Your failure, miss. So what does that make you?

There were times when she could cheerfully have cut off her head, just to drown out the voice.

But which was worse? That shrill, little voice inside, or the deadening solicitations from the people around you.

They could never leave you alone with your infirmity. Suddenly you were everyone's parcel, marked fragile. The chorus followed you ... 'you all right, dear? Everything all right? You must be so tired. Take the weight off your feet.' You weren't just your own cripple, you were everyone else's as well. The moment they caught

197

sight of you, you were elevated to cause of the day. Public cripple No. One.

That's why she'd forced herself to mend.

That's why she'd hated her own weakness.

And she had promised herself there'd be no more displays of that weakness – or any other.

On the runway the RAF VC10 reared its head and lifted out of Berlin. Foster was mumbling about the Cabinet meeting on her return, the statement to Parliament, the need, he 'honestly felt', to get a grip on the colleagues closest to her, assert authority. After all, her first days as PM had been out of the country. Foreign Secretary was better. He could take over the gallivanting ... time of crisis. She tuned him out.

On board was a message just in from Air Force One. David Bradley, already on his way to Washington, intended calling for a meeting of the security council. Heads of government invited.

Then she remembered. In the chaos after the shooting, she hadn't even had time to tell him goodbye. He'd simply made his arrangements and she'd made hers. Officials had communicated. The master and mistress had been swept up by their delegations and sent home.

She held the message up to the light and read it again.

Every time she cleared him from her mind, he put himself back.

Chapter Forty-five

Crises had always done a great deal for David Bradley. To him they made the difference between showman and president.

He wasn't angered or upset by the attack on the Russian President. It simply focused the mind.

Piece by piece his timetable was constructed as he crossed the Atlantic – the day like a slab of meat, carved and re-carved into tiny slices. Phone calls to world leaders, emergency Cabinet meetings, Defence, the national security. All the implications to be weighed and assessed.

Washington would be running on its favourite fuels – black coffee and hype.

Bradley wasn't like his predecessors, wasn't a concensus builder. Didn't see the job as being chief American mediator, didn't much favour Clinton's informality – the pressure groups and the kids wandering in, discussing, discussing ... and then the next day's headlines ... 'Still no decision from the White House.'

Didn't want Jimmy Carter's isolation. The guy who preferred reading it all on paper to dealing direct with humans.

Had little time for Ronald Reagan's good natured bonhomie, which inspired only back-biting and disloyalty from his closest colleagues.

Nor did he want an army. He'd served in one of those and was glad to leave it behind.

David Bradley considered his role was to make decisions. The more crises you confronted, the more decisions you made.

Sure you consulted. But each day you had to press buttons. Send signals.

The public had to know that if ninety odd missiles came up on a radar screen, inbound on Washington, the main man wasn't going to wake up half the lobby groups in the city to establish a view.

He was damned if he was going to run his administration like that. And he was damned sure the staff was going to know that.

By five a.m. Air Force One had landed him at Andrews, more awake than he had been in months. By seven he had his diary cards, his press reviews and the news from Berlin. Shilov was hanging on. Harry had phoned Moscow to confirm it.

'Good flight?'

The butler served them breakfast in the family dining room.

'Best in the world, Harry. What you got?'

'Trouble. Listen, David, this is going to be a crazy day so I'll say what I have to and then leave you in peace. I'm not qualified to talk about this nuclear thing, or Shilov, but you have a serious domestic problem, that we need to address right now.'

'What's it called?'

'What's *she* called?' His shoulders hunched. 'She's called Alison Lane.'

Bradley reached for a slice of wheat toast, smearing it with butter.

'OK, let's have it.'

'When you upset Norton at the summit – you seem to have made a good job of it. If you searched his house, you'd probably find it full of your effigies – with pins in them. Anyway, Norton has powerful friends. Larry D'Anna – for one. Magazines, newspapers . . .'

'So?'

'So they're asking questions. They've put out feelers.'

'Let them.'

'OK, David. OK.' Harry laid his hands on his lap. 'I suppose I'm asking the question as well.'

Bradley drew a line under his scribblings. 'I'm not going to let them or anyone else dictate how I live my life. Alison Lane is an unmarried woman, who I once fell for in a big way and might . . .'

'So it's true.'

'That much is true. We had an extraordinary relationship. It was in Oxford. 1966. We were gonna get married. Then Vietnam came along. I went off and left her.'

'End of story?'

'Yes. Except that now I want her back.'

Harry looked at the floor. Once you cross the line from honesty to hypocrisy, he thought, the lies come easy. The deceptions. They're like bricks. Build one, and then there's another on top of it. All of a sudden you've got the foundations for a whole life of lies. Hard to go back and start again.

'The problem is, David, they want to find some way to use this story against you ... And she's helping them. That interview where she said you'd never met ...'

'It was a slip ...'

'It was a lie. It happened and she said it. No instant corrections afterwards – the way Reagan used to churn them out. She's saddled with it. A pure eighteen-carat lie, out there on the record. And sooner or later someone'll ask you the same question.'

'So I tell them – no comment. Presidents don't comment on their personal life. You know that ...'

'She's a prime minister for Chrissake. This isn't some bimbo – the kind your predecessors indulged in. It's a prime minister. I know it was years ago. But she's denied it – that's why it's dangerous. She's made it dangerous. I've been in this city a long time. I've watched snowflakes turn overnight into avalanches. And that's in summer! I'm telling you ... I sense trouble with this one.'

'What do I do about it?'

'Don't see her for a while. Communicate by telephone. People are already noting the long looks between you guys and a lot of very private conversations behind closed doors. Don't add to it, David. You both have a lot of enemies, especially her. You're not just giving them the ammo, you're loading the gun for them.'

Bradley got up from the table and put on his jacket.'I have to tell you ... that's not going to be easy.'

Deval sighed. 'What can I tell you? I'm not so old and worn out that I can't see her attractions. She has authority, she has charm – she's a lot better looking as a leader than you ...' He grinned. 'Listen, it comes down to the person you are. In the old days you always pushed the boundaries. You did it in Vietnam. That's why you're sitting in this office right now.' He drank the last dregs of his coffee. 'In my experience presidents fall into two categories – those who don't believe they can do anything – they're in the minority, always whining about oversight committees, terrified that if they turn out the light, they'll trip over a special prosecutor; and the others who believe the world's up for grabs. Mandate, schmandate – I'm here and you're there – like Kennedy. The Charles Atlas brigade – kicking sand in people's faces, and enjoying it. Right?'

'Right.'

'Which are you?'

'D'you have to ask?'

Deval took off his gold-rimmed Dunhill glasses and rubbed his eyes. It was a punctuation mark – nothing more.

'Let me put this in context, David. This could blow over. It could. But I doubt it. There's a lie on the table. A lie from a world leader, about a very personal and unusual subject – a love affair thirty years ago between two people who went on to lead their countries. That's big time. Be assured that if you're ever forced to answer the same question she did, you either compound the lie – or finish her completely. What I'm saying is that if the scenario develops you may be obliged to choose between her . . .' he paused for a moment and replaced his glasses, '. . . and this job.'

Bradley didn't answer.

'The only thing you have going for you right now, is that with Shilov shot, there's an international emergency. So people are looking at other things. That may not last long.'

Bradley put his arm on the chief of staff's shoulder. 'You know, there's a funny thing about this story. I really believed that with all the leaks in this place, all the kissing and telling and kissing again – that this thing was safe. Why? Because only two people knew about it. Me. And I didn't tell anyone . . .'

'And?'

'And my mother.'

As Harry promised, the day was truly crazy. For everyone. Even Emily Laurence at the quiet end of the administration, had felt the heat. Now, close to 7.30 at night she was enjoying a cup of coffee, the size of a small bucket. Mrs Bradley was thankfully out of town, so the duties of shepherdess, cash-carrier and chief muzzler had fallen to someone else.

On her desk lay the latest edition of the *Washingtonian* and she was scanning the In Search Of columns, because one day, according to her best friend, there'd be a description that would 'leap out and french-kiss her to the ground.'

Hadn't happened of course, but it was a nice thought on a snowy morning.

When the door opened she had expected almost anyone except the person who entered, looking remarkably like the president of the United States, in his shirtsleeves, and minus the winning smile that had won him so many electoral college votes two years before.

She stood up hurriedly, unable to disguise the page she'd been reading.

'Good evening, Mr President.'

'Was never going to be.' He stood in front of her desk, lips pursed, eyes unimpressed. 'I want to talk to you, Miss Laurence. Maybe you can shed some light on what my mother has been doing, recently.'

Emily blushed.

'Doing and saying.' Bradley leaned forward and closed the magazine on her desk.

Chapter Forty-six

London felt deeply unwelcoming and proud to be so.

To Alison there were no concessions from the winter night. When the rain stopped, the wind would start, when the wind died away there was always the drizzle. Insipid. Incessant. You could live a lifetime on interval wipe.

And Foster never seems to leave my side, she thought, except when I'm lonely, when I could do with the company, when I don't want to talk politics.

Where are my friends? I mean, I've had so many over the years. Only this is the strange thing about Britain. When you get on, when you really make it, so many of them drift away. They don't like to say 'well done' or 'terrific stuff' – sticks in their craw, because you've made it and maybe they haven't. They're afraid to ask what it's like, in case it's really wonderful. That'd undermine their own lives. They couldn't bear it, going round believing someone else is having an amazing life – and they're not. We can be so mean-minded.

Such a contrast with the political managers. To them everything you did was 'bloody amazing.' 'You really got 'em going with that speech, knocked 'em dead in the debate.' No praise too overdone, too fawning, too outlandish.

So it's the parents you call, isn't it? They're the ones who'll tell you if you were great, or simply average. Not Mum, because she's star-struck by the whole thing. But Dad's still got a sharp knife. He can cut through the crap.

And what had he told her? 'It's too late for David. You're on opposite sides of the world. You've got to accept that.'

No one else would tell her the truth.

If she wanted to hear it.

'Welcome back, Prime Minister.'

'Prime Minister.'

'Prime Minister.'

There's a moment when she wonders if they're addressing *her*.

And then you're back in the study, gazing out on to Mountbatten Green, the oak desk looks so small, and the room is so ordinary. And there's no power there, of any kind – except what you bring to it.

'Don't you want to go home, Dick?'

But he shakes his head. Doesn't he have a home? Maybe all he possesses is a collection of pin-stripe suits, white shirts, flowery ties. Goes out at night to the park, changes behind a tree, comes back in the morning.

'Shilov's condition's the same,' he's holding up a news agency report. 'Wife's gone back to Moscow, though. Mounting unrest among politicians ...'

And in that moment she can see Katya quite clearly, sitting on the Aeroflot plane, heading back into the Russian night. She didn't know if her husband would live, she didn't know what she'd find when she got to the Kremlin. But she'd be sitting so straight and dignified, emotions tied up in a bundle for later, working through the options.

Why can't I be like her?

'I've sent the messages you wanted.' Foster looks awkward. 'But there's no reply from either Sir Henry or Mr Harper. I ...' he blushes slightly, 'I took it on myself to call the clinic and arrange for the physiotherapist to come round, er ... seeing that you hurt your back.'

'That's very thoughtful.'

'Different lady, they said ...'

'Oh.' Alison looks down at the stack of red boxes on the carpet by the desk. 'Listen, Dick, I think I should go to New York tomorrow. The security council ...'

'If you want my opinion ...'

'Situation's very serious, very fluid ...'

'I was about to say that the political secretary thinks it'd be a bad idea ...'

Her eyebrows lifted. 'You've spoken to him?'

'I thought it prudent. His feeling is that since your sudden appointment there's been no time to consolidate your position at home. Naturally the news from Berlin has dominated, the shooting ... but you haven't yet made any Cabinet changes, and he felt there was a need to stamp your personal imprint quite quickly. In fact ...'

'In fact, let the rest of the world get on with it. Is that what you're saying?'

'We just felt that in order to prevent any murmurings ...'

'Which've doubtless begun already ...'

'But before they take on any momentum.'

'How many murmurings, Dick?'

'Preventive action, Prime Minister, that's all we had in mind ...'

'I said how many?'

He shook his head. 'Five, six. I don't know ...'

'And Harper?'

'I just don't know, Prime Minister.'

Even for Cindy Tremayne, blessed with the acquaintance and favours of a Cabinet minister, an opposition front bench spokesman, assorted MPs and advisers, this was the ultimate playground.

Not nervous, she told herself, recalling Primp's breathy phone call. 'You've got your chance. Seven p.m. Downing Street.' But keyed. Poised. There was a lot to remember.

They had her name at the big iron gate on Whitehall. 'Any identification? Fine. Someone'll meet you inside.'

Up the street and the clouds have cleared. Moon's come out to play, she tells herself – and haven't we all. Past the big iron barrier in the road, the black front door, already open because they radioed ahead. Shirtsleeved security, perched inside on the right.

'Miss Tremayne? This gentleman will show you the waiting room, if you wouldn't mind, for just a few minutes. You can leave your coat there.'

It's quiet. Hardly anyone about. Place is so much bigger than you think from the outside. Long corridor to the back, waiting room on the left. She hung up the raincoat, plain white uniform underneath. Starched, professional. 'Nurse Tremayne.' That's what one of the MPs liked to call her. 'Nursey.'

She put down the blue holdall. Few towels inside, lotion, and a closed metal compartment that Keith Harper had said was none of her business.

'Just stand it as high as you can, turn the side towards her and open the catch. When you've finished, close it up again and walk away. You'll have done the business.'

Cindy checked her handbag. Passport inside, money. She could go now. Should go now. But then if you buy a ticket, you have to take the ride. The story. The experience. You couldn't pass up a thrill like this. She couldn't.

The messenger's back and it's up the wrought-iron staircase, past the portraits and photos of all the old PMs, seen off by mortality, or treachery or the whim of an ungrateful public.

More stairs.

He knocks at the door.

'Come in, be right there.' And it isn't just any voice. It's her. Head girl – as the papers have started calling her.

Now there's a bloody thought on a winter's night.

'You're Miss Tremayne, aren't you? I'm Alison Lane. Thanks for coming.'

'Very pleased to meet you.' And Cindy looks hard at her. For she's younger than the early fifties they've given her. Very blonde. Strong face, strong body. And wouldn't she have to be, to survive?

'Sorry to hear about Lillian. She all right?'

'Fine now. Nothing serious.'

So normal.

'I had a slight fall while I was away. Couldn't get to the clinic ... they told you about my back, didn't they?'

'I read the file before coming.'

'Oh good. Tea? Coffee?'

So normal.

'No thanks. Where would you like me to unpack?'

She's standing just inside the door with the picture of a ship on the wall, and the moon staring through the skylight.

'Why don't you come into the sitting room? I set up the portable table the way Lillian's done a couple of times.'

'That'll be fine.'

Too bloody normal. This woman is very deceptive. Dressed in a simple red tracksuit. Nicely spoken. Could be Kensington. But there's an edge to her that comes from somewhere else. A sharpness. An economy. Means she's trained in a rough school and still works there. She doesn't just look. She's working out the angles. Yours and hers. Eyes seem to go everywhere.

She's put a couple of sheets on the table. 'Shall we get going then?'

'Right.' Cindy turns away, hears the track suit coming off. Admit it, you're excited by all this, aren't you? Admit it – it's a hell of a thrill, a prime minister undressing behind your back.

She's settled on her stomach, sheet pulled across the back. There's nothing awkward about her. She's in charge.

Cindy lays the holdall on the floor, unsnaps the clasp. Clear view of everything. And now you move.

Almost immediately she can feel the woman's pain.

She can see the heavy, multiple tracks they left on her spine. Miracle that she's walking.

'You mess around with people's backs and you're never sure what will happen.' Words from a class many years ago.

'How long've you been with the clinic?'

'Not that long. Few months.'

'Like it?'

'Very much

'Why?'

Cindy poured some lotion on to the lower back. 'Why do I like it?'

'Mmm.'

Clever question, that one. Casual but not. Forces me to show who I am.

'The people. It's extraordinary what some women will say when they're on the table. They get relaxed. They want to talk. Some even cry. I could write a book.'

Alison coughs. 'But you won't.'

'I take the trust very seriously.'

Pile it on – the pressure. Five minutes, ten, fifteen, and she's close to sleep. Practically exhausted. Ask how she feels.

'Fine.' Languid moan. Very sensuous, this woman. She enjoys it. Odd that you never think of prime ministers as sensual, the same way you can't imagine your parents having sex. But Alison Lane is intensely physical. She's letting her body take a walk with me. No inhibitions.

There's silence in this sitting room with its pleasant striped wallpaper, the beige carpet, oatmeal sofas. No'clocks to tick. Just her breathing – and mine.

'Would you like to turn over – away from me?' You always add that phrase to cover their sensitivities – except with Primp.

But Alison just turns towards her, showing a body, full and cushioned, a luxurious body, thinks Cindy, a place where people would want to make a home – in the warmth and the light freckled skin, curving like a mountain road. And who has the run of you?

'Just the shoulders and legs now,' Cindy's voice rises . . .

'Fine, whatever you think. Feels really good.'

She closes her eyes and Cindy starts on the feet and ankles. And the patient's breathing is deep, relaxed. From the calves up to the knee, sheet rising as we go. Take it very gently. Thighs need a little work, very English there. But she's soft, and they're slightly apart, and just once the skin trembled with the touch, just the hint of a chain reaction, lights turning on across the body, deep inside . . . keep walking with me, very, very slow now.

And you're an inch away, move her thighs, rock them gently, ride the sheet up . . . touch once as if by mistake, just a finger brushing at the door . . .

She's still breathing hard, eyes closed.

Go on. Again.

And then a rock out of nowhere smashes the atmosphere. 'I think we'd better stop there, Cindy.' Voice suddenly firm and level.

Oh God. Oh God. Oh God. 'I'm terribly sorry Miss Lane. I don't know what I was thinking of.'

'Don't you?' She sits up. Sheet pulled up to the neck 'Would you step outside for a moment, while I get dressed.'

Cindy reaches for the holdall.

'Leave that, would you.' Command not question.

And Cindy can't help feeling like the schoolgirl, banished from class by the headteacher.

Back in the safety of the red tracksuit, Alison glances round the room.

I don't believe this. I don't believe someone would go this far. But then if you have strangers in the queen's bedroom, this is minor league.

She opens the holdall, seeing the metal compartment, the glass eye, the tiny window that housed God knows what . . .

Little bitch. Bloody little bitch. A cheap, cheap shot. The cheapest of all.

'Come in, Cindy.' She doesn't look at all contrite. Confident, experienced. How the hell did she get into the clinic?

'Talk to me, Cindy.' She goes up very close to her. 'I've no interest in threatening you, or making a scene, although I could – and maybe I will. I just want an answer to a question, and then you can go on your sordid little way, pick up where you left off. I don't give a damn what you do. I want to know who organised this. That's all.'

Cindy shrugs. She's not nervous or upset. Very confident, in fact. They chose well with her. Whoever 'they' are.

'Nothing to say?'

'I've got plenty to say. Just wouldn't do me much good to say it.'

'You've been threatened?'

'Something like that.'

'Just a name, Cindy.'

'I think it's past that. I'm leaving anyway.'

'Then leave behind the name.'

'This is so strange.' Cindy shakes her head. 'You know I didn't mind the idea of it all. I knew it was a risk. But I thought . . . hey, it'd be a real lark. After all, I know politicians. I mean 'know'. OK? I thought you'd be the same. Hot air. Lot of pompous crap. And look at you! You don't shout, you don't scream, although by rights you should, after what I've done.'

'So?'

'So what do I owe any of them? Not much. Nothing. You're different. You don't seem to me to be polishing an image. I'm not sure what you're doing here. Yes, you're tough. You probably play the game, same as the rest of them. We all play games. But you seem to know the difference. There seems to be a person still in there. Anyway,' she shrugs, 'you don't need this from a tart like me, do you?'

Alison doesn't answer.

'Keith Harper,' says Cindy and raises her eyebrows.

Chapter Forty-seven

'Why didn't I shout at her?'

I know why.

I have to admit something to myself. Something I never thought I'd feel. But I did – I enjoyed it. Put me at rest for the first time in ... God, days. Truth is, she turned me on, for just a moment. Not in a way that challenges my sexuality. But there was one moment ...

She snapped shut the folder on her desk and went over to the sofa. You don't think of this again, Alison. Once and once only. Now it's over. You have urgent business. Urgent, right?

Sir Henry had called. Sir Henry was on his way. Together they had more important things to consider – like the immediate future of Mr Keith Harper. Call your mind back. Go on, it's wandering. Get it back.

She sat and stared at the gold-framed mirror above the fireplace. This wasn't a warm room. The ceilings too high. Narrow and white and clinical. And the desperate presence of Keith Harper was still there, hard to shake, the smell of anger and desperation.

Not that he'd surprised her. For thirty years she'd known politicians every bit as prepared to crawl around in cesspools and garbage. Harper was the rule – not the exception. You only had to take the whip's office that he so ably managed. There, intimidation was dish of the day. Oh, it could be subtle. Could happen over a sherry in the club. Might be just one of those soft, lilting voices from the Welsh valleys, reminding you of a little indiscretion you'd long ago forgotten; or, a couple of the big boys to kindly help you through the correct voting lobby, when – oh, dear – you might have forgotten which one to go for.

Not long ago, she recalled, those same kind-hearted boys had all but broken down a lavatory door in the Commons, where a diminutive Labour MP had been crouching to avoid a vote. Forced him into the lobby with his shirt caught in his zip. Fine moment for the mother of parliaments.

Keith Harper fitted well within *that* establishment.

Now, of course, there'd have to be the ritual revenge. The destruction of the man's political career, his removal from the government. That wasn't in doubt; only the manner of it needed careful planning.

Sir Henry was shown in shortly before 9.30.

'My dear.' He took off his raincoat, showering the carpet in the process. You could see it on his face. He liked the off-duty calls, the grand doctor summoned to an emergency, the only one who'll do. Routine was all very well, but it was in the hours of darkness that you earned your money. 'Filthy night, isn't it?' He retrieved a handkerchief and blew his nose.

'In more ways than one.'

She offered him the sofa she'd vacated and watched his reaction as she spoke. He was no more surprised than she'd been. In fact, she'd never known Sir Henry surprised by anything. It was a face that took in, but didn't give out. Neither warmth, nor information – just the social mask, as and when circumstance demanded. A little small talk, a grin, a wink. He knew the tricks – when he chose to use them.

'So.' Alison finished the story and stood with her back to the fire. 'I should simply sack him outright, shouldn't I?'

'Of course you should, *should*, I emphasise ... but you can't afford to. He's the centre of your power base.' Sir Henry frowned. 'Such as it is. He got you the job – or at least he was one of the prime movers. Brought you the trade unions, didn't he? Anyway, confirms what I've always known. It's your allies you have to worry about. If I were you I'd sack him in a week's time, in a month, when you've had time to bring in some of your own people. But get them there first. Sack him now and it'll be suicide. I'm afraid those are the practical limits of power.'

'I have to go to New York tomorrow. The security council ...'

'Not a good time, my dear ...'

'Maybe there are no good times.' She grimaced. 'There is, believe it or not, an international emergency. Shilov may well die. In which case the emergency will rapidly become a crisis. I should be there ...'

Sir Henry inclined his head in deference. She turned and looked out of the window.

'I take it — you know about my little slip on television.'

He nodded. 'You didn't help yourself, if I may say so.'

'Will you watch my back, while I'm away?'

Sir Henry moved his hand to the coffee table and put the metal device from the holdall in his pocket. 'Haven't I always?'

'Will you, this time?'

She turned round and he met her gaze with what he hoped was a sincere expression. Of course, it wasn't good to lie to a prime minister. But if you had to, it was best to choose one who was unlikely to hold the office much longer.

Keith Harper knew it had gone wrong. Cindy didn't show at the restaurant beside Victoria station. He waited an hour, walked twice round the concourse and thought about going home.

Bugger Cindy. She and her antics would have been the icing on an already tasty cake. A wonderful headline for the tabloids. 'Who strokes the PM?' What the hell? He still had plenty.

Inside the station he rang Levinson at the Baker Street hotel where they'd installed him.

'We're getting close, OK? Something went wrong with Cindy. But we still have plenty to go on. Are your people ready in Washington.'

There was silence for a moment. 'Right. They're sitting on the edge of their seats.'

'Did I wake you?'

'Uh-Uh. Just reading. Story's ready to go when you say the word. We can top it with the political implications, as seen by a high, and very unnamed, government source.' He chuckled. 'You up for this?'

'What d'you think I've been doing it for?'

'Right.'

'I'll call you later.' Levinson was really lightweight. Or maybe that was just the manner. He was oddly wide-eyed for someone clearly so devoid of scruples. The kind of person who could shatter lives with a smile and a shrug, as if to say — hey, this is nothing personal. Just business, fellah.

Keith would have been surprised, though, to see Levinson put down the receiver and smile towards the light in the bathroom. Surprised too, at the figure who emerged and came over to him. She was outrageously overdressed in a silver ankle chain, with a silver tag, that only the influential and acrobatic had ever been in a position to read. 'To Cindy with love from Cindy,' it said.

Footnote from an admirer.

They were all long nights. That was the abiding feature of Downing Street. The government had a thousand leak points. And they all leaked late. Someone would open their mouths or their trousers too wide and suddenly, wherever you looked, there was a cat peering out of a bag.

Then the night news editors would be on the phone, the political correspondents, the dawn reporters – who was going to rebuff the latest, slur, smear or inaccuracy?

Foster sighed. This might be one of those nights – with the comings and goings, the closing of doors, and now a wild-eyed chief whip, waiting in the hall downstairs, demanding an audience.

He hurried down the corridor to meet him. 'I phoned your home hours ago.'

'I didn't go home.' Keith removed his coat. 'Is she in?'

'I'll have to see.'

'Bollocks! I'm going up.'

'Haven't you had a bit too much to drink?'

'What if I have?'

And yet, by the time he reached the study door, Keith had calmed himself. I have only one chance, he thought. One chance left to get close to this woman. He knocked quietly and went in.

'Alison?'

She didn't look up. A single lamp was illuminated on the desk, shadows lay across the striped wallpaper.

'I . . .'

'Sit down, Keith – before I have you thrown out.' The words were controlled, quiet.

He tried to speak but his voice didn't seem to be where he'd left it. 'Listen, love I . . . I actually came to say I'm sorry. Isn't that ludicrous, me coming here to apologise? This whole thing . . . it was so stupid and unnecessary. I was so hurt. Believe me I didn't know what to do. I just wanted to lash out . . .'

'I'm glad you did. Shows me what worthless scum you really are. Now get out of my sight.'

'Alison, listen to me ... there has to be some way we can piece this all together .... I just want to make it work, to be with you ...'

'You make me sick.'

He swayed for a moment, but the words seemed to pull him upright. In that moment she could see the flame ignite in his eyes, the dirty, ruffled collar, the cheap pretensions, as the anger gripped him. The index finger of his right hand shot out towards her. 'And you ... you're finished. Finished.' She could see him transforming before her eyes. The monster, shedding its cloak. 'D'you understand that? I can pull the plug on you anytime I want. Your lying on television, your cosy, private sessions with David bloody Bradley. You're in this office because I and my people put you here ...' The voice was little more than a croak.

'Get out, Keith ...'

'Don't think that we won't get little Cindy to dress up a story as well, by the time I put the papers on to her. There's enough muck and innuendo to bury you ...'

Alison got up from the desk and went over to the door. 'If that's what it takes to stay in power, stroking the egos of creeps like you, I don't want it. Not now, not in the future, either.' She opened the door and stood aside. 'It's not necessary for you to come here again. I hope I make myself clear?'

Eleven o'clock. In the study you got the time from Big Ben. Upstairs in the bedroom there was the clock over the arch at the Horseguards Barracks. No shortage of chimes. Like calls to battle.

It was good to have this one in the open.

Less good, though, to go away.

So stay and fight your corner, said the voice. That's what you've always done. You like fighting. They all say that. You fought your body. Made life so tough for it, that eventually it gave in and got better. You fought for this job.

But in New York, I can do something, she told herself. In New York I can have a say in the whole crisis. I *can* make a difference.

Oh yes?

And in New York there'll be one David Bradley. My oasis.

You're not going for him, are you?

I'm not going to make a choice between him and my job. I'll see

215

him and come back. Then I'll turn the bloody Labour Party inside out, on its head.

But I need to see him. I need the strength.

She stared at the White House telephone on the desk, only it wasn't the one that began to ring.

'Yes, Dick.'

'Another visitor, I'm afraid.'

'Shop's closed. Goodnight. No more visitors. I'm going to bed ...'

'I think you'll see this one.'

And in the seconds that followed she was running down the stairs, taking them two at a time, not caring about protocol or decorum, shrieking the way few, if any British prime ministers have ever been known to do, within the confines of the building.

Chapter Forty-eight

He had put on his best suit, like a Sunday boy home from school, standing in the hall, red-cheeked, unsure what to do, where to go.

Dad.

'What are you doing here?'

'I had to come.'

'I don't believe it.' She led him upstairs to the flat. Dad with the unfailing antennae, always knowing when to call, when to be there, all through her life, especially the times when the candle was flickering low.

'Right.' She flung open the sitting-room door. 'Let's have a drink. C'mon, Dad, take off your tie. Relax. It's me – Alison. I'm not the bloody Queen.'

Shy smile. Sunday boy on special outing. 'Can't stay long. I promised your mum I'd get back tonight.'

'You drove up all the way?'

'Your mum and I ... we thought ... I don't know, we just thought you might need a friend.'

He looked round the room. He's cowed by it, she thought. They all are. I can't just have a person in and say ... let's be normal. Even Dad. They all behave as though it's Disneyworld and I'm Mickey Mouse.

'Listen, stay the night, for heaven's sake. I'll show you round. We'll do the tour.' She poured him a whisky. 'Bring your glass.'

Alison on his arm, leading him from darkened corridor to darkened landing, pointing out pictures and inscriptions, the sword in the Cabinet room, the table shaped like a whale, brown leather chairs, yellow carpet, blue pencils and pads, the trees of St James's Park spiky like witches' fingers against the skyline.

Back in the flat she cooked him an omelette, and when he'd eaten he perched uncomfortably on the armchair, startled momentarily by the noise of the front door opening and closing.

'Just the boxes, Dad. Papers. They bring them all through the

217

night when things are going on. It's probably stuff on Russia and the Ukraine.'

'Don't you ever sleep?'

'So pampered I hardly need it. Stewards doing my shopping, taking the cleaning, typing the diary. Like being married to thirty people at the same time. They're all wonderful wives.' She laughed. ''Specially the men.'

'Not lonely?'

'No time. You forget Dad, Alison and I are used to each other. Had to be.'

Later, they sat in front of the fire, each with a second glass of whisky to distance them from their thoughts.

He took her back to her childhood, the fairy tales and sunny days, the teachers and friends, the landmarks of a little life in a London suburb. And she too, began turning the pages.

'You remember the Christmas dances? Us girls at one end, the boys at the other . . .'

'You didn't put up with that for long,' he grinned. 'Always the first to rush over and take your pick . . .'

'Was I?' She laughed. 'I never told you about this bloody awful dance at my first Party conference. I still had that limp, and I got paired off with this northern lad. Well, I thought everything was going fine till he looked at me halfway through the Twist and said . . . "you're a pretty lass, but I never seen such bloody dancing in all my life." He was so embarrassed when he found out why. Sent flowers to my room. He'd have married me next day, if I'd smiled at him.'

Uh-oh. Wrong turn, she thought suddenly, getting up, switching on the television. *Newsnight* was showing her picture, quoting her statement on arrival from Berlin, someone else speculating about her hold on Foreign Affairs . . .

'Popular girl, aren't I? Talk of the town.'

'D'you mind?'

'Not yet. I expect I will, when they get it wrong.' She laughed dryly. 'I should think I'll mind even more when they get it right. For now I can't quite believe they're talking about me. Alison this, Alison that. Who the hell *is* this Alison Lane?'

'I'm beginning to ask myself that as well.'

The tone caught her off guard. 'She's a lot tougher than she used to be. She wouldn't have survived otherwise ...'

'And one day they'll take it away from you, love. What then?'

'Jesus, Dad. How much forward bloody planning d'you want? I've got a job to do. *The* job. Number One. Most important handbag in Britain. See ...' She pointed to the screen. It was a picture of her coming down the steps of the plane. 'Look at me. Talking. Talked about. Analysed. Probed. I'm the bloody evening meal for each and everyone in this country – to be chewed up, or left on the side. But for the little time I may have here ... I'm it. OK. So don't tell a climber who's just reached the top of Everest, that one day he'll have arthritis and won't be able to make it up the stairs.'

His eyes turned down towards the floor. 'I shouldn't have come.'

'Maybe you shouldn't have.' She got up and stood in front of the fireplace. 'I know I've been a single girl all my life. So in your eyes I've probably never grown up. No ties. No kids. But in some ways, I've lived ten lives – the kinds of lives you and Mum couldn't even imagine. The things I haven't done have been a lot harder than the things I have. They've required some pretty difficult decisions over the years. So when you come in here and tell me ...' she stopped and looked down at him. He seemed suddenly like the family Labrador, kicked hard in the balls and sent to its basket for chasing sheep. How can you do that? The man's your father. Not an aide or a flunky, or a worm from the other benches. Can't you turn it off?

She waited a moment, letting the sharp taste drain away. 'It's been a hell of a day, Dad. And you don't know the half of it.'

It was about two in the morning when someone stuck a blade into her chest. And she sat upright in bed, knowing instantly what was wrong.

In dressing gown and slippers she hurried down to the study, unlocked the door and stared at the coffee table, where she knew she had placed Cindy's metal box.

The coffee table gleamed back at her – bare.

Keith had taken it. Had to have done. Nobody else had been in the room. Nobody. Must have slipped it in his pocket when she wasn't looking. How the hell could she have been so stupid? Keith

219

was the only one to come into the room. Except, of course, Sir Henry.

She stood still for a while, mouthing his name over and over again, not knowing why.

Chapter Forty-nine

'Is that your final answer, Harry?'

'Isn't ... "go to hell" clear enough for you?'

'I hoped you'd be more sensible.'

'Just fuck off, Clark. Do the world a favour.'

'You're a stupid man, for someone who was once so clever. The ironic thing is that at this point, I know far more than you do about the whole affair. David Bradley, Alison Lane. You haven't even got a clue, Harry. But I'll break you anyway, because you deserve it.'

The phone went dead and Harry sat at his desk, counting the now familiar symptoms of guilt. The eyelid that wouldn't sit still, the creeping nausea – and the growing need to tell someone.

But he couldn't have told David. Didn't want to admit he'd been stupid enough to have an affair. At his age. In his position. Just another Washington idiot, like so many others. And he had prided himself on being different. Pride? Now it would come out in the worst of all ways and they'd be joking that the whole White House had its dick hanging out ... and Jane? Oh God! Too awful to contemplate.

Norton had said ... 'You haven't even got a clue.' What did that mean?

Somewhere in all this, there were details he'd missed. Something else. Something about Lane.

It peeved him, niggled him, sat in front of him on the desk, daring to be addressed.

Harry knew he couldn't leave it alone.

As a lawyer he had become a formidable researcher. Never went to court without digging a hole in his case. And then he'd dig deeper and again and dig around the first one.

There's no such thing as a complete picture, he would tell his juniors. But you're either more or less complete than your opponent. You work harder, you go to bed later. You suffer for your work, just as artists suffer for their art.

So he knew how to pick up a telephone, knew how to use a library, knew how one document led to another – and with age had come the delight of remote control.

Six calls, four of them transatlantic had set the hunt in train. If there was any delight at being fifty-one, he reflected, it was that your friends started moving into useful positions. A journalist in London, a visiting professor at Oxford, a doctor in Harley Street, and an enquiry agent who had retired to Britain to escape all the clients he'd upset. Then an archivist in Army Records at Quantico.

There were dates and times to be discovered, there were biographies half-written, half thought about.

He would get it, he promised himself.

The only question was whether it would get *him* first.

Harry didn't see the president until much later. He put on his coat and together they stepped on to the Truman balcony. The sun had begun grilling the capital in defiance of winter tradition. Across the south lawn large tracts of snow had melted into swamp.

'It'll freeze again tonight.'

The chief of staff shook his head. 'Time was when the climate did what it was supposed to do. Froze your pipes in winter. Bleached your hair in summer . . .'

'And Washington was a sleepy, southern town.'

'Still is – in some departments.' Harry shrugged. 'So why the smiles?'

'Miss Lane says she'll join me at Camp David tonight and we'll fly on to New York tomorrow.'

'She agreed just like that?'

'I told her several other leaders would be there.'

'And they won't.'

'Right.'

'Jesus, David.' He breathed deeply. 'So you're celebrating?'

'It's kind of premature. Shilov is still in a coma and the news from the Russian border with the Ukraine is lousy. For now I think celebrations would be unwise.'

'So to take your mind off all this, you invited her – with a straight lie.'

'Let's not kid ourselves, Harry. We didn't exactly lose our virginity today.'

Right, he told Bradley silently. Never more right than that, my friend.

The president looked sideways at his friend. 'I want to have some time with her.'

'You'll have an evening,' he winked. 'Until midnight.'

'That's exactly what my landlady once told me in Oxford. If you can't do what you want by midnight ... you're no bloody good. Whenever I had a girl in my room, she used to climb the old narrow staircase with her squeaky, flea-infested dog, and shout outside the door. 'Time up – out you go.'

'Maybe I should play landlady.' Stupid, thought Harry. Stupid thing to say. 'Be careful, David. Please,' he added.

Which of course was even more stupid.

'I'm not invited to Camp David. Can you believe that? The fucking secretary of state doesn't get to go to Camp David when the British prime minister flies in. What in Christ's name's going on?'

Norton stood up. He wore his anger in the shape of two bright red patches that stood out from each cheek, as if they'd been sewn on.

'The guy doesn't like you.' Till's merit in the White House was that unlike many people he could see the obvious. The disadvantage was that he would tell everyone.

'Makes me feel like some kind of leper. And there's a ripple effect. Once it gets out that I don't have the president's ear, let alone even his courtesy, I'm finished inside State. They'll be using my office for the fucking discotheque. And I'll still be there.'

Till burst out laughing.

'I'm serious. If I had any pride I'd resign.'

'We're not in it for the pride ...'

'Yeah, well right now, I'm barely in it, at all. I get about as much time with the President as the Burmese ambassador. We'll meet in New York tomorrow ... I won't have spoken to him, he won't have spoken to me, there won't be any kind of agreed position ... I might as well take round the tray of fucking doughnuts.'

'Ain't that bad.'

'Sure. The only guy Bradley sees is the White House counsel.'

'Fox dressed in human clothes.'

223

'Same guy.' Norton swung himself a half circle in the easy chair. An ideal time to sound out Till. The house in suburban Maryland was quiet. The family away, thank Christ. Otherwise his wife would be shoving it up his arse, that he was being walked all over and he ought to fight back. What the hell did she think he did?

She'd find out though, soon enough.

He reached over and poured Till a bourbon and a mound of ice. 'I've been talking to an old friend of mine ... .you know Larry D'Anna?'

'That guy's a friend?'

'I use the term loosely.'

'Larry's pretty loose himself. At least he was with the Party finances ...'

'Still a powerful guy. The newspapers he has ... you should know that.'

'So what's his angle?'

'He's taking a very personal interest in the affairs of the president. And I mean affairs ...'

Till grinned. 'So that's why you're pissed at not going to Camp David ...'

'I'd give plenty to know what happens out there.'

Till looked thoughtful. 'What exactly would you be prepared to give?'

Norton caught his eye. 'Favours, recognition, still the only usable currency in this city.'

'How far have you thought this through?'

There was a line of sweat on Norton's upper lip. 'I want to expose him, destroy his credibility, limit his options for manoeuvre. I want more than a lame duck. I want a laughing stock duck; a can't-get-himself-out-of-bed-on-crutches duck; the biggest duck casualty since records began.'

'That's a lot of wanting.'

'Look at it this way ... We're midway through the guy's first term. It's time to start positioning yourself. If you want to come along for the ride?'

Till nodded, drained the bourbon and got up to pour himself another.'

Norton frowned. 'Make yourself at home.'

'Thanks. I will.' He grinned. 'As a matter of fact I'll be at Camp David myself tonight.'

'I know, you beautiful little putz.' The secretary of state smiled for the first time that day.

It was nearly twenty-four hours later that Harry saw Jane. She had been working nights at the hospital. He had been working nights. Jason had been baby-sat to distraction.

He tiptoed in and sat in the kitchen, listening to the silence.

And then as he looked up, he saw her standing in the doorway, with an expression she'd never worn before.

She knows. She knows. And that silence is the sound of my life coming to an end.

'I got a letter today, Harry.' So quiet, so level. 'It told me you'd been seeing someone, even gave me a name and a few other details as well ...'

'Jane ...'

'Listen to me Harry. I don't believe everything I read. After all I'm a doctor, aren't I? I make my own diagnoses. Set my own questions and then answer them. I even checked with the White House to see if there was someone by the name I'd been given ...'

Harry, like time itself, is a thing of the past.

'They told me there used to be but she'd just left town. For good. Gone back home to California. Couldn't take Washington. People are very understanding. They like to help.'

'Listen, Jane ...'

'Don't, Harry. You see that's good enough for me. I don't own you ...'

'Maybe you do, more than you think.'

'If you ever meet someone, Harry. Just tell me about it, OK. Lies – I can't deal with, but the truth I can handle, however bad. I give it to my patients' families, and they cry and they weep, and then they go home and somehow as the days go by, they get on with their lives. I cried and wept a lot today, Harry. Now I'm getting on with my life. With our life.' She kissed him on the cheek. 'Goodnight, Harry.'

He fell asleep where he was, head cushioned by his arm on the kitchen table.

Chapter Fifty

Katya knew she should return to Moscow.

She leaned over the inert body of her husband and looked hard into his face. 'You'd want me to go, wouldn't you? At least I can try to get them talking, keep the old bastards at bay, make them see reason. I've known that little pisser of a vice-president since he was six . . .'

But Shilov didn't answer, half-buried as he was under wires and bandages. Half-alive.

She touched his hand, as if that might stir him, force him to make the connections. And yet the hand seemed strangely cold.

'I need your strength to help me do what must be done. Please!'

She sat back in the chair and dried her eyes. The last thing he wanted was a snivelling cry-baby. He'd never had one before. He wasn't going to get one now. Not when so much had to be done. Not when Russia seemed to be hurrying towards a black hole.

Such a terrifying country, she reflected. Like a violent, uncontrollable horse. Everytime you loosened the reins, it would gallop towards the cliff, bent on its own destruction. There was no kinder, gentler Russia. There was a manageable Russia – with the lid shut tight. Or there was no Russia at all.

She looked at the clock. Another half hour and then she'd leave him, order up the presidential plane, shout her way on to it – loud and angry. As long as he lived, she'd possess his authority. They couldn't refuse her.

Watching him, it occurred to her that she hadn't seen him that peaceful for so many years. Not since their student days, when they would lie for hours in the woods on the outskirts of Moscow, because that was the only place you could be alone.

There you could imagine you lived in a beautiful country, far away from the red banners and the slogans, the deadening pettiness that went with them, the food queues, the scavenging and dishonesty.

But it required great imagination. It was as if the magnificent Russian soul that her husband spoke about, wasn't really so magnificent after all. It was a fragile, capricious being, always hostage to the abuses and corruption of its people.

Maybe a part of it still existed somewhere. Maybe it had died, like so much else. Maybe she would find out in the days to come.

In the distance, Katya heard a door slam shut.

She had always believed in signals. The little things of life, pointing the way to the bigger things. Everyone had a path to follow. All you had to do was read the signposts correctly along the way.

She got up, aware that the atmosphere inside the room had changed. Shilov lay more still, more peaceful than before.

'I'm leaving now,' she said quietly, and bent to kiss him.

Yet, at the last moment something stopped her. Somehow a kiss like that seemed too final.

What had he said once? . . . 'If it hurts to say goodbye, then don't say it. Just walk out. Go. But leave the door open. Then anything is possible.'

'The only doors that ever close for good are in the mind. Others – you can force open, pick the lock, smash them down with an axe. But not the ones inside the head . . . So leave the door open.' She could still hear the words, the way he had uttered them.

Rapidly now, Katya turned away without looking at her husband, and went in search of the doctors.

She spoke to them for no more than two minutes, holding herself so straight and calm, that they marvelled at her self-possession. And yet they seemed genuinely shocked by her words. One of them stared after her in disbelief, as she walked away down the corridor, past the nurses and the trolleys. He was still staring long after she'd disappeared.

'You think,' he told his colleagues, 'that you've seen it all. Until the day – like this day – when you haven't.'

Through the trees around the clearing, the moonlight sketched shadows over Chukovsky's encampment. The six helicopter gunships had turned into fifteen – dragooned together, their missiles slung beneath them. For now they were lifeless and awkward. Once ordered into the air they were the favoured killing machines of

Russia's forward units, on special operations.

'Colonel, you should see this.'

The young major handed him a computer print-out. Chukovsky read it briefly and passed it back.

'Is that all, Colonel? No reply?'

'What d'you want me to say?'

'For the sake of Jesus Christ, say something. And pretty fucking quickly. What I gave you was the official Ukrainian communique issued in Kiev forty minutes ago. It accuses you of an act of war against a Sovereign state and demands the withdrawal of all forces, within twenty-four hours. Still nothing to say? Uh? Where is this little adventure to lead. Perhaps you'd like to share this State secret . . . ?'

'They won't do anything.' Chukovsky's voice was calm.

'How can you be sure?'

'Because they want the missiles intact. Anyway it's out of my hands. I'm now obeying orders from Moscow. Or hadn't you noticed?'

The major snorted. 'There aren't any fucking orders out of Moscow. No one has a clue who's in command. They're running around, scared out of their wits that Shilov will die, or they'll be a coup, or God knows what else might happen . . . The only reason they haven't told you where to get off, is because no one's strong enough to issue the order. And besides, the hardliners are quite happy for you to make a point. Mother Russia baring her teeth. You're just playing into their hands . . .'

'Maybe. That's not the point.'

'What is?'

'I told you. We have to defend the missiles. If we clear out. If we remove the troops, they'll seize the silos and the missiles, and we'll have lost everything.'

'Meanwhile, you're content to start a war?'

'I didn't attack the silo in the first place . . . I didn't kill a twenty-year-old captain.'

'But you're escalating the conflict. Ukraine . . .'

'Somebody has to solve the question of these missiles. Finally. The leaders got nowhere in Berlin. Maybe this will focus their minds. It's vital. We need the world's attention. Now.'

'So you hold the world to ransom.'

Chukovsky got up and went over to within a few inches of the major's face. 'I force the world to see this issue. Now. In daylight.'

'A fine argument, my friend.' The major spat on the ground. 'I wonder if the history books will manage to see it that way.'

He must have slept for an hour. No more. And yet he knew that the sleep had gone.

In the forest you were never alone. Birds, animals, all moving to the rhythm of their night.

He could well remember the time he had climbed up from the silo and surveyed the universe beyond the clearing. He remembered the promise he had made himself, never to use the weapons, never to destroy the beauty that he saw around him.

Chukovsky didn't think of himself as a religious man. True, he had been baptised in secret, soon after birth ... but he had hardly made the decision himself. To him the church had always been part of Russia's folklore. A cultural heritage, irrelevant to the life around him.

So he didn't know what made him kneel down on the forest floor, and pray to a God he had never spoken to, and never even imagined.

Chapter Fifty-one

'Why do we have to keep on meeting like a couple of old queens out of school?'

Tom Marks, the Trade and Industry Secretary, glared at Harper across his double espresso.

'Speak for yourself, my friend. It's Ms Lane you should be asking.' Keith made a point of the Ms.

'Still bitter and twisted, I see. For God's sake, Keith give it up. I'm not surprised she won't jump into bed with you. Can't say I know many who would. Look at yourself, man. You're no oil painting, are you?'

Keith sat back and surveyed Marks with evident enjoyment. He had chosen the café well. A small brasserie, just behind Oxford Street. The place full of guide books and Italians. Not a soul speaking English. Even so, he leaned forward almost whispering, watching the colour ebb away from Marks's face, the fingers begin a little dance on the table. Rage, incredulity. It was all there, thought Keith, building nicely.

'Christ, Jesus, Almighty!' Marks pushed away his cup in disgust. 'I can't bloody believe it. Alison Lane? Cool as a mountain stream. You've *got* to be joking . . .'

'The Americans say Bradley's crazy about her. This morning she went haring off to Camp David. Told everyone there was going to be a crisis meeting of foreign leaders there. I happen to know she's the only one. And if what I think will happen, happens . . .'

Marks looked round to make sure no one was listening. 'It's the lies I don't like. Combination of lie and innuendo. And then there's this being in bed with the Americans – in more ways than one – that's going to piss the Party off mightily. Most of them loathe Bradley and everything he stands for.'

'There's also the film.'

'What film?'

'Delivered to me, this morning. Film of a little incident between Ms Lane and her masseuse.'

'I don't believe . . .'

'You want to see it?'

'Dirty bastard.' Marks shifted his bottom off the plastic seat, from where it appeared to have stuck fast. 'I don't get this. Any of it. I just don't . . . whole thing smacks almost of a concerted campaign. But who . . .?' He put his hands together on the table. 'We're going to have to bury this, and bury it now. There's too much at stake. We've got the Party faithful out all over the bloody country, swearing undying allegiance to her, selling her on every bloody soapbox from here to Flugga Mugga. Historic change of course. Bloody hell!' He wiped his forehead on his sleeve. 'If you don't get rid of this, she isn't going to make it. New prime ministers are fragile enough as it is. We couldn't take this amount of scandal. Party's been out of power too long. Seventeen years and now this. There's no other way, Harper. You'll have to kick it under the nearest rug and sit on it.'

'Too late for that.'

'What?'

'I said it's too late. The Americans have the story and they're not exactly blushing virgins. They've got the film as well. Don't you see what I'm saying?'

'So what do we do?' Marks's voice climbed into descent.

'Stay calm in the first instance.'

'We have to do something, man. Fast.'

'I can't save her, Marks. I've tried thinking of everything. But it's not in my power. You've got to know that. Talk to the rest of the Cabinet. Talk to the Unions, the party managers. Get everyone prepared, because she's going down – and there's not a thing I can do about it.'

Marks had begun flapping his head up and down, like a rag doll.

'Listen to what I'm saying. There aren't any quiet ways – she's got to go in a blaze of publicity. Get it out. Get it over and move on. Otherwise the story will never go away. It's too close. Too sensitive. Too many ramifications. If she's hit with this at the start of her term, she'll never recover . . . you know that, as well as I do.'

Marks's face twisted into a sneer. 'I'm not blind, my friend. Don't think I can't see your role in any of this.'

Keith put on a choirboy expression. Calm Keith. Reasonable

Keith. 'I'm simply warning everyone to be prepared, learn their lines, so we're not all caught looking even more stupid ... It'll be a bad week. Course it will. I'm not saying it won't. An awful week. But it doesn't have to be a mass grave for everyone. Think about that.' He shrugged. 'As for me ... I stand ready to serve the Party in any way I can.'

'You pompous shit.'

Marks got up and left the café without another word.

Keith could see Levinson in the cinema queue, just as they'd arranged. But he wouldn't greet him. They stood separately as the dismal matinée audience shuffled in out of the daylight. He couldn't remember the last time he'd seen a movie in daytime. God, not since they'd played truant from school and got a clout round the ear for it.

He hadn't even looked at the film's title. Something like Black Dogs, or Red Dogs.

Didn't matter anyway.

It was funny to think this was how Denise spent her time. Whatever it was at the local flicks, she saw it. Lined her stomach with coffee and sat bug-eyed as one film blurred into another and one more day got clocked up on life's meter. No wonder she'd become so boring. Her whole existence took place on a screen. Bugger all in the way of participation.

Levinson joined him in the neighbouring seat, Coke in hand. He offered a wet hand.

'So are we ready?'

Keith surveyed the auditorium. 'Let's get the story out of Camp David. If it comes, you can go for the next day's papers. Understood?'

'My people have already psyched up some of the editors ...'

'Did you hear what I said? Only if we get something out of Camp David ...'

'I hear you. I hear you. This isn't the slither of cold feet, I hope?'

'Keep your bloody voice down.' Keith could see a couple of heads turning in their direction. 'I'm the one who set all this up, if you remember. So don't talk to me about cold feet.'

They sat in silence for a few moments. On the screen Keith could see a train bearing down a mountain pass. Anxious faces. Just like his.

In the past, he reflected, he'd never been the one to press the big button. Not by himself. Of course he'd helped. Any number of ritual muggings. MPs set on in the parliamentary equivalent of a dark alley. Careers and reputations beaten up for the greater good. Fighting the good fight.

'Look at this place,' a fellow MP had told him, his first day in the Commons. 'Look at the building. Grand isn't it? Then take a look at the buggers walking around. Half of them would be better off managing a public pisshole. Be more honest, wouldn't it?'

Rough game you played, in your suits and ties, in the bars and tea-rooms and on the terraces. All the honourable members, shafting each other with a cucumber sandwich in one hand and a young blonde researcher in the other ... if they could get it. Bloody rough game.

He turned towards Levinson. 'All right. But Camp David's got to be the lead. If you get it – ring the number I gave you. If you don't, we'll have to think again. But either way we don't have to meet any more. That's one advantage, I suppose. Just don't mess it up.'

Levinson offered his hand again, but Keith ignored it. He knew perfectly well where that hand had been.

'May I speak to you, Prime Minister?'

'Of course, Dick. Sit down.'

They were three quarters across the Atlantic, 35,000 feet high. Every hour putting them another six hundred miles further from London.

'What's on your mind?'

'This is difficult, Prime Minister.' The face once again gammon pink. 'I don't know how to begin really ... but it's something I feel I have to say ...'

'Then you'd better say it.' Alison gestured to the cabin around her. 'I'm not exactly going anywhere.'

'That's just it, I'm afraid. I don't think I'm going anywhere, with you. Not in this job. I just feel it's not going to take me in the right direction ... and I have my future to consider, my children ...' His voice trailed away.

'I see. May I ask what's brought you to this realisation? After all, we've only been working together for a week now. I wasn't aware I'd presented a major threat to your children during that time – nor any other members of your family, come to think of it. Not so far, anyway.'

'I don't think it's going to work. I mean I feel very nervous about some of the things I'm hearing ...'

'From me?'

'Not just from you. But there's some talk among the Press. Some kind of groundswell against you. It seems to be building ....'

'When does it not build? Have you ever known a prime minister who didn't have to watch out for the Ides of January, February, March and then all the way to bloody Christmas and back again. What d'you think politics is ... ?'

'I just think this is different.' He bites a piece of gammon from the lower lip. 'This ship doesn't seem to have a direction ...'

'And you want my permission to bravely jump before it capsizes.'

'I don't mean it that way.' Foster's cheeks are carrying a film of sweat, embarrassment and fear. 'This is all so awkward ...'

'But you need to think of the future. That's what you said. Your children. My goodness I never realised I was so life threatening. According to you, staying with me is just about as healthy as a weekend in Chernobyl. Well ... Dick Foster.' Her fingers locked together under her chin. 'This is your immediate future. You will work with me during this trip, because I don't have anyone else. When we return to London, you can draw up a shortlist of replacements, preferably people who have a little more backbone and loyalty in them, than you. After that you can dig a hole in the ground and live in it, as far as I'm concerned. Is that understood?'

'I ... I'm very sorry, Prime Minister.'

'So am I, Dick. I had no idea you were as weak and pathetic as this. Perhaps politics isn't for you at all. Maybe you should give the hole in the ground serious consideration. You could possibly find work as a gardener. Something quiet and intellectually untaxing.' She smiled sweetly. 'That should suit your talents.'

* * *

So what am I doing? Chucking it all away?

It's Harper and his friends. They got me in. Now they want me destroyed with rumour, and a lie I should never have told.

Why did I?

I could so easily have said, yes, Bradley and I knew each other. Course we did. Not well, mind. But we had a drink a couple of times. Why not. What would have been so astronomically mundane as that?

And yet I couldn't let the genie out. That moment, in the middle of the interview – I thought – if anybody learns of this, even the barest details, then the whole thing'll be public property. The pain, the memories. The realisation of what I lost. I couldn't have gone through that.

So what now? Sir Henry will look out for me. Do whatever he does below the surface – pressure, suborn, threaten . . . who knows?

'Haven't I always?' he said, when I asked him to watch my back. And he has. That's true.

Only this time, it wasn't much of an answer, was it?

Chapter Fifty-two

From Dulles airport in Virginia the presidential helicopter carried her north over the state line into Maryland, where the snow lay speckled and uneven across the landscape, patterned as if by the paw-prints of a giant beast.

They bent low over the forests with the rotors slashing at the wind. As the machine banked hard towards a clearing, Alison could make out the toy people in parkas and fur hats, the snow driving at their faces.

She knew him instantly, the giant in blue, at least three inches taller than the others, laughing as his cap was torn off in the slipstream, springing after it.

Alison felt a pang of embarrassment. They were all in jeans and rough boots and she had worn a suit – a bloody suit for God's sake – with patent leather shoes. The prize cow from England. Trust a Brit to get it wrong.

Doors open and she was making excuses in her mind. This was what you got when your Party'd been out of power for seventeen years. No one knew these things. No one had the faintest idea how you dressed at Camp David. Last time Labour had been in government, they'd gone into the ark two by two. Bugger! The other woman hadn't made mistakes like this. That at least was certain.

Carefully she let herself down the steps, as the Marine guard saluted. Bradley stepped forward and for a moment it seemed she almost fell into his arms.

'Prime Minister . . .' he grinned. 'Great welcome.'

Introductions through chattering teeth as the cold swirled around them. Presidential aides, a pool camera, White House lenswoman. Bags of American informality and ease, while her own sphincter squeezed ever more tightly.

Bradley's arm cossetted her through. 'I was going to treat you to the presidential golf cart. It was the only thing Ronald Reagan was ever trusted to drive. But it doesn't go too well in the snow. Walk?'

The wind bit at her face and legs. 'Of course. That'd be very nice ...'

'I mean you Brits don't feel the cold, I seem to remember.' His eyes laughed at her.

They walked in silence for a while, feet crunching on ice.

'We have a lot of work to get through tonight.' Business now. Business first and last, she thought. 'Have the others arrived yet?'

'Ah.'

She stopped and turned towards him. About fifty yards back three secret servicemen slithered to a halt. 'Ah' was not the answer she wanted.

Bradley seemed to be hiding behind a tree of his own making. 'They ... uh ... cancelled at the last moment.'

'I see. They just ... uh, cancelled. All of them. One by one.'

A quiet 'Yup.'

'You liar!' Came out just like that.

'Yes. I'm afraid so.'

'You admit it?'

'Can't deny it.'

'God! What's the matter with you? Don't you hear anything I've been saying ... ?'

'Everything. Every word, Prime Minister.' More teeth. 'I just had a query or two on interpretation ...'

She turned away from him and took a few steps off the path between the trees. But then, quite suddenly, she didn't want to fight. She could see the image of a little girl stamping her foot in the snow, because someone had taken her toboggan, yelling out loud across the park, trying to throw rocks at the sky. You can't go on like that. Not when all your friends have run away. In the grown-up world, he lied and she lied. But on a snowy day in Maryland, there was a single truth. She was glad to see him.

'You like my coat?'

He peered at her as if from the trenches. 'Sure.'

'Can you lend me some jeans?'

Camp David is an upmarket holiday village, a series of guest cottages, with tiny kitchens and bars and televisions and all the freedom of a zoo.

237

When the president is there, air-space in the region is closed to all but the official. Noisy dogs and very silent human beings patrol the forests around. The seat of power becomes a high-tech log cabin, like a wooden white house – a tree house. Birds eat crumbs from your table while the man with the Great Seal turns sausages on the barbecue and discusses what he wants to do with the rest of the world, for the rest of the day.

Jeans and sweats *are* the order of the day – any day. For long ago American presidents gave up wearing ties simply to prove they were gentlemen. Fashions changed – and real gentlemen went and did other jobs.

Bradley led her to the cabin and pushed open the door. Someone had already placed her luggage on a rack. I expect, she thought, that someone would hang up my clothes if I asked. Someone would polish my shoes, or lick them if I really wanted it, turn down the bed, fasten my dress – or unfasten it, if it ever came to that . . . no doubts on that score. But everything in front of her spoke simplicity and warmth. The country-bright sofas. Wooden sills, wooden floors polished to a diplomatic sparkle. Little house on the prairie, it said. Only the outsize white telephone hinted at power and the world beyond.

'If you need your people, they're somewhere out there.' He pointed vaguely through the windows, but she could see only the trees, sagging under snow. 'If you want a maid or a butler, we have those too. If you need me . . .'

I do. Something inside her spoke the words, but they didn't come out.

'If you need me, just pick up the phone.'

He stood there, uncertain what to say next.

When you speak, she thought, you use your eyes, and you angle your head, and you hold your hands in front of you, feeling for the cuffs that aren't there. Some people make decisions when life rules out all the other options. You make them right up front. Choices. And yours are different from mine.

'I shouldn't be here like this. Nor should you. Not when there's a spotlight on us, when people are talking and sniffing and looking for evidence . . .'

'People always talk . . .'

'It's more serious than that,' she interrupted. 'It's damaging and it's painful, for all sorts of reasons . . .'

'But you're safe here. For just a night. Nothing's going to happen, Alison . . .'

She shivered slightly. 'If you leave the door open the warmth will go.'

'I could close it from the inside, or shut it behind me on the porch.'

'Is that a question?'

'If it were, would you answer?'

She couldn't help smiling. 'If I answered, would it be the one you wanted?'

Gently, almost imperceptibly, he licked the side of his mouth and it reminded her the way she used to do that in the darkness of the cinema, a teenager sitting next to her boyfriend, getting ready in case he kissed her. You didn't want your lips too dry. You had to be prepared.

The scene changed again and she could see him in her room at Oxford in the middle of the night, twenty years old, eyes peaceful, heart peaceful, only his hands moving. You've loved once and you know you'll do so again before morning.

And she would run her finger down his chest, as if it were a zip, releasing the energy below, watching him stir, hearing the breathing become more urgent.

Like the tide, he was, coming in, slamming against the shore.

'What do you want from me, David?'

'I want to find the person I knew.'

'What for?'

'Because I cared very much for her.'

'And if she's gone?'

'Then she's gone. But what if she hasn't?'

'It may not matter.' Her eyes left him, as if to look into herself. 'If she has another life.'

'She could have both.'

'Is that the American way, to have it all ways, and death is just an option . . . if you want to go?'

'I don't want to take anything away from her . . .'

'Then how does she keep what she has . . . ?'

'By adding to it.'

Dialogue in the third person. Always safer. The fiction that you're talking about other people. 'You used to be so good.' Her eyes seem to find him again. 'So plausible. You could argue a case.'

'And this one?'

I'm so tired of fighting.

'You still argue well.'

Outside the window a pile of snow cascaded softly from the trees. If their eyes could reach out, she thought, then they would touch. There was a moment when they dared each other to step forward. Like standing in the sea thirty years before, wondering who'd be the first to strip. Only neither moved. Then or now.

A moment that sits forever in the space between you.

And you can spend a lifetime wondering why you never went for it. When it was there on offer and you wanted to.

Why didn't he move?

Why didn't I move?

Moments are just that.

And this one has passed.

Dinner comes. Simple and large.

They sat at a farmhouse table. Till and Foster on hand, talking cameras and press pools and a scattering of others. The Brits had removed their ties as a concession to informality – the Americans in designer leisure, as if born in it.

There's another difference, thought Alison. They have expectations. They expect to succeed, expect to be happy, expect things to work. And we're always surprised if they do. We trail around, head held low, palms on the ground, waiting for a brick to drop on us. That's why it does. What brick can resist the temptation?

They talked Russia. Shook their heads over the turkey, basted and glistening, tutted at the pecan pie, sighed long and loud over the cognac. Life was hard and likely to prove it once again.

Bradley did the carving himself. 'We have to involve the security council. Has to be an international concensus on this thing.'

'Why?' Alison's sharp little word. Sharper than they'd expected. 'Look at Bosnia. Whole thing winds up in a talk shop. A few UN troops get sent out to provide target practice for the warring parties.

And they settle it on the ground anyway.'

'What would you do?'

They all seemed to be munching more quietly, ears extended to pull in her answer – if she had one.

Bradley collected a sliver of white meat, smothered it in mashed potato, and was about to despatch it, when he put down his fork and stared at her quizzically.

'As I understand it, your Party generally favours the use of sanctions in these circumstances. Right?'

'Right.' She tilted her head in acknowledgement. 'But times are different. And maybe, Mr President, I'm different. There isn't time for resolutions, for condemnations. Right now there's a missile silo in the Ukraine that the Russians and Ukrainians may be about to fight over. If we don't sort out *this* silo, there are dozens of others waiting to flare up in our faces.'

'So?'

She looked down the two rows of faces, and at David Bradley at the other end.

'I'll announce my proposal in New York tomorrow.' She caught David's eye. 'Meanwhile, your turkey's getting cold.'

Till has a friend in the secret service. One of the friends Till tries to have everywhere.

Pressman's friend is Till. Anyone's friend. Listen and spin. Listen and spin. That's the job. Can't do it without friends in all the places. High and low. Especially low.

Till sits in his cottage with the head of the secret service detail.

Truth be known, they're not too fond of Bradley either. Doesn't do what he's told.

And to think they have him for life. Not just the four-year term. This guy gets a nanny in dark glasses and a plastic earpiece until the day he croaks. If he doesn't behave now, think what he'll be like when he's a crotchety old fool, curmudgeon – or the way Till puts it – 'pain in the butt.'

Secret serviceman is bitter because he was told to get lost. Presidents can do that. Most of them don't know they can. But if the commander in chief tells you to back off, you shrivel up and die. And Bradley did just that. Tonight.

241

And I know why, Till thinks. My knowledge is my power.

'I shouldn't be telling you any of this.'

But she does.

And he sits where he was at the end of the table, now that everyone has shuffled away into the forest and the peace of the night lies around them.

She tells him about the foreboding she feels, about her lie on television, about Harper and Cindy – about the row with Dad.

If she leaves out anything – then she leaves out Sir Henry, not knowing why.

'Nature of the beast,' he says. 'You always feel you're on the brink.'

'In Britain you are. I could be gone tomorrow. You at least know you have four years in office. You're also head of state. That's like dry land. I don't have that refuge. My feet are wet all the time. Even Foster, born into slavery by the look of him – even he wants to desert.'

'I can have him shot.'

She smiled. 'Does it ever get to be fun?'

'Moments. In retrospect.' He gets up, turns down the light, leans against the wall, notes the fullness of her breasts against the blouse. Breasts to feed men, not babies, he thinks, wondering where the thought has come from. 'What will you do?'

'Fight. What else can I do?'

'D'you have enough friends?'

'Maybe. Early days. Depends if they think I'll make it. Coups like mine are notoriously unstable. I shouldn't be here. Shouldn't have left Britain. Not now. Certainly not for any international crisis.'

'Why did you?'

'Wanted to show off. Always easier to score goals away, than at home. Thought I could make a difference. I still think that.'

'Then you will.'

Not an awkward end to the conversation. Quite a natural pause – the way two travellers might stop along a country road to check directions.

David Bradley went over to Alison's chair, knelt beside it and touched the fine blonde hair and the dimpled face. Somehow his hand found hers and the fingers locked.

In the darkness of the forest an animal pauses to sniff the night, drawn by the lights and the sounds from the big house.

There's no thought for the cold – only for the prey, for the victims.

When you watch someone, you join their life. You leave your world and attempt to enter theirs. You read their intentions, and actions. From then on, they talk to you. They act for you. They belong in part to your vision.

When he rose from the frozen ground, the animal became a man, who shuffled away from the big house and went looking for his friend.

He wakes up Till, who wasn't sleeping anyway.

It's as good as anything they'd imagined.

In his mind David's rushing back down the path, same feel, same sensations, hurrying as if, after all this time, the same person will be waiting at the other end.

'Don't move me too fast.'

'It's been thirty years.'

'I'm an old lady. I need careful handling. I'm not used to being pawed.'

'I'm not pawing you.'

'Maybe we should wait.'

'What for? The millennium?'

'Maybe we've forgotten how to do it.'

'We used to do little else.'

'I don't remember.'

'Think back to the bathroom, old lady. Things you used to do with a bar of soap.'

'Only 'cos you asked me to.'

'I'm asking again.'

'Nicely?'

'Nicely.'

'Haven't got any soap.'

And then the white phone on the bureau starts buzzing and the rest of the world seems to walk in and watch.

'This isn't going to work.'

'Yes, it is.'

'No,' she says. 'I have to answer it.'

Chapter Fifty-three

Katya put down the phone and stared out over the traffic of central Moscow.

They didn't live in the Kremlin. Her husband had insisted on keeping their three-room flat from the old days, and she'd agreed. Image was vital. Nowadays the president was poor and the crooks were rich. So things had changed.

And other things had stayed the same.

All morning she had held court among the powerful and the corrupt. How was the president, they salivated? How serious were his wounds, what could they do for him and for her? And for the cause of peace?

And as she answered, she could see their eyes making the calculations. Where did they stand in the order of succession? Would they rise or fall? Could they claw themselves an extra slice of power while the larder was open?

To each she had conveyed what she termed 'the president's instructions.' Stay calm, stay loyal, prevent retaliation.

And in mock solemnity they had nodded back their assent. One or two had even stooped to wiping perfectly dry eyes with a handkerchief. Of course they understood. They would obey the president without question. Only ... only the silo in the Ukraine refused to back down. For now, dear lady, it was out of contact. Out of reach. They could do little except wait. Russia, did she know, was a big country ...

Maybe it was the smile, barely repressed on the lips of the armed forces chief, Marshal Tenko, that made her lose her footing. Made her realise the presence of men without care or restraint. Men of bad will.

And now in the last few hours they had made sure the new reports were brought gleefully to her door; men and material had poured over the border into Ukraine ... and Russia was once again on the cliff, getting ready to jump.

Katya didn't know what brought her the image of Alison Lane. Perhaps it was the expression of sympathy and understanding she had seen in Berlin. Only she couldn't let it go. Without thinking she had ordered the Kremlin operators to locate the British prime minister as a matter of great urgency, wherever on the planet she might be.

'I have to go to the Ukraine. I need you to come with me. A symbol of international concern and resolve. The situation is deteriorating very rapidly. I need your presence. Will you come?'

The voice, bounced by two satellites to the Russian Far East, downlegged, as they like to put it in Seattle, and beamed through White House communications to the State of Maryland, losing none of its brittle control.

To a cottage in the woods.

And even allowing for the fact that politicians fear a direct question like the onset of typhoid, the answer had been unambiguous.

'I'll return your call in thirty minutes. Please wait beside the phone.'

So Katya knew she was dealing with a woman of unusual decisiveness. A serious woman. And for a moment she felt relief.

Only when she caught sight of herself in a mirror did she see the avalanche of pain the other side of her eyes.

How long before it smashed through her defences and broke her?

The room at Berlin's Charite hospital had been sealed. And yet two plain-clothed guards from the Russian embassy sat outside day and night.

No one entered or left, and they asked no questions. The shifts changed every eight hours, and the hospital administration continued to give twice-daily bulletins to the reporters and television crews, installed at the front of the building.

Only a handful of doctors knew where the president had been taken. They had arranged the transfer by themselves, in the low hours of the night, when the corridors had been all but deserted, when death moves quietly about its business. They had used a tunnel once reserved for the East German communist leaders. No nurses or orderlies had assisted. They had kept their word. And it was they alone who supplied the information about their patient.

Of course, they had misgivings. But then, they reasoned, they had had those before. Plenty of them, during the twenty-eight years when Berlin had lived with a wall, and its citizens had died trying to cross it.

What they were doing was strictly against the ethics of the medical profession.

And yet, once you started down such a road, it is virtually impossible to turn back.

The president's wife had known that when she looked at each of them in turn and extracted their promise.

I can't think of him lying in a tiny room in Berlin. I mustn't. I may only think of him when it's over.

And yet that figure was no longer my husband. The face, plain and white like cardboard. The body immobile. The mind, gone on a journey, who knows where. Not the man I have carried in my hands and my heart.

When I knew him he possessed the force of ten devils, pulled by a train. A man machine, energised by all the could-be visions that might have so changed the world.

Now silent. But not at peace. Never at peace.

I will return to you soon.

Chapter Fifty-four

'You don't want my advice, do you?'

'No. Yes.'

'Which?'

'You tell me.'

He pulled away from her. The flushed cheeks made her seem younger, more vulnerable.

'I know what I have to do, David.'

'Great. Then do it.' Back away into a corner. See if she'll follow.

'I don't have too many choices any more ...'

'We could talk about that.'

'For Chrissake, I'm being squeezed by the bloody snakes. All about you and me. Mainly. Thirty years ago. This is what gets me. And I had to lie about it. D'you believe that? I don't know any more if I'm going to be sleeping in Downing Street or under Charing Cross Bridge.'

'Then go home ...'

'And lose the chance to make a difference. In Russia I might be able to *do* something ...'

'Too risky. Too unprepared. Could easily blow up in your face ...'

'So you're saying forget it ... ?'

He nodded.

'I can't.'

Somewhere, he thought, I've played this scene already. Only the roles were reversed, and the issues were just as blurred ...

'Listen to me, Alison ...' He saw her head shake. 'All right, don't listen, but I'll say it anyway. World leaders, and you're one of them, can't just go jetting round the world – like some kind of do-gooders tour. Doesn't work that way. Can't work that way. This Russian woman could be lying. They could have set a trap for her. She doesn't know what she's getting into. And you don't either. Bottom line, Alison. You can't afford to bet on less than a pretty-damn-close-to certainty. And you don't have it here.'

'You went off to Vietnam. Bush went to Panama. Mitterrand went to Bosnia. People do this . . .'

'When it's prepared . . .'

'No! When it's important. How many times do leaders sit on their fat arses on fat cushions and order people into war? Tell me. You've done it. If I stay in power much longer, maybe I'll do it too. Who knows? But just sometimes you've got to set an example, David. You have to get out of the sleaze bucket of party politics and opinion polls and lead from the front. Not from some armour plated fucking car with bodyguards.'

'Jesus! How you can even think about something as stupid . . . ?'

'I haven't seen you this angry for a few years . . .'

'I haven't had so much cause . . .'

She sat up on the sofa and draped her feet over the side. Her blouse stayed half-open, the way it had been when the phone rang. Even angry, David required a serious effort to pull away his eyes.

'Call her back, Alison. Offer tea and regrets. Advisers. Blankets. Offer her anything she wants, except your presence. You're not a mediation service, you're a leader.'

'I don't want your advice.'

'Then why are you here?'

She looked away. 'I don't know, David. I really don't know.'

He'd give it one more try, he thought. Moving closer, despite the imminent storm warnings . . .

'You're not elected to take risks like this . . .'

'I took enough risks to get here.'

'That's different. When you get the job, things change.'

'They shouldn't . . .'

'They have to. It's called responsibility.'

'Not in my world. I didn't take the job to sit in a chair. Didn't you ever have any sense of what you wanted to achieve . . . ?'

'Yes.'

'And did this sense involve any risk-taking – albeit in the cause of truth, liberty and the pursuit of happiness?'

'Don't patronise me. Of course it did . . .' He could see where she was taking him.

'So risks are fine under certain circumstances?'

248

'Right.'

'You mean when they pay off.'

'Yes.'

'When the world holds its breath, and you come home with the trophy. Against all the odds, all the predictions. Our boy shoots the apple off a baby's head at a thousand yards, and becomes the hero of the day ...'

'Yes, yes, yes ...' He couldn't help feeling a grain of admiration.

'So all it has to do is work. That's your bottom line. That's how you get from being idiot to genius, from fool to sage, from coward to a citation for bravery. All it has to do is work.'

'It won't.'

'It will.'

And there was the wire.

There were the words, he thought, that stop time in its passage. He could see it in her. Still, after so many years. The Alison who would always stand up from the crowd, spear in hand, who'd argue with all the finesse of a battering ram, who'd always go after just one more dragon. He'd seen it in Oxford at the political meetings, in the lectures when she'd argued with the tutors. There had to have been thirty years in which she'd refined the art, developed it, channelled it into the lady who *would* win. The lady with her blouse unbuttoned and the fine blonde hair in all directions. In a cabin in the woods.

'Then call her,' he said.

She put out her hand and touched his forehead.

Something mundane about the final act of betrayal. It's the plotting that's fearful, the steps, the intention. The nights when you wonder where your soul will go.

And then the thing builds a life of its own. And you, the creator, can only sit back and watch it grow.

As he dialled the number on his cellphone, Till felt no remorse and no trepidation. He was calm. He felt good about himself. At peace with the final move.

He could picture Norton in the front room of his colonial, just over the DC line. Guarded voice, because the pushy wife was back. She of the rasping Southern stiletto, she of the ambition. Only now he'd have something to tell her, and it would be plum pie and he could do it up, down, and kissing her kazoo all night long, if that's what he wanted. And anything else he wanted. So long as she got it first.

In turn, Norton would make a call of his own. To the prize skunk Larry D'Anna who would get the printing presses spinning for the devil himself, and all who would smile at his works.

Till lay down on the bed, and pictured the first of the White House news conferences that he'd be facing in just a day and a half. 'I'm sorry guys, I have nothing for you on this one. We do not, repeat not comment on the president's personal life, nor his past, nor any sleazy innuendo that happens to be circulating.'

And then they'd tear him to pieces and the crews would be out, and they'd be digging into every crumb of dirt they could lay their hands on. And he'd love it.

Wouldn't be long before someone talked. A someone in London, or from the Oxford days, or from Camp David or Berlin. The networks would throw dollars at anyone who even whistled the right tune. He'd see to that. Stoking the fire, if it were needed. He'd help it along.

Norton's call rang more than one telephone in the nation's capital.

By means of an extraordinary chain reaction, it activated the pearly-grey, see-through box that Champagne Tripp kept beside her bed, for those special conversations.

What she loved most about it was the classically understated, banana-shaped receiver. For if that 'tiger' of a husband ever called when he was away on business, and wanted a little caressing by remote, she could nestle it against her ear, coo softly into the mouthpiece – and leave her hands perfectly, but perfectly free.

Which was exactly what Tiger wanted that night.

'You ready?' he croaked, when she picked up the phone.

'Chrissakes, honey. Gimme a moment – I was just writin' a letter. Can't be spread out on the bed, stark naked, twenty-four hours every day, just in case you call.'

'Well drop 'em and get movin'.'

Tiger could be an arsehole when he wanted, she reflected, as she moaned distractedly down the telephone. But it was a small price to pay for the luxuries, heaped upon her. In any case, on this occasion, it was over before it had begun.

She pouted down the line. 'That was quick, honey. Didn't you want to wait for me?

'How long d'ya need? Haven't got all day. Busy man. Things to do, people to see.'

Jerk.

She mouthed the word at the telephone, hearing the rustling of tissues and clothes in the background . . .

'Wanna know something?'

She smiled. 'Only if you tell me you love me.'

'Listen. Remember you asked me to find out about Ruth Bradley? Well, now there's more.'

And so he told her what he was hearing. What someone influential had taken the trouble to phone in, just in case he needed to know. Just a rumour. Not to be spread around. But watch the papers next day. And no calling the lady to warn her, OK? Things were pretty delicate, and might just backfire.

Champagne reached for her address book and opened it at B. 'Don't worry. You know I never tell anyone your little secrets.'

' 'Bye, honey.'

' 'Bye, sugar.'

Please, Mr Jack Daniels, tell me I didn't do this.

The bottle was on the sideboard and Ruth Bradley was on the bed.

Her first thought after hearing from Chamapgne Tripp, was to buy an air ticket, go to Europe that night and disappear. Turkey or Egypt. Someone would take her in, give her sanctuary. Hide a stupid old fool, until the fuss had died down.

But David would find her.

And she was too old to go chasing round foreign countries where they didn't speak American.

She'd just have to face him and admit what she'd done. A ghastly, ghastly error.

Only he wouldn't see it that way. He'd look at her, the way he used to when he was a boy, with deep pools of disappointment in his eyes, and a kind of unspoken blame.

And when she thought about it, that was the most upsetting thing of all. For she had so wanted David to be proud of her, because no one else was, or ever would be again. He was the last person she had. The very last in the world who still loved her. And now he would despise her, just the same as everyone else.

Outside the window, it was snowing all over again in Georgetown.

Please, Mr Jack Daniels. Tell me I didn't do this.

And gradually Mr Daniels did as she requested, the way he always did.

In a while she pulled up a chair to the window, watching the snow, feeling nothing at all.

Chapter Fifty-five

The helicopter lifted off at first light, sucking the snow from the treetops, turning towards a sunrise, pale as a watercolour.

'If it goes wrong,' she'd told him, 'you'll read about it in the papers.' Standing in the wooden holiday home, coat on, bags already gone. 'I have to go and do this.'

'You said that.'

'D'you understand why?'

'Does it matter?'

She shrugged. 'Maybe. Thirty years ago you went to Vietnam because you had to. Now I have to.'

'And afterwards?'

'I'll either be prime minister or you can look for me under the Bridges . . .'

'I didn't mean that.'

'I know you didn't.' She reached up and put her arm round his neck. It was like pulling on the branch of a tall tree. 'Don't count on me, David. I don't know what I'll be able to do, when all this is over.'

And then a formal handshaking in the clearing.

'By the dawn's early light,' he said quietly, removing his right glove and pulling hers off as well, so that skin touched skin. I remember him doing that, she thought, the night when the gloves were all I wore . . .

Alison climbed on to the steps but he wasn't releasing her hand.

'Let's do lunch one of these days, Prime Minister.'

'I know a little place in Oxford.'

'Perfect. I expect I'll find it on the map.'

Only their eyes said goodbye.

'So who's coming, Colonel?'

Chukovsky sat in the tent, watching the troops go through the exercises. One thousand men, and Moscow kept sending more. His command, his operation and yet someone else was now giving the orders.

The major went and stood looking down into Chukovsky's face. 'No one's coming, Colonel. Isn't that right? We have twelve hours before the Ukrainian ultimatum runs out. And no one is fucking backing down ...'

'You forget yourself, major ...'

'And you forget where you are, Colonel Chukovsky. Even now, even at this ludicrously late stage, you can inform Ukraine that we're withdrawing. You can order the troops back to Russia. You can close down this encampment. You can terminate this pathetic farce. You. Commander fucking designate, Russian land forces, Ukraine.'

'I suggest you keep such thoughts to yourself, unless you wish to be removed from further duties and arrested.'

'You're mad.'

Chukovsky stood up. 'Wrong, major. I'm desperate, and the world ought to be desperate with me. To settle this question once and for all, and bring this long-suffering planet a little peace and a little confidence. Do I make myself clear?'

Clear?

He watched the major's departing back. Somehow the prayers he had whispered, kneeling on the floor of the forest, had given him a new sense of determination. The weakness had passed.

Keith Harper gave it the final push.

Alison *seen* at Camp David; so very close to the president of the United States; touching, cuddling little escapade; late at night in one of the guest cottages; blouse undone ...

Jesus Christ!

He couldn't help the stab of jealousy that seemed to pierce right into his head. It had taken half an hour to get a grip.

So he'd talked to them one by one. The Cabinet. The young, the Scottish, the Trade Unionists, the anxious and ambitious. Some had ranted. Others had sat across from him, eyebrows scraping the ceiling in disbelief. One woman, the chief secretary to the Treasury had wept. One friend for Alison, he thought. Maybe two at most. When they know you're down, and about to be carried from the ring, there aren't too many people to cry for you. They backed you.

They betted on you. But they're not impressed when you lose.

Salutary lesson, he thought, for the time, when I'm the one out there ... and the final right hook goes in.

There's no such thing as a bulletproof politician. They don't make them, so you can't buy or sell them. And just when you think you beat the system, you, the first of your kind, the only one ever to do it – the system will bring you down.

You're a glorified temp. That's what someone had told him. Bloody 'here today, gone tomorrow'. Country run by temps. Called a democracy.

'Funny, old ...' he wasn't going to say it out loud. Not like the last woman PM, crying her eyes out all the way to Buck House and back.

And yet she'd had a point.

Marks had been the last one in. Stayed behind, like the prefect after school. Talked to his people, he said. But the damage went deep. Party was already lining up for therapy. Thrown off one leader, about to throw off another. 'What the bloody hell's going on?' was the cry coming down from the regions.

'They want it done rapidly. They also want it done on medical grounds.' Marks spoke very quietly and slowly. 'Nervous exhaustion, spinal complications brought on by stress.'

'Bollocks! That went out with the Kremlin.' Keith pointed his index finger at Marks's nose. 'She resigns because her personal life has got in the way of her politics. Best interests of the Party and the country. Happy to serve in any capacity. Maybe at some future date ... etc, etc. Anything else, and the country'll throw up all over us, and the Tories'll be in for the next fifty years. Grow up, Marks, for God's sake. She's going to have to take it. All there is to it.'

'And what about you, Keith. What's going to happen now to Mr Keith Harper, eh?'

'The National Executive will meet, the general secretary will call for a one-day emergency conference at Queen Elizabeth Hall. And the Party will choose itself a new leader.' He smiled. 'Just the way we did a few days ago.'

'And with all your intimate knowledge of the candidates ...'

'The Party will choose ...'

'But who, Keith? The candidate of the Left, the safe pair of hands, the bold image ... which is it to be? Which one are you?'

'You don't seem to be hearing me, Marks. I said the party'll choose.'

'Tough lady, your prime minister.'

Harry had flown to New York to chaperone Bradley at the United Nations. Not before he'd made his calls again, done the rounds. Answers soon they'd told him. Any moment. But in the interim things weren't going well.

'Ambition.' The president nodded his head. 'That's what always turned her on. That and some other things.' He stood at the sideboard and poured the coffee.

'Ambition or desperation?'

'Maybe both. But you didn't come here to discuss that.'

'No. I didn't.' Harry took a sip from the tiny espresso cup. 'My newspaper friends tell me there's an article that isn't exactly going to make your day – slated for tomorrow's tabloids ...'

'Just the tabloids?'

He shook his head. 'There's a head of steam on this one. The networks are already trying to decide how they'll handle the thing. It's scheduled to come up at the Affiliate meetings in a couple of hours' time. So far nobody knows the strength of the story. Nor do I, by the way. But they're working out contingencies.' He put down the coffee cup. 'So what are yours?'

'State of denial.'

'You mean ignore it, laugh at it, hope it'll go away? Uh-uh, not this one, David. Each time you get out of a car, or walk through the Rose Garden, or wave at a passing pigeon, they'll be shouting the questions at you. Until there's an answer that works and an answer that satisfies. You can't do a Reagan and pretend you don't hear.'

'I can for a while.'

'And then?'

'Then's another season. No news conferences scheduled for a while. And when there are, there'll be something else to worry about. Plenty to choose from. Somalia, Bosnia, violence on the streets. Besides we'll get one of our guys on *Time* magazine to do a piece knocking the thing down ...'

'They don't get a story like this every day.'

'They're not getting it any day. Not from me.'

'And Alison Lane?'

'Right now, the best thing I can do for her is shut up. Period.'

'This isn't gonna be easy, David.'

The president rose to signal the meeting was over. 'That's why they pay us.'

Chapter Fifty-six

In the stale, endless hours of Sunday, Alison Lane drops down through clear skies on to Moscow's Vnukovo airport.

Even as the plane taxis in, Russia pulls its curtains and goes to bed. The runway lights are doused and the plane sits alone and untended in the moonlight as if it's come to the wrong place.

She can see there's no guard of honour, no flowers from the rented schoolgirl. Only a lady in boots, frail and small at the bottom of the steps, blown there by the wind.

Katya reaches out to grasp Alison's hand, and her gratitude comes in short, cold sentences. The exhaustion has attacked her English. She's running on emergency power, way beyond her limits.

Inside the VIP reception only half the neon strips are working, half the room closed off. Little clusters of mineral water, some steps of bread, smeared with red and black caviar. Regulation welcome kit, it says, for visiting inconsequentials.

'We leave in twenty minutes if that's convenient.'

Convenient.

As if, thinks Alison, we're off to a tea-party in the Ukraine – and don't want to miss the cakes.

While they watched in silence, a miniature tanker emerged from the darkness to fuel the plane. Only when they boarded did Katya feel like talking.

'You are so good to come, my dear Miss Lane. I did not think you would. Not for one moment.'

'Can I help?'

'They are playing political games with me. I knew it would happen. Now they say I can't use the presidential plane, because he's not with me. Tomorrow it'll be something else . . .'

'How is he, Katya?'

For a moment she looked puzzled as if she hadn't understood the question. 'Nothing changed.' Staring straight ahead, somewhere else. 'Nothing. Doctors, you know doctors. I . . .' She stopped as if arriving at a roadblock. Perhaps there was simply nothing else to say.

'And you?'

'What can I tell you, dear friend? I try to follow where the days take me. I try to put out fires by blowing on them. It's not so effective.'

Foster came through to the forward cabin, bringing the outside world on his clipboard. 'We've got clearance for a military airfield, south of Kiev. After that, seems we're on our own. No facilities on offer. Ukrainians are telling us they're facing an emergency, an armed incursion by Russia, so we have to take sufficient fuel for a return flight. No guarantee of safety.' Monotone delivery, message and messenger become indistinguishable. 'Foreign Office is of course strongly recommending not going. Secretary of state requests an urgent radio linkup. Insists it's far too risky.'

'How many Press are we carrying?'

'Twelve, including a TV crew.'

'Why don't you tell them what you've told me, in case anyone wants to get off.'

'They won't.' He looked at his notes. 'Met report forecasts lousy weather down there. Drifting snow. High winds. Pilot says it's borderline for an old bus like this. Your call, of course.'

'I'll talk to him.'

'One last thing, Prime Minister.' He handed her an envelope. 'Came just a minute ago over White House communications. I'll leave you in peace, for now.'

Alison broke open the seal, but stopped before unfolding the paper inside. There was a time when David had written to her almost every week. How many letters had she collected during that year? Collected and later destroyed. Only one had been stored, deep inside, where the mind refuses point blank to tear up its memories. 'There's not a city been built where I can't find you, not a forest where you can lose me, not a river where you can submerge, but that I will see your shadow in the water.' She hadn't recited those words in decades, but they were still there, still familiar.

As she opened up the single sheet, Alison could see them in the same order, just as she had remembered, clustered together on the page.

Not a city been built, not a forest, not a river ... thoughts from another time ...

'Good news?' Katya raised an eyebrow.

She folded the paper and put it in her bag. 'No news. On the contrary – a very old story.'

'I prefer old stories.' Katya stared out into the darkness. 'The endings were happier.'

For the first time since his liberation, Chukovsky had returned to the silo, taking the lift to the control room, checking the systems as he went. You didn't become a colonel in the Strategic Rocket Forces Command, without acquiring unbreakable habits. Like staring at the thin pencil-shaped killer, standing, spitting smoke on its haunches, just a wall away from you.

Even now the Ukrainians would be attempting to break the launch codes that were held in Moscow.

It might not be long before they did.

As he made his way to the surface he could see the major's face peering down at him. What was that strange expression? Not a smile, surely.

'What's happened? Fresh food arrived?'

The young officer shook his head, a child with a secret, dying to tell. 'Visitors. Important ones.'

'Dracula.'

'The president's wife, for God's sake. She's on her way here, left Moscow about an hour ago, says she's bringing a message from the president ...'

'I'm sure we'll all be very excited to hear it ...'

'No, but listen, Colonel – there's someone travelling with her. They just announced it on the radio – British Prime Minister, Alison Lane, of all people, two women ...' he began to giggle. 'Did you ever believe ... ?'

'Quiet man! Wait a minute ...' His thoughts had begun sprinting in different directions. Why Lane? Why the president's wife?

'Colonel ... ?'

'Listen to me ...' Maybe he was missing something. He had to look at all the angles. Nothing was ever what it seemed, or where it seemed. No one lied until they actually opened their mouth. A gift was nothing but an object whose price tag was hidden. Catechism from Soviet life. Think hard.

And then he saw it.

An idea that caught fire in his mind and started to burn.

'Colonel ... ?' Much louder now.

But Chukovsky wasn't listening.

In that moment he had decided what he'd do. And maybe he *was* crazy. Maybe that's what happened when you slept and worked next to a nuclear warhead.

Only he knew he had never thought more clearly in his life.

Out over the English Channel the storm clouds had merged, drawing a curtain towards the south coast.

The elderly couple could feel the dampness in the air as they hurried out of the bungalow with their suitcases and loaded the car. The cat was packed squealing into a box. Last of all came a plastic bag with the supper they would have eaten in tired tranquillity in front of the television – if it hadn't been for the call from Sir Henry.

'Mrs Lane? Alison asked me to give you a ring. Going to be a little bad publicity breaking in a few hours. Might be as well if you went somewhere else. Only a couple of days. Soon blow over. It's just that you'd have to deal with quite a few reporters, and that wouldn't be pleasant, as I'm sure you already know. Fact of life, I'm afraid. Very little we can do about it.'

'But what's happened?'

'Much ado ... as usual. Old story plus a bit of new innuendo. Typical tabloid stuff. One gets used to it after a while.'

'What?'

'Just let the Downing Street operators know where you are. Don't worry. It'll all be fine.'

So they hadn't waited. Margaret Lane had rung their friends the Taggarts who lived along the coast in Sidmouth. Met on a cruise years before, swigged back the rum and oranges like nobody's business. Bloody good times, they'd been. And yet somehow never saw much of each other. Devon's finest, they were. Two old clotted creams. Daft as brushes.

'Of course you can come. Must come.' Taggart in organisational mode. Thirty years as a tax inspector behind him. 'Climb into the

261

old jalopy and get a bloody move on. If I were you, I'd stay the night somewhere and we'll see you lunchtime for a wee dram. What's that? Course we won't say anything. Quiet as a pigeon's piss. Sorry. Yes, yes. Stay as long as you like. Best news we've had in months.'

Only it wasn't the best news at all.

Not when they turned on the car radio and heard the midnight bulletin, with the trickle of poison running right through it.

Chapter Fifty-seven

Sir Henry stared at his toast, seemingly unsure what to do with it.

Across the breakfast table the radio held court, and Wendy could see her husband pretending not to listen as the reports from Washington poured into the dining room.

Along the US Eastern Seaboard, it was three a.m. and yet the coffee cups were already rattling. First editions of the major papers were in the television and radio newsrooms. The story was on the runway, cleared for flight.

Sir Henry chose marmalade over butter. A large dollop from a silver serving spoon.

This was different from all the other scandals and rumours. Too much meat on this animal, too many legs. Too big a mouth.

This time the Press had done a number, just as he'd known it would.

In his mind he ticked off the points as they came up. Relationship in Oxford. Love that had never died. Alison's denial, broadcast and re-broadcast. Shots from the Berlin summit. Little bricks to build a scandal. You could see it being constructed, statement by statement, times and places, places and times, looks and handshakes and the damning indictments of all those 'highly influential sources', interviewed on condition of anonymity.

'Car's outside, Henry.' Wendy got up from the table.

But he didn't answer, sitting there, watching the structure rise.

Of course there were tell-tale signs. But who would spot them? The Labour party, just a little over-rehearsed, the lines a little too finely-honed, the message off pat. Surprise on their lips, but no surprise in the tone. No rush to defend their precious lady, no counter-accusations of smear and slur, no 'too ridiculous for words.'

Go on like this, he thought, and she'd be sentenced and hanged by midday.

'Poor taste. Dangerous precedent. Lack of judgement.' And from one Labour MP ... 'If it's true it's crap. If it isn't it's crap.'

As for Downing Street, the Press office had run up the No Comment flag and was waving it wildly from the chimney pots. All around town, the government's officials and advisers were coming to work, and lying down beneath their desks.

'What does it mean, Henry?'

'Haven't got a clue.'

'Balls.'

'I beg your pardon.'

Wendy leaned across the table, daring him to look away. 'Is it true?'

'I've no idea.'

'Yes you have. According to the papers you bring home. You were well aware this was going on.'

Henry's hand had been reaching for a fresh piece of toast, but it stopped in mid-air. 'You looked at those papers?'

A smile began creeping across her face.

'But they're secret. They're some of the most confidential documents that exist in this country.'

The smile completed its journey. 'I know.'

'For God's sake, Wendy. I thought we had an understanding.'

'You had an understanding. I didn't. What have I ever had? Certainly not you.' She sat down again. 'Oh God, Henry, as if it bloody mattered. Just a lot of stupid papers ... games, all of them. I used to think ... what kind of job is that? You go to the office every day in a big shiny car, in a smart suit, with the shirt I've ironed the night before and the cufflinks I've put out, and then you play ... games. That's all they are ... until someone loses.'

'I don't believe this. I simply don't believe after all these years you could do a thing like that ...'

'It's exactly because of all these years, as you put it, that I could.'

He sat silent at the head of the table, not knowing how to answer.

'You can tell me one thing,' she said. 'And then we'll drop the subject, and I'll go back to being the dutiful, boring wife you married to do the washing up.'

'What?'

'Why didn't you protect her, watch her back, as you always put it? I thought that was part of your function.'

'Wasn't in the plan this time.'

'Why not?'

'Just wasn't.'

And that, she thought later, was the real turning point. Slowly she began clearing the plates and cups from the table, but after a few moments she stopped and went over to the dining-room door empty-handed.

'What's in the plan for me, Henry? I think I need to know that.' The voice was sharper than he'd ever known it. 'What's going to happen to me?'

'You've handled it well so far.'

'Thanks.'

'It's not a compliment, Harper. There aren't any prizes on this one. For any of us. Let's just get through it, OK?'

'People seem to have learned their lines.'

'Yeah, including the bloody Tories. It's more fun than most of them could dream of ...'

'Not so much.' Keith smiled into the receiver. 'They're a little surprised to find we're not defending the castle. Wait and see, worst'll be over in forty-eight hours.'

'And the lady herself?'

'Who cares? Somewhere in the Ukraine. One of our people is going to ask a question in the House this afternoon ... Does the prime minister intend to return to this country in the near future, and in what capacity?'

Marks snorted.

'Thought you'd like that one. All my own work.'

'Don't get too cocky, Harper. If she comes back with a triumph from the Ukraine ... peace in our time ...'

'She could come back with bloody Noah's ark, but it wouldn't make any difference. Ever heard anything as stupid – PM dashing off to a crisis zone? No protection, no planning, no clear aim in view. You think this is the way prime ministers are supposed to act? You wouldn't catch the bloody Tories sticking their necks above the parapet. No, my friend. No more. The moment she's back, the National Executive will call an emergency conference, and Miss Lane'll be invited to step aside ...'

'Invited?'

'Carried out on a pig's back, for all I care.'

Cindy Tremayne was changing planes in the scrum of Karachi airport when she caught the picture on the television screen. The face and the caption ... 'Special Relations?'.

She couldn't make out what the BBC Asia newsreader was saying but she didn't need to.

Bloody hell, she thought. It's happened and I was a bloody part of it.

And she could see the attractive blonde woman in the small cramped flat on the top floor of Downing Street, lying there, with her back being massaged and her reputation already slipping away.

Hard to believe, when you thought back. Being right there, at the centre. The power, the dignity. All the fine words used by all those fine people. You imagined they'd be so different from everyone else, at least in their private lives. But they weren't. Just more so. More insecure. More desperate. More needy.

It had been fun for a while. But it wasn't right. Alison had done nothing wrong. Not in Cindy's eyes. Just got caught up with the hard crowd – the Keith Harpers, the aggressives, the ones who always wanted more.

She'd get a new life once she arrived in New Zealand. She'd heard it was green and pleasant and maybe wouldn't ask too much of her, or about her. Just another Brit wanting twelve and a half thousand miles of scandal-free distance from the old country. Not the first.

'Well, thanks for coming with me this far.' She turned and held out her hand to Pete Levinson, and then laughed a little nervously and hugged him, because it was ludicrous just to shake hands, after all the other kinds of shaking.

'I could ride further, if you want. They told me to get lost for a couple of months.'

'Let's just leave it here, while we still like each other.'

He smiled. 'You're the best, Cindy. Best ever.'

'That's the problem.' She pulled away from him.' I was too good, wasn't I? Don't ever get too good, Pete. People don't like that. OK? Just remember I said so.'

Taggart got up from the sofa, switched off the news and turned to the Lanes.

266

'I think they're all shits . . .'

'Jim, really.' His wife looked at the wall.

'No, I think it's got to be said the way it is. The bloody BBC should be ashamed, broadcasting that kind of character assassination. Cos, that's what it was. Make no mistake. Wouldn't be surprised if they're jamming the bloody switchboard with protests all over the country. Got a good mind, myself . . . .'

'It's all right, Jim.' Margaret Lane went on calmly sipping her whisky. A woman to whom all problems had solutions, all evil would be vanquished. She could never believe, she once said, that bad people would win in the end. 'It's really all right.' She shrugged. 'That's what happens in politics. Alison can look after herself . . .'

'But what about you?'

'What about us, Jim?'

'I just meant all the scandal and everything. Bit difficult to cope with, I'd have thought, having to go to ground and all that . . .'

Margaret Lane sat up in the chair and fixed him with her finest British Empire smile. 'If you think we're going to hang our heads and start weeping because people are telling lies about Alison, you've got another think coming. We're proud of our daughter, Jim Taggart. Always will be. And we're going to tell that to anyone who asks, and go on telling it, till this nonsense is dead and buried. I hope I make myself clear.'

She turned and looked at her husband for reassurance. He shook his head at her and thanked God silently for the thousandth time that he had married the right woman.

Deval was on the phone soon after six a.m.

'I was about to call you.' Bradley turned down the TV sound. He hadn't slept for most of the night.

'They're crucifying her. All sides.'

'I know.'

'They're going to turn on you by the time the morning shows get going.'

'Till's been briefed. No comment on the president's personal life. We never comment on former relationships, real or imaginary. Nor on personal rumours or speculation. The press knows the rules.'

Deval snorted. 'Since when? There haven't been any rules I can remember for years.'

'Come up with something better, Harry, and we'll go for it. OK? For now there aren't too many other fig leaves that fit.'

Till couldn't help enjoying himself as the 9.30 White House briefing approached.

If Bradley thought he could hold them off with a little sign saying 'No Go' – he'd think again in a while. All the TV networks had requested permission to carry the briefing live. They were turned down, reminded tartly that it was off the record – as usual. If there were any special announcements to be made they'd be notified in the normal way.

The long narrow room was crowded. Winter outside, the heat of the chase within.

From the veteran UPI correspondent came the 'what you got, Cliff?' that set it all off. And from then on Till could barely hear himself speak.

He stood smiling for a full half-minute while the tremors subsided and the reporters realised they were shouting solely at each other.

'We've no further news from Berlin on the condition of the Russian leader.' Till looked meaningfully at his notes. 'The president is being kept fully informed. I understand he has spoken to Mrs Shilov during the night.'

'Jesus Christ, Cliff' A gasp of frustration came out of a hundred mouths as the dogs sensed their quarry slipping out of reach.

'The relationship, Cliff. The relationship.' ABC's White House correspondent rose, face contorted, an inch away from his trade-mark tantrum. Immediately after the briefing he'd have to go live into the network with fuck all to say, which meant his contract negotiations would be even more dicey ...

'Quit stonewalling.' An ageless blonde from the rival CBS, stood up shaking her perfect perm at the presidential spokesman. 'You've seen the papers, you've heard the bulletins. Start giving. The nation expects, Cliff. Bring the president out. Let's hear what he's got to say.'

'The president is spending the morning in telephone discussions with our allies,' he smiled, 'including the British. We're monitoring developments in Russia with the utmost care.'

He gathered his papers. 'That's all guys. Thanks for coming. No further announcements expected today. It's a wrap.'

He turned to his right, stepped down from the podium and disappeared through the door, as the howling followed him.

Back in his office, there were phone calls from sixteen of the country's principal editors, the presidents of the four major networks, twenty-three foreign news moguls – and the list was mounting.

'Way to go,' he muttered. The phone calls would keep coming. The more Bradley ducked, the better they'd learn to shoot.

Chapter Fifty-eight

The reports, coded from London, were received in flight over the Ukraine. Maybe a little worse than Alison had expected, more barbed and vindictive. But then, she told herself, you shouldn't be surprised in British politics. The mother of parliaments could be a real bitch when she chose.

Skimming through the lines, she noted the absence of any robust defences, any smoke screens, any standard ministerial diatribes against the Press. This was a frontal attack, with the party fully behind it. Foster had been right. Tricky, clever, little Foster. Only even he hadn't jumped in time.

'I'm sorry, Prime Minister. For what it's worth.' He was sitting opposite, having brought her the papers, gauging her reaction.

'For what it's worth, Dick Foster, don't go away thinking this is the end of Alison Lane. Tell that to anyone who asks. It's an authorised comment, OK?'

She shut the papers away in her briefcase and stared into the clouds. They were flying into a gulley, between two walls of solid grey. Nothing could be done about events in Britain. Not from this distance. But in the Ukraine, by contrast, she still had a small chance to make an imprint, to leave a mark.

If there was some point to it all, to the struggling and suffering and pushing of the last thirty years – then maybe it was here.

Standing by the open door of the plane, they could see the airport stretching away in stagnant desolation. At the perimeter the control tower seemed to lean on a single leg, its plaster facing half crumbled away, old signs and notices ripped from the wall and stacked against it. Broken windows, empty hangars, their mouths frozen open in shock. Dirty snow. The crows in sole possession, calling out to each other across the emptiness.

At the foot of the steps were the only visible signs of life –

two ancient minibuses, spattered with mud, ragged curtains at the windows, and a single black Volga sedan, its bonnet coated up against the chill. It was like an invalid who should have stayed in bed.

'This is one of the old Soviet bases. You see the long runways. They were for the heavy transport planes, closed up when the Union disintegrated.' Katya had put on a red fox shapka, pulled tightly down over her head. 'There are many like this – relics, you say?'

'Relics. Just like us.'

'Better let me go first, Prime Minister,' Alison's detective pushed past them to the top of the steps. 'Just clarify the situation. Think it'd be wise.'

But even as he reached the ground, a figure in a long black leather coat swung easily from the Volga and approached the plane. The young, swaggery walk of the nouveau powerful, she thought, thug of the day, with a voice that scythed through the wind.

'Prime Minister, Mrs Shilov. I come from the president's office.'

Alison stayed where she was. Let him shout, let him come to me.

'The president regrets he was unable to meet you. He is, as you understand, in the midst of a crisis but you are free to go where you wish.'

She nodded.

'You'll be aware that our ultimatum to the Russian government runs out in just over six hours. Please give yourselves time to leave the area and be out of Ukrainian airspace by then. This is for your own protection. The matter is, of course, up to you.' He spread his hands like a priest offering absolution. 'I hope your mission is successful, Prime Minister. For our part there's nothing more we can do.'

'I wish to talk to your president.' Her own voice seemed so frail by comparison. A tiny echo across the airfield.

'I regret that's not possible.'

'Then make it possible. We are trying to negotiate. That means talking. Everyone. No communication barriers.'

He smiled. 'The Russian military commander knows where to find us. He is, after all, situated on our territory. We are listening on all frequencies ... when he wishes to announce his withdrawal.'

'You are not helping the situation.'

The hands returned to the black leather pockets. 'Forgive me, Prime Minister, but you are arguing with the messenger. I convey what I am told – no more, no less. I can make no deals.' He looked at his watch. 'I may only observe that time is still passing – and there is very little left.' His eyes flicked towards the vehicles. 'The drivers know where you wish to go. You'll understand if I don't travel with you.'

The detective, Katya and Alison in the first car. The others in the minibuses. Crew on the plane. The little expeditionary force on its way into the Ukraine.

You couldn't see where the fields ended and the snow began, the roads cleared only by the tracks of the other vehicles, skidding, slithering across the country.

'You are new to this job.' Katya leans towards Alison.

She nodded.

'You are an adventurer?'

'I never thought so.'

'But you have struggled.'

'Yes.' And she could remember hearing that a conversation in Russia is always a grope towards the meaning of life. No small talk. History has never given them that luxury. Your subjects are death and freedom and lies because you must confront them each day. You bump into them on the street. They are all around you.

'Is the truth important to you, Alison?'

'It has to be.'

'So you try always to tell it?'

'I try . . .' she could see the television screen back in Berlin, the colour spreading out across her cheeks. The simple denial of a simple fact. 'I don't always succeed.'

'So there is a place for lies in government?'

'There's a place for confidentiality.'

'May I share a confidence with you?'

Cold suddenly in the car, limping along in the slush.

'If you wish.'

'And you will inform no one.'

'Of course.'

'Then I will tell you when this is over. For now you will need your strength and your concentration.' Katya stretched out her hand and Alison felt the force of the fingers, like tensile claws.

As she did so, the Volga slid to a halt in the forest clearing and the engine fell silent.

'You're keeping watch on her?'

'The Pentagon, the DIA, half the agencies we possess. The plane was tracked throughout Ukrainian airspace.' Harry spoke softly, easily, trying to reassure the president.

'And on the ground?'

'Difficult. Satellites are still being re-tasked and there's heavy cloud over the region.'

'I want her tracked, dammit.'

'They're working on it, David.'

'They'd better be. If she clears her throat, I want to know about it.'

'David ... this close interest of yours ... you've seen the reports. Hour by hour. A pundit here, a pundit there, TV, radio, the Press, they're talking about nothing else. I haven't seen this level of hype since Iran-Contra. If you want her monitored so closely, there's going to be a leak. I can guarantee it. Hundred per cent ...'

'Do it, Harry. Every move she makes. No questions on this one. Just do it.'

Chapter Fifty-nine

There are helicopter gunships, missiles, there are troops encamped beneath the trees. Straight out of the briefing books, straight off the pages of Nato threat assessments – and they shouldn't be here.

Someone has let them out.

Alison can see the silent, fair-haired colonel, standing at the entrance to the field tent, apart from the others, a danger all on his own.

He walks towards them, eyes armed with a cause.

He talks quietly to Katya in Russian and she listens, probing, not pushing, not insisting. Simple enquiries.

'This is Colonel Sergei Chukovsky of the Strategic Rocket Forces Command.'

'Yes.' Alison is motionless.

'He welcomes you to Silo 318. A tent has been prepared for you and your advisers ...'

'I don't need a tent. I want to talk. Now.'

'He says we should wait a while.'

'He's in no position to make demands.'

'On the contrary, he claims to be in the best possible position.'

Alison looks into the large, tired eyes. Know your opponent. Know your target. If you can see how he's put together, then you can see how to take him apart. That's politics. But not here, beside a missile. All the rules are different.

'We've come as a sign of international goodwill. You can't order the leaders of the world around. Doesn't work like that.'

Look at him, though, as the words reach him in Russian. He doesn't care what works or what doesn't. Couldn't care a fig about leaders or protocol. He has an idea. A light to see by, and a path to follow.

And me? I'm prime minister of Great Britain and Northern Ireland. I hold the highest political office in the land, I'm supposed to make the decisions others carry out.

I shouldn't be here.

Behind her in the trees a group of commandos snaps to attention. But there's something wrong, something out of place. Only as her eyes accustom to the dying light of the forest, can Alison see the machine guns in their hands – pointed straight at her.

Three hours go by and David Bradley takes calls from a satellite station in California. It's a grey windowless warehouse, sitting beside a six-lane highway, and the name on the sign is 'Keep Out.'

There are little specks of doubt on the things he is hearing.

They have pinpointed the silo and the helicopters. But it's too quiet and too inactive.

The hours are inching past. The sun is moving out of the Ukraine, and they don't like what they don't see.

'She's in talks, David. Long and difficult.' Harry leans against the desk. The hotel suite is forty-eight floors above the reporters and TV trucks gathered in the streets.

'You believe that? They don't all sit there navel-gazing. People take breaks, walk around, communicate. The press are with her. What about them? They should be filing reports, clamouring for phones. And they're not. No calls. No radio traffic. There's nothing from Klimak either.'

'What d'you mean? We've tried hotlines, faxes, even our ambassador in Kiev has been round to the Presidential residence, but they turned him away.'

'So you're telling me there's silence on this, right across the world. And we, the United States, can't get any answers.'

'David, for now there's nothing you can do.' In that moment, Harry catches sight of the president's expression, eyes staring into the middle distance, calculating. Shouldn't have said that, he tells himself. Not to this guy. Should've kept my mouth shut. This one time.

'We haven't met before.'

Keith Harper tried to place the voice before turning round. It was certainly more polished than the other drinkers at the bar, more rounded. Always happened when he needed peace – some doddery, old fool from the constituency would crawl out of the furniture,

275

wanting to talk about schools or the bloody health service. Only now, when he looked at the face, he knew this was different.

There was confidence in there, an in-built superiority. The mottled after-dinner skin, the manicured hands, the hint of a handkerchief protruding from the sleeve. Power.

'To whom do I have the pleasure?' he had to raise his voice to be heard. But the figure seemed to draw him imperceptibly towards the corner of the bar. Only when the light hit Sir Henry's face full on did Keith know who was with him.

'This is a surprise.' He took a sip of beer and licked his lips.

'A pleasant one, I hope.'

'I'm not sure you're the kind of person associated with pleasant surprises.'

Sir Henry smiled. He took that as a compliment.

'You seem to be heading ever onward, ever upward, if I may say so.'

'Kind of you to notice.'

'Oh, but I do.'

'Well the Party has been forced to make changes. That much should be clear today of all days.'

'Yes, of course. So nice when a Party can agree and come to democratic decisions . . .'

Keith took another swig of beer and seemed emboldened by it. 'So what did you want?'

'To pay my compliments.'

'Why?'

'You've played it very cleverly.' He raised his eyebrows.. 'If I may say so.'

'I'm not sure I get your drift. I said *the Party* had been making some changes . . .'

'Suggested by you.'

'Some of them.'

'And some of them seem to have paid off. Don't they?' Sir Henry's eyebrows lifted the barest fraction.

'Listen,' Keith smiled for a moment. 'Why don't you and I play a little game? I start a sentence like this . . . 'I've come here today because . . .' and you finish it for me. OK? Shall we have a go?'

'So black and white?'

'So black *or* white, Sir Henry. Let's finish the sentence and then decide, shall we?'

Sir Henry inclined his head. It was good to be reminded that Harper was far from stupid.

'As you wish. I simply wanted to tell you, as I tell all prospective candidates for the leadership that they can count on our unbiased support. You are, I take it, a candidate for the leadership?'

'News to me.'

'I see. Well, perhaps it won't be news for much longer.'

'Is that the kind of assurance you gave Alison Lane?'

'You're quite a politician, Mr Harper.'

'My constituency seems to think so. I've been their MP for twenty-six years.' Harper finished his beer and put the glass on the ledge beside him. 'Anyway, how do I know you're on my side? You people haven't exactly put yourselves out for Labour in the past, have you?'

Sir Henry grinned. 'Those pictures you received, the ones featuring Alison Lane and her physiotherapist. Your pictures, in fact. Who do you imagine sent them?'

Chapter Sixty

Alone in his room above New York, Harry Deval assembles his bag – the enquiries, the little unanswered questions and the big ones.

Only now can he think himself back to the city of Oxford. End of the summer term, 1966. Vietnam building steadily into the headlines, the counter movements learning to tie their shoelaces and going for walks.

You'd think everyone was involved – at least from the newspaper cuttings. But not David Bradley.

He's a volunteer, by golly – one of a kind, recorded in Army archives at Quantico as a committed soldier-to-be. So they paid his air fare home and cut him a uniform. Didn't get many like that. People with a brain, willing to use their hands.

And there's the High Street, warm and crowded on a summer night. Bottles of booze in every fist, students ebbing and flowing away. Careless, they were. As if the future were simply an open door, admission free.

David stays outside the celebrations. Hasn't got anything to feel good about. He's making the supreme sacrifice for a young guy, kissing his girl goodbye, the girl he promised to marry, the girl who won't wait for him, because she can't love a fool in a stupid war.

You see ... Harry's friend had found a friend of hers. And eventually she'd talked.

Time: 7.30, perhaps. Bags already packed in the college. The London train ran at eight, in those days. Said his piece, had young David, walks back to his room, calls a cab from the porter's lodge.

Funny how everyone keeps records. Old, half-eaten by time and termites. The more trivial, the more there are. You don't pass through life without leaving paper behind.

Only Bradley's state of mind is unclear. No papers for that.

And yet by 9.30 that night he's in London's Paddington station. And there's nothing to show that he ever phoned back, went back or looked back to Oxford, ever again.

Alison?

She's in there too. One more year to go. Heading for a First Class degree. Straight A student – only they don't use the term in England.

Last meeting with her tutor – 6.30, same evening.

Says she can't stay long, the old bag remembers. Always in a hurry but more so that day. Hurried and sad.

How does she remember?

Well, she remembers because of what happened later, and what Alison became. And because a wasp flew in the open window and stung her.

Christ knows how, but the local police records have made it.

7.40. pm. Not 7.41. Not 7.39. Exact time of incident. Female student, Alison Lane, hit by van, registration so and so, driver so and so.

Ambulance is summoned, 7.46. Admitted Casualty, Radcliffe Infirmary, 7.59.

And they don't hang about.

Casualty sister, houseman, professor of surgery. All the reports in there.

All bleak.

Pulse barely there. Shock trauma. Severe spinal damage.

A young woman who isn't going to see night turn to day.

Prime minister-to-be. A. Lane. Miss.

Harry takes off the Dunhill spectacles and listens to New York, as the certainty comes to him across the miles and years. The complete and utter conviction that David Bradley knows nothing of this. Not the accident, not the injuries, not the struggle young Alison Lane undertook in order to rise and walk.

Bradley has no idea.

I could junk this, he tells himself. Bin it, pretend I never knew, and so he'd never know, and the world can take its own course.

But Harry can't do that.

Not this time.

After all the lies and obfuscations of his own life – he decides that little piece of truth deserves to be heard.

Chapter Sixty-one

Her own thoughts travelled that way in the hour between sunset and dusk.

A time to wonder what might have been.

'I refuse to wait any longer,' she had said. And that was an age ago, before they had posted sentries around the cars, taken her with her advisers to a field command post, and the others somewhere else.

'I demand to begin negotiations. I demand communication equipment.'

And the silence had seemed so conclusive. Served as it was with the evening stew in tin pots, with a bucket of water and a pile of plastic mugs.

She sat in a corner of the tent with Katya, while they examined options that weren't. And realities.

Odd thing about power, she decided. It wasn't real. It relied on other people giving it to you. Recognising you. An acceptance that you're the one.

Withdraw it and suddenly you're stuck back down in the world of the ordinary; protesting, demanding – to no avail.

Like judgement day. When the powerful find out they're not. And the meek inherit, the way they were promised.

'What's their aim?' This to Katya, just a whisper.

'World attention. Blackmail, possibly. But I doubt it.'

'The deadline has passed ...'

'That too, they have calculated. Ukraine will not attack with you here. You've bought them some time.'

'You too.'

'The purpose, Colonel. This is what I'm asking myself.'

'That should be clear enough.' Chukovsky bit the end of his thumbnail. 'In a few hours' time, the world community will realise that a prime minister is here, and held against her will. They'll put unbearable pressure on Moscow and the Ukraine, there'll be meetings in the security council and a settlement will be forced on all the parties concerned.'

'Will, will, will . . . what makes you so sure?'

'What would you do, Major?'

'You asking me? Personally I'd infiltrate a single agent into this command and kill you. That's what I'd do. And the moment you become too great an embarrassment to our so-called leaders in Moscow, the moment they stop fucking around and decide something – that's exactly what they'll do.'

'I'm grateful for your thoughts, Major.'

'I thought you would be.'

As they watched the television news the Lanes and the Taggarts could see the little bungalow near Brighton, with the reporters staking out the road.

'Neighbours say they have no idea where Alison Lane's parents have gone. They left no forwarding address, simply took the car out of the garage and slipped away into the night.'

Taggart pressed the remote and blacked out the screen.

'Look at the bastards. Like bees round the proverbial . . .'

His wife threw him a warning glance. She'd already warned him his language was 'on the fruity side' and after all, these *were* the prime minister's parents.

Margaret Lane got up from the sofa and smoothed her skirt. 'I'm away to bed, if nobody minds. Seen enough news for today. Although I'm a little surprised there was nothing from the Ukraine. I know they mentioned communications problems. But there should have been a report about what Alison's doing, instead of all this speculation . . . you know. I mean it's very unusual, isn't it? Shouldn't we ring the BBC or Downing Street.'

'Everything's unusual these days,' said Taggart, gazing philosophically towards the window. 'Bloody unusual, if you ask me. Still, I'm sure there's nothing to worry about.'

'Why, Jim?' Mrs Lane was staring at him.

'Why what?'

'Why are you sure there's nothing to worry about?'

'Well, of course there isn't.'

'No, but how do you know?'

Taggart sniffed. 'Stands to reason.'

'Let me tell you something, Jim,' Margaret Lane opened the doo
to the hall. 'I never realised what an awful windbag you are. Thank
for putting us up. But we'll be leaving in the morning.'

'What are the Brits saying, Harry? She's their prime minister.'

'Not worried. Not concerned. Fault with her radio system. They'l
let us know.'

The president ran a hand through his hair. 'So they're doin
nothing.'

'Right.'

'You contacted the Ukrainian ambassador here.'

'He promised to call within one hour.'

'One hour then. That's all I'm waiting.'

'David.' Harry produces his file from the briefcase – the little ba
of facts on Alison Lane, the little pieces of history that he's fitte
together.

'What's this?'

'Just read it. Spend an hour of your life. I think you should.'

Chapter Sixty-two

The Ukrainian ambassador has called Deval. He has failed to make contact with Kiev. He wants to explain, wishes he could, perhaps in another hour ...

Harry takes the elevator to the forty-eighth floor, past the secret service, along to the presidential suite. And for a moment it seems like a different man at the desk. Different colours in his face. Different lines. Something inside him has re-arranged.

'You didn't know about it, did you David? The accident? All the rest ...'

And Harry can see him trying to play back the day. Retrieve the sights and the voices.

'Nothing. Thirty years and nothing. Wouldn't she have said ... ?' He closes the file and pushes it away from him. 'Listen, I'm not going to go back over everything. I'm going to act on it.'

'Right. We've got to discuss all this, bring in the Cabinet, take soundings.'

'Not this time.' And if you look carefully, Bradley's eyes are carrying a decision. An impetus that wasn't there before. 'I want you to call the networks. I'm going to make an announcement in two hours.'

'What the ...?'

'I'm announcing the resumption of the summit ...'

'Jesus Christ! The summit's over, David. There's no venue, no agenda, and there's no one to sit down with. Listen to me. Listen very carefully ...'

'No, Harry. Make the arrangements.'

'What arrangements? We've had no contact with State. Congress has no idea what's going on. The allies need to be called. You're not just one man with a plane. You're an office, for Chrissake. An institution, the highest, most protected and most valuable on this planet. Do I even have to be telling you this?'

'I wasn't elected to be an office, Harry. I was elected to do

283

something with it. That means taking action. What're we gonna do? Wait a year for the UN?' He shakes his head. 'You talk about the presidency as if it's some kind of divine relic . . .'

'It is.'

'Well, I'm not.' Eyes already travelling.

'Your judgment's clouded, David. I can't put it more strongly than that.'

'You're saying I'm doing this for Alison?'

'Of course I'm saying it. Everyone's gonna say it. You risked the security of the United States for a woman you love. That's what the American people will say. The truth.'

'Let them say it, Harry. But I left this woman for dead, thirty years ago and never knew anything about it. I'm not going to do that again.'

'You don't have the right to take that risk.'

'It's why I was elected. Remember? The man who took risks and won. What did I do in Vietnam? Disobeyed orders right from the top, saved lives. The people elected that person. Remember the campaign, the commercials . . .'

'You're starting to believe your own propaganda . . . that's dangerous . . .'

'You get paid for results, Harry. That's the only propaganda that matters. If I don't bring them home this time, then I'll take one final executive action . . .'

'Why, David? You have to make a choice. Her or the job. Choose her, if that's what you want. But make a choice.'

'No choice. I want them both.'

'You can't . . .'

'Look at my predecessors. Look at the crap they did and got away with. Most of it illegal. Why d'you think Bush overwrote so many of the White House computer discs before he got out of office? You've seen some of it. Jesus, this doesn't even rate next to Nixon or Kennedy. I'm not doing anything illegal, Harry.'

'There are worse things than illegal. There's ill-advised. There's imprudent. Hair-brained. Want me to go on?'

'So tell me the stakes aren't high.'

'Course they are.'

'So you take drastic action.'

'You order drastic action. You're commander in chief. You order –
they do.'

Bradley got up and poured two whiskys from a decanter on the
sideboard.

'Seems to me I've been away from the action far too long. Seems
to me I've lived in the dark. This woman nearly died because of me.
D'you understand, Harry?' He drained the whisky and poured
another. 'It's not enough to make decisions from the safety of a big
chair, behind bullet-proof glass. I've never in my life been paid to
sit around while others do things. Never led from the back. Not me.
Not on this planet.'

He handed his chief of staff the other glass.

'Make the calls, Harry. We can't wait any longer.'

'Now I know he's crazy.' Norton sat on the edge of his chair,
watching the network special.

David Bradley in a New York studio, dark suit, plenty of Max
Factor, seemed normal enough. Summit back on, where better to
hold it than at the site of the missile silo in the Ukraine?

Take the medicine direct to the patient.

This time they wouldn't leave without a solution.

Mrs Darlene Norton sat scraping her nails with an emery-board.
'Looked pretty damned convincing to me.' The low drawl was
deceptive. 'Why did you tell them you were ill, for Chrissake? You
should be on that plane same as the rest of them.'

'I told you why.'

'Tell me again.'

'Because he's gonna fall flat on his arse, and I don't want to be
part of it. I have to keep my distance . . .'

'Yeah.' She stood up. 'I might just keep some distance of my own
for right now.' She let him stare at her slim, tanned legs, disppearing
all the way up into the short, silk nightgown. Let him look all he
wanted. She wasn't going to give him any tonight. Not after a damn
fool trick like that.

Clark, she reckoned, could be a real schmuck when he dropped
his guard.

Sir Henry heard it all on the BBC World Service. Two a.m., London time, alone in the downstairs kitchen.

So Bradley didn't want to play it safe. Must be really hooked.
Much more than he'd realised. If he was going to risk everything
for her.

Why did these leaders all think they were gods?

So many of them did.

Believed all the hype and the praise, the trappings of power.
The special lifestyle, removed from normal people and normal
considerations.

In the end they all lost their judgement. Became overwhelmed by
their own self-importance.

Thought they could have it all.

Funny thing was ... the more they talked about accountability,
the less there was.

People didn't know what went on. And if they knew what, they
seldom knew why.

Not the real reasons.

Bradley's mistake was to think he could get away with it.

When the broadcast was over, Sir Henry took his solemn thoughts
up to the bedroom and sat in darkness on his side of the bed.

Not, of course, that he had played it any better than Bradley.

Wendy was gone, and there was nothing to indicate whether she
ever intended to return.

'You spoke to Klimak?'

'The message has reached him. I know that.'

'What did it say?'

'It said you'd be arriving to continue the summit beside the
missile silo. And if he wasn't there he could forget about Ukraine's
international reputation, forget about aid. We'd blacken his name
and that of his country for all time. By fair means or any other.'

'Those exact words?'

'More or less. And to the Russian vice-president.'

'And Norton?'

'Says he's sick. Deputy secretary will stand in. Defence and NSA
are going with you. They're really sick – with worry, but privately
wouldn't miss this for the world.'

'Congress?'

'Shock from the senate majority leader and a few others, but most are on board. Plenty of God speeds and good lucks.'

'That simple, Uh?'

'There are still people in this country who like decisions. Any decisions. Plane's at Kennedy, fuelled and ready. Some Press on board. Secret service. Counter assault. New wash cloth. Amazing what you get when you ask for it. Trouble is, nobody says "no" to the president. Maybe some day we'll learn.'

'Thanks, Harry.'

Deval has to stand almost on tiptoe to touch Bradley's shoulder. 'For what it's worth, David, I'd do the same thing.'

Chapter Sixty-three

Katya woke her before dawn and for a moment she thought she heard a different sound. A low, persistent rattle in the distance, the grind of heavy machinery on the move.

She opened the front of the tent, but the noise had gone. Above the trees, thick clouds were pulling hard from the east.

'When it's light, I'm going to demand transport to the plane. We're going to walk to the cars and buses and drive away. What'll they do – shoot us? I can't allow myself to be a virtual hostage. That's the worst of all options. For everyone.'

'I regret very much that I brought you here.' Katya's voice just a whisper in the dark.

'You shouldn't. People face this kind of lawlessness all over the world, every day of their lives. And governments never hear about it or never do anything. The leaders all go off in protected convoys, on so-called familiarisation trips, exchanging one set of luxuries for another. But this time it's different. I get to make a stand, where it counts.'

She lay down again and tried to sleep. But now there was a face in front of her that she couldn't shake.

And what would you do, David?

You'd do the same, wouldn't you? Always said so. Can't get others to carry your convictions.

And maybe for the first time in thirty years I understand why you went to Vietnam, why you felt involved. Everyone else was having parties and celebrating the end of the summer term in Oxford – and you walked the other way.

Without me.

You threw away the person you loved. And now I've thrown away my career.

Perhaps there's some sense to it, somewhere.

He couldn't explain it to anyone on the aircraft. Just how good it felt to have the leash untied, to be going out of a sanitised, protected, cushioned little world – and into trouble.

Felt like the first time they'd been helicoptered into battle inside North Vietnam, over the jungle, low over the treetops, the wind and the rotors tearing at your tunic, the hunt in your blood.

And we're not killers at all, because right is on our side. The mantra, repeated over and over again to ward off conscience.

Should I be here, now? Was Harry right? Could I have done this differently?

Not when I look back.

Not when I see Alison Lane, student of mine, lying in the gutter of an Oxford street, that soft summer day, with the rain crying gently over the city.

I don't have a choice.

I made one thirty years ago. And it was wrong.

Now there's no choice at all.

Wherever Air Force One travels it is the most closely monitored flight on the planet. That night it was shadowed into Ukrainian airspace by F-14 fighters, with US airbases on alert throughout the European continent, and governments warned that the protection of this one aircraft was their duty, and America's right.

The president was on an emergency peace mission. No hostile action would be tolerated. And US armed forces world-wide stood ready to enforce the threat.

Throughout the night, Harry had been busy.

Chapter Sixty-four

David Bradley looks back on this time as the best and the stupidest thing he ever did, brushing aside the secret service to stand by the open door of Air Force One, smelling the damp cold, hearing the snow falling from the trees.

He says it was the longest two minutes he ever waited, before the line of black cars emerged from behind the hangar, the Ukrainian colours in full view, doors opening, security men running hard to keep up, and the Ukrainian president, stepping towards the aircraft, the short squat body slipping on the tarmac.

Bradley took hold of Klimak's hand and felt it start to crush his own, in something more than diplomatic enthusiasm.

He remembers telling him ... 'how good it was to re-start the talks.'

And Klimak, jaw frozen, muttering simply, 'Do you always threaten weaker countries?' Do you think this is acceptable behaviour for a superpower? Bradley answering 'yes' to both.

There's a picture he likes to recall of Klimak scowling, while two secret servicemen force their way into his limousine to sit either side of their president, rejecting all efforts to have them removed.

Such an uncomfortable ride across the countryside, with the counter assault team right behind and Bradley in bullet-proof vest, no room for his legs, jammed as they were against Klimak's. No conversation between them.

And you don't attend public events and the glittering international occasions without savouring those moments of delicious embarrassment.

Klimak again, exiting from the car, stiff and awkward, confronted on his own territory by a Russian colonel, informed that the summit is about to begin and that all the other participants are ready.

'You're very welcome,' says Sergei Chukovsky, newly-shaved and luxuriating in false modesty. 'I am most grateful you could be here.'

And as Bradley's eyes scout the territory, he can see a blonde lady in a coat, pencils and files under her arm, scribbling notes on a paper in front of her.

He remembers what she said. Probably always will.

'You're late, David. I expected you hours ago.'

And as he tells the story, himself, there wasn't anything else that needed saying.

Most of this is in the public record, thanks to the cameras. The six-hour talks, the minute details, the lengthy and laborious route towards an agreement.

Nobody ever gives in at a summit and says ... 'OK, you've won. I change my mind.' Each concession is dragged from the sections and sub-sections of draft after draft, that the experts on both sides agree to put before their leaders.

So it was in the Ukraine.

But there are two meetings that didn't get recorded.

Sergei Chukovsky taking the American president into the silo that he had commanded on behalf of the Strategic Rocket Forces. Just the two of them.

Seventy metres below ground they inspected the launch control, and the missile, still fuelled in the shaft beside it.

Bradley leaned on the table and examined the colonel in the dim neon light.

'You took a big risk.'

'So did you, Mr President.'

Bradley grinned. 'I guess I'm paid to take them. What's your excuse?'

Chukovsky paused and looked around the narrow complex. 'I watched my captain die here in this silo. A boy, but a boy with good ideas, big ideas, all about the new Russia. He saw a different future. This was for him.'

'Would you have used the missile?'

'No. I promised myself that years ago. Way before the cold war ended. But I thought we waited long enough for an agreement. No more people were going to die.'

They emerged into sunlight, more cameras, and the signing of an agreement in principle.

The four summit powers to guard the silos in the Ukraine, until new arrangements could be concluded. All disputed missiles ceded to the control of the United Nations.

'Peace in our time?' A reporter shouted at Bradley.

'It's a start. That's all.' He searched for the requisite soundbite cliché. 'Peace isn't a destination. It's a journey. We travelled a way today. No more than that.'

And then they cordoned off a section of the wood. Alison Lane and David Bradley once again in protected space.

'So you came to get me.'

'I came for a summit. Your idea.'

'And released me in the process.'

'I can leave you if you want. The fact is we did what we couldn't do in Berlin.'

'That's not the way it'll be seen back home.'

'How so?'

'The Press were with me. They know what really happened. They know I was a hostage till you arrived. "Bradley releases Lane." That'll be the headline. Then the ... so-called love story. Then down at the bottom of the page, that we got an agreement on nuclear missiles which may or may not hold. I know Britain, David. I know the Press.'

'I shall tell it another way.'

'I shan't.'

They walked for a moment, conscious that the space and time were restricted.

'Why did you never mention the accident in Oxford?'

She shrugged. 'You *have* been busy. Why? What for, David? It was a long time ago. Everything was a long time ago. Would it have made any difference if you'd known?'

'Yes.'

'No. You had something you wanted to do with your life. Something you needed to do. I wasn't going to show up, like a cripple and say ... hey, remember me?'

They stood for a moment, and then a thought pierced her.

'Is that why you came? Because of the accident?'

'No.'

'Yes.' She smiled. 'Doesn't look as though we'll ever get the same answers, will we?'

'I don't need any answers. I know what happened thirty years ago and I know what happened at Camp David.'

'It was like re-visiting an old house, where we were once happy. It was the past. Not the future.'

'I don't accept that.'

'You have to David. You have to return to Washington and go back to being a president, and I have to go to London.'

'You said we'd do lunch in Oxford.'

'Did I?' She took his hand. 'Then we will.'

Only when Bradley had gone, did she get the chance to see Katya.

They sat in an empty Field-tent, while the summit set was cleared behind them.

'So, my dear. It worked.'

Alison leaned against the long table. 'It worked because David Bradley flew in, like the knight of old. Let's not kid ourselves.'

'You remember, I asked if I could share a confidence?'

'Yes.'

'Perhaps now is the time.' And as Alison looked there were tears, freshly squeezed from her eyes.

'What is it?'

'My husband . . .'

'So go to Berlin, Katya. Now. He's strong. He's holding on.'

'My dear, he died four days ago, while I was with him.' Tears flowing free down the steep, grey cheeks. 'I couldn't tell anyone. Russia would have broken apart if they had known.'

'I don't . . .'

'I had no choice. I knew that. It was almost as if he were telling me what to do. The moment I was about to kiss him goodbye, he'd already gone. Like he couldn't bring himself to part. You know what he once said . . . if it hurts to say farewell, then don't, just walk away. And that's what he did.'

'But the doctors . . . and the bulletins . . . ?'

'I made them promise. They're good when it comes to questions of life and death. They're used to that. They'll announce the death tonight and I'll go to Berlin and take him home.'

Alison could see the first hint of darkness, the forest closing in around them.

'You're a remarkable woman, Katya.'

'You won't break my confidence?' Tears and more tears, like a river bursting its banks, sweeping away the levy.

'I won't break your confidence.'

They held each other for a long time without speaking, until the advisers moved in quietly behind them and suggested it was time to leave.

Chapter Sixty-five

'Harper?'

'D'you know what time it is?'

'It's Marks. We have to talk.'

'Go to sleep.'

'But she's got an agreement in the Ukraine. What about that? What about public opinion?'

'Don't be stupid. Why d'you think I called in the Lobby correspondents last night? I told them what the Americans are telling their people, privately of course. That she blundered into something she couldn't handle, and Bradley had to rush in after her. The agreement's OK as far as it goes – but the experts say it's full of holes.'

'You hear the Russian leader's died?'

'See? That'll keep any thoughts of triumph off the front pages. Now the whole nuclear thing'll be up in the air again. That's the line I'm flogging and I suggest you do the same.'

'So we go ahead as planned?'

'You've got a bloody short memory. There's an emergency conference fixed for the Queen Elizabeth Hall, day after tomorrow. It's all been decided. Get some sleep and stop panicking. You're like a little girl.'

'You can go now, Foster. I expect you want to get back to your children.'

They had reached Downing Street way after midnight. A single light in the study, Mountbatten Green and St James's Park deserted in the middle distance. The first editions of the national papers covered the coffee table.

Foster hadn't taken off his coat, hadn't been asked to. 'I'm sorry things turned out this way. But you know, even now you could go to the people. That was a very brave thing you did back there. You deserve some credit, really . . .'

'Maybe ...' she gestured towards the pile of newsprint. 'But they've already sold their version. And what would I achieve? Split the party. More scandal. At the end of the day, I told a lie in public. And that's still on the record. My record. I also took a dangerous, foolhardy decision, had to be rescued by a foreign leader who has more experience and sense than I do.'

'I don't ...'

She stood up. 'Listen, Dick, this was a caretaker administration at a time of crisis. Let's leave it at that, shall we?'

'If only there'd been more time.'

'How d'you mean?'

'Time to make enough friends. You don't need much time to make enemies. They're all around you in politics. Come with the job. But real friends – the people who'll back you when it's tough, who'll go out on limbs for you, who'll take some heat on your behalf – takes years to cultivate those kinds of relationships. Years, if ever.' He blushed. 'I wish I'd done better by you.'

'Goodnight, Dick.' She held out her hand.

'Goodbye, Prime Minister.'

'What's up, Harry?'

The satellite link to Air Force One was clear as a local call.

'*You're* up for one thing. Jesus, David. Talk about returning hero.'

'Tell me.'

'In the last hour calls to the White House are running fifteen to one in your favour. Congress is going crazy – both parties. The Cabinet wanted to give you a ticker-tape parade along Pennsylvania Avenue. Anyone'd think you'd found Elvis. Did you?'

'Harry ...'

'I can't tell you ... every five minutes they're bringing flowers here. Lee Greenfield's re-recording "Proud to be an American" ...'

'Finest taste, as always.'

'Don't knock it, David. Been a long winter.'

'They'll get over it.'

'Let's hope they don't. You could ride this all the way to the next convention. Reagan would've killed for the part – flying in like that, rescuing Lane ...'

'Is that how the story's playing?'

'Isn't that the way it was?'

'And in London?'

'They're killing her.'

'How bad?'

'The embassy thinks she'll be out – day after tomorrow. Labour's calling a special conference, where she'll be forced to step down – health reasons, maybe. And if she doesn't go quietly, they'll push her. She doesn't have many friends. Papers cite lack of judgement, foolhardiness, lying about her personal life ... I'm sorry to dampen your landing, but you asked.'

'That's always been my problem.'

'I'll be there to hold your hand at Andrews.'

'Thanks, Harry, but I'll hold my own.'

Darlene woke Norton on the sofa where he lay.

She flicked on the television.

'You better watch this.'

And he hadn't got much choice. Seeing the turnout at Andrews, the congressional leaders out there in force, a band, well-wishers, streamers. Messages of congratulation pouring in to stations all over the country – and the president's approval rating, like a summer in Washington – well into the nineties.

'Gonna fall flat on his face, huh? Isn't that what you said?' The Southern drawl was right up against his ear. 'You fucking idiot. Had to distance yourself from the president, didn't you? Arsehole! Know something, I'm wondering why I wasted so much time on you in the first place. You really piss me off.'

He watched her turn the magic, tanned thighs away and flounce out of the room.

If he hadn't been scared of her, he'd have gone upstairs and bent her over the side of the bed.

In your dreams, he told himself. In your dreams.

Chapter Sixty-six

She had been home for three days when Sir Henry visited.

Even the Press had got tired by then. Gone off, leaving their tripod marks in the front garden, and mother shaking her head over the plants.

She'd told them there were errors of judgement, the Party had made its decision, she was stepping down, would resign her seat at the next election.

What else was there to say?

They walked beneath the chalk-white cliffs at Saltdean, dodging the waves that hurled shingle on to the pathway. The air was bright and good, and she wanted him to feel the cold.

'Why didn't you watch my back ... ?'

'I tried ... This time it didn't work. You can do almost anything except when a straight lie is sitting there on the record.'

You're a glib bugger, she thought. Always got the answer ready.

'What are you going to do now?' he asked.

'Find something.'

'I'm sure you could find something the other side of the Atlantic.'

'I've already turned that down, thanks. I can find my own occupations.'

'He rang, didn't he?'

'Of course he did.'

'So why did you turn him down?'

'Don't want the job. Not good with consolation prizes. Winning or nothing really.'

'That's pretty arrogant if you don't mind my saying ...'

'I bloody well do ...'

'You want a function. I'll give you one. You go there and watch out for your country. You watch for the intelligence operations they mount against us, the secrets they fail to give us, the way they play us off against their other allies. You care for your country – you do something for it.'

298

'Lousy, twisted argument, that one.'

'They're all lousy arguments. You want to do something useful. Then do it. You want to make a difference to this country, then do it ...'

'Wouldn't work. Too many split loyalties.'

'They all are, my dear. That's the trouble with loyalties.'

'It's no way to start a life together.'

'It's a way to make a difference.'

'And go through all the pomp of being First Lady ...'

'Tell me another way you can do more for your country.'

'I can't do it.'

'Then bury yourself in the country. Write your memoirs. Raise flowers.'

She could have slapped his face then. Wanted to for the first time since they'd known each other.

'What have you fought for all these years ... to be an ex-prime minister, to hug babies for the UN? You pick yourself up and you take the crap, because you want to do something. Use what you have, use his position. But at the end of the day ... *do something* that makes a difference. Or is your petty pride too great?'

And then she did slap him, full and hard on the red, right cheek, the kind of satisfying clap that imprints all five fingers on the skin.

So that he knew he'd got through to her, made her think.

'Wouldn't he come back for tea?'

'I didn't ask him.'

Her mother always seemed to find something to do in the kitchen.

'It's the first day David hasn't rung.'

'I told him not to, any more. He's there, I'm here. And he, at least has a job to do.'

Her mother and father exchanged glances.

'You seem to be shutting all the doors, love.'

She wasn't going to get into that.

'I'm going to New York tomorrow. Interview at the United Nations. There's talk of some kind of ambassadorship. I think it'll be worthwhile.'

'You didn't mention anything ...'

'Wasn't confirmed until this afternoon. But I'll go up to London tonight. Plenty of things to sort out with the flat.'

'Anything we can do, love?' Hurt emblazoned on the two elderly faces.

'Stop worrying both of you. I'm alive and well. Life goes on. OK?'

'Come to bed, Keith. I want to christen it.'

He stood by the window, looking out over St James's Park. Still couldn't believe it. You worked and you schemed and then you schemed again . . . .and suddenly it was there in your hands. The unthinkable. Crown Jewels. King of the world. You of all people, Keith Harper.

It had been some arrival. Denise leaping around the building, flirting with all the staff, yelping like a puppy and threatening to invite all the relatives. They wouldn't take long to reduce the place to the dignity of a Happy Eater on the M4.

Have to keep them well out of sight.

As if there wasn't enough to think about.

He sat on the bed and swung his legs under the blanket, aware suddenly that Denise was naked, pressing her body against his side.

'I said I wanted to christen it.'

He turned away. 'I'm really tired, love. OK? Tomorrow.'

'Listen, Keith Harper, you only ever get one First Night. So why don't we put on a real show?'

'I told you love. Lot on my mind . . .'

'But it's been ages.'

And then he knew why. Even now, even after all that had happened, he would have given the last change in his pocket to have Alison lying beside him. This had been her bed, and she had lain on this same mattress, staring at these same walls. The imprint was hers, the smell. Part of her lingered on.

After a while, Denise gave up, switched off her body and went to sleep. As the hours passed, he couldn't help wondering if the longing and the disappointment would ever leave him alone.

Chapter Sixty-seven

Alison could hear the police sirens all the way down Lexington Avenue. But they meant nothing to her.

As she returned to the hotel her mind was full of the interview she'd attended at the UN. One down – and a second scheduled for the morning with the Secretary General. The questions had been sharp, incisive – so had the answers. And she'd found herself enjoying the chance to flex her claws again. You didn't want to lose your edge.

From what they'd told her, she liked the sound of the job. Liked the idea of troubleshooting flashpoints and crises. There'd be sacrifices and tradeoffs, but it was well away from the ritual muggings of Westminster. And she needed that. Once the dogs had been turned loose on you, it took a long time to return to normality. You kept finding scars you never knew you had – ones they'd opened and left behind.

Three times that day she had picked up the phone to call David Bradley, but each time she had replaced it. He wasn't the answer to her problems. He was part of them.

The only solution, she decided, was work. Work would fill the gap that he left in her. Had done for thirty years. She'd have to hope it would do so again.

She undressed, put on a bathrobe and ordered her dinner from room service.

And it failed to occur to her when she heard a knock on the door just three minutes later, that even by the superfast standards of New York, this might be a little hard to credit.

So it was a full five seconds extra before she recognised the face of David Bradley.

'What the hell are you doing here?'

He smiled and moved past her into the room.

'I thought it was time you bought me dinner.'

'But how did you get here?'

'I took a plane and about sixty motorcycle outriders helped me through the traffic. "The President," it says on my schedule, "is having a private dinner with friends in New York." '

'What friends?'

'You.'

'I don't even need to ask how you knew I was here, do I?'

'No.' He sat down in an easy chair. 'I don't suppose you do.'

She stayed where she was, beside the door. 'I'm not even dressed, David. And you shouldn't be here. What about your army of secret servicemen?'

'They're fine. They've closed off one of the elevators. They're staked out along the corridor, and most of them have already eaten. So don't worry about them. If you could just order for me, that'd be quite sufficient.'

'I don't know what to say?'

He leaned across and took the menu. 'I'll have the grilled chicken, if that's OK. And some wine. Say that.'

They ate by a candle-light on the dinner tray, Alison still in her bathrobe, fastened by the single cord. She could see his eyes, distracted, the hint of another appetite, his hands unable to stay still.

Bradley finished the chicken and pushed away the plate. 'So what are you going to say to me?'

'I thought we'd said everything, David. I couldn't be happier about the way this all turned out for you – but I can't be part of it. I have a life of my own. And what's more I have my pride.'

'You can have more than that.'

'That's not the way it'd be seen.'

'That's the way you could see it.'

'Listen to me. I fight for what I have. I've always fought. I had to. So I don't want gifts. Not even one . . . .' she stopped for a moment. 'Not even one as generous as this.'

His little finger touched hers. 'I'm asking you to carry my ring, that's all. Everything else is your own. Your job. Your life. Come and go as you please. Hell, you're going to be away a lot anyway . . . .'

'But even so, I'd be judged simply as your wife.'

They both seemed surprised by the feel of the word. For a moment, neither of them spoke.

And strangely she didn't mind the way it sounded, leaning forward, doing nothing to prevent the opening of the robe. Was she daring him, she wondered, or daring herself?

'Things have changed,' he said, voice much quieter. 'White House women aren't the same as they used to be.'

'I'm British.'

'I'm very happy you are. Means you can't challenge me for the Presidency. There are some compensations.' He could see the faintest swing of movement below the robe.

'Why, David? What am I to you?'

'I'll show you.'

She couldn't help laughing as his hands undid the cord, couldn't help the pleasure being squeezed from inside her, couldn't help the sounds and rhythms that he brought out of her, played and played again. And she went on grinning to herself, eyes tight shut, just as she had done in the rooms of Oxford.

It seemed as if three more decades were to pass before they spoke.

'You feel just the same.'

'There's more of me.' She turned towards him and ran her hand down his stomach. 'And there's less of you.'

'That's not very flattering.'

She giggled again. 'I didn't mean there. I meant your waist.'

'You still laugh in bed.'

'That's because you're still funny in bed.'

'Why?'

'You treat me like a meal. Only not everything was meant to be eaten.'

'That's what you used to say in Oxford.'

'You're better than you were in Oxford. You don't rush your food any more.'

'And you taste better.'

'Couldn't you put away your tongue for a moment? I haven't seen your face for the last fifteen minutes.'

'Can't you take it?'

'Too much pleasure for an old lady. I might overdose. I'm not used to it.'

They got up for a while and finished the wine, and then she

303

began to laugh again, low down . . .

'Where are you now, for God's sake?'

'Last outpost of the empire.'

'Well, come back to Rome for a moment.'

'Why, do I get an answer to my question?'

'Yes.'

'What is it?'

'The answer's no.' She smiled at him in the darkness. 'But ask me again in a few minutes.'

Chapter Sixty-eight

They all went to the same place. But they all remember that day for different reasons.

Champagne Tripp remembers the day, because it was the last time she squeezed herself into her pink outfit. And she still believes the outspoken senator from Wyoming made an assignation, that he intended to follow up.

Ruth Bradley remembers the day because her son forgave her – over breakfast in the family quarters – the way she never thought he would.

David remembers the day, for the beginnings of a question mark that somehow never went away.

Shortly before six a.m. Alison Lane, as she still was, dodged the cameras and the satellite trucks, and the twenty thousand reporters, and thirty thousand police that filled the capital. And she met Sir Henry at a metro station half way up the line to Shady Grove, in Maryland.

Washington's suburbs still dozed in the snow. Only the very early and the very cold saw her, scarf about her head, knee-length black boots, grey sheepskin coat. Not a bride-to-be. Not out there in sleepy-town USA.

They walked for a while around the empty parking lot, until he broke the silence.

'Thank you for seeing me. I realise it couldn't be a busier day.'

'You said it was urgent.'

'I thought it important that we clarified our arrangement. Since you're going to be pretty well protected after today.'

She didn't answer for a moment, just listened to the boots on the soft snow, watching the lights turn on in the blocks along the Pike.

'I don't think we have an arrangment any more, Sir Henry.'

'I'm sorry, my dear. I don't follow. I thought our conversation on the coast a while back was pretty clear.'

'You made me an offer and now I'm turning it down.' She stopped in the snow and faced him. 'Our arrangement is over, terminated. I'm not doing this for you. I can't. I know that now. I'm not going to burrow and ferret for you, as I have done over the last thirty years. This is where it ends. It has to.'

Even in the dawn light, she could see the surge of anger, the way it burst inside him, the way he sought instantly to control it. The pleading, reasonable tone that took its place.

'I think you should see this in context, my dear. In the context of the relationship that we've enjoyed for a very long time.'

'What does that mean?'

'I'm offering you a chance to do something of the utmost importance.'

'That's exactly what I'm doing. I have a new career at the UN, and for the first time in thirty years I'm going to have a personal life. Can you understand how much that means to me? All of it on my terms. Not for you. Not for anyone else.'

'I still don't think you've grasped what I'm saying. Our relationship has been based on a number of mutual favours. Without my help ...'

'Get to the point, Sir Henry.'

And the anger was returning to him. First in the eyes, now spreading outwards, tightening the face and the lower lip.

'The point, my dear, is that I made you, your career, your chances and I'll be the one to decide when this is over. Is that clearer ... ?'

'So that's where we've got to, is it? Threats, little tantrum perhaps, intimidation. Good old weapons, tried and tested.' She took off her glove and rubbed her eyes. 'Go home. Go on. Go back to London. It's over. The time has moved on. And ...' the voice seemed to hold a threat of its own 'don't let me hear this again. D'you understand? It's finished.'

'Not for me.'

She shrugged and walked away, back to the metro, not knowing or caring what happened to him.

Harry Deval remembers the day with considerable trepidation. For the fourth time that morning he was tying Jason's tie, standing him

306

up against the wall of his west wing office, while Jane made final adjustments to her hair.

It was past eleven o'clock, when his secretary knocked at the door.

'What is it, Jean?'

'There's a man been calling for you all morning. I've explained the circumstances. You'd think he'd understand.'

'Who is he?'

She lowered her voice. 'He's from one of the British Services ... you know ...'

'So put him on to NSA. For Chrissake there are channels to go through. I don't meet with these people. Period.'

'I tried. But he won't speak to them. Says it's vital he sees you. Can't wait. National Security. He's at the south-west gate. Now.'

'Jesus, there's a wedding in the East Room in forty-five minutes ...'

'It's OK, Harry.' Jane touched his arm. 'Do what you have to do. I wanted to go up anyway and make sure David's all right.'

Harry made two phone calls and then sat at his desk and waited. Even as he replaced the receiver, there was a knock at the door and the elderly man was shown in.

'A thousand apologies, Mr Deval, I'm ...'

'I know exactly who you are. What you don't seem to realise is what the hell's going on here today. Don't you read the papers, watch television? What in Christ's name is the matter with you people? You have your own contacts, your own channels. If it wasn't for the fact that the president is marrying a Brit ...'

'A British national?' The man took off his hat. 'That's precisely why I thought you ought to see the file I have with me and communicate the contents ...'

'I'll look at it later.'

'You'd do well to look at it now. I understand you've been conducting a few researches of your own recently in England. There are one or two details here, which I believe you missed.' A folder seemed to make its own way across the desk to Harry. 'I didn't want there to be any question about our commitment to the Special Relationship, in the years to come.'

He put his hand on the door and was half-way through it before Harry caught him.

'Where you going?'

The old man waved the gold embossed card in front of him. 'I have an invitation.'

All of them have one peculiar recollection.

Of seeing David Bradley moving through the crowd in the East Room, surrounded by glitter and smiles, a mass of hands shaking almost all his movable parts. A little bit of White House magic in the air, the kind that accompanies every great occasion in the capital of the Americas.

And then Harry Deval catches his arm, still smiling and joking and leads him firmly to the exit, back to the Cross Halls, into the shadows where he can't be seen.

'Just signing a piece of paper,' the word goes out. 'Only take a second.'

Then, just as suddenly, he's back into the crowds, with the winter suntan and the campaign smile, trying not to step on everyone's feet as he makes it across the room to Alison.

She too, remembers that moment, thinking she heard her name being called. Just as she thought it, thirty years before on a street in Oxford. Only this time she doesn't turn, catching sight instead of the elderly man in the crowd – the red face, the studiedly ill-fitting morning coat, a rose in his lapel, half-smiling, because he only ever had half-emotions; half there, half somewhere else.

'Alison!' David's hand tight on her arm, a new urgency in the grip.

'What is it?'

His eyes taking a moment to decide.

'Nothing.'